"Deese is a master wordsmith, deftly weaving a story that readers won't be able to put down. This latest book has crossover appeal for fans of contemporary romance seeking realistic and endearing characters."

—*Library Journal*

"Deese's novel has good dialogue, vivid description, and plenty of emotion."

—*Booklist*

"Sometimes a love story ends in tragedy and a tragedy leads to a love story. And sometimes a hero turns a bit villainous and a villain turns a bit heroic. In this unique story within a story, Deese delivers all of the above with the finesse of a clever storyteller. *The Words We Lost* is thought-provoking and tender, capturing the transformative beauty of surviving."

—T. I. Lowe, bestselling author of *Under the Magnolias*

"A poignant, masterful exploration of the enduring power of friendship and love, and the links that sustain and nurture us through all of life's complications and losses. Deese once again takes readers on an emotional journey filled with heart and hope."

—Irene Hannon, author of the bestselling HOPE HARBOR series

"Few things in life can be depended upon as reliably as the magic of a Nicole Deese book. No one breaks my heart and pieces it back together, better than before, quite like Nicole. *The Words We Lost* more than lives up to the standard of beauty and brilliance we've come to expect."

—Bethany Turner, author of *Plot Twist* and *The Do-Over*

# The Roads We Follow

## Books by Nicole Deese

*Before I Called You Mine*
*All That Really Matters*
*All That It Takes*
*The Words We Lost*
*The Roads We Follow*

### Novellas

*Heartwood* from *The Kissing Tree:*
*Four Novellas Rooted in Timeless Love*

A FOG HARBOR
······ ROMANCE ······

# The Roads We Follow

## NICOLE DEESE

BETHANYHOUSE
a division of Baker Publishing Group
Minneapolis, Minnesota

© 2024 by Nicole Deese

Published by Bethany House Publishers
Minneapolis, Minnesota
BethanyHouse.com

Bethany House Publishers is a division of
Baker Publishing Group, Grand Rapids, Michigan

Printed in the United States of America

Library of Congress Cataloging-in-Publication Data
Names: Deese, Nicole, author.
Title: The roads we follow / Nicole Deese.
Description: Minneapolis, Minnesota : Bethany House, a division of Baker Publishing
    Group, 2024. | Series: A Fog Harbor romance
Identifiers: LCCN 2023051460 | ISBN 9780764241192 (paper) | ISBN
    9780764242762 (casebound) | ISBN 9781493445165 (eBook)
Subjects: LCGFT: Christian fiction. | Romance fiction. | Novels.
Classification: LCC PS3604.E299 R63 2024 | DDC 813/.6--dc23/eng/20231102
LC record available at https://lccn.loc.gov/2023051460

Cover design by Susan Zucker Design
Cover images Shutterstock

Baker Publishing Group publications use paper produced from sustainable forestry practices and postconsumer waste whenever possible.

24  25  26  27  28  29  30      7  6  5  4  3  2  1

*In honor of my father-in-love, Bill Deese,*
who enjoyed many cross-country road trips
and all the family bonding time they entailed.

If there are road-trip adventures to be had in heaven,
then I hope you'll save a seat for me, Dad. I love you.

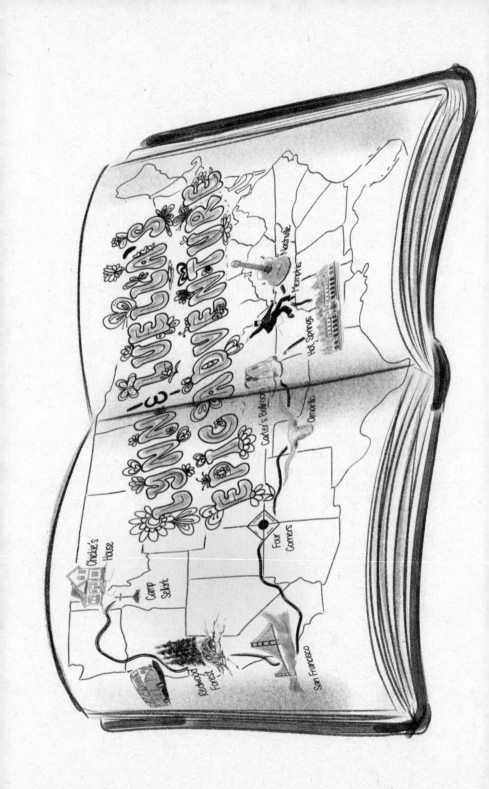

# 1

## Raegan

I breathe in the fresh dopamine hit of a dark roast brewing somewhere behind the coffee shop's counter and remind myself that turning off my GPS location from the family tracking app is not one of the seven deadly sins. Nor is my decision to keep today's meeting with the acquisitions editor from Fog Harbor Books off the shared family calendar. Don't get me wrong, I'm not ashamed of my love for the written word. It's just that I've learned the hard way why some dreams are worth keeping to yourself, especially when those dreams involve seeking a professional's opinion on the unpublished manuscript you've been revising all year. And especially when the world you live in is far more likely to accept an up-and-coming country music artist over a wannabe author who writes in secret under the cover of night.

The thought triggers the same herd of nerves I've worked to corral since I first spotted the email in my inbox last Friday. There's no need to close my eyes to retrieve the message. It's still right where I left it, burning a hole in my prefrontal cortex.

Raegan,

I'll be in Nashville for a publishing conference next week. Any chance you might be available to discuss your manuscript while I'm in town? My afternoons are open.

Chip Stanton
Acquisitions Editor
Fog Harbor Books—San Francisco, CA

After a quick adjustment of the claw clip restraining my curls at the back of my head, I rise up on tiptoes to search the few patrons seated inside the memorabilia-heavy Cup O'Country Coffee House. I've only met Chip in person once, but his flaxen hair is easy to spot at a corner table near the back. As if sensing my perusal, he shifts his attention from his laptop and offers me a friendly wave. I immediately respond in kind.

Before our first meeting last December, my only reference for acquisitions editors came in the form of a Hollywood stereotype: a grumpy, overbearing stress case who wields their red pen like a dagger and has never cracked a joke in their life. Thankfully, Chip's demeanor couldn't be more opposite. He has the kind of smile that instantly sets a person at ease, and even though he looks to be about my age, somewhere in his mid-to-late twenties, his knowledge of books and the publishing industry leaves no guessing as to his life's passion; he's living it. It's an observation I can't help but be the tiniest bit envious of. And yet, for what feels like the first time in my adult life, the outcome of today's meeting holds the potential to change that.

I push down my rising hope as I zigzag through the entryway and around country-music display cases scattered through the coffee shop. An editor doesn't ask for an in-person meeting if he hates the manuscript he read, right? Seems like a brief email would suffice. I'm pondering this line of thought for what is likely the hundredth time when my hip makes contact with a tall object, causing it to teeter. Just as I throw out my arm to steady it, I realize the item in question is a life-size cardboard cutout of a beloved country music legend. Luella Farrow.

My mama.

From her place in the center of the room, she smiles back at me in all her crushed-velvet-jumpsuit-wearing glory. In her right hand she holds up the shiny CMA Award she won for Song of the Year only a few months back, an iconic night for more reasons than one. From her mouth is a speech bubble with text I've read a hundred times in a hundred different locations on the internet. But this time I read her words through an entirely different lens. *"Don't confuse your talent with your worth; only one of those is subjective."* Much to my surprise, the timely quote from her award speech serves to boost my confidence in the way only a pep talk from my mama can. Ignoring the niggle of guilt I feel over the secrets I've been keeping from my family, I thank her under my breath and set her right.

By the time I've reached Chip's table, he's standing with his hand outstretched. "Raegan, hello! It's so good to see you again."

"You too." We shake hands. "Thanks for taking time out of your busy conference week to meet with me. I was surprised to learn it was here."

"We rotate locations," he says easily. "And it was my good luck that this year's location was near your hometown."

Fresh hope buoys to the surface as his words anchor in a tender, uncharted place in the center of my chest. Could that mean he . . . he liked what he read?

He glances around the quiet coffee house. "I think this is the first place I've been to in Nashville that doesn't have a line waiting outside the door or music turned up so loud I can hear the bass line in my sleep. Good recommendation."

"The summer heat keeps this coffee house pretty low-key during the afternoons."

He nods and gestures to an empty beverage on the table. "Said heat is why I ordered the iced coffee special. May I order you one, as well?" He leans in and lowers his voice. "In full disclosure, I will be ordering myself a second round. I have absolutely no shame when it comes to caffeine intake."

I laugh. "An iced coffee sounds perfect, thank you."

It's remarkable how in only a matter of seconds Chip confirms he's exactly how I remember him being last winter—easygoing, personable, real. When my niece Cheyenne had been hired to sing for an office Christmas party in San Francisco last December, she'd begged me to fly down and spend a long weekend with her and her lively roommate, Allie. I'd agreed without hesitation. Partly because any escape from home is a welcome one, but also because over the course of the year, those girls have played a significant role in my life as a closet writer. Apart from the man ordering me an iced coffee, they remain the only two souls on earth to have read *The Sisters of Birch Grove*, my only completed full-length novel to date.

At just seven years my junior, my musically gifted niece grew up reading my short stories as a girl, so when I agreed to start a weekly accountability call with her and Allie to aid in our collective creative motivation, I hadn't expected it to help me as much as it did. Each Wednesday night on video chat I'd read them one chapter of *The Sisters of Birch Grove*, and in exchange, Cheyenne would sing the lyrics to a song she'd been working on, and Allie would share whatever scene she was revising from her already contracted fantasy trilogy.

Little had I known, however, that this so-called *office Christmas party* I'd been invited to was at none other than Fog Harbor Books, Allie's publisher. She introduced me to Chip, and within the hour, she must have told him no less than fifteen times, in fifteen different ways, just how much he'd regret letting me leave the party without asking to review my manuscript. I was both mortified at her forwardness and flattered at her adoration of the fictional world I'd grown to love more than any place I'd visited in real life.

By the end of that night, Chip had asked to review my manuscript. The moment had coaxed all kinds of fairy-tale-like feelings, though it didn't take long for the fear to set in. I'd spent the next four months tweaking and polishing before I had the courage to send him the novel that took me the better part of two years to write and revise.

Chip now strides back to our table, having made our coffee orders, and his smile takes on a new quality. And unlike I predict, he doesn't sit down across from me. "So I have somewhat of an unconventional request to make of you before we get started."

"Oh? What is it?"

He ticks his head left, and for the second time in five minutes, I lock eyes with my cardboard mother.

"My girlfriend is a huge fan of your mother's. Would you mind taking my picture so I can send it off to her before my brain switches fully over to book mode?"

"Sure, of course," I say cheerily, even though I feel a twinge of disappointment for Allie's sake at the revelation that Chip has a girlfriend. When I saw them together last December, their chemistry had been off the charts. I figured it was only a matter of time before they started dating. Guess I was wrong.

"Thanks. Charity's borderline obsessed with that new remix song—the one about the bridge."

"'Crossing Bridges,'" I supply.

"That's the one." He points with a grin. "I swear I hear it everywhere—the grocery store, the gym, my dentist's office, and somehow it's playing in every rideshare I climb into. Pretty crazy how a song written decades ago has the power to take today's music fans by storm."

Due to years of living under the scrutiny of the public eye, I nod politely at his unassuming observation. But it wasn't only music fans that had been *taken by storm* with the resurgence of "Crossing Bridges" these past eighteen months. My family had been stunned to watch a song Mama cowrote decades ago with her ex-bandmate soar to the top of the charts—skyrocketing there from the remix version used on a popular mini-series, a show that's now been streamed millions of times over. Seemingly overnight and without warning, the spotlight on Mama—and our family-run music label—had brightened considerably. Unfortunately, the bright lights of fame aren't always flattering.

I banish the thought trail before it can gain traction and instead tap into the camera app on my phone to grant Chip his favor. Nothing says *icebreaker* quite like cautioning a business professional on how to avoid papercuts from posing with a cardboard replica of your mother. Then again, after living nearly three decades as the youngest child of a famous entertainer, this moment ranks low on the weirdest-things-I've-been-asked-to-do-for-a-fan list.

Back at our table, I'm halfway through my first sip of iced coffee when Chip abandons all things country and pulls an about-face in conversation. "I loved your book, Raegan. More than loved it, actually. And I sincerely hope I can convince you to let me pitch it to my publishing board next month."

My straw slowly sinks back into my plastic cup as I blink up at him for a full three seconds. "You . . . you want to publish it?"

He laughs as if this isn't the most serious question I've ever asked another living soul.

"Let me put it this way, I think *The Sisters of Birch Grove* has the potential to be the modern-day *Little Women* of our time. It hit all the right notes for me—nostalgic, moving, witty, romantic. It's an expertly paced family drama and exactly where I suspect the market will be trending by this time next year. Don't tell Allie I said this, but she was spot-on in her recommendation when she said I'd regret not asking you for your manuscript that night. The entire time I was reading, I kept forgetting it wasn't yet a published work." He plants his elbows on the table and drums his fingers. "Please tell me you have ideas for a sequel—and perhaps a book three, as well? I guarantee readers are going to want more from Birch Grove."

*A modern-day* Little Women*?* I bring a trembling hand to my mouth and release a sound that's something between half sob, half laugh. "I'm sorry, I'm . . . you think readers would want a series of Birch Grove novels?"

He nods demonstratively.

"This is surreal," I whisper and fall back against my seat.

"In a good way, I hope?"

My eyes turn watery. "In the best possible way."

His smile softens as he reaches for his laptop. "I have a whole list of questions and comments I jotted down while I was reading, but first, I've been dying to know if Birch Grove was inspired by a real town."

I shake my head and work to regain my composure. "Not unless you count my internet travels. I've never actually been that far north."

"Then that's even more remarkable." He opens his laptop and scans whatever document he's opened. "Before I get too far ahead of myself with story questions, I should ask if you have a literary agent you'd like me to reach out to on your behalf. It's best I touch base with them as soon as possible so we're all in the know at the same time."

"I don't have an agent," I say quickly. "I'd like to represent myself."

He stares at me for a beat before he nods. "Okay, that's not a problem. We have several authors at Fog Harbor who are self-represented. Typically they opt to use an entertainment lawyer for contract review and negotiations, but if you'd rather use one of your family's attorneys, that's understandable. I'll just need their contact information within the next couple weeks. If my pitch to the publication board goes as well as I hope, things could move pretty quickly after that."

The euphoria I experienced from moments ago is placed on pause, making way for my climbing anxiety. "Actually, my preference would be to handle as much of this process on my own." And as far away as possible from certain sisterly opinions.

"With all due respect, Raegan, the legalities involved in a publishing contract can be difficult to navigate, seeing as each contract is drafted for the individual author. Given your unique background and high-profile family, I'm certain your legal team will require specific provisions for your—and their—protection."

He relaxes into his seat as if I'm a totally reasonable individual who will simply accept his sound logic at face value. Only, it's not his logic that has my insides churning. It's the lack of one small, but absolutely critical, detail.

A detail I fear has somehow been lost in translation.

The pulse in my throat moves to my ears, muffling the sound of my own voice. "I'm sorry, but I think there's been a misunderstanding. I realize now I never should have expected Allie to relay my wishes for anonymity to you but . . . I have no intention of publishing under my own name."

His brow crimps slightly. "Meaning . . . you were hoping to use a pseudonym?"

"That's correct."

At my confirmation, the confusion in his eyes deflates to an understanding I can feel in the depths of my soul. So he didn't know, then. Chip came here expecting to sign a book deal with a celebrity's daughter. Not an anonymous nobody.

He opens his mouth twice before he manages to speak. "May I ask why?"

And it's right then the phone I left face up on the table after picture-taking vibrates. My oldest sister has the most impeccable knack for poorly timed communication. As soon as Adele's name appears on the screen, I flip it over, knowing the action will in no way silence her for long.

"I don't want my writing to be tied to my family name," I say. "I want my stories to stand on their own, unattached to my family's achievements."

For so many years, my dream of publishing a novel lived in a protected cocoon, safe from expectation, pressure, and rejection.

Safe from the reality of being known as only one thing: Luella Farrow's youngest daughter. While the literary agents I've queried in the past promised huge book deals and placement on prestigious bestseller lists due to my family's connections and resources, I've never wanted the Farrow name to be a stepping stone for my success as an author. I've only ever wanted to know—*needed* to know, even—that I'm a storyteller by talent and not by fame.

Yet once again, the answer to that ever-elusive question remains up in the air.

I can almost hear Adele's reply to my musings: *"When will you finally accept what I've been telling you, Raegan? You'll always be a Farrow first. Your name is not a filter you can take on and off. It's permanent. What you do affects all of us."*

My phone vibrates again. I ignore it. Adele has had me at her beck and call nearly twenty-four hours a day for years now. She can give me one hour.

The short buzzes indicate she's left multiple texts. I don't look at the screen.

"You've obviously given a lot of thought to this," Chip continues.

"I have, yes."

His nod is slow, yet his expression remains open, empathetic even. I've just set fire to his hope of signing an author with access to a built-in fan base of hundreds of thousands, and yet he's still here. Still sitting with me. That's more than the last literary agent I queried ever did.

"It's no secret that a known brand is an easier sell than an unproven one," he begins. "The marketing strategy that's been used for decades by clothing designers, product labels, automotive branding, and music bands is essentially the same for authors and their books." He releases a long exhale. "I wish I could tell you that the current marketplace is kinder to debut novelists than it is . . . but I believe in your story too much to mislead you. Starting from scratch by using a pen name with no backlist to work off of and no real visibility is a tough sell to any publisher. In our industry, like so many others, names and connections are important."

"Of course," I whisper around the growing lump in my throat. "I understand." I swallow and lift my head. "I appreciate you taking the time to review my manuscript, Chip, and I apologize again for the misunderstanding about—"

The abrupt shake of his head cuts off my polite attempt to wrap up our meeting. "When it comes to your talent, there's no misunderstanding. I'd want to publish this book if you were writing as Luella Farrow's daughter or as Big Bird."

Despite my increasing heartache, a mournful laugh escapes me. "I promise you my pen name is better than Big Bird." I'd planned to use Sunny Rae—a combination of my two childhood nicknames—but when I think it over now, it sounds almost as ridiculous as Big Bird.

"I'm sure it is," he concedes, "but regardless, creating a marketable pen name will require a lot of time, energy, and diligence. If that's the route you decide on, I can send you information on how to grow your socials, along with advice on how to utilize any of your past writing efforts for contest submissions in order to grow in name recognition and visibility. Earning some accolades under that name would be a good start."

"I understand." I drop my gaze to the condensation slipping down the sides of my cup and process what he's actually saying: the path he's describing now won't involve a publishing contract from Fog Harbor Books, at least not until I establish a reputable foundation for my pen name.

Chip studies me for a long moment before he adds, "As counterintuitive as it might be for me to say this to you, you could also look into self-publishing as an option."

I meet his gaze, stunned again by his forthrightness and honesty. I'd done my research on self-publishing. Truth is, I've enjoyed all sorts of books by many authors who've chosen that option. Yet when I think about finding the time to learn an entirely new business *and* execute it well while also doing my best to remain anonymous, it seems about as plausible as joining the witness protection program to escape my family responsibilities.

"I appreciate the option, but I don't think it's the right one for me," I say, as disappointment continues to weave its way through my ribs.

For the briefest of moments, I allow myself to imagine how incredible it would be to sign a publishing contract with Fog Harbor Books as someone else. Someone born into a typical family with typical jobs and who grew up in a typical home with typical siblings. Someone who's never had to question if their achievements are based on their own merit or a family member's. Someone whose every life decision isn't discussed and dissected like an agenda item at a monthly business meeting.

He nods as if he's not surprised by my response. "I'm sorry I can't offer you something that will work for us both at this time, Raegan."

Suddenly unable to speak, I can only swallow and nod.

Chip looks down at his laptop screen and then begins to read out loud without preamble, "*The Sisters of Birch Grove* is both universally relevant and deeply personal. Readers will wonder what window Farrow snuck through in order to write such a detailed observation of a family." His smile turns pensive when he glances my way again. "I wrote that after I read the last chapter—after the sisters finally reconcile. It's obvious you know a thing or two about family dynamics."

Yet another reason for a pen name, I suppose. As Raegan Farrow, the readers familiar with my family would be wondering what parts of my stories are true and what parts are fiction. But when I write, I'm *not* analyzing the divide between my life and my characters. I'm simply writing the narrative that speaks to me.

Writing has been the only thing that's truly been mine since the day our father died and left Adele in charge of everything . . . and everyone.

". . . touch base in the future."

I blink Chip back into focus as he's politely wrapping up our meeting. I clear my throat and thank him again for his time, knowing that realistically this will likely be the last time we meet under these circumstances. Neither of us has made false promises as to what the future holds for my publishing journey or lack thereof.

Perhaps I should be content with my current reader audience of two—Cheyenne and Allie. Maybe that's enough. Maybe I need to make it be enough.

As I gather my things, Chip's attention returns to his laptop. So this time, when my phone buzzes, I give in to the pull and tap the waiting string of text messages from my oldest sister.

Adele:

Where are you? Why does the tracking app show you're offline?

Adele:

What do you know about the meeting Mama put on the family calendar for tonight? There's no way I can break away from the office before seven.

Adele:

Did you pick up the outgoing packages from my secretary yet? They need to go out by four. I don't trust our new mail courier. Please confirm.

Adele:

Please get Mama to reschedule tonight's meeting for some time after next Wednesday. Please confirm.

Adele:

Why is Hattie's location showing she's near the courthouse??? There's nothing on the calendar regarding her custody appeal until next week. Are you with her? I'm walking into an important meeting. PLEASE CONFIRM ASAP.

Reality presses down on me with such force it's an effort to switch mental gears in order to say a final good-bye to Chip as I take a step back from the table. Only, his reply comes in the form of a furrowed brow as he seems to contemplate me.

"Before you go, there's something I overheard at the conference that's been bothering me, especially in light of our conversation here today. At the risk of beating a dead horse, can I ask if . . ." He stops himself and then starts again. "Does part of your reasoning for anonymity have to do with a publication rumor involving your mother?"

"What rumor?" I shake my head. "I haven't heard anything."

"Really?" His brow rumples further. "Interesting. I swear I heard something about a biography collaboration."

Relief comes swiftly. "My mother would never agree to anything like that. I know that might seem odd, given her gregarious personality onstage, but my parents made a commitment early on to each other and to us that they'd keep their private lives private." And given the fact that Adele is the reigning Nondisclosure Queen of our family, there are few people who could write anything of substance without having to go through her first. My oldest sister is a star player in both offense and defense when it comes to matters of family. "Chances are good it's nothing more than a rumor."

He bobs his chin twice. "Perhaps I'm mistaken, then."

"Perhaps." Then again, *if* there was something unsanctioned in the works and I failed to give Adele a proper heads-up, she'd skewer me. "But if you hear anything more, would you mind letting me know?"

"Certainly. I'll keep my eyes and ears open for you."

"I appreciate it." I try to hold my smile even as I feel the vibration of more texts rumble against my palm again. Any chance I had of appealing to Adele's good graces at this point are long dead and buried. "Bye, Chip. I hope you have a good trip back to California."

I'm only a few steps away from the cardboard cut-out of my mother when I hear him call after me, "Do whatever it takes to get your book on the shelves, Raegan. Your future readers will thank you for it."

I hesitate for the briefest of heartbeats as my mind is whisked away to a fantasy life where I can be both an accomplished author and a dependable sister. But then I look down at the leash tethered to my palm, and the spell is broken.

# 2

## Raegan

By the time I pull through the privacy gate of Mama's estate in Brentwood, the all-too-familiar itch on the inside of my wrist has already begun, made worse at the sight of Adele's black Lexus parked in the driveway. Using the pad of my thumb, I rub at the pink patches snaking up my forearm and release a weary sigh—for the stress hives, for the 9-1-1 summons on my phone screen, and for the dream that felt so close to being realized if not for my name.

I slip through the front door unannounced and head straight back to Mama's kitchen—though for the last four years, it's been my kitchen, too, ever since Adele insisted that the best thing for Mama after Daddy's passing would be for me to move in with her. One might argue that Mama's longtime house manager and trusted friend for decades, Jana, who's here five days a week plus most Sunday afternoons to swim with her grandbabies, would suffice for companionship. But arguing with Adele is a lesson in futility.

I scratch again at my forearm. My hives have crept their way past my elbow, and as much as I want to learn the reason behind Adele's urgent texts regarding my middle sister, I will be of no use to her or anyone else if I don't first locate some antihistamines.

I'm rummaging through the medicine cabinets when I hear Adele's assertive tone barking orders from the living room. She's using legal jargon I don't understand, yet it comes as no surprise that she's on the phone after summoning me here. Benjamin Franklin had it wrong; death and taxes aren't the only two things that are certain in life.

Hiding behind the Pepto Bismol is a box of expired Benadryl tablets. I down two with a tall glass of water just in case expired equals less potent, then go in search of answers. *Where is Hattie?* I stride down the hallway from the kitchen toward the formal sitting room and library, listening for Mama's low hum or the light sweep of her rhinestone slippers against the hardwood floors. Maybe she can shed some light on whatever drama happened today. But the only thing I hear is the low rumble of Adele's stern voice echoing in the quiet.

As I round the corner into the parlor, the blood in my veins chills. Hattie—almost eleven years my senior and three years Adele's junior—is passed out on the sofa, where three bulky black garbage bags are parked near her feet. Her snores are light, but the thick, dried rivulets of mascara on her cheeks are not. The rare sight of her disheveled appearance keeps my eyes locked on her still form as I move to tuck a throw blanket over her bare feet and legs, all the while searching my brain for a narrative that makes sense.

"Apparently," Adele says from somewhere behind me, "Hattie's custody appeal hearing was moved to this afternoon. And she went alone."

I spin to face her. "*What?*"

"And she lost."

"No, *no*," I repeat while shaking my head, as if that action alone might force either the circumstances or the verdict to make sense.

Adele tips her head to the hallway and leaves the room. I

follow her lead, lowering my voice when I say, "How did that happen? I didn't know anything about a reschedule."

When we stop, Adele studies me in a way that says *it's-your-literal-job-to-know, Raegan*. "The judge granted *him* the full six weeks he requested this summer with the children, starting today since this is their usual weekend." Adele almost never uses our ex-brother-in-law's name in conversation. As far as she is concerned, Peter San Marco's name, or Cheater Peter as I refer to him in my head, takes up far too much real estate in our lives as it is. Adele is still dealing with the scandal he caused nearly two years ago at Farrow Music Productions.

Adele's gaze cuts to Hattie's sleeping form in the den. "Imagine my surprise when I was minutes away from walking into a meeting with our legal team when my phone alerted me to Hattie's location. I texted you *and* called, but it went straight to voicemail." She searches my face. "Where were you this afternoon?"

"I took an hour to have coffee with a friend." I keep my tone even as I supply an answer, but my heart is an erratic drumbeat in my chest. I push aside her clear frustration with me and instead process the injustice for my nephew Aiden and niece Annabelle. And then, with a clenched jaw, my sister Hattie. "How can he do this to her? She's their *mother*." I've never come so close to hating anyone in all my life. "He can't just . . . he can't just take them from her, can he? The longest they've spent apart is three nights, per their agreement."

"I'm well aware of the previous arrangement, Raegan. I was the one working with her lawyers. Which is why I was shocked to discover she'd gone to the appeal hearing alone and represented herself. You and I both know she was nowhere near ready for something like that." Adele sighs and straightens her skirt. "It appears the cheater struck a compromise the judge favored. He gets them for six weeks this summer, and in turn, Hattie will have the same schedule next summer."

I shake my head. "But why is he so insistent on six weeks? They're only eight and nine."

Molten fury ignites my sister's gaze. "Because he wants them to meet Francesca's family in Greece."

I open my mouth only to shut it again. There are no words for this kind of revulsion. Francesca is not only the twenty-something Cheater Peter left our sister for; she was also the top-grossing female artist at Farrow Music Productions right up until Peter—the former legal advisor at the label—amended Francesca's contract to include an escape clause that allowed her to walk away without penalty not long after he walked out on his family.

Sympathy compresses my next breath as I think of the pain Hattie must be in tonight.

Once upon a time, Hattie was the life of the party, the one who planned events and holidays, family excursions, and weekly dinners at our folks' estate. But that version of Hattie feels almost as foreign as the version we'd been introduced to after she married Peter San Marco.

"How is she?" I ask.

"Mama said she took an anti-anxiety pill the minute she walked through the door. She fell asleep here about twenty minutes later."

I gawk at Adele. "But Hattie doesn't like taking pharmaceuticals."

"Yeah, well, she also doesn't like having her kids taken away from her."

There's no argument for that.

We both crane our necks and peek in on her together. If Adele and I are unified on one thing, it's our mutual disdain for Hattie's ex and his manipulation skills for obtaining whatever he wants at any cost. If not for the surprise resurgence of "Crossing Bridges," the family label would be in a world of trouble. Adele has been tight-lipped on the details, but I do know that shortly after she exposed Peter's affair and fired him, Peter went public with outrageous claims regarding the mismanagement of our artists and the poor morale inside the studio. Naturally, he painted himself an innocent bystander-turned-hero instead of a con man. He sued Farrow Music Productions for wrongful termination and won. After that, Adele tightened everything that could be tightened. Finances. Personnel. Interviews. Nondisclosure agreements. Mama's public appearances. And the choke hold on her two younger sisters.

Adele lowers her voice. "You and I need to discuss how these next six weeks will play out in order to keep Hattie out of the media." She says this as if *discuss* is something we Farrow sisters do. Only, I can't even recall the last time she invited me to be a part of any decision—much less the ones involving our family. "That goes for Mama, too. I need her to stay focused on her appearance at the Watershed Festival next month. She's one of the main headliners on one of the biggest stages for country music. There's a lot riding on her performances there for the label."

I glance down the hall behind me. "Where *is* Mama? Is she home?"

"She left with Jana a few minutes before you showed up. I was on a work call when Jana dropped Hattie's bags off, and the next thing I knew, Mama was saying something about needing to run a quick errand before the family meeting tonight."

Though Jana is technically on Mama's payroll as her house manager, she's been more of an extension to our family than a Farrow employee. She was the one responsible for teaching me my alphabet and taking me to the library when my parents worked tirelessly to build the label and Mama's career from the ground up.

My gaze catches again on the giant trash bags in Mama's parlor. "Are those bags filled with . . . Hattie's belongings?"

"Jana couldn't find Hattie's luggage set anywhere." Adele shrugs absently. "So I told her to be resourceful and bring her stuff in whatever she could for now."

"Jana didn't need to do that. I can stay with Hattie until she gets settled into a routine at home and—"

"No." Adele shakes her head. "We can't risk that. Hattie doesn't do well on her own; you know that. It's best she stays here until the kids return. It will be easier for you to keep an eye on her if she's across the hall. Maybe you two can find some hobbies to pass the time." So this is how Adele planned to discuss Hattie's next six weeks with me: by making all the plans and then informing me about them later.

It's not that I'm not supportive of Hattie; I am—and I have been. But to just throw a live-in roommate on me without consideration to any plans of my own breeds a special kind of annoyance reserved for bossy older sisters.

"There is no amount of arts and crafts that's going to distract her from missing her kids for six weeks, Adele." I draw in a breath, then slowly let it out. "Plus, don't you think six weeks is a long time for you to assume I have nothing else going on?"

She raises one perfectly groomed eyebrow. "I checked the family calendar. Your schedule looked plenty open to me—is that not accurate?"

If there is one advancement in technology I wish I could go back in time and smite, it would be the invention of the shared family calendar. I *loathe* it. And unlike Adele, who doesn't get questioned about adding secret meetings without contact information, I get questioned about everything.

"That's not the point—"

"It's exactly the point. If you can't bother to keep your schedule updated on the calendar, then how can you expect me to factor in your plans? As I said before, the most important thing is to keep Mama and everything she's associated with in good standing until she performs at the Watershed Festival in Washington."

Before I can offer a rebuttal or even think of broaching the subject of Tav coming to town, a horn blares followed by music coming from somewhere outside. And not just any music, but the chorus of a song we all know by heart: "My Darlin' Daughters Three." The song Mama wrote for us not long after her career went solo in the mid-'90s.

Adele starts and moves toward the front door. "What on earth is that?"

"Doesn't sound like an ice cream truck," I quip, but Adele isn't up for my humor. Come to think of it, I can't remember the last time I even saw her laugh.

Our mother's distorted voice projects over what I can only assume is either a bullhorn or an intercom speaker. "Girls, can all three of you come into the driveway, please? I have a surprise for you."

Adele doesn't hesitate to be the first outside, regardless of the fact that Hattie and I are still in the parlor and one of us looks like the only thing that could wake her is the second coming of Christ. I move toward my groggy sister on the sofa and rock her shoulder gently. "Hey, Hattie? Mama's asking us to go outside together. She says she has a surprise for us."

"Later," she mumbles. "Too . . . tired."

"I'm sure you are tired," I say, fighting off a yawn of my own as I feel the antihistamines hard at work in my body. "I'm really sorry about what happened at the appeal, Hattie. I wish I would have known about the schedule change . . ." I swallow back the guilt. "You can get through this, though." *Somehow.*

The only indication she's heard me is a scrunched-up brow.

There's another short horn blast from the driveway, so I leave Hattie on the couch and head for the front entrance. I don't get far.

Adele is halted two steps lower than me on the front porch, and I don't have to wonder where her gaze is fixed. There is only one option. The metallic gold vintage tour bus with tinted windows donning a bright red bow attached to the rooftop is not exactly subtle. Nor is the voice of our mother, who is standing just inside the open bus door, gripping a bullhorn.

"Well, don't you two just stand there catching flies," our mama calls from the shadowed steps inside the bus. "Where's my second-born?"

Adele twists back to stare at me as if she's the commanding officer and I'm her recruit.

"She's sleeping," I direct at the gigantic brick of gold on wheels.

We've moved several steps closer when a siren loud enough to wake the drunks still sobering up from a night of barhopping on Broadway blares. I cover my ears but can still hear Mama's twangy bellow over the loudspeaker. "Harriet Josephine Farrow, your presence is requested in the driveway."

"She's had a hard day, Mama," I try again.

"Which is exactly why I decided to switch up my original plans for our meeting tonight. Hard days only stay hard if you allow them to. There's no sense in wallowing over what can't be changed now. It's time for some good ol' fashioned cheering up, and this is just the ticket."

An instant later, Hattie staggers out the front door. Her black joggers are twisted so that the center drawstring is hooked on her right hip bone, which has become further pronounced in the months following her divorce. Hattie's build is the female version of my father's—tall and willowy, with long, lean limbs perfect for running track or walking a runway. Once on the porch, she makes a sad attempt to smooth the frizzy blonde mess atop her head before giving up. She stops short at the same place Adele and I did.

It's then our mama steps down from the bus entry. She stands there in her adorably petite high-waisted jeans, rhinestone belt, and glitzy black tank top with the words *Drama Mama* scrolled across her ample bosom. My mother doesn't own a single piece of apparel that isn't encrusted with something sparkly. One of my many questions for heaven is why Adele was the one blessed to receive the majority of our mother's genetics when the only things she ever wears are neutral-colored power suits and three-inch block heels. And a blazer. *Always* a blazer. One would never know there's a fabulous figure hidden underneath all those CEO-worthy pleats.

I, on the other hand, share neither the lean build of my father nor the hourglass figure of my mother. I'm instead the lucky recipient of a recessive genetic makeup that fashionistas on social media have coined "The Pear." No buxom bosom or thigh gap for me, folks. But I do have enough hip and booty curve to win a Hula-Hoop contest any day of the week. About the only feature I share with all the Farrow women is our hair. Each of the four of us lands somewhere on the spectrum of curls, though it's only me and my niece Cheyenne who've chosen to embrace our natural ringlets.

Mama uses the handrail to climb down the bus steps, and it's only then I wonder how she managed to get this giant rig here in the first place. She hasn't driven herself anywhere in decades, and Jana certainly doesn't have the credentials to drive something this large.

Mama waves at whoever is still inside.

"Girls, this is Eddie. He's the miracle worker behind this secret project of mine." After introducing us each by name, she addresses him directly. "You're welcome to stick around for some sweet tea and pie."

Eddie, who looks like the all-American mechanic on one of those TLC shows, gives us an awkward salute-wave and then glances at his phone. "I appreciate the offer, Ms. Farrow, but my ride is almost here. And thanks again for all the signed merch. My wife and kids will have a whole new appreciation for what I do. Feel free to give me a call if you need it moved before you leave."

"Thanks, sugar, will do." Mama tugs on the arm of his monkey suit until he hunches low enough for her to plant a kiss on his cheek. Eddie's skin flushes three shades of pink.

Our mama has truly never known a stranger.

As Eddie begins his long trek down the driveway toward the privacy gate, Mama's hands go to her hips and she looks at each of us appraisingly. "Would any of you like to take a guess at who this beauty is behind me and what she's doing here?"

My gaze is still on the retreating mechanic when Adele steps up to the plate and inspects the sparkly motor coach in front of us as if she's suddenly become an expert in transportation. "It's certainly not the tour bus I told Raegan to rent for your travels to Washington next month." Adele looks to me. "I requested a new model, black in color, and a few feet longer."

"You did. And that's what I secured. Give me just a minute and I can pull up the confirmation code." I dig for my phone in search of the confirmation email when Mama's voice brightens. "Don't bother, sweetheart. I canceled that one."

"You . . . *what?*" Adele chokes on the words. "Why on earth would you do that?"

"Because it makes no sense to travel to a festival honoring my legacy in country music on a bus that holds no legacy." Mama's smile broadens. "Which is why I paid Eddie to revive Old Goldie from her long slumber and give her a much-needed facelift. I adore how the gold shimmers in the sunshine, don't you? Eddie said it's called metal flake paint. It's even better than the original and far better than boring black."

"Old Goldie as in . . . as in the old tour bus you've been storing since the '90s?" Hattie asks, coming out of her stupor.

"That's the one." Mama beams. "She's been completely renovated inside, as well—everything feels bright and open, and all the furniture has been replaced for a more comfortable ride and stay. But the best part is all the history on the walls—I had Eddie and his team reframe all the pictures inside for us. I can hardly wait to show you around." She beams at us. "This will be the best summer we've ever spent together."

I side-eye Hattie, wondering if I'm the only sister out in left field, but it would appear by all three of our slack-jawed expressions that none of us has any clue what is happening right now. As usual, Adele takes the lead before anyone else can. "What are you talking about, Mother? Only I'm going on the road with you to Watershed. Just me and you in a rented tour bus with plenty of space and a private office I can work from inside. Your band is meeting us there, remember?"

Our mother's face looks as if she's been waiting for this moment all her life. Never mind all the times she's stood backstage at the Ryman or the Grand Ole Opry or any one of the hundreds of venues she's performed at worldwide, waiting for her name to be announced. Every morsel of her anticipation seems to be sitting on the edge of its seat, waiting for whatever comes next.

"Actually, I've been working on a new plan—with the help of Jana. She's been wonderful at sorting out all the logistics." She scans our faces and speaks as if there's a drumroll behind her. "Prior to the festival, I want to take my three daughters on a cross-country road trip that will end at one of my favorite places on earth. Just the four of us gals together, plus a driver. I'd like to leave in a week."

Nobody dares to breathe, much less speak. We just keep staring. At her, the bus, and then at each other.

"Mama," Adele says as if she's launching in with one of a thousand reasons why a trip like this can't work, and for once, I'm grateful for her assertiveness. The four of us on a bus for any amount of time sounds more like the opening of a true crime podcast than a luxury cross-country girls' trip. "You have several more rehearsals with the band scheduled, as well as choreography, and one with the stylist—"

"I can play and sing those songs in my sleep, just like the band can. And choreography? I'm not Beyoncé. I've had the same three moves since before you were born. The four of us can certainly take a couple weeks to meander the country together before the start of the festival. I'll only need twenty-four hours to rehearse. Tops."

Adele shakes her head. "While I appreciate your confidence, Mother, I think it would be best to schedule a . . . a girls' trip *after* the biggest festival of your career. There are just too many variables involved to risk something untimely happening before the show. We simply have too much at stake at the label right now for anything to go awry." She glances at the three of us for confirmation. "Maybe we can meet for a short getaway in August? A long weekend some-where, perhaps?"

"No, that's too close to when my kids come back home. I'd rather go beforehand. I'm not willing to give up a single hour of time with them for anything," Hattie replies with a directness that surprises me. Despite my role as youngest child, I'm usually the one to play middle-man when it comes to the communication between my older sisters.

"Hattie, I assure you, I wasn't trying to suggest that you . . ." Adele stops and clears her throat before she begins again in a consoling tone I rarely hear from her. "I know firsthand how difficult the next few weeks will be on you. When Cheyenne left for college, Michael and I—"

"Cheyenne is *nineteen*. Aiden and Annabelle are eight and nine and about to leave the country for the first time under the care of my cheating ex-husband and his mistress. Don't try and compare our circumstances. They're not the same. *You and I* are not the same."

"You're right," Adele retorts coldly. "We aren't. I, for one, wouldn't have dared go to a custody appeal without proper representation or a single member of my family—"

"So I suppose you think it's my fault I lost, then?" Hattie laughs darkly. "Of course you do. Feel free to add that to the tally of my sins, big sister. Lord knows you've kept a record of them."

"That's enough, girls," Mama interjects. "You're missing the whole point of this trip."

"What do you think, Rae?" Hattie swivels toward me. "You're the tie-breaker sister. Are you good with getting out of here for a couple of weeks?"

As much as I want to side with Hattie, my antihistamine-fuzzy mind can easily recall the plans I didn't add to the family calendar. The one involving Tav asking me to *"please hear him out over dinner"* once he's back from his music tour. At the moment, I'm not sure what I'm dreading more about the upcoming conversation—having to come up with a response or reopening a wound that's barely had time to form scar tissue. It's a tough call: stay home and meet up with your ex to discuss all the reasons he couldn't love you as much as you loved him, or live on a tour bus with your two sisters and hope you're not starring in a reboot of *Survivor*.

My mother and sisters watch my silent mental debate.

Adele narrows her eyes in that intrusive way of hers. "Please tell me your hesitation doesn't have to do with Octavian coming back to town."

"What? No," I lie and cross my arms over my chest. "My relationship with Tav has nothing to do with this."

"Wait, your *relationship*? I thought you ended things for good after what happened on his last tour," Hattie says, looking first to Adele and then to Mama for answers. "Did I miss something?"

Adele and I eye each other. Hattie has missed more than a few *somethings* over the last year to be sure, though most of those are what the media has been circulating about the fate of Farrow Music Productions due to the scandal involving her ex-husband.

"We're not together. Tav just wants to talk through some things, as friends," I clarify, unwilling to add more. Adele instructed me to keep the details to myself.

"It's not worth it," Hattie says flatly. "If you need any inspiration for what begging a cheater to love you looks like, look no further than my train wreck of a life." Hattie sweeps a hand down her coffee-stained T-shirt and rumpled joggers.

"We were on a break when he—"

"Didn't you ever watch the show *Friends*? Spoiler alert: 'on a break' is a big neon sign for toxic."

"He didn't cheat on me, Hattie." At least, not technically. "He was up-front with me about . . . you know what?" I shake my head. "Forget it. None of this even matters—we're supposed to be talking about Mama's trip—"

"That's right." Adele jumps in before I can finish my thought. "Bottom line, Mama, a trip of this length needs to be planned much further in advance. It's clearly bad timing."

Mama crosses her arms and widens her stance in front of the bottom step of the bus she's still guarding as the air conditioning blows her hair around her face. "Let me tell you three a thing or two about bad timing. Bad timing is when you're having a contraction with your first baby mid-chorus of 'Silent Night' during a Christmas special on national television. Bad timing is when Hattie decided to chop off her bangs two minutes before she was supposed to walk the aisle as a flower girl in a destination wedding for a band member. Bad timing is when Raegan locked herself in George Strait's cabana bathroom and we spent the whole night hollering her name only to find her passed out on the floor on top of her *Magic Tree House* chapter books. Bad timing is what parenthood is made up of; this road trip is a choice. So I'm asking you to choose to make the timing work. For my sake."

Hattie steps toward Mama. "I'll go."

Adele and I aren't nearly as impulsive as our middle sister, though our reasons for hanging back are not the same. Adele has a corporate calendar she'll need to contend with, as well as a husband and a college-age daughter to check on. Whereas the majority of *my* entire world is standing right here in this driveway—as long as you don't count the characters who live inside a fictional world far away from this one. But they've never counted for much in this crowd anyway.

And maybe it's for this reason more than any other that I step toward the gold tour bus. "I'm in, too." I smile sweetly at my oldest sister. "Don't worry, Adele. I'll make sure to update our road trip on the shared family calendar ASAP."

# 3

## Micah

I t's been a week since my kid brother, Dr. Garrett Davenport, broke down the genetic findings of my blood test into bite-size chunks while we fished the Saint Joe River in north Idaho. And even still, I was banking on a lab error. There had to be some other less life-altering explanation for the results. *Run it again,* I'd told him as I'd cast, *you know that can't be right.*

Without argument, Garrett had agreed.

But now, as I lean against the kitchen countertop in the house I grew up in, phone in hand, I know by the slow breath Garrett exhales before he speaks that the fear keeping me up at night is about to be realized.

"I'm sorry, Micah. I wanted there to be another explanation as much as you did. I ran the test multiple times. It's confirmed." Pause. Breath. "Frank Davenport is not a blood relation of yours."

*I'm not my father's son.*

Just like that, I'm teleported to another fishing trip only a couple weeks ago. Three months to the day we buried Mom, to be exact.

The trip when Garrett first suggested we should both go in for a simple screening to determine if either of us showed any pre-markers of the kidney disease that took our mother. Only, instead of being given a clean bill of health, inconsistencies surfaced, and another round of tests was suggested.

One that has been run multiple times, according to my brother.

*I'm not my father's son.*

Despite the number of workshop trainings I've taught and attended for the school district on how to reconstruct old narratives and create new neuropathways in the brain, there is no reframing technique in the world powerful enough to remove the barbed wire of betrayal slicing me open at present.

Garrett drops any trace of his doctorly voice in exchange for the brotherly tone I know best. "Where are you right now?"

"Mom and Dad's."

The tense silence that follows creates a boomerang exchange back to my ears. Our mom has been gone for three months, and now, according to a DNA test, my dad is . . . not my dad.

"Okay, listen," he says, "I'm going to cancel my last appointment at the hospital and meet you out there. I don't think you should be alone." My brother is a hero to many, myself included, but I don't want to be rescued tonight. I need to think, to plan. I need to follow through on the reason I came. Now so more than ever.

"I appreciate that, Gar, really. But I'll be fine."

"*Fine* is a four-letter word. You're the guy who taught me that, remember? Nobody is ever just fine."

"You shouldn't listen to everything I say."

"You're my big brother. It's written into the bylaws of life."

I know he's only trying to lighten the mood, but suddenly I'm consumed by the second part of an equation I hadn't put together until now. If our dad is not my blood relative, then Garrett is not my . . . he's not fully related to me, either.

We're half brothers.

"Don't cancel on your patient," I repeat as a sledgehammer strikes my temples. "It's been a trying week." Understatement. "I'm not planning on staying out here long."

My gaze catches on the infamous houseplant we nicknamed Jumanji inside Mom's office where I've been sorting a mountain of paperwork so Dad won't have to when he returns home from Alaska.

"What about meeting up for a quick bite to eat, then? Or better yet, why don't you come over tonight. You know Kacy would be happy to have you join us."

"Kacy needs a break when you get home from work; twins are a four-handed job. Probably double that most days." I pause, picturing the mischievous grins of my twin nieces. "I'll call you tonight once I'm home. I don't want you worrying about me."

"What are you even doing over there?" Something close to suspicion laces his tone, but I pretend not to notice. "Dad said he put the garden sprinklers on automatic before he left, and the mail's been stopped, right? I don't blame you for wanting to search for answers wherever you can, but this isn't your burden to bear alone, brother. I'm here, too."

"Jumanji needed water." A half truth told by a half sibling. "I've been coming out every couple of days."

A knock sounds in the background of our call, and a female voice interrupts a moment later with news that Dr. Garrett's next patient has been checked in and is waiting for him in exam room number five.

"Listen, Micah, as far as Dad's concerned—" his sigh is heavy—"I think it would be best if we waited until after he comes home to—"

"I'm not going to interrupt his fishing trip. It would be nearly impossible to get a message to Dad out at sea anyway." How strange that such a simple word like *dad* can inflict so much pain each time I say it. "This can wait until he's back."

Garrett's voice dips low. "I'd bet my medical license he doesn't know about this, Micah."

It's the same conclusion I've come to in the dead of night, as well, but a second opinion from a reliable source is always appreciated when dealing with life-altering information.

"So your working theory is that Mom managed to keep her pregnancy with me a secret from him until after they eloped?" I ask.

"That's what makes the most sense to me, considering the timeline involved."

So Garrett had been up at night thinking, too.

On the one hand, this explanation makes the pain slightly more bearable. But on the other hand, if Dad knew my mother had become pregnant with me by another man before they married, then I'd have someone to direct my questions to, a full story instead of the tiny crumb I've been handed at the age of twenty-nine. But while Frank Davenport is many things to many people, a secret-keeper he is not. The man can't hold an ace in his hand without biting his lower lip or breaking out into an anticipatory sweat. There's not a chance in this world he could have been hiding something this large from me or my brother.

Before Garrett married Kacy, the three of us Davenport men spent time outdoors together nearly every weekend. If we weren't out hiking a trail near Camp Selkirk or singing our hearts out on the open road, then we were fishing on the Saint Joe River and prepping our catches for Mom to grill. Dad gave Garrett and me his passion for nature, but really what he gave us was himself.

He wouldn't have hidden something like this from me. Nor would he have allowed my mother to. He loved his family too much to hide the truth.

"I'll talk to him when he gets back," I confirm for a second time. "He deserves this time away to clear his head. Thanks again for funding his charter passage."

"My part was easy," he offers. "You're the one who had to convince him we'd be okay if he actually left."

To some, spending a month on a deep-sea fishing excursion with an old friend in Alaska while grieving the love of your life might sound detrimental, but I can't fathom a better activity for my dad to be doing in this time. His mind and heart work best when he has a fishing rod in his hands.

"You'll be okay, too," Garrett adds quietly. "Just please don't do anything . . . impulsive."

*Like quitting your job without securing a new one,* is what we both know he doesn't add.

I make no promises as I flick on the light in my parents' kitchen. "You should get to your patient, doc. I'll call you later."

As soon as we hang up, I go in search of the real reason I came over today. It wasn't only to water Mom's beloved houseplant—that thing could survive a year outside in the Sahara. I came for the old-school answering machine I used to make fun of when I was a know-it-all kid in middle school. My parents were never fans of the ever-changing technology of cell phones. Dad kept his old flip phone until it drowned in the river one glorious day a handful of summers back, but he refused to give up their landline or the answering machine that still sits atop their counter. Last week was the first time I appreciated the thing in my life.

I tap the faded Play button and lean my back against the fridge door to relisten to a recording that has puzzled me for the past five days. The instant Luella Farrow's voice fills the room, the image of her waiting on my parents' front porch with sorrow-rimmed eyes and an overnight bag clutched in her hands pushes all else aside.

When working with my students at school, I encourage them to find alternative terminology when speaking of the villains in their stories for the same reason I don't encourage the label of victim, either. It's too easy to slip into the mindset of either extreme. Both are equal in their danger. But I'd be lying if I said I haven't thought of Luella Farrow as the villain in my mom's story for most my life, which is precisely why I'm still struggling to reconcile the woman I met three months ago with the version of her I grew up secretly despising whenever I saw her picture in supermarket magazines or heard her name whispered behind closed doors. And yet, a death-bed summons from an estranged best friend is hardly the time to be psychoanalyzing someone's true character.

"*Hi, Frank . . . it's Luella. I've been wanting to check in on you. I know you have your boys nearby, but if you ever need to talk, I'd answer day or night. I know how hard these first few months can be. After Russell died, I couldn't sleep more than two hours at a time. Sometimes I still have trouble staying asleep in an empty bed."*

I've memorized the Southern cadence of her phrasing and the way she pauses for breath right before she launches into the reason for her call.

*"Anyway, I'm calling because I found something of Lynn's I think you should have. It didn't feel right to send something of hers to your doorstep unannounced. So I'll keep it safe until I hear from you. I pray for you and your boys daily. I wish . . . I wish . . ."*

The line goes quiet for so long one would think the call had disconnected. Only, when Luella's husky voice returns, her raw words prick my eyes.

*"I wish I wouldn't have waited until good-bye was all we had left. She deserved better than that. Maybe we both did. I loved her, too."*

This time, when she drawls out her unlisted phone number, I jot it down. And before I can talk myself out of it, I punch in the numbers and make the call. The superstar herself answers on the third ring.

"Hello?" she asks, her accent bright and full.

"Hello, is this Ms. Farrow?"

"I suppose that depends on who's asking, sugar."

"This is Lynn and Frank Davenport's oldest son, Micah." I hate how the introduction leaves a strange residue on my tongue.

"Oh dear, is Frank . . . I mean, please tell me he isn't—"

"He's in Alaska for most of the summer, ma'am. Deep-sea fishing."

"Oh goodness sakes, that's a relief. You had me worried for a minute." She seems to switch mental gears. "You and your brother have been in my nightly prayers. How are you doing, darlin'?"

It's been months since I heard a maternal voice dote over me, and for a moment, the knot of grief wedged in my throat won't allow me to answer. When I do, it's far more honest than I intend. "I'm . . . doing the best I can, thank you."

"You're a school counselor, correct?"

Technically, I'm an unemployed therapist for the school district, but for the sake of brevity, I simply say, "Yes, ma'am, for the past five years."

"That sounds like commendable work."

*Commendable* is not one of the labels I'd give myself at the moment.

"What can I do for you, Micah?"

"I've been taking care of my parents' house while my dad's been away—trying to lessen the stress load on him by sorting through some of her things before he returns. I heard the message you left and was hoping to inquire after what you found of my mother's."

"That's thoughtful of you," Luella says with a touch of nostalgia. "I used to tease your mother about all the things she used to collect when we were young. She was forever hanging on to scraps of paper and pressed flowers when we were on the road. Once she scolded me for nearly tossing out the gum package we purchased in some tiny town in Oklahoma. Like everything else, she wanted to save it for Chickee."

My mind flashes back to the picture my mother kept of her grandmother—Chickee, as she called her—on her nightstand. The woman had died long before I was born, but Mom had grieved her absence until her own last breath. Chickee had taken on the impossible role of trying to make up for my mother's two neglectful, abusive parents. She'd been the one to give my mother a home, the same home I'm standing in now. As well as a family. And I suppose, in a way, she's partially responsible for giving Garrett and me the same.

"They had a special relationship," I state with care before realizing Luella would have known that. She would have known Chickee, too. I'm hopeful she knows far more than that.

Luella clears her throat. "I recently had an old tour bus remodeled. It was in storage for quite a while. When the crew demoed the bunk room, they uncovered a stack of travel journals that belonged to your mother. She always documented our travels for Chickee—started with our first cross-country trip from Idaho to Nashville. I figured your family would appreciate having them."

I work to connect the hemispheres in my brain until I can recall the detail I'm searching for. "Would this bus you restored be the one called . . . Goldie?"

Luella gasps. "You know about Old Goldie?"

*I know a lot more than that.* "The last tour you took with my mother was in 1994 aboard that bus, correct?"

"Yes, yes, that's right. Goodness, I . . . I didn't realize she spoke about those days much with anyone but your father."

Truthfully, she hadn't spoken much about them, which is why I've been conducting my own research since Garrett first noted the discrepancy within our family blood types. I wove a loose timeline of events through commentary online and stories about an old band that broke up just as they were about to strike gold. Yet lurking underneath it all was a story problem needing to be solved, one circling a secret conception that dates back to the summer of '94. The same summer Luella and Lynn went their separate ways after an unknown scandal did them in. The same summer Frank the bus driver eloped with a woman who had actively sworn off ever becoming a wife or a mother.

"Are you headed out on a tour soon?" I ask the question casually, as if I'm seated across from a student and not speaking to a three-time CMA Award–winning artist.

"Not a full tour; it's a three-day country music festival not too far away from your neck of the woods. I'm headlining the Watershed Festival at the Gorge Amphitheater in Washington. It will likely be my last time performing for a live audience, and I've always dreamed of playing there again." She says this with a confidence that surprises me. But with a hit single that's still making waves, it's hard to imagine her stepping off the stage anytime soon. Of course, I never would have imagined her sending the award she won for Song of the Year to my mother nearly five decades after they cowrote it, either—information I only learned after the ornate box was delivered and opened.

Not too long after Luella sent it, she had stood on my parents' doorstep.

"But before that," she continues, undeterred by my mental twists and turns, "I'm taking my girls on a special road trip. I'm planning to stop in many of the same places I stopped with your mother when we first left Idaho in the '70s." She sighs. "Time is a strange thing. I can still remember the smell of our old Lima Bean VW Bus. Of course, those were the days before we could even dream of affording something like Goldie. We loved Old Goldie—that gold pin stripe down the center of her all-black body. She was the prettiest thing we ever laid eyes on." She chuckles then. "I recall your father staring at your mother as if he thought the same about her." Her chuckle is softer this time. "Franklin was smitten with Lynn years before she gave in to his charm." There's something sobering in her tone. "Your dad may have driven us around the countryside, but he was so much more than a bus driver to us. My Russell used to say Frank was the glue that held the lot of us together. What I wouldn't give to have him with me and my girls this summer."

And just like that, my mind hits a series of speed bumps, slowing down my thoughts long enough to glimpse a detour sign up ahead. With all the times I've been on the open road with my father, sharing the wheel and the drive time after he retired from the school district and took on contract tours whenever he "needed to gain some fresh perspective," I know the value of a good driver. And I can picture exactly what Luella means about my father being the glue. She isn't wrong. He was the one who inspired me to go into psychology.

"I'm sure he'd appreciate hearing that," I reply. "I'll be sure to pass it along."

Unlike the stereotype, I didn't become a licensed therapist because of a messed-up home life when I was a child, or because of some need to right the wrongs of a past generation. I became a therapist because my parents loved hard, fought fair, and modeled the healthy boundaries and communication skills they attributed to their faith in God. At least, that's what I'd grown up believing, anyway. Now I can't decide what's worse: believing the wrong narrative about my childhood or being blindsided by a backstory I never saw coming.

*I'm not my father's son.*

"I'd really like to get those journals from you, Luella."

"Of course, darlin'. Just let me know where you'd like me to send—"

"Actually, I'd rather not risk them to a mail carrier. They're too valuable." I take a breath and formulate a plan I know Garrett would label impulsive if given the chance. "If it's not too much to ask, I'd like to collect them from you in person."

There's a muffled sound on the other end I can't quite decipher, followed by, "I'd love nothing more than to have you visit. I used to dream about what it would be like to have Lynn's boys over to introduce to my daughters, as well as to eat some proper Tennessee BBQ. But of course, dreams make everything seem simpler than it is." Another pause. "Please know that anyone in your family is welcome to come with you."

Her statement pricks goosebumps down my arms. A week ago, I never would have imagined such a reaction over meeting Luella's family members, much less that I'd be traveling to her home. But a week ago I still believed my family didn't have any skeletons in their closet.

"Garrett and his wife, Kacy, have two-year-old twin girls, and he's recently taken a promotion at the hospital where he works. He's not in a place where he can get away easily."

"That's understandable. Unfortunately, we're planning to hit the road this coming Saturday. I don't suppose you'd be able to come this week for a night or two, would you? You'd be welcome to stay at my home in Brentwood. Otherwise, I'm afraid such a trip might have to wait until we're back from Watershed in August."

"I'm in a bit of a job transition this summer, so my schedule is fairly flexible." Job transition? More like gainfully unemployed. But before I can backtrack my response, the impulsive thought returns. If there's one regret I've heard most often in my line of work, it can be summed up in two words: *missed opportunity.* "At the risk of sounding too presumptuous, may I ask if you've already secured a driver for your road trip?"

There's a short silence on the other end of the phone. "At the risk of sounding too presumptuous, are you asking because you might know a driver who'd be interested in taking a two-week cross-country road trip fueled by more estrogen than a sorority house?"

I can't help but smile at that. "I should disclose that I'm hardly as qualified as my father, but I have clocked a lot of miles with him at my side in all different kinds of rigs, and on many road trips. He used to volunteer us boys to drive for choir competitions and basketball tournaments. It was his way of giving back to the community—by farming his sons out for community service work."

"Why, Micah Davenport." Her voice is pure Southern sunshine now. "I do believe this phone call has just crossed the line into providential territory. If you're serious about driving for us, I'll cancel the company driver my daughter hired the second we hang up. I'd be absolutely tickled to have you join us. I can't think of a better tribute to your mama than to have you along." She sniffs and coos into the phone. "I'm so glad you called today."

"Glad I can be of service to you, Ms. Farrow."

"Luella. Please call me Luella."

We spend the next few minutes talking through the logistics, including a phone call I'll need to have with her eldest daughter regarding paperwork, but all the while my mind never stops running the hypothesis that started the instant Garret first flagged my screening test for discrepancies. Once we hang up, I push inside my mom's old music office in search of any tidbit of information I can get my hands on. If I'm going to drive their bus, then I need to figure out how to steer the narrative in the direction I need it to go.

There are two people who know what transpired on that summer tour in 1994, which resulted in a country girl from out west becoming pregnant by one man and eloping with another within the same month. One of those people is in heaven, and the other is Luella Farrow.

I may not be my father's son, but I think she could know whose son I am.

# 4

## Raegan

This morning is not the first time I've joked about changing my name to Cinderella. Barring the evil-stepmother component of that particular fairy tale, the rest of it has hit pretty close to home all week. I've spent the last seven days running a million odd errands in preparation for our departure, checking off the to-do lists Adele emails me from her corner office every morning, while also keeping Hattie from sleeping the day away. When I first moved in with Mama after Daddy died, Adele added me to the company payroll as a "strategic assistant," a title I've since come to realize is as ever-changing as the music industry itself. My duties are often a reflection of whatever Adele requires of me in the moment. Most recently, I've been tasked with being the gatekeeper of any potential threat to our family—inside or out. I can't exactly blame Adele for being protective. After everything that happened with Peter, she's ultraparanoid about who we invite into our lives.

Which is why the text from Chip Stanton that pops up between my packing tasks for the morning stops me dead in my tracks.

Chip—Fog Harbor Books:

> Hey, Raegan. I wanted to follow up with you about the rumor we discussed last Friday at the end of our meeting. I have an update whenever you have a free moment. I'm at the office early this morning.

I abandon the box of pantry goods on the counter and let myself outside to the pool patio. The July humidity is far from comfortable to linger in, but it's about the only area on the property I can guarantee privacy at this hour.

Chip answers on the first ring.

"Raegan, hey." The first thing I notice is the lack of buoyancy in his greeting. "I'm glad you called, though I wish I had a better reason to reach out."

I drop onto the corner lounge chair at the far end of the infinity pool and skip past any polite small talk. "Did you hear something more about that rumored biography?"

"Yes and no," he begins unsteadily. "I went to dinner last night with a college buddy I reconnected with at the conference in Nashville. We got to talking about our upcoming projects. He happens to work in freelance editorial for several publishing houses—mostly in nonfiction. I thought I'd broach the rumor with him, see if he'd heard anything at all. Turns out he was asked to submit a quote for a sensitive project with Willow House Press a couple of months ago." Chip slows his cadence, as if selecting each word with care before he speaks. "Nick doesn't think the project is a biography—"

"Oh, thank God." I squeeze my eyes closed and exhale a breath I didn't even know I was holding. There are gobs of opportunists all over this city looking to trade lies for a big payout, and dealing with one is the last thing we need right now. Not with Mama's festival around the corner. And certainly not when we're about to board a bus for the next two weeks. "That's a relief."

"Raegan," he says in that grounding tone again. "Nick confirmed the project has to do with your mother. He said it's already been contracted out to a popular ghostwriter in our industry. He also claims it's one of the most secretive deals he's ever been asked to submit a bid for."

"But you just said it wasn't a biography."

"Right. Because authors of biographies aren't usually kept under lock and key—even the unsanctioned ones. Nor do they require a ghostwriter well-versed in celebrity gossip and scandal."

"Scandal . . . like a tell-all?" The words feel sticky and wrong on my tongue.

"That would be my guess, yes. At the moment, Nick feels slighted by Willow House, so it's possible I might be able to eke out more information from him if he gets wind of anything else, but he and I both know the editor in charge. She's well-known for her shrewd business dealings and targeted subject matters."

Perspiration gathers at my neck from the oppressive heat, and yet an icy chill licks up my spine at his words. This can't be happening. Not now.

"I'm sorry, Raegan. I wish there was something more I could give you on this." He sighs and hesitates. "Do you know anyone close enough to your family who would be willing to sell them out?"

Immediately, a face etched in smug disregard for any of the sins he's committed against my family materializes in my mind.

*Peter San Marco.*

Just the thought of him makes me want to scream. Hasn't he taken enough from us—from Hattie? He won the lawsuit money, not to mention the shared custody he fought for and the entire summer with his kids and girlfriend in Greece.

"Possibly" is the only reply I can form back to Chip. "What can be done at this point?"

Chip goes quiet. "Not much, I'm afraid. Even if you uncovered the author's identity and tried to negotiate with them, there would still be a binding contract between the author and the publishing house—in this case, Willow Creek Press. It would be a massive and costly legal undertaking to break it, especially considering the kind of resources they've already forked out. The fact that your mother has never collaborated on a book deal tells me the publisher must believe their source is solid enough to create a mass amount of sales, especially given her recent spike in popularity."

My hope deflates. "It's pretty much the worst-case scenario, then."

"The length some people are willing to go for money is truly despicable."

*Not money,* I think. Peter has money thanks to the massive lawsuit he won after Mama's song went viral. If he's the one behind this, it's personal.

I think back to when Adele was appointed the CEO of Farrow Music Productions after our father's death, leaving Peter in the same position he'd worked at in the legal department since he married Hattie.

Is it power he wants? Retribution?

"Do you know when this . . . this book is supposed to be released?"

"Nick said there wasn't a release date specified on the paperwork he was sent, but I'll do my best to find out. It has to be recorded somewhere. The world of editorial is relatively small, and we're a surprisingly connected bunch. Dirty, underhanded deals like this tarnish the integrity of an industry many of us are working to improve. The best we can hope for is that the timing of this release will be overshadowed by something more deserving."

And yet, even with his conversational push toward optimism, I feel the distinct lack of hope at nearly every angle I consider. "I appreciate you telling me, Chip. I know you didn't have to do that." Especially considering he has no professional tie to me whatsoever.

"It was the right thing to do." Another pause. "Take care, Raegan. I'll reach out again if I hear something more."

The instant our call ends, a barrage of unknowns hit me at once. I don't want to believe the author is Peter for numerous reasons, but who else would be conniving enough to write something salacious about my mother? And who on earth would even be able to? Anyone with personal connection or access to our family has already signed their soul away in nondisclosure agreements via Adele.

*Adele.*

My sister will be here in less than an hour.

True, unadulterated panic fills me as I try to imagine how I'll tell her. I pace the length outside Mama's infinity pool, which feels as never-ending as my anxiety, before I make the distinct mental switch to go into storytelling mode. A big glob of scary details always feels a bit less overwhelming when I think of them as the plot points in a story. It reveals the things I know, but more importantly, the things I don't know yet.

If I were to boil Chip's update into a story synopsis, the plot would be about a secret book deal with unknown content that may or may not have to do with Luella Farrow, written by an anonymous author and set to be published on an unknown date. It's far from a compelling story, and there's no way Adele will be satisfied with that level of information. She'll demand more, which I don't have and won't be able to acquire with only minutes to spare before we spend the next fourteen days together on a bus.

After several long, cleansing exhales, the Armageddon-level crisis resizes to one I can pack up and take on the road with me. But the plain truth is, it would be reckless to pull the fire alarm on this without filling in some of the vital plot holes first.

At a quarter past ten, I push all thoughts of the tell-all into a mental file marked *Later* and rap on the bathroom door, informing Hattie of the time, as she still needs to take her luggage down to the bus before Adele arrives with her proverbial clipboard. Honestly, for a woman who's been walking around in the same Oreo-encrusted gray T-shirt for the better part of a week, spending an hour in the bathroom seems a bit overkill for the start of a road trip.

"Hattie?" I knock again. "Adele just texted. She's on her way. You should probably move your bags down to the bus."

"Almost finished in here. Did Jana drop our driver off yet? Mama said they were headed to pick him up a while ago. Seems odd that the driving company wouldn't drop him off." Hattie's tone is so normal sounding it almost makes me forget her sobs on my shoulder last night after she hung up with Aiden and Annabelle. They'd arrived in Greece with Peter two days ago and were yammering away at all the gifts Francesca's family had given them. "Also, isn't loading the bus a job for our driver?"

"I don't know a thing about him or the company he works for." Driver vetting is not in my jurisdiction of family responsibilities. I might have been in charge of securing the original tour bus for Mama—with Adele's approval—but she's big on checking credentials of contracted employees herself. "I took my luggage down last night." The same thing I suggested Hattie should do in order to keep the peace this morning.

"Would you mind taking mine down for me? Please? I really can't handle an Adele-lecture on how much luggage I'm bringing."

I rumple my brow. "How much luggage *are* you bringing?"

"Only two bags," she answers quickly. "I consolidated this morning."

I recite every Scripture verse I know about patience before I can muster up a reply. "I'll take them down for you, but there are still some loose ends to take care of before we can load up."

"Thank you, Sunny Bear. I'll help with whatever you have left as soon as I'm done in here."

As I walk into the room across the hall from mine to play volunteer bellhop, my eyes drop to the giant, dusty hardcase bag on the floor that looks as if it could double as a bomb shelter for children in WWII.

"Where did this brown suitcase come from?" I call back down the hallway.

Hattie is usually a designer-bag kind of gal. I can't quite see how this monstrosity would fit into her personal luggage collection.

"Found it in the garage. There's a duffel bag near the closet, too."

"Where's the Dolce and Gabbana set Mama bought you for Christmas two years ago?"

"Don't have it anymore."

"What? Why not? You loved that set."

"Raegan, I'm trying to put mascara on—do you want me to talk, or do you want me to finish getting ready so I can help?"

"Fine."

It takes two tries on the count of three to heave the mammoth eyesore to a standing position before I stack the duffle on top of it. Thankfully, there *are* wheels at the bottom. A relief, considering nothing else about this suitcase is modern or convenient. I can't remember the last time I've seen leather straps belting the girth of a suitcase.

It's a precarious task dragging the bags down the stairs, but finally, I arrive at the front door and slip on my shoes. I prepare for the heat wave I'd only just escaped a few minutes ago when I was out back. Sadly, the blacktop of the driveway will be even hotter.

The low hum of the air conditioner from the goldenrod motor coach sounds like a jet engine even from across the drive. I'm only a few steps out when I feel the remaining anti-humidity gel in my curls surrender. There is no lotion or potion that will keep these curls intact during a Tennessee summer. Halfway across, I break for breath, readjust my grip on Hattie's bags, and wonder how I got suckered into doing this again.

The wide luggage compartment at the side of the vintage bus is hinged open and resembles a mini garage door of sorts. The middle shelves are filled with supplies and totes, leaving the top and bottom shelves open. Bottom shelf it is. There's no way on earth I'd be able to lift the Brown Behemoth any higher than my knee. If I push the bag all the way to the back, it won't be visible for Adele's judgment. Although, if I'm honest, I'm feeling pretty judgy myself at the moment.

As soon as I heave the bag onto the shelf, it jams on the leather belt buckle. It takes three pushes and a hip check to make it budge an inch. Only, when it does, I hear a disturbingly loud pop followed by the clang of something solid hitting metal. *No*, I think. *Please no.* Cautiously, I bend and confirm that Hattie's luggage straps have indeed popped open. Worse, some of her clothing has been catapulted to the opposite side of the shelf.

After a choice word or two, I squat low enough to shimmy my upper body into the opening and retrieve a handful of my sister's random belongings, noting a pair of animal-print panties in the corner. I work to shove everything back where it belongs, which proves to be a difficult task, seeing as the belt loop of my shorts is caught on something along the wall. I try to reach around to unhook myself, but the space is too tight for such ninja maneuvering.

The fear of confined spaces has never been at the top of my list, but I'm beginning to reconsider that now. I scissor my leg from left to right, worried I might lose my shorts altogether as the entire bus sways with the motion. When I hear the whoosh of the bus door opening close by, followed by the distinct sound of footsteps on the stairs and then onto the pavement, relief comes swiftly.

"Hello? Jana? Is that you?" I call out. "I think my shorts are caught on something—a screw, maybe? Can you unhook me, *please*? This is far from the most flattering way to die."

There's a notable silence before a throat clears. A male throat. "That is a rather curious predicament you're in."

Mortified, I flail to the left side of this hot box and catch sight of the man who has an unobstructed view of my derriere. The stranger dips his head low enough for me to catch a brief peek at his shaggy brown hair and dark eyes. "Hey there."

"Um, hello," I say as sweat prickles the base of my neck. "Are you . . . the driver?"

"That would be me, yes. I was just inside getting acquainted with the rig." Before I can respond to this, he ducks out of view and adds, "I was also doing my best to become one with the air conditioner. Humidity doesn't mess around in these parts, does it?" His northern accent comes from the other side of me now—the stuck side. "Ah. I think I located the culprit. May I?"

"Um . . . sure?" On second thought, maybe I do want to die like this. It would be less embarrassing than facing the stranger who's had an up-close and personal view of my backside.

"Would it make you feel better if I told you I'm a card-carrying Red Cross member who's medically trained and can help you?" His honeyed voice dips with restrained humor.

"Strangely, it does," I admit.

He laughs, and then without further ado, I feel a swift yank near my right hip followed by an immediate release that causes my bent-over body to sway.

"Here, take my hand," he instructs. "I'll guide you out so you don't smack your head."

In a different life, one where there's still an ounce of dignity left to my name, I'd politely decline his offer and emerge from this underworld unscathed from humiliation. But not even my pride can will that to be the case.

My already hot-as-fire face flames as I reach for his extended hand.

As soon as I'm upright and shielding my gaze from the sun, the blood rush to my head makes me feel a bit woozy. Yet the longer I stare into the melty brown eyes of our bus driver, the worse my symptoms become. This stranger doesn't look at all like what I imagined, given his profession, and I can't decide if the stereotype is a myth or if this man is simply an anomaly of epic proportions. I work to straighten my shirt as self-consciousness consumes my entire body.

"You doing okay now?" the man, whose eyes are the color of milk chocolate and whose hair appears more auburn than brown in the sunshine, asks.

"Yes. Thanks," I say. "I don't know what I would have done if you hadn't been certified in first-aid training."

His face breaks into an amused grin. "Glad I could put it to good use on someone other than Bob the half-bodied mannequin. Honestly, he was a bit oblivious about the whole thing. Not very grateful, either."

"Torsos can be so entitled sometimes."

He's smiling in earnest now, and I can't help but join him. "Your accent isn't as strong as some of the locals I've met since I flew in. You from Tennessee?"

"Born and raised." I give my decade of voice lessons a mental high five at the compliment. Like my mother and my sisters, I can turn my Southern charm on and off at will. I swing my gaze to the bus. "I didn't realize the driving company Adele approved was out of state. She's usually not big on outsourcing."

"Driving company?" He gives a shake of his head. "Luella was actually the one to hire me. I was supposed to come by yesterday afternoon to get everything in order and meet the family, but my flight was delayed so I opted for an airport hotel. Luella's house manager . . ." He looks up and to the right as if trying to recall it. "Jane, maybe?"

"Jana," I correct.

"Yes, that's right. The two of them picked me up and took me on a mini tour of downtown before they dropped me off here in time to rescue a damsel in distress."

"Poor timing for you."

"That depends on how you look at it, I suppose."

Something flutters low in my abdomen, and I glance around the driveway for the women. "Where are they now?"

"They said they were going to pick up the coffee orders before everyone arrived." He extends his hand to me again as if this is our real first meeting. "I'm Micah, by the way. Any chance you'll be joining the Farrow women on this epic road trip, as well?"

*Joining the Farrow women?* The question barely has a chance to register when Adele's Lexus flies up the driveway and brakes to a stop beside us. She looks the two of us over from her driver's seat. Her eyes round as she focuses on the state of my frizzy hair and makeup-less, flushed face. This homely look is certainly not Adele-approved.

"So which Farrow sister is this?" Micah mutters under his breath. "Wait, let me guess—Adele, right? She has the look of a firstborn."

It's then I realize Micah doesn't think I'm one of them, the Farrow sisters. It's also then I make a split-second decision to play along rather than correct him. It would be nice to make a first impression without muddying the waters with my last name. "Ding, ding, ding."

Micah's smile doesn't wane as Adele pops open her trunk and steps out.

"Hello," she directs at our driver. "You must be Micah."

"I am, yes. It's nice to finally—"

"Did my mother give you the last of the paperwork?"

Micah blinks. "Uh, yes. I have most of it filled out in the bus."

"Great." Adele nods. "I have one more nondisclosure agreement for you to sign before we leave. I'll have it ready for you on the dining table inside."

"Sure thing," he says as Adele takes our measure.

"Micah was just helping me with the luggage," I add for no reason other than to break the odd way Adele is studying him.

"I'd appreciate some assistance with mine, as well." She nods toward her trunk. "The black bag can go in the luggage storage, and everything else can go inside. The ice cooler will need to be unpacked into the fridge. Please organize them per the color code of my nutrition protocol; it will make things easier on the—" Her words halt abruptly when her gaze zeroes in on my hand. "What on earth are you holding?"

All eyes drop to my right hand, which is still clutching a pair of animal-print panties. On instinct, I drop them to the ground, which seems to answer her first question while the awkward silence fills with a dozen more.

"Those *aren't* mine," I all but squeal in defense, stopping myself from blurting out the identity of the true owner. There are levels to sisterhood loyalty I'd never cross.

Adele's eyes drag from the sexy paraphernalia on the blacktop back to my face, which I am certain is now a brighter shade of crimson than Adele's red leather purse. She closes her eyes and seems to take a cleansing breath as if she's already had enough of this day even though it's not even noon yet. "Let's just get ready to leave, okay? I need to check on a few things inside. Have you seen Jana?"

"Sounds like she's still out on a coffee run with Luella."

Adele doesn't bat an eye when I refer to our mama by her first name. I was twelve before I realized this wasn't the normal practice of children everywhere.

After a curt nod, she walks toward the house, her block heels clacking against the driveway.

"Is she always like that?"

"Pretty much," I say as I move to collect the blue toiletry bag from her trunk.

He clears his throat for longer than what should be humanly possible. "Um, I think you might be forgetting something?"

I twist back to see him pointing at the cheetah undies on the pavement.

"It'd be a shame to lose those," he deadpans as he moves toward the trunk. "They look expensive."

"Seriously, *they aren't mine*," I hiss emphatically, swiping them up and tossing them back into the open luggage compartment.

His chuckle comes out low. "Guess I'll need to take your word for that."

He reaches with both hands for a cooler that's half the size of Adele's trunk, and it's a chore to drag my eyes away from his tan, sculpted forearms. If these are the arms of today's bus drivers, then it's a wonder why more people don't choose this mode of transportation. I sling Adele's toiletry bag and laptop satchel over my shoulder, then reach back to collect the long garment bag, nearly tripping over the tail as I work to follow our bus driver inside. Three strides into the air conditioning later, he sets the ice cooler down and heaves out a hard breath before closing the door and twisting around to face me. "You never answered my question."

I blow a chunk of frizzing curls off my forehead and plant my feet on the top step. "I'm not discussing those panties with you one more—"

"Not that." He shakes his head. "I'm still wondering if you're coming with us?"

With two cumbersome pieces of luggage slipping off my shoulder, I lay Adele's garment bag on the arm of the white pull-out sofa that stretches from the dining table to the driver's cockpit. "Pretty sure they wouldn't be able to make it five minutes on the road without me."

His next laugh determines just how much I enjoy the sound of it. "What's your name?"

I drop the last of Adele's bags at my feet and work to catch my breath. "Just call me Cinderella."

# 5

## Micah

Thanks to Cinderella, the second thoughts I've experienced since boarding that plane yesterday have eased considerably. After Luella and her house manager had dropped me off to get acquainted with the tour bus parked at her grand estate, Garrett's most recent lecture regarding my impulsivity had started to ring true. *"You do realize how ludicrous it sounds to be joining a random family for a two-week road trip in hopes it might solve the origin questions in your own family, right?"* Of course I did, and yet it wasn't enough to stop me from trying.

Out of the corner of my eye, I watch the beautiful woman I just met sort and put away each of the prepackaged meals and green drinks inside the fridge and wonder what her actual staff title is around here. If Jana is the house manager, could Cinderella be a personal assistant of sort to the sisters? I wonder how many employees it takes to run a property of this caliber. Definitely more than the grandmotherly Jana who drove ten miles under the speed limit and mentioned her arthritis flare-up at every intersection we approached. Luella, on the other hand, pointed out famous venues and landmarks like she was my personal tour guide. As she talked, it was nearly impossible to drive down Broadway without wondering how many places my mother and Luella had performed at together back in the day. And even more impossible not to think how different her life would have been if Luella hadn't pushed her from the spotlight all those years ago.

"Have you known the Farrow family long?" I ask Cinderella as I walk the length of the front lounge, which boasts white leather sofas on either side of me.

"All my life," she replies simply.

"Then can I ask you about these framed pictures on the wall? They look like they're all from the same time period." I've lost sleep over how I might broach the subject of my true parentage with Luella, but maybe I've been overthinking it. Maybe this beautiful brunette with the out-of-control curls, witty mouth, and close family connection will prove an invaluable resource.

She lifts a Greek yogurt out of the cooler with her left hand, and I'm not disappointed to discover there's no ring on her finger. She glances at me over her shoulder. "They are, actually. They're all from the last road trip this bus traveled—a music tour. What do you want to know about them?"

At her reply, my mind sharpens. It's what I'd thought when I studied them alone earlier. I'd recognized a couple of the framed pictures as duplicates of the ones my mother kept in her music office. Again, I'm surprised by how easy this seems. Perhaps God decided to throw me a bone.

"I was just trying to place the people in them. I recognize Luella, of course. She must have discovered the fountain of youth in the last thirty years because she looks the same."

Cinderella rises from where she's been squatting in front of the fridge and smooths her palm over the curve of her right hip where her belt loop is frayed from the escapade in the luggage department.

I swallow and glance away, though my pulse kicks up considerably as she nears. Her green eyes gleam with unmistakable curiosity.

"That fountain of youth's name is Elizabeth Harrington, and she's one of the most highly esteemed aestheticians in the industry." She smirks at me a bit. "Pro tip, you should really save those types of compliments for when she's around to hear them. Flattery is anything *but* overrated where she's concerned. You'll be sure to see that reflected in your tip, too. Just don't let Adele overhear you."

"Why not?" I muse. "Adele doesn't like to receive a compliment?"

"Adele doesn't like a lot of things."

Whatever hope I had at masking my growing interest in this fairy-tale-like enigma disappears in a blink. Honesty has long been the quality I'm most attracted to in a woman, and this one doesn't need any extra help in the attractive department.

Her eyebrows bunch puzzlingly as she looks from me to the picture frames and back again. "Wait, how did you know these photos were taken thirty years ago?"

For a second, my mind goes blank. Did I seriously just give myself away on my first question? *Real smooth, Davenport.* But then I remember the time stamp on the bottom right of the picture of my mom and Luella standing in front of Old Goldie in Amarillo. I know that one well; one just like it was in the oak chest Mom stored in her music office at home. I could only find three pictures of this time period in total. One of my mother and Luella in front of the white chapel at Camp Selkirk at roughly eighteen, this one, and another with Luella and Russell at a courthouse on what appeared to be their wedding day. My mom was the only other person present in the photo outside of the judge.

Thankfully, enough of the time stamp peeks out from the frame to save my hypocritical hide. If honesty happens to be among the qualities *she* admires most, then I hope my lies of omission won't completely annihilate my chances of getting to know her better on the road.

"The date on this one here—" I tap on the glass of the photo closest to me and point to the month and year. "I did the math. Thirty years ago this summer." Consequently, also nine months to my birth date.

"Wow." She stares at me, blinks. "You have freakishly good eyesight."

"I wear contacts."

"Still. That's . . . weirdly observant. You're not really an undercover FBI agent posing as a driver, are you?"

Though I can tell she means this to come off as a joke, the truth hits a little too close to home for me to laugh it off. Not FBI, just a guy who spent his entire life believing the best man he's ever known is his father when in reality his father is actually someone's best-kept secret. Or in this case, possibly two someones.'

I'll never forget the look on Luella's face after she left Mom's bedside—the resolve in her eyes, the fresh tears on her cheeks. Whatever happened behind that closed door had to be more than two friends finding peace after thirty years of fractured friendship and silence. It had to be something significant. Perhaps something that, if outed, would devastate a newly grieving husband and son after all this time. Something that would be big enough to end a childhood friendship and convicting enough to seek amends on a deathbed.

I blink the introspection away as Cinderella points to the furthest frame in the wall timeline, the one hanging above the dining table. "That one there is Luella with Adele and Hattie. I think they must have been around seven and ten—and that's Frank Davenport with them. He was the bus driver. At that point, he'd been driving them all around for several tours, maybe three or four?" Her finger swings to my mother standing on the opposite side of the frame. She's leaning against a tree in a long denim skirt and orange striped shirt, and she looks frail—even more so than on the day she died. The bottom of her Taylor guitar rests on the toe of her suede-fringed boot. I've played that guitar dozens of times, but I've never seen this picture of her before. My gaze automatically dips to her flat midsection, as if I might be able to discern a secret baby inside her womb. But not even the best contact lenses in the world could detect such a thing. "That's Lynn Hershel, who eventually became Lynn Davenport. She and . . . she and Luella were childhood best friends. They started a band together and toured for quite a while after getting signed in Nashville, decades before Luella went out on her own." She pauses, and I involuntarily hold my breath as she speaks again. "Lynn passed away recently."

When her eyes draw back to mine, I know this is the moment I should tell her that the Lynn she speaks of is actually my mother, but I care too much about the quiet thoughts lurking behind her eyes to interrupt whatever connections her synapses are making. Interruption is a therapist's worst enemy; permission their greatest advocate. Not that I could call myself much of a therapist these days. A license is only a piece of paper.

I hold her gaze for three, two, one . . .

"Sorry, I just . . ." She shakes her head.

"Did you know her?" I ask softly, ninety-nine percent sure I know the answer, but life has been too full of surprises lately not to ask.

"No, but . . ." She pauses. "This might sound super weird."

"Believe me, I'm well-acquainted with weird."

She sighs. "Drivers probably have more weird conversations than hair stylists."

I remain strategically quiet.

"I haven't said this out loud to anyone, but since you're going on this trip, too . . ." She bites her plump bottom lip, and I have to fight to concentrate on her next words. "I feel like this road trip is connected to her somehow—to her death."

"How so?" I ask.

"Closure, maybe? I don't know, it's just a theory right now. But I do know grief does strange things to people."

I wasn't prepared for her answer, but unlike the tenderhearted beauty before me, I've learned how to train my emotions before they have a chance to register on my face. "Theories can often be right."

"I guess we'll see." She points to several other photos, mentioning band members standing in front of memorable venues and national landmarks, but the one face I'm looking for above all the rest appears to be absent from every single photo. I nod along and ask appropriate questions to encourage conversation, but I'm distracted in my search all the while.

Finally, I ask.

"Did Luella's husband ever tour with her and their children?" I've done an exhaustive search on Russell Farrow online, but what's on the internet is as generic as a Wikipedia page. Birth and death dates, survivors, career focus, and notable contributions to the music industry, net worth, etc. Nothing personal. Nothing that would reveal he was a cheater who had a secret son by his wife's best friend.

"He did, but he was out of the country during this particular tour."

Her answer comes so easily and yet it doesn't compute, which is why my reply is unfiltered. "Out of the country—why? Where? For how long?" I run the math equation in my head again. For me to have a March birthday and be born full-term at eight pounds, six ounces, I had to have been conceived between late June and early July. Russell Farrow would have had to at least be in the same country to have an affair with my mother.

By the questioning expression on her face, it's clear I've tripped too far over the suspicion line. Just when I'm searching for a way to patch my blunder, the bus door opens to reveal a tall, too-thin woman with bright red lips and animal-print sandals. She climbs the stairs and meets us in the main living quarters on the bus.

"Ah, there you are, Sunny Bear. I've been looking all over for you." The woman's gaze swings from Cinderella to me. "Hello, I'm Hattie. And *you* must be our driver."

By the way she says it, I'm a hundred percent certain her definition of driver is not the same as mine. My hypothesis is confirmed when she extends her right hand toward me, grasps mine firmly, and then covers our hold with her left hand. Unlike Cinderella, there's an indent where a wedding ring used to be on her left index finger. If she wants me to notice, she's succeeded. Only, the fact that this woman is quite possibly my half sister is enough to make me retract my hand as if she's been holding it to an open flame.

"Micah," I supply. "It's nice to meet you, Hattie."

"Wow." Her eyes widen. "Has anyone ever told you how much you resemble a younger version of Ryan Reynolds? Seriously." She tips her head to the side. "I'm somewhat of an expert on him these days. I've been watching a lot of his old movies—*The Proposal* is my favorite." When her perusal of my features lingers a bit too long, I'm positive I've never felt more uncomfortable in my life.

"Um, I don't think I've seen that one."

"Really?" She pulls out her phone. "Here, I'll show you. Apart from your widow's peak, you two could be brothers. Can I take your picture?"

"*Hattie.*" An exasperated voice from my right causes my gaze to jump from the middle Farrow sister to the woman beside me— Sunny Bear? Is that what Hattie had called her? If that's her actual name, it's no wonder she prefers Cinderella.

"*What?* I was simply going to do a quick photo comparison of Ryan in *The Proposal* and Micah here." Hattie blinks her thick black eyelashes as if she's not at all embarrassed of her blatant attempts at flirting. "There's nothing indecent about giving a compliment to a handsome man."

In this moment, the perspiration gathering at the back of my neck would beg to differ.

"I'm an unattached woman," Hattie continues, undeterred. "According to ChatGPT, that's the proper terminology. *Free* is synonymous with *cheap*, and I'm definitely not that."

"Yes, Hattie, but you being an unattached woman doesn't mean that he's an unattached man who wants to be ogled. He could be married with four children for all you know."

I choke on my own saliva at the quick—yet odd—defense from Sunny Bear.

"So are you?" Hattie's point-blank assertiveness makes me forget the question.

"Am I what?" I ask.

"Married with four children?"

Both women seem to await my answer, which in and of itself is not complicated, but there are other complications that should very much be considered in this strange and awkward conversation. Like the fact that Hattie and I possibly share fifty percent of our DNA. "I'm not married, and no, I don't have children. Just twin nieces."

Hattie's grin is triumphant as she looks to my advocate, but before any more can be said on the topic, the bus door opens again. Adele enters holding a to-go coffee in one hand and a phone to her ear with the other. Luella follows her eldest daughter inside. Though I only saw her an hour or so ago, the surreal feeling I get each time I'm around her hasn't faded.

Adele halts her stride when she catches sight of Hattie. Her eyebrows raise ever-so-slightly as she scans her outfit, and I get the distinct impression that this is not typical road-trip attire for the middle Farrow sister. Without pausing her conversation on the phone, she continues on through the bunk hall and into Luella's bedroom at the rear of the bus. She closes the door behind her, leaving the four of us to stare at one another. Unlike her animal-print-wearing daughter, who is likely down one pair of matching unmentionables due to an unfortunate luggage incident, Luella is wearing all white with flashy silver accessories. She holds out a coffee tray with four drinks inside it.

"Forgive me, Micah, I wasn't expecting that coffee run with Jana to take so long. There was more traffic on this random Saturday morning than before Willie Nelson's last concert, but I knew I'd need to butter you up before asking you to maneuver Old Goldie through a coffee drive-through line." Her eyes hold a kindness I don't expect.

"There's no need for buttering me up, ma'am. I'm happy to drive wherever you want to go—coffee drive-throughs and all." I take the flimsy tray from her and allow her to pass out the drinks.

"Ah, what a gentleman you are. Thank you, Micah," Luella says. "I regret not being back in time to introduce you to everyone myself like I'd planned on, although I know you and Adele were acquainted last week on a call." She tiffs and shakes her head. "Some days I think she's forgotten how to communicate face-to-face since she's on that phone so much." She hands a coffee to Hattie, then places mine on the table. I'm expecting it when she hands one to Sunny Bear, but instead of leaving the last drink in the tray for when her youngest daughter joins us, Luella takes the last coffee for herself. The drink carrier is now empty.

She blows on the steam swirling out the spout of her coffee even though it's close to a hundred degrees outside. "Other than Jana requesting a proper good-bye hug from everyone, I think we're ready to push off."

Confused, I glance at the two ladies standing nearest the exit and wonder, not for the first time, why nobody has addressed the whereabouts of Luella's youngest daughter. Had plans changed? Or maybe the pick-up location had changed? "Will your youngest daughter be joining us farther down the road, then? Raegan, isn't it?"

Luella removes her lips from the coffee lid and shifts her gaze from me to the far end of the lounge.

"Uh, right," Sunny Bear stammers. "I was going to—"

But Luella cuts her off mid-sentence. "You see, this is why I always say proper introductions are a lost art in today's world." Luella *tsks* and makes a beckoning motion in two directions. Mine and Sunny Bear's.

"Micah, please allow me to introduce you to my youngest daughter, Raegan. And Raegan, please allow me to introduce you to Micah Davenport, Lynn's oldest son."

I was wrong.

*This right here* is without a doubt the most uncomfortable feeling I've experienced in my entire life. If there was any way I could go back in time and filter every thought I've had about Raegan upon meeting her through this one vital piece of information, I would agree to it without hesitation. Because as it stands now, I'm not sure whether to turn myself over for waterboarding or forfeit my license as a therapist.

For reasons I can only guess at, the stunned expression on Raegan's face morphs into something unreadable. But then Hattie steps between us and blocks my view of her entirely. "I've always wanted to meet Lynn's sons." I'm so caught off-guard by the spontaneous hug she gives me that I nearly miss when Raegan excuses herself, disappears down the stairwell, and exits the bus.

There's so much I don't understand in this moment, but I do know I have to follow her.

As politely as possible, I remove myself from Hattie's embrace, slip out the exit, and jog to catch up to Raegan before she makes it through the front door of a mansion that could hold at least four of my childhood homes inside it.

"Wait! I think we should probably—" But my words falter as soon as she rotates to face me. Her cheeks might be as flushed as they were when I cut her free from the luggage compartment, but her wide-eyed expression is new.

"You're really Lynn's son?" It's the bewilderment in her tone that throws me off balance.

"Yes," I admit simply. "I am."

"I . . . I don't . . . I don't even know how to process that." Her head shake is one of self-deprecation, if not full-blown humiliation. "There I was back there, just babbling on and on about those pictures." She slaps a hand to her face before peeling it back to say, "You know, stating your last name when we first met would have been *really* helpful."

I shield my eyes from the sun and do my best to match her tone. "I could say the same about your first name, *Cinderella*. I honestly thought I was talking to an employee of the Farrows."

"I *am* an employee of the Farrows," she says without a hint of spite. "The irony of *being* a Farrow and *working* for them is what makes me Cinderella. It's rare that someone doesn't know how I'm connected to my family, and I just wanted to . . ." She blows out a hard breath. "It doesn't matter. I was wrong to pretend to be someone I'm not, but if I'd known who you were from the start, I wouldn't have spoken so casually about Lynn's death *to her son.*" She looks at me as if I might have a remedy for how to fix this sad excuse of a first impression, but I'm too self-aware that my own defense on this is weak.

"I feel really stupid," she says, turning toward the house again.

"Please don't," I stammer, working to pluck all thoughts of how adorable this woman is when she's flustered from my mind. *What is wrong with me?* Isn't there supposed to be some kind of internal alarm to prevent awkward scenarios like this from ever happening? This woman could be my half sister. "You're not stupid. I apologize for not telling you my full name from the start." As well as for the rest of what I cannot tell you.

When her eyes find mine again, I'm so stunned by the tenderness I see reflected in her gaze that I can't even recall my full name, much less my reasons for being here, until I finally snap to and realize she's asking me another question.

"How did this even come about?"

I have the strongest desire to disclose everything to her, but that simply isn't possible. I can't blow my entire mission before I've even left Luella's property just because I'm an idiot with a crush—one that needs to die *right this second.*

"I'm here because your mom found something of my mother's." The truth. "When we spoke on the phone last week, she mentioned this road trip, and one thing led to another and I ended up offering to drive the bus. I thought it would be a good way to get to know your family a little better."

"But why would you want to do that?" The lack of hostility in her voice is as mesmerizing as a north Idaho sunset. I can hardly tear my eyes away from her face.

"Because our mothers shared a history I want to better understand." It's the most honest version I can offer her.

"They didn't speak for over thirty years," she lobbies.

"I know," I admit. "I can't say I understand much about the events of the past, but I do know that." When she says nothing, I take a deep breath. "I also know I'm a stranger, but I promise you, I don't mean you or your family any ill intent."

She studies me for several seconds without making a sound. "Why were you asking all those questions about my father earlier?"

I hold her gaze and speak as candidly as I can. "I'm trying to piece together the timeline of my mother's life. I want to understand how all the pieces connect. There are giant gaps in her story I'd like to fill in, especially around the time she and your mother were music partners."

"Why not ask your dad—Frank? He was around during that time, too."

I nod not only because she has a point, but also because I wish it were that simple. "Because my dad just lost the hardest battle of his life, and the last thing I want to do is make it worse by asking him questions that could spiral him to an even worse place." It's an effort to swallow the lump of emotion that lodges in my throat.

Raegan's eyes glisten. "I'm sorry. I know those words sound hollow, but I lost my dad four years ago, so I say them not because they help, but because I get it." She swallows. "I really do."

"I believe you do." Her father's death is a fact I know all too well. "You weren't wrong earlier when you said grief does strange things to people."

She nods then and waves me the rest of the way down the walkway and inside the entryway of Luella Farrow's grand estate. She ticks her head toward what looks to be a den of some sort. The air conditioning is almost as sweet of a reprieve as Raegan's benevolence.

"Okay," she starts. "To answer your question, my father was stuck in Germany for eight months in 1994. Farrow Music Productions was a new label at the time, and he was there with a team of employees trying to secure an international tour for the following year.

It ended up being a huge legal disaster after their work visas were deemed fraudulent. The entire crew was detained in a hotel for months with armed guards that kept them inside until it was sorted out between the embassies. Which didn't happen till right before Christmas."

"You're saying he missed the entire tour that summer," I repeat, taking it in.

"That's right, he did."

I can't concentrate on all the details of her story because I'm too busy doing the math in my head. Twice. The numbers don't add up. Conception. Pregnancy. My March seventh birth date. And then the August sixteenth elopement date between Frank and Lynn Davenport.

I shake my head. "And you're absolutely sure of those dates—that your father was in Germany from May through December 1994?"

She bobs her head. "You can probably Google 'music producers stuck in Germany with forged work visas' and confirm it for yourself. My mama has talked about how hard it was to take my sisters on tour that year as a single parent. It was just our two mamas together back then trying to keep their budding careers afloat." She stops and looks up at me. "Does that help fill in some of your timeline?"

"It does." I clear my throat. "Thank you."

Of all the conflicting feelings I've had in the months following my mother's death, this is by far the most conflicting one of them all. Because even though Russell Farrow was the only lead I had to go on due to the overwhelming circumstantial evidence, if he's not my biological father, then Raegan Farrow is not my biological half sister.

And I'm one hundred percent certain I've never felt more relieved about anything in my entire life.

# 6

## Raegan

Something happened in that driveway with Micah, and then again in Mama's den. Something I've struggled dozens of times over to describe in my fiction. Something not nearly as cliché as a spark but not nearly as dramatic as a divine revelation either. I suppose, at the very least, it was a connection, one unlike any I've experienced before.

I run our conversation over in my head again, trying to sort it out as Micah loads our remaining totes onto the bus as if his sole reason for being on this trip is to live up to the job title he's accepted. Yet I know it's more complicated than that. He told me so himself. And perhaps it's that—the depth of what he shared with me—that's the most disorienting part of it all.

Still is.

From my place on the bus sofa, I watch Micah from the corner of my eye as he situates himself in the driver's seat and speaks logistics with my mama for what is obviously not the first time. How many phone calls had the two of them shared? And why hadn't Mama told me she'd been in contact with Lynn's family members since her death? The questions are like an irritant in my eye. Small in size, but noticeable enough that all I want to do is flush it out.

Mama has been different since she came home from saying her final good-bye to Lynn in April, and strangely, I was the only one who seemed to notice her frequent musings about a past she'd rarely spoken of before. How I'd hear her in the den playing old songs I'd never heard her sing. How I'd walk in on private conversations with Jana—likely scheming about this very road trip. I'd mentioned it to Adele once, telling her how I'd stumbled upon her digging through old boxes of photo albums and journals at midnight more than once. And how she started sharing bits and pieces of her history with me that I'd never heard before. For most of my childhood, Luella Farrow had fought to prove her place in country music, but suddenly, in the quiet of the night, it was as if she was trying to prove she'd once been a regular girl who'd lived in a regular world with regular friends.

The dichotomy has been disorienting to say the least.

Adele dismissed my concerns, saying it was normal for people Mama's age to have bouts of nostalgia and that it would pass. Besides, she had the festival coming up, and Mama loves nothing more than being on stage playing for tens of thousands. I tried to seek Hattie's opinion on the matter as well, but she was too distraught over Peter filing for temporary custody for the summer to focus on anything else. So I stopped bringing it up. Instead, I stuffed it all down inside—all the strange things I saw and overheard as Mama's roommate. Only, now I'm starting to wonder if I'd missed something. Perhaps there was someone else Mama had been talking to these last few months.

I watch her place a hand on Micah's shoulder, and the realization hits me anew: this man is Lynn Davenport's son. I allow the fact to roll around in my brain a half dozen times until I accept it as truth. Lynn Hershel-Davenport's past connection to Mama has never been a secret. Her name even appears on the official Luella Farrow bio page as a former band member, though from all Mama's stories, especially the ones as of late, I know they were much more than that—best friends who parted badly because one of them couldn't handle the mounting pressures of fame. Right up until this moment, I believed the only thing I would ever share in common with the woman in my mama's vintage photographs is my given middle name.

And yet . . . here is her son.

It's a chore to tear my eyes away from his profile as he taps in whatever address Mama has given him into his map app, but Hattie's concerning sighs and manic scrolling of her photo album on her phone switches me into a different mode. I knew this moment of panic would come for her, I just hadn't expected it before we pulled out of the driveway.

I touch her leg in an effort to distract her. "Hey, I meant to tell you I repacked everything from the brown bag into a blue duffle." *Minus one pair of panties*, I think.

She barely reacts. Not a good sign.

"Hattie?" I try again, switching my tactic. "What time is it in Greece right now?"

Maybe if I can get her talking about Annabelle and Aiden, it'll help her internal spiral.

"Nearly four," she answers robotically, looking at a picture of Annabelle pulling a wagon full of apples at an orchard last fall. It's an adorable photo, one that could easily belong on the front of a blank stationery card for people who despise corny, canned messages. Like me.

"And what time did you agree on for your video call tonight?" It's a stipulation of the summer custody agreement. At least three video chats a week and a phone call on the off days.

"Eight their time."

"Oh, well that's not too long to go, then," I say, using my most cheery voice. "I'm sure they're going to be thrilled to see you—and maybe you'll have something fun to show them from on the road, too." Although, I haven't a clue where our first stop will be. Every time I've inquired about the driving itinerary, Mama just says she'll let us know.

Hattie shrugs as her tears well inside her perfectly lined eyes. The reaction is enough for me to push aside her uncharacteristic forwardness with Micah earlier. I can't say I don't know what's gotten into her . . . I do know. She's hurting. Tenderly, I place an arm around my fragile sister, the way she used to do with me when I was younger and knew I could talk to her about anything. I do my best to blink away the series of haunting images that invade my memory every time I see Hattie cry. Even though Micah and Mama are still engaged in conversation and Adele hasn't bothered to come out of the back room since she boarded, I keep my voice soft.

"I have no doubt Annabelle and Aiden miss you just as much as you're missing them right now. I also have no doubt that being on the road will speed up the time and give you some great content to share with them."

"I sure hope so," she says, perking up a bit. "It just feels wrong leaving on a trip without them."

Having no kids of my own yet, I have no firsthand experience with that feeling, but I do cherish my role of being an auntie. I adore both my nieces and my nephew, even though Adele's daughter, Cheyenne, is now taller, smarter, and probably all around adultier than I am. She's currently in her third year at the University of San Francisco as a business major, music minor. I miss her terribly.

I lean toward the sink counter, rip off a paper towel from the bolted-down holder, and hand it to Hattie. She blots at her eyes and sniffs.

"In good news, your makeup is on point today," I attest confidently, wishing I'd taken an extra twenty minutes to shower and freshen up in the house. My gaze finds the bathroom door on the opposite wall of the bus. It's going to be a learning curve figuring out how to get clean and ready in a two-by-two rectangle.

Hattie smiles up at me. "Thank you."

"Anytime." I tap her knee, and she sets her phone down on the cushion beside her. I hope the relief I feel is not as obvious as it seems.

Back before she had Annabelle, Hattie worked as a part-time event planner for Farrow Music. She loved collaborating with the artists for album-release parties, publicity campaigns, music videos, and more. I often wonder if she misses it. Every once in a while I can still see a glimpse of the confident, fun woman she was before she married a man who only wanted her when she was packaged a certain way—a rich trophy wife and mom whose only interests were his interests. It's no wonder Hattie struggles with her identity—she hasn't been allowed to have one for over a decade.

I'm just about to broach the subject of her considering looking into some part-time work on her off days with the kids when Mama steps into the front lounge. She stands with her back to the driver's cockpit and calls for Adele—*twice*. Shockingly, my oldest sister graces us with her presence without a phone affixed to her ear.

Mama smiles at each of us and clasps her hands. "I've told Micah we're not to start any day of this special journey without a prayer asking God for protection, guidance, and some good honest fun. Who'd like to pray for our first day?"

Our eyes dart away from one another, but nobody volunteers as Prayer Tribute. For reasons I can't fully articulate, I can pretty much pray in front of anybody *but* my two siblings. Truth is, I'd rather be caught holding a dozen random pairs of panties than be vulnerable in that way with them. Our faith journeys are not something we share with each other anymore.

"Gracious heavens, one might think I've raised a bunch of heathens. Raegan, why don't you—"

"I'll pray," says the deep voice to Mama's right.

My neck jerks up so fast I'm on the verge of whiplash when Micah meets my gaze and then dips his chin just enough for me to know he's taking one for the team. A team I'm uncertain I should join and yet . . . perhaps I already have. Perhaps what we shared back in the den was the initiation of two strangers forming an alliance.

He prays for our trip—for clear roads and no traffic and easy parking and for *good honest fun*. He says the last part with a near-perfect impersonation of Mama, and we all chuckle a bit as we say *amen*.

And then Micah takes the driver's seat again and slowly begins to pull the bus out of Mama's driveway. It's strangely captivating how at ease he seems behind the steering wheel. This bus is massive, and yet nothing about his movements make him seem intimidated.

Mama situates herself on the sofa opposite Hattie and me. There's a marked furrow in Adele's forehead as she lifts her phone and says, "I still haven't seen the email come through with the itinerary you promised, Mama. Can you send it over now, please? I need to forward it to my assistant at the office and—"

"I've had second thoughts about that promise, darlin.'" Mama says this with all the ornery conviction of a child who reveals the fingers they've crossed behind their back. "I've decided it would be more fun to keep an element of surprise for you girls."

On instinct, Hattie and I press our backs against the sofa and brace for the oncoming turbulence. Adele might be Mama's right-hand gal when it comes to her work, but they are two very different people when it comes to . . . everything else.

"I abhor surprises, Mother, you know that. That was not a part of the original deal we made when you decided to pull Old Goldie from storage and do an HGTV-style makeover on her. As far as I'm concerned, that was surprise enough. I was clear when I told you I needed to be available to the label while we are away. Furthermore, it's not safe to be gallivanting around the country without a known plan. What if there's an emergency or we have a breakdown somewhere?"

"I do have a plan, a solid one at that if you must know, and I've informed our driver of it, as well," Mama says before she makes a show of counting each one of us—including Micah. "And if there's an emergency, then there are four other passengers aboard this bus who can call for help. It only takes one finger to dial 9-1-1, and all of us are able-bodied enough to use our legs and walk if the need arises. Believe it or not, I'm a survivor of the BCP years." Mama doesn't wait for someone to ask what her abbreviation stands for before she lands her own joke. "Before Cell Phones."

Micah's unexpected chuckle from the front causes my own lips to twitch.

"I'm not okay with this," Adele states, as if that was news to anyone.

"Well, I'm not okay with you working eighty-hour weeks, so we'll have to strike a compromise for the sake of this trip, sweet pea. My vote is for you to sit back and enjoy today's ride while it's still today. Let tomorrow and all the days after that take care of themselves. It's biblical, after all."

To say Adele isn't pleased with Mama's pep talk is an understatement, but she does as Mama suggests and settles herself at the dining table without further comment. She's probably planning a mutiny for after dinner.

As soon as Micah pulls onto the main road, Mama slips one of her paint-by-number canvases from her bag along with the high-end felt markers she's opted to use in place of actual paint, and I smile at this newfound hobby of hers.

"I think I'll be Micah's co-navigator for the day," Hattie announces ten minutes into our drive. She stands and stretches, and then makes her way to the jump seat beside Micah. An option I hadn't even considered until now.

A flicker of something I don't want to name pinches in my chest at her bold assumption, only I have no logical reason to protest. Micah is a grown man. And according to him, he's an unattached man. Sure, he's a good handful of years younger than my sister, but who am I to judge?

Hattie situates herself quickly. Conversation between them seems to flow as easily as Adele opening up her laptop and getting to work at the table. I can't hear a word they're saying, but that doesn't stop the sour feeling in my stomach as I observe them.

It turns out, the sour feeling never fades. In fact, it grows worse over the next two hours.

Every time I try to focus on the list I've been keeping in my notebook, nausea creeps in. It's so bad that at one point I have to put everything down and close my eyes. Slowly, I breathe out through my mouth and in through my nose the way I saw both my sisters do while in labor.

It doesn't help.

"Raegan, are you ill?" Mama asks.

"I'll be okay."

"You're white as a northerner in winter. You're carsick, aren't you?"

"I'm just a little nauseous," I mumble quietly, leaning my head against the wall, but the world keeps moving, which means my gut keeps churning.

"You're carsick," she says as if it's a clinical diagnosis. "I thought you grew out of that."

I don't bother to tell her that I'd thought I grew out of it, too, yet the times I've sat sideways on a couch in a moving vehicle as an adult are zero.

"Hattie, your sister needs the front seat," Mama spouts abruptly.

My eyes ping open wide. "What? No, I didn't say—"

"Raegan needs to look out the front window. It's the only thing that helped her when she was young."

"But, Mama," Hattie protests, "Micah and I are having a nice conversation up here."

"*Now*, Hattie," Mama demands. "You can come paint next to me. I have plenty of extra canvases for you to choose from."

And just like that, Hattie is making her way from the cockpit to the sofas.

"Go on, Raegan," Mama says with a quick jerk of her head. "You look terrible."

My stomach churns something fierce, but this time I'm certain it has more to do with *who* I'll be sitting next to rather than where

I'll be sitting. I'm feeling so pukey that when I stand to make my way toward the cab, I have to brace myself against the wall for a few breaths.

I feel Micah's eyes on me as soon as I take the passenger seat and latch my seatbelt. We're on I-40, and it's a route I've driven a thousand times. If there are levels of carsickness shame, then I must be near the top. We're still in my home state for goodness' sake.

"I can pull over at the next exit and stop for Dramamine," comes the masculine voice to my left.

"No." I manage a whisper. "I can't take that anymore. It gives me hives."

"Okay, well you should open your eyes, then. Concentrate on those clouds in the distance, and don't look anywhere else. Take slow, deep breaths."

I'm too woozy to respond, so I do as he suggests. And within a few minutes, I feel infinitely less nauseated.

"Better?" he asks, as if he can read my mind.

"Much," I admit quietly. "That's one more punch to add to your Red Cross card."

There's a laugh in his voice when he asks, "And what happens when I reach ten punches?"

I don't trust my equilibrium enough to turn my head just yet, but my brain is finally coming online again. "That's for you to decide."

"But I'm curious what you would choose?"

My only response is a side-eye. I don't understand this game.

"If you got to choose any prize, what would it be?" he tries again.

"Time travel."

"Oh."

It's crazy how a single utterance can reveal so much. In this case, it says, *Congratulations, Raegan, you discovered the only wrong answer to this hypothetical question.*

"Sorry." I chance a look at him this time. "I should have disclosed ahead of time that I'm not good at that kind of stuff. Carsick or not."

"No, no, you did perfectly. I should have specified that the use of magical portals are definitely allowed in this game. Please carry on. I'd love to know where you would time travel to. Past or future?"

It's a harder question to answer than I realized. If I went back in time, back before Tav and I got entangled in a losing game of *I Can Love Him Enough for the Both of Us*, and back before my father passed and life as we knew it went haywire, would it have made a difference to my writing dreams? Or would it be better to travel to a time five or ten years from now and hope things might be stable enough to try my hand at publishing again under different circumstances? It's this thought that plucks at a string a little too close to another, and suddenly I'm picturing the terrifying aftermath of a tell-all that, if real, could have consequences too big to even speculate.

"I'm starting to wonder if you just slipped through a magical portal while sitting in that jump seat. . . ." Micah turns his questioning gaze on me as the bus rolls on.

"Sorry, no. I just realized that transporting to a different time won't really solve much of anything. Things are . . . what they are." I must be far sicker than I thought to admit such a thing, and yet as soon as I speak it, I feel it anew. This bizarre intimacy we stumbled into earlier.

Micah's nod is slow yet attentive. "I can relate." He adjusts his grip on the steering wheel. "It's been a heck of a year."

The sudden onset of empathy weaves like a ribbon through my rib cage the way it had before at the thought of losing a parent so suddenly.

"How long was your mother sick?" I ask, though I'm fully aware of how inappropriate this question is given the amount of time we've known each other.

"Six weeks from diagnosis to hospice."

I swallow and run my fingers along the rough seam on my jump seat. "That's so quick."

"Sometimes I hate myself for being glad it went as quickly as it did in the end." He keeps his eyes straight ahead but speaks in a measured tone. "What kind of son prays for God to take their mother home to heaven over waiting on a miracle?" He expels a slow breath. "But seeing someone you love in that much pain is . . . it's unbearable."

"A merciful son," I say in response to his question. "I, on the other hand, begged God to save my dad after his heart attack. I was too selfish to pray for what would be best for him because a life without my dad felt like the most unimaginable thing in the world. Still does some days."

"That's not selfish," he says.

"And praying for your mama's freedom is nothing short of loving."

We glance at each other then, realizing just how bizarre it is to be having such a raw conversation with a near stranger. Yet, perhaps Micah is more legend than stranger. I've known his name my whole life, like a comic-book character born in a parallel universe to my own. He was the baby born to a woman who broke my mama's heart and nearly her passion for music all at the same time. After the Lynn & Luella's tour of '94, Mama didn't sing publicly again for close to three years. I was a toddler the first time she took the stage as a reinvented solo act—one who started from the ground up in nearly every way.

"What was he like?" Micah asks. "Your dad."

"The perfect balance to my mother." I laugh to myself. "Dad was levelheaded and logical, a goal-setter by nature. He was hardworking, innovative, and wise. No matter how many birthdays he had, retirement was always at least five years away. . . ." I pause there for just a minute. "He loved his family, and he never stopped cheering Mama on."

"He sounds like he was a great man."

"The best," I agree.

Micah's lips part, and he looks as if he wants to say something more on the subject but then seems to reconsider. "You speak like a writer."

A quick rush of air escapes me. "*What?*"

"It's not just the words you use, but how you string them together."

My heart begins to race, and I'm utterly speechless at—

"Also, your sister may have mentioned you enjoy writing." He carries on as if this is a natural conversation. Hardly.

"There's no way she just came out and told you that."

"Why not? Is it a secret?" Sudden interest laces his tone as he glances in his mirrors and changes lanes. The sun is high in the sky now, radiating off the paved highway and causing those mirage-like squiggles to appear in the distance. I squint my eyes, wishing for sunglasses.

"No, it's just not something I discuss with people much, so I know Hattie wouldn't volunteer that information at random."

"You might be surprised at the information people volunteer when the right questions are asked."

I'm still struck by the implication that he asked Hattie a question about me when he hits me with: "So what kind of writer are you, Raegan? Fiction, nonfiction? Sports columns? How-to guides? Advertising? Obituaries?"

"Obituaries?" I blurt with a laugh, realizing how much better I feel sitting in this jump seat over the sofa in the back. "Do I really seem like the kind of person who writes obituaries?"

"What? Not cut out for the rigid *deadlines*?"

I roll my eyes. "Are you positive you're not a dad of four? Because you sure tell jokes like you are."

"Positive."

I take a minute to secure the words in my brain before I expound. "I write fiction. Mostly contemporary."

"About what?" he prompts.

"Anything that interests me. But most recently, about family." These words do come naturally. "I write about the struggling individuals who make up a family—the nuances of their roles, limitations, expectations, and pressures—and how the community around them either helps or hinders what they want most."

"And what do they want?"

"What all of us want, I suppose. Acceptance, freedom, love, a place to belong." I swallow and return my gaze to the steaming pavement ahead. "People who they belong with." I think of Allie's words when she described *The Sisters of Birch Grove* to Chip the night of the Christmas party. "A friend once described it as a love story dedicated to an entire town." Something in my chest stirs as I recall the many journeys of the residents of Birch Grove. I miss them. I miss writing.

"Wait—this is an actual book you've published? I admit, I mostly read nonfiction, but I usually enjoy at least one novel during the summer. I'll download yours at our next stop. I'm intrigued."

The cramp in my chest expands as I admit, "It's not published. It's only a hobby for now."

"For now," he repeats. "But you don't want it to stay that way."

He can't possibly know how right he is. I think back to my conversation with Chip, and regret and desire war within me. "The timing's not right for it to be anything more."

"Why's that?"

I screw my eyes into slits and examine his profile. "Ya know, you might be the nosiest bus driver in history."

"I had a really good teacher," he quips as a white Honda Pilot passes us on the left. "My dad always peppered us with questions when we rode in the jump seat, so you can thank him."

I study the time-to-destination numbers at the bottom of the navigational app on his phone. "Where are we headed? What's in Memphis that's worth stopping at?"

"Afraid that's a question you'll have to ask your mother." He winks. "I'm just the driver, remember?"

Only something inside me knows this man is so much more than that.

# 7

## Micah

Graceland in Memphis, Tennessee, was not the destination I'd been expecting Luella to request for our first stop of the trip. For one, it was only three and a half hours away from her property in Brentwood, and for two, no one on board this renovated motor coach seems too excited about the idea of touring the King of Rock and Roll's grandiose estate. With the exception of Raegan. Unlike my other passengers, she's never been before. Something else we have in common.

As soon as I pull Old Goldie through the famous music-note gates of Graceland, it's clear this is no ordinary tour. The red sign posted on the black security box out front reads: *Closed until 3:00 p.m. for a private tour.*

"Roll on up to the speaker, Micah sweetie," Luella says, making her way up to the driver's cockpit. "You can let the security team know Jana Barkley's guests have arrived."

"Jana's guests?" I ask.

"Yes, Jana helped me arrange all the lodging and private events for this special trip. Everything is reserved under her name so only those who need to be in the know are privy to our comings and goings."

I glance at Raegan in the jump seat for clarification. "Mama's presence can cause a bit of a stir if we don't have certain protocols in place."

Outside of the hat and oversize sunglasses Luella had worn to pick me up from my hotel this morning, I hadn't given much thought to all the safety measures involved in an excursion like this. What a different life my own mother led from Luella, raising her two sons at home and only sharing her musical talents with a rural school district in north Idaho.

After gaining clearance from Graceland's security team, I steer Old Goldie through the gate and up the slight incline to the driveway. "How do you know the staff at these places won't tell their social media followers where you'll be?" The longer I consider it, the more difficult the idea of keeping Luella's anonymity under the radar for a trip across the country becomes.

"Confidentiality clause. Jana sent one out everywhere we're going. Adele made sure."

"Ah yes," I say. "I signed a couple of those myself." Along with a brick of other paperwork Adele sent prior to my flight out.

I flick my gaze to the rearview mirror, where Adele is typing furiously on her laptop at the dining table. I suppose a legal agreement does make sense, and yet this life of VIP tours, disguises, and secret identities is as uncommon to me as the South's humidity meter. Once we're parked, I lend a guiding hand to each of the four Farrow women as they exit the bus. I'm expecting to wander around the property on my own during their tour when Luella unexpectedly links her arm through mine.

"Did you know your mother had the biggest crush on Elvis when we were girls?"

I laugh, surprised. "Not sure I did."

"So it's safe for me to assume she never told you about the time we won concert tickets in a dance-off to see him on our first road trip together in '75."

"A dance-off? Are you sure you're talking about *my* mother?"

She swats me with her free hand, and despite myself, I smile at her feistiness. "I most certainly am. The dance-off was sponsored by a local radio station, and wouldn't you know, your mother was the last woman standing in that entire dance hall! She had moves I'd never seen before." Luella laughs heartily. "Talk about being in the right place at the right time. And that concert . . . wow. It was a night to remember. It's hard to believe Elvis died just six short years later. We stopped here again together many years after he was laid to rest on our way back to Nashville. Of course, I didn't know at the time it would be our last tour."

The blazing heat is unbearable, yet the date she mentions manages to block out the potency of the sun's rays momentarily. "Are you referencing the summer of 1994?"

"That's right. It was just me, your mom, Jana, my girls, and of course, your mother's not-so-secret admirer, Franklin. The band rode in a separate bus—it was less complicated that way. Single-parenting on the road wasn't the easiest thing I'd ever done, especially without my Russell that summer."

Her reference reminds me to confirm the story Raegan told me about Germany as soon as I have a minute alone in my bunk tonight.

"I'm sure it wasn't," I empathize. "Were there any other stops you made after Graceland?"

"Not that I can remember, but that was over thirty years ago now. If we did stop somewhere, she might have mentioned it in her journals."

I picture the thick plastic box Luella handed me this morning and where I'd tucked it deep into my bunk for safekeeping.

"Chickee made her promise to record all our adventures on the road, and your mother was faithful to do so, even after your grandmother passed away." Luella stops at the end of the walkway just before Elvis's front porch steps, allowing her daughters to go inside the mansion before us. "When you're young, you think you'll always remember the moments that mattered most to you with vibrant clarity." She shakes her head. "But that's simply not true."

Her admission darts through my chest just as a gentleman in a three-piece suit opens the front door to Elvis's former home and introduces himself as Charles, our VIP tour guide for the day. I'm tempted to excuse myself right then from today's excursion in lieu of time with my mother's journals when Raegan rotates in our direction from inside the marbled foyer. Her gaze locks with mine, and my feet make their own decision to join her. I'll have plenty of time to crack open the journals after we stop for the night.

During the ninety-minute tour, we see no other tourists and very few staff members. But the expectation that Luella will host a private meet-and-greet for a handful of employees after we finish up here has been implied by Charles more than once. Luella doesn't so much as bat an eyelash at his comments. Maybe it's all part of the agreement Jana sent out beforehand. Or maybe she's simply too busy hunting for the exact background of a photo she took with her two oldest daughters in Graceland more than thirty years ago.

"Here it is!" Luella confirms with a spark of exuberance I'm realizing is quite common for her. "This is the very same fireplace we took the picture in front of, girls. You were in the middle, Hattie, and you were to the far right, Adele."

Unfortunately, neither of them is paying attention. Adele has been quite invested in whatever's going on in her inbox for most of the day, and Hattie has been single-minded about getting to a secluded location with good enough cell coverage in time to take a video call with her kids. At least *her* preoccupation is understandable. I've been around enough struggling families after divorce to see Hattie's desperation for what it is—critical to her survival.

Luella frowns as she regards her two oldest daughters in all of their distracted glory. This is hardly the first time she's tried to engage them in a walk down memory lane today. And despite my own unresolved issues with the woman, I'd be an unempathetic jerk not to feel sorry for her unseen efforts. Raegan must feel similarly as she twists away from yet another plaque of information on the wall to look between her sisters and her mother.

"I'll take the picture," she announces with a peace-making tone that catches my ear and causes me to analyze her anew. Even though I've instructed myself to only be a bus driver and *not* a therapist for the next two weeks, that part of my brain is more difficult to remove than I thought. "I just texted Jana to send me a pic of the original photo so we can get the re-creation just right. I should have it in just a second."

"Thank you, darlin', but what I need most is for your two sisters to *get off their phones* and pay attention."

Luella's stern reprimand is not unlike that of my own mother. And it works.

Adele and Hattie snap to attention, looking as if they've been sent to their rooms without supper rather than asked to participate in a day their mother obviously took time and forethought to plan.

"I'm ready, Mama," Hattie says cheerily, exchanging her phone for a tube of glossy lip stuff.

Adele slips her phone into her blazer pocket and joins the group without a word. Her compliance is less eager than Hattie's but more efficient as she silently situates herself where Luella is pointing without asking questions that could delay the process.

I step behind Raegan as she sets up the shot, referencing the old picture on her phone. She ducks to avoid shadows and even asks Charles to open the blinds at one point in order to get the re-creation as close to the original photo as possible. It's as endearing as it is telling.

"How about I take one with all four of you now?" I reach around her for the phone she's holding, and Raegan startles at my nearness.

"I wasn't here when they took the originals," Raegan says simply.

I hold her gaze. "But you're here now, aren't you?"

"Come on, Sunny Bear." Luella waves her youngest in while her sisters remain planted in their spots. Raegan crouches low in the front and pastes on a smile, clearly uncomfortable. I'm beginning to see why Raegan identifies with Cinderella more and more. Now, if only I could figure out why her nickname among her family is Sunny Bear.

I take three shots in total and then check the screen. I'm startled by how deceptive the images appear. I used to tell my students at school how easy it is for a picture to lie—for a social media post or YouTube video to mislead an audience—but this might be the first time I've watched it play out in real time. These four women are all beautiful, intelligent, successful, wealthy, and privileged beyond ninety-nine percent of the population, and yet something acute is missing from all of them. I just haven't put my finger on it quite yet.

I hand the phone back to Raegan.

"Perfect," Luella chimes. "Thank you, Micah."

"Mother, it's nearly four," Adele states. "We should get your obligations to the staff here finished up before the public tours begin again."

Luella checks her own watch. "But the Lisa Marie is up next, and I was hoping to get some family pictures out there, as well. It's the best part of the whole tour. Don't you remember how fascinated you and Hattie were with that tiny 24-karat gold sink? Raegan's never seen it."

"Hattie and I were fascinated by everything at that age. We're fine to skip it this time around. Raegan can go, but we are too pressed for time to add anything more without being seen. I also need to make a phone call to HR once we're back on the bus. Apparently, I'm the only one who knows how to properly deal with a disgruntled ex-employee."

The announcement seems to spark Raegan's interest, and she turns to face her oldest sister. "What are they disgruntled about?"

Adele briefly meets her sister's gaze before slipping her phone from her pocket again. "That I hold people accountable to what they sign."

Raegan's eyes and tone grow instantly concerned. "What happened? Did they leak something? Is that why you fired them?"

Adele's eye contact is far more pointed this time when she addresses her youngest sister. "If you'd like to weigh in on how I lead the family business, then you're more than welcome to attend one of the monthly board meetings you've been invited to for the last four years, Raegan. If not, then please kindly keep your judgment to yourself."

"But I'm not judging, I was just trying to—"

"Why don't you go take that tour of the Lisa Marie for Mama, okay? We'll meet everybody back at the bus later."

Adele turns toward the tour guide with a pasted-on smile. "We're ready when you are, Charles."

"Oh! My kids are calling—they're early!" Hattie glances around the room with panicked eyes as her phone continues to alert her of the incoming video call. She takes a quick step away from the group and answers with a grin. The sound Hattie makes when their faces come into view on the handheld screen is half sob, half laugh.

"Mom! Mom!" Her son and daughter cheer. "Can you see us?"

"Yes, yes. Hi, Annabelle! Hi, Aiden! Hey, wait a minute, why do you both look so grown up already? I thought we made a deal. No growing up this summer!" Hattie's teasing tone resounds inside the parlor, and with a quick glance to my left, I confirm I'm not the only one captivated by her animated conversation. Hattie might struggle with who she is as an unattached single adult, but she certainly knows who she is within this dymanic duo.

Raegan catches my eye, and we exchange smiles as the banter between Hattie and her kids continues.

"Would the two of you like to know where *I* am?" Hattie's voice grows more dramatic, and both kids stop talking immediately. "This is Charles. He's our tour guide today at a special place called Graceland—where Elvis Presley used to live. He's offered to let me show you some really fancy old cars in the automotive museum."

The kids begin to talk over each other, and I can no longer make out what they are saying, other than that there's obviously a lot of excitement, especially from Aiden.

Like the trooper Charles has shown himself to be since our crew first arrived, he escorts Hattie—and by default, her children—from the room and toward the promised cars. Adele and Luella follow suit only a few seconds later, leaving Raegan and I alone on the main floor of a mansion that if sold could put a massive dent in world hunger.

"Looks like it's just you and me." I state the obvious and hold up the brochure, which pinpoints the location of the Lisa Marie on the jetway. "Here's hoping the walking outside part is shorter than this looks."

"Please don't feel obligated to join me."

"If that's not your subtle way of uninviting me, then I'd like to go. I can't remember the last time I toured a dead celebrity's private jet. Oh, wait, yes I can. It was never."

She laughs obligingly. "I hear company is always better when touring a private jet. Let's go."

When I pull the front door open, I immediately stifle a groan from the hellish wall of misery that consumes us as we step into the open air.

I used to think the idea of frying an egg on a sidewalk was a myth; but now it feels as if I could fry an egg on every surface of my body in direct view of the sun. And then there's the issue of the humidity. How do people breathe in this part of the country without worrying about aspirating? I tug at the neckline of my blue polo, wishing there was a slab of ice I could pay to lie on for an hour or two.

"You doing okay?" Raegan glances at me, but I'm already looking at her. She's not even broken out in a sweat, and we've been walking on this hot black tar for more than five minutes.

"How do you look so normal right now?"

"If that's how you compliment women up north, you should really work on that."

My brain is quickly overheating. "No, I mean, how do you look like you could endure several more miles in this sauna and think nothing of it?"

She shrugs. "I'm acclimated. I've grown up in this all my life."

"I'm sorry."

She rolls her eyes as we approach the base of the jetway steps. "Just stop focusing on it so much. It's not as bad as you're making it out to be."

"You're right, it's far worse. The only reason I'm still walking is because my desire for air conditioning is weaker than my pride. Barely."

When we hike the steps up to the jet and enter the cabin of the Lisa Marie, I'm sure I've never been more thankful for the cool blast of air that greets us from the sealed-off cockpit area and saves me from making an even bigger fool of myself.

"See? You made it," Raegan offers. "Good job."

I wipe the river of sweat flowing from my temples with the hem of my shirt. "Yay me."

Before she can roll her eyes at me this time, an automated voice comes on over the loudspeakers, informing us we are on a self-guided tour of the 1958 Convair 880, the Lisa Marie. We both snap to attention as if at any moment, the King himself might come through that cabin door and tell us to behave while on his aircraft. We meander through the entire jet only a few feet apart, pointing out details to each other after "the voice" prompts us to view the stunning 24-karat gold sink, the private library, and the queen-size bed with attached seatbelts near the rear of the plane.

"This is all pretty crazy, isn't it?" Raegan muses. "One man's talent was responsible for all this . . ."

I weigh her tone for any trace of irony. Sure, Luella's mansion in Brentwood isn't Graceland, but in terms of wealth comparison, her property could easily be considered a great-grandchild to this one. No private jets or vintage automobile museums that I know of, but an impressive dwelling and estate to say the least.

"It is," I venture, "but your family's talent has built a pretty impressive empire, as well."

She twists back. "*Empire* is a bit of a stretch. And it's not my family's talent, just my mother's."

An interesting distinction to be sure. "But all of you have an important role to play when it comes to Farrow Music Productions, right?"

Raegan leans against a curved wall. "In theory? Yes. In reality?" She shrugs. "Some roles are more critical than others."

I think back to Raegan's interest in Adele's HR issue at the office. "Do you want to be more involved in the business side of things?"

"Definitely not. Although working so closely with my sister would provide me plenty of writing fodder, I'm sure."

I smile at that. "I certainly don't envy the ex-employee she referred to today."

Raegan's expression morphs into something indecipherable. It's the same expression she wore earlier back in the manor. "Me either. There were quite a few layoffs earlier last year, but as far as I knew, things have been pretty stable at the company for a while now. It's partly why I was so surprised to hear her mention a recent firing."

"Any idea who it could be?"

She shakes her head. "Not a clue."

I'm about to ask another question on the matter when her phone rings. We both startle at the loud sound inside such a tight enclosure. She pulls the phone from her back pocket and looks from the screen to me before deciding to swipe right. It's only then I realize it's a video call.

Two in one afternoon. These sisters are popular.

"Sorry, but I need to take this," she says to me, while ducking into the conference room area . . . which is only a few yards from where I'm standing. I can't see the guy on the other end of the phone, but I can certainly hear him and the guitar he's strumming when the call picks up.

"Hey, Rae Rae. How are you? I texted you earlier—was hoping to get your thoughts on some lyrics I'm stuck on."

"Oh, right. Yeah . . . um, I'm actually in Graceland at the moment. On board the Lisa Marie. We stopped here for a private tour."

"No kidding? I just told the guys we need to book a show in Memphis sometime. Feel like I owe it to Elvis to add a stop. How's the trip going? Everybody still alive so far?"

She laughs, and I notice how different it is from the laughs I've heard from her today. This one is more controlled, almost practiced sounding. "So far, yes. But it's only been a few hours."

"You'll make it; you're a survivor."

There's an uncomfortable pause so I take a step to the right in order to catch a peek at Raegan. Her free hand hangs at her side, and she flexes it into a nervous fist over and over. Interesting. Who is this guy to her? They're far too polite to be romantically inter-twined, and yet they're clearly more than casual acquaintances. The tension between them is confusing.

They both start talking at once when I hear Raegan say, "Were you calling to play me the chorus you're stuck on?"

"Yeah, but if it's a bad time . . ."

"No, go ahead. I'm not sure what my connection will be once I'm back on the road. I have a couple minutes to listen now."

The guitar starts up again, a slow finger-picking melody with a minor bent. "I don't have a strong hook for this chorus yet. That's why I'm asking my muse for her help."

A gruff voice with a country twang fills the jet, and I take an-other step to the right. I catch a brief view of the singer. Blond. Scruffy jawline. Cowboy hat. "'When you left I thought I'd drown in a river of my own tears; my lungs still cry out for breath yet the air they crave is no longer there. . . .' And then maybe something about how we belong together." The guitar stops abruptly. "What do you think so far?"

"Wow . . . that's a really different sound for you."

"The guys have been challenging me to go deeper, dig up a new emotional well. You like it?"

"It's definitely deeper. What's it for?"

"Our next tour. Gage said our list needs a good breakup song, something that will spark the tears."

Raegan's hand flexes several times before she speaks. "Is there a story behind those lyrics?"

"Nah, it's just fiction," he provides. "Which is why I thought you could write it better than me. I'm hoping to have it finished by the end of week. That is, if you think you might have some time to spare?"

"I'll do my best."

"Thanks, Rae Rae. I . . . it's not the same back home without you." A thick pause. "I miss you. I hope you've been thinking about what I asked you last time we talked. I know I have."

"I have, too." Her fist squeezes closed and holds so long her knuckles blanch white. "Tell the band I say hello."

"Will do. Talk to you later."

I watch her lower the phone and exhale several times with her back still to me. I manage to turn away before she heads in my direction. I don't bother pretending to be busy as there's nothing to occupy myself with other than my phone, and that's a bad habit I don't need to pick up again given the challenge I extend to my students to plan mental breaks from screens. Or rather, a challenge I used to extend to my past students. Back when I had a stable career path.

"Sorry about that, that was . . ." My eyes meet hers, waiting for her answer. "My ex, Tav."

*Raegan has an ex-boyfriend.* And by the sounds of it, that relationship status is either brand-new or questionable at the moment. A wave of disappointment swoops in at the revelation. It takes me a second to find my bearings, and when I do, all I can come up with is "So he's a musician?"

"He's actually the lead singer in a band that signed with Farrow Music a few years ago. He's been working on his songwriting."

*Sounds like you're working on his songwriting,* is what I don't say. "Country music?"

"More of a hybrid of new country with a bit of pop, too. They're an eclectic sound. I'm proud of him," she says with an added edge to her voice. "He's wanted this for a long time. He's on a short break from his tour right now, at home in Nashville."

"And you're here," I fill in the blank, stating the obvious.

"Yes," she says on an exhale. "I'm here."

I study her face as a million new questions compile in the silence that passes between us, but there's only so much a near-stranger can ask without risking a complete shutdown. And truthfully, Raegan having a complicated relationship with an ex who is obviously still connected to her is probably for the best. I don't need any added complications right now. I need to read my mother's journals and utilize the time I have with Luella to figure out who my biological father is. That's why I'm here. Nothing more.

"We should probably head back to the bus. I have a few hours of drive time left before we get to our stop tonight."

"You're probably right," she affirms with a nod. "It's been a long day."

When we exit the jet, I will myself to make it across the entire tarmac without breaking into a sweat. I last four seconds.

---

Our darkened tour bus is tucked in for the night just two hours past the Arkansas state line in a private RV park owned by a famous friend Luella didn't bother to name and I didn't bother to ask. Between the jet lag, the drive time, and all the extra variables that come with life on the road with four adult women I've known for less than twelve hours . . . I'm spent.

Now, in the privacy of my bunk, I'm closer in proximity to each of the Farrow sisters than I ever would have imagined I'd be, but the one directly across from me has been quiet for most of the evening. Raegan spent the last leg of our drive head down in her notebook, writing sentences at lightning speed only to cross them out seconds later.

More than once, I wanted to ask to read whatever she was busy working on.

And more than once, I wanted to banish myself to a dark corner so I could regroup and focus on the real reason I'm here.

With my blackout curtain completely closed, I prop myself up on my side and immediately regret the move. My shoulder scrapes the bottom of the hard wooden bunk bed above me where Adele is sleeping with a white-noise machine that could wake the dead. Speaking of, if I ever wanted to know what the inside of a coffin is like, my present reality can't be too far off. My dad never mentioned the sleeping arrangements when he spoke of his glory days as a tour bus driver before he married my mom. How did he do this? He's a full three inches taller than my six-foot-two frame and thicker around the middle, although I suppose he wasn't nearly as bulky in his late twenties. A lot of things were different back then.

I set my flashlight on my phone to the brightest level and illuminate my coffin before reaching for the box Luella gave me earlier. Once I remove the lid, I stare at the half dozen or so journals of varying sizes inside. The moment feels almost as surreal as it did when I found a few treasured photographs and postcards in my mom's music office after she passed.

Not for the first time, I wonder why my mother never requested her journals back from Luella. She had to have known where she'd left them all these years. Why would she trust a woman she hadn't spoken to in nearly thirty years with such personal possessions? And what all had my mother told her oldest friend in those intermittent hours of lucidity only days before she crossed into heaven?

I run my thumb along the spines of the journals and then order them by the dates listed on the inside covers. Some span a year, while others span several years. It's clear my mother wasn't a daily journal keeper, but a situational one.

As I crack open the oldest journal in the pile, dated May 1975 with an earthy green canvas cover and a worn yellow peace sign on the front, there's a charcoal drawing of a building I'd recognize anywhere on the very first page: the old chapel at Camp Selkirk, near my hometown in north Idaho. It looks exactly the same today as it did fifty years ago, as does the mountain range behind it and the river flowing just below it. My mother's first month of entries as a Camp Selkirk employee are fairly limited in details, other than to describe her daily tasks doing grounds maintenance work at the summer job Chickee made her get once she turned eighteen. It's clear this job was not my mother's first choice but equally clear that Chickee's hopes for her to *"meet friends"* and *"get a life outside of playing my guitar in my bedroom"* were top priority. I flip through several pages of sketches of flowers, trees, and plenty of peace signs in various styles, and I smile at the number of times Mom mentions how much she dislikes keeping this journal for Chickee when it would be far easier for her to simply *"ride back home and tell you the events of the day in less time than it takes to come up with these dumb words."*

Though it was rare for my mom to open up about her life before she had Garrett and me, her stories about Chickee were always a highlight. From what I can remember, after Chickee rescued my mother at the age of fourteen from her father's house, armed with nothing more than her walking cane and a hardback Bible, her degenerative illness eventually took away her mobility. But from the way my mom always told it, Chickee refused to allow her illness to limit her mind or her faith, and she certainly didn't allow it to limit my mom. She was a woman of prayer with hundreds of prayer rocks lining her garden to show for it.

I yawn, about ready to give in to the heavy call of sleep, when I see an entry that features far more exclamation marks than all the others I've read combined . . . as well as a name I recognize.

*June 2, 1975*

*Dear Chickee,*
    *I'm overwhelmed! I can hardly hold my pen without feeling faint from everything that happened at the chapel tonight. I wonder if you*

*could hear the singing from your porch? There were hundreds of people everywhere! All the inside seats were taken, and people were sitting outside on the dirt and grass. The speaker was so passionate! I'm not sure I can describe it all in words, but I never want to forget this night or this feeling. I didn't know if I would ever believe what those preach-ers you listen to on the radio say . . . but tonight I believe. We stayed in that chapel till after midnight. There was so much praying, crying, and singing that when the speaker finally asked if there was anyone who wanted to make a decision to follow Christ, I couldn't wait to shoot my hand up. I know you're probably in shock over that; I think I'm still in a bit of shock. But I wasn't alone. Luella, one of my cabin mates, held her hand up, too. We prayed together, and then about thirty minutes later we were walking hand in hand to get baptized in the river under a full moon with dozens of our friends. I've never seen so many hippies in one place, and I couldn't stop crying. I don't think I'll ever be able to top this moment. I don't think I ever want to.*

*I know I've grumbled about you making me spend my summer at camp, but tonight I want to thank you. I think God might have prompted you to send me here. What do you think?*

*Starting tomorrow morning I'm going to start playing the guitar for Luella during the morning chapel. She has a beautiful voice, and she's asked if I'd accompany her as she's still learning how to play.*

*I love you,*
*Lynn*

I pause for a long moment, so moved by the experience my mother recorded all those years ago, and yet saddened by the fact I never heard that story from her in person. Garrett and I have attended that same camp, sang inside that same chapel, and were even baptized in that same river, and yet I never knew my mother had led the way in all of it. I read several more entries, detailing the guitar lessons my mother was giving Luella in exchange for voice lessons. Apparently, Luella had dropped out of an elite music program in Atlanta, much to her parents' disapproval, and busked her way to her aunt's house, located in a town about an hour from Camp Selkirk. Another fact I hadn't known.

I continue reading until my eyes lose focus.

*July 7, 1975*

*Dear Chickee,*

*For the last week, Luella and I have been leading the song service in the evenings. At first, my nerves were so bad I told Luella I was too afraid to harmonize with her for fear I might lose my dinner onstage. But she told me stage fright means I'm focusing too much on myself and not enough on who we're singing to—God. So that shut me up right quick.*

*I haven't told her everything about my life before coming to live with you yet, but I will. I trust her, and I think trust has a lot to do with what takes people from being average friends to best friends. I also think playing music together must do that, too.*

*Between you and me, I feel like each time we play and sing together something in me begins to change. Like maybe I can truly become someone else, someone with a different story, someone _free_. Luella talks a lot about wanting to fall in love. She can be a bit of a flirt around the guys, but I told her last night that I don't care a thing about falling in love. All I care about is never losing this new peace I've found.*

*I've asked Luella what she's planning to do after camp closes for the summer, but all she'll say is that she hopes to follow the music.*

*I love you,*
*Lynn*

*August 4, 1975*

*Dear Chickee,*

*You made me promise I would write this all down after we spoke on the phone tonight, but I don't feel much like writing. I don't feel much like praying, either, which is the other thing you told me to do. I think I'm going to take a walk around the trails and then try again later.*

*I'm back. My head is a little clearer now although my heart still feels torn in half.*

*The longer version of the story: Luella met a man with a deep Southern accent (similar to hers but different) who came up to her after chapel last night. He said he drove all the way from Tennessee trying to find an original sound and that he felt God lead him to our camp. He also claims that Luella is exactly who he's been searching the country for all summer long. He works for a recording label in Nashville and offered Luella a chance to meet his partners and see about making an album together in country music.*

*The short story: Luella told Russell Farrow the only way she'd go to Nashville in pursuit of a record deal is if he offered her a packaged deal: me and her, together. Russell said if she showed up in Nashville, he'd give her whatever deal she wanted.*

*The even shorter story: I don't want to leave you.*

*The shortest story: you told me to go.*

*I love you,*
*Lynn*

# 8

## Raegan

The rocking motion I wake to is smooth enough not to be an earthquake but shocking enough for me to forget where I am for several heartbeats. The privacy curtain attached to my cubby is slit just enough near my feet to allow in a spear of light from inside the bus. It's my only indication that life outside this dark cocoon exists.

Adele's white-noise machine is turned up so loud I can't even hear myself cough as I clear the sleep from my throat and peel back the thick black fabric to peek out. Adele's curtain is open, her bed made with a gray and white down comforter and matching pillowcase. She must have left her sound machine on for the rest of us. Micah's privacy curtain is closed, but seeing as the bus is moving, it's safe to assume he's behind the wheel. I slide my head out just enough to glance at the bunk above mine. Hattie is still up there. I know this because her socked foot is sticking into the narrow passageway between bunks. At least I'm not the last one up—not that I'm trying to impress anyone with my promptness, seeing as Micah said the majority of the morning would be spent crossing through Arkansas. Adele might not enjoy Mama's daily surprise destination plan, but I'm enjoying the spontaneity more than I expected.

I search for my phone under my pillow and pull it out, guessing the hour to be around eight when it's actually nearly nine. Before I have enough time to evaluate if I should be ashamed of myself, I notice the text notifications on my phone.

Chip—Fog Harbor Books:

> I sent you an email from my personal account. Please read it in a private place and don't forward it on to anyone else. If I can do more for you, I will.

My stomach is empty, but I have that sinking sensation in my core like I'm going to be sick. I brace myself as I tap into my inbox and pull up his email.

Raegan,

I hope you'll see my text first, but just in case, please only read this attachment in a private location, and please delete this email as soon as you've read it. I broke more than one rule to get this to you, but I thought maybe if you had a piece of real evidence you might be able to identify the author behind the ghostwriter. I've had no luck on that part yet. For the sake of my source, I won't disclose how I came about this excerpt.

Chip

My fingers are shaking as I note the file name: *Luella Farrow: Lies to Legend. A true story of friends, family, fame, and fraud.* I click into the attachment.

*Proposal by: Anonymous*
*Proposed Word Count: 75,000*
*Sample Chapters: Included*

I'm so disoriented by the title that I scroll to the end of the document for context before I attempt to read a single sentence. There's a short summary at the top promising exclusive information on Mama's early history in music, followed by an account of her personal and professional mistakes, milestones, and failures, and the fraud that's long plagued Farrow Music Productions.

My stomach lurches as I read the attached three sample chapters.

Fire fuels my veins as I read an exaggerated tale of how my mother left Idaho as a poor nineteen-year-old young woman and embarked on a reckless dream with little more than a guitar, an orphaned friend, and a stunning talent which, according to the author, she used to hitchhike her way across the country and do whatever it took to find fame in Nashville. A gross misrepresentation.

In these short early chapters there are some details that ring true, others that are mostly true, and still others that are blatant lies. Despite myself, I have to admit that the writing is decent, even if it feels generic and soulless. I read on, mentally filtering through a narrow list of suspects who might have enough intimacy with my family to know any of these early memories—true or not. Peter, unfortunately, still remains at the top.

What strikes me most, other than the audacity of someone who would willingly sell out my mother for money, is how none of us had any clue this was happening right under our noses. I think of all the times I researched late into the night in search of a single detail I needed in order to finish a scene or add to a location or character in my fiction work. How does a person go about writing an entire book about someone's life without extensive interviews and supporting documents? I'm my mother's daughter, for goodness' sake, and I wouldn't even claim to be able to write her entire story without fact-checking with the source throughout.

I'm almost to the end of the final paragraph of chapter three, the last chapter provided in the sample, when I read a sentence I'm not at all expecting, one revealing the secret wedding anniversary date of October 21, 1980, that my parents managed to keep private for over forty years. When Mama and Lynn first signed with their label, they'd agreed to certain stipulations; one of those was in regard to their marital statuses. For this reason, my parents planned a wedding in secret at the courthouse—which they never shared with the public, even after their "secret romance" made the tabloids. For the sake of Mama's fans and her record label, my parents "got married" two years later in front of thousands. Only a select few knew of my parents' private tradition of celebrating their real wedding anniversary by eating hot chicken at sunset.

There's no denying it now. This is happening. Whoever the author is, it's someone with intimate access to my mother's history and possibly the label, as well. Someone who has likely sat at our family dining table . . . or is, at the very least, close enough to someone who has.

Before I throw off my covers, I open my notes app on my phone and pound out every key phrase I might need to jog my memory in the future, and then I do as Chip asked and delete the file. It's painful to watch it disappear from my inbox when it's the only piece of evidence I have to go off of, but it's the right thing to do. I have no doubt Chip risked his job—possibly more—by sending it to me in the first place.

In the tiny bathroom on board the bus, my movements are robotic as I change from my pj's, reset my high ponytail, and brush my teeth, all while my motion sickness works in tandem with my anxiety. How exactly do I go about making an announcement that will derail not only the rest of this trip but possibly the mental health of both my sisters—one for a company she's fought to stabilize after so much upheaval, and the other for a bully ex-husband who refuses to let her heal?

I don't believe in hate, and yet I can't think of a synonym that better describes what I feel at the moment for Peter San Marco.

Adele's back is to me at the table when I approach the front lounge. The bus sways a bit on the highway, and I brace a hand to the wall for stabilization. I want to offer up a prayer for guidance and help, but the words in my heart feel as jumbled as my nerves. All I manage is a simple, *Please, God.*

It's then, as I watch my sister stretch her neck from side to side and take a drink from her green breakfast smoothie, that I see the screensaver on her open laptop. It's a picture of her standing in front of Farrow Music Productions with the entire staff two Christmases ago, back before so many things flipped upside down. They're all wearing Santa hats and grinning as if they could all see the bonus checks Adele would hand out moments after the shot was taken. I skim their faces, wondering which of them was fired for breaking the office confidentiality clause. At the thought, something clicks in my author brain. What if the disgruntled ex-employee Adele's been handling has been syphoning information from the office? It's more than likely they would have worked with Peter during his decade there—could the two be in cahoots somehow? Could the ex-employee have been a spy for Peter?

I recognize that even though the accusation has the potential to be a far greater threat to my mother and to my entire family, it's still only speculation at this point. What if I'm wrong and I turn everybody on Peter and it's not him? A shiver runs the length of my spine.

I need more information.

Too bad everything I need is locked inside Adele's hard drive.

I'm just about to clear my throat and ask Adele if we can talk in private when my sister slides the laptop toward herself and banishes the festive picture for the password key with a swipe of her finger. In a split-second decision, I'm stepping closer to peer over her shoulder. My heart pounds in my ears as I watch her type CheyenneAvery04. My niece's full name and birth year. Not a great password for a CEO to keep, but one I won't soon forget.

I tuck the knowledge away as guilt presses in.

She starts to turn when my voice squeaks, "Morning!"

She jumps and smacks a hand to her chest. "Raegan! Are you trying to kill me?"

"Sorry." I wince.

She breathes out one of her overly annoyed sighs. "Why are you standing so close?"

I do a quick glance around me. "Um . . . I was just going to ask you if Mama is still asleep?"

Adele looks at me as if I'm a few cards short of a full deck. Maybe I am. "Hardly. She's been awake since six *not* doing any of the pre-festival tasks I've asked her to do in the mornings." She rubs at her temples. "I swear, it's like she enjoys working against her own best interest."

"Oh, I don't think that's—"

Adele's scowl tells me whatever I think is not welcome at the moment.

"I'm certain two weeks will never feel as long as this again," she adds.

I can't argue with that.

Adele points toward the front. "Mama just brought Micah a third refill of coffee about ten minutes ago. She's in the jump seat."

I frown, failing in my mental efforts to understand how time works. "How long have we been on the road?"

"Two hours."

"Did Mama say where we're headed yet?"

"No, but she hinted at something involving swimsuits."

If anything could shake the intrusive fear of a corporate spy working against us from my head, it's imminent swimwear. "I really hope you're wrong."

"So do I," she says through an almost empathetic-looking smile.

And it's right then, in that exact millisecond, I'm tempted to unload the heavy burden I'm carrying into the capable arms of my big sister in hopes that the two of us might problem-solve it together. My palms grow damp, and despite the low-level motion sickness I've experienced since the moment I climbed out of my bunk, I shove it down and open my mouth to—

"You're not eating enough green veggies," Adele says matter-of-factly before looking to her laptop screen again. "It's why the dark circles under your eyes are still present after a full night of sleep. Drink one of my kale smoothies at lunch today—it will help."

And just like that, the warm, sisterly moment is gone. Who was I kidding? Adele is a solo act, a take-over, take-charge type. Do I really want to pour more kerosene on that fire before I'm certain who she should be pointing the torch at? Definitely not.

"I'll try that, thanks," I lie. I'd rather drink from the gray water tank than have one of her uppity smoothies.

I move toward the front unsteadily, knowing it's only a matter of minutes before I reach the point of no return with my nausea, and yet the idea of sitting beside Micah again makes me feel a bit squirrelly. Yesterday at Graceland with him was . . . confusing. As was the way he searched my face after Tav called. I don't know what it is about him, but every time we share the same space, I have this weird compulsion to divulge far more about myself than I do with anyone else. And right now, that's a very, very bad idea.

I'm holding far too many unlit explosives to suddenly become an oversharer. An overthinker is bad enough.

By the time I reach the closed curtain separating the passenger lounge from the driver's cockpit, Micah's voice has already woven its way to my ears. Only, I'm surprised by the content of their conversation, or rather, by the timeline he's rehashing—the tour of '94. Again. If he wants to fill in the holes of his mother's life, shouldn't he be asking questions about decades earlier? Our mothers' journey together *ended* in 1994.

"Russell's homecoming from Germany that Christmas was a gift from heaven," my mama says.

"Sounds like there's a story there."

"I tend to reserve the good ones for a captive audience."

"Don't think I can get much more captive than this, ma'am."

Mama laughs. "You have your father's humor."

Still hidden from their view, I lean against the wall behind Micah's seat and listen to a story I used to hear every Christmas Eve—told in dual-perspective.

"It was Christmas Eve of 1994, and I hadn't heard a peep from Russell in nearly two days. I was worried sick! The embassy was operating on holiday hours, and my contact there hadn't returned my calls. The last thing I'd heard was that there was to be a mediation between the two embassies to finally resolve the visas, but then there was nothing but radio silence." Mama pauses, and I lean closer to the curtain. "There had been so many deep losses to grieve that year, and I was certain I wouldn't survive another if something terrible happened to my husband. When I finally stumbled to my bedroom around midnight, I'd convinced myself that this would be our worst Christmas and that somehow I'd have to pull myself together for the sake of the girls. There were a few wrapped presents under the tree courtesy of bandmates and friends, but I felt as if my heart had been removed from my body, and all that was left was an empty shell. You ever felt that way, Micah?"

"Pretty close, ma'am."

Mama sighs. "Just as I reached my bedroom door at the top of the stairs, ready to cry myself to sleep, I heard the sound of jingle bells coming from the driveway outside. Given the late hour, I thought I must be delirious, but the bells continued. And then I heard the front door open. I was so petrified, I froze like a statue right there in the hallway, trying to think of how I could protect my daughters as I was certain I was about to be murdered by a burglar disguised as Old Saint Nick. What a headline that would make."

"Woman Attacked on Christmas Eve by Candy-Cane Wielding Santa?" Micah replies with a hint of amusement. "A true American horror movie if ever there was one."

"Exactly!" Mama exclaims. "But when that jolly old Mr. Claus climbed the stairs and appeared with his fake pillowed belly, long white beard, and red velvet hat, his eyes were the only thing I could see. For the first time in months, my heart felt like it could beat again. My Russell had returned, and I needed him more than I'd ever needed anyone in that moment."

I can hear the tears in Mama's voice, which cause my own eyes to mist with the memory of the last time I heard my daddy tell his version of that story five Christmas Eves ago. How he'd paid the taxi cab driver handsomely to give him the rented Santa suit hanging in a bag in the back seat from a costume shop across town. The way my straightlaced father spoke of undressing in an airport taxi cab after barely catching his red-eye flight from Germany ranks as one of the funniest stories in my family's vault of memories.

"When Russell finally wrapped his arms around me, after all those months, he whispered, 'Merry Christmas, Lulu. I hope you can forgive me for running a bit late.'"

"Lulu?" Micah repeats.

"That's what he called me," she says. "To be honest, I hardly remember a time when he called me Luella. The day we were married, he told me he would agree to share my name with the world but he would never agree to share my heart with anyone else."

"A true romantic, then?"

"Oh, he was so much more than a romantic, sweet boy. He was my hero." I smile at the admiration in Mama's voice and slowly pull back the privacy curtain, bringing a close to story time and hopefully an end to the crashing waves inside my core.

"Good morning," I say.

"Good morning, darlin'! I didn't realize you were awake. I've been warming up your seat for you." She scans my face and frowns. "Goodness, you look pale. Here, let's trade."

Mama holds her hand out to me, and we gingerly exchange places.

"Your mother makes for a great road-trip companion," Micah says as soon as I'm seated. "She's kept me well-entertained."

After I buckle up, it's a struggle to keep my eyes trained on the horizon like I should when the view to my immediate left is far more appealing. I chastise myself for thinking like a romance writer and not like a regular human being who can simply turn unwanted attraction off. Because that's what I need to do with Micah—turn it off.

"Wait—you can't stop there, Luella," Micah calls out to Mama.

"I need to know how Russell knew about Raegan before you. Did the angel Gabriel come to him in a dream?"

Mama slaps him on the shoulder. "You're closer than you realize!"

I lean my head against the seat. "My dad bought her a—"

"Don't you go spoiling my story now, Sunny Bear. How much longer do we have until we arrive, Micah?"

"We should be at our destination in roughly twenty minutes."

"Plenty of time, then," Mama says as he continues on the interstate. I notice for the first time how rich the scenery around us has become. I know we're in Arkansas by the exquisite Ozarks and thick evergreen forests. It's beautiful.

We pass an interstate sign that proclaims: *Hot Springs, Arkansas 15 miles* and another highlighting a popular destination called Bathhouse Row.

Mama moves up to the stairs. "Can you see this in the mirror, Micah?" She lifts the gold necklace out of the neckline of her shirt that she's worn around her neck since before I was born. It glistens in the sunlight, and I can tell the instant Micah catches the reflection of it in the rearview mirror.

"Is that three angels holding hands?" he asks.

"Yes. It's the gift Russell brought home from Germany for me that Christmas. Oh, how he loved to tell this story on Raegan's birthday." Mama reaches forward and squeezes my shoulder. "When he left the American embassy and was headed with the crew to the airport, he told the driver he couldn't go home without a single Christmas present for his wife and daughters, but there wasn't a store open. You see, it was nearly Christmas Day in Germany. But the driver's wife's family owned a jewelry store, so he pulled over to the side of the road and made a single phone call. Russell said a few blocks later their driver pulled up to a store that looked like it could be a replica in my little porcelain Christmas village I put out each year. He only had five minutes to pick something out, but he said the instant he saw this necklace he knew it was the right one. Naturally, when he gave it to me, I assumed the three angels represented me, Adele, and Hattie. But when he slipped it around my neck he told me that as soon as he saw it he knew the three angels represented his three daughters. Of course, I'd laughed at him—we'd tried for years to have another baby after Hattie. I told him I was too old now and that he had it wrong. But wouldn't you know it, I found out I was pregnant with our Raegan three years later at the age of forty-one! It's what inspired the song 'My Daughters Three.'"

"That really *is* quite the story," he says, regarding me again. "Guess you're one of the select few in history whose births were prophesied ahead of time."

"You should have seen these two girls when they were young. They were obsessed with our Sunny Bear here. For years, it was like she had three mamas fussing over her. And now she's the one who's often taking care of us. She's always there to help when there's a need." Mama presses a kiss to my head. "I don't know what this family would do without her."

Her assessment rubs against a sore spot. Is that what I'm doing now—taking care of them by keeping the tell-all a secret?

Mama turns then, saying, "Looks like Hattie is up and about. I better tell her to unpack her swimsuit."

The second she's out of earshot, I address Micah. "Please tell me whatever Mama has planned today doesn't have something to do with that bathhouse sign I saw a while back."

"Sorry, but I'm locked in a verbal contract with your mother. I'm not allowed to disclose that information to any of—"

I swipe his coffee from the cup holder. "You will if you want your caffeine."

He eyes me as if trying to size up my threat. "You do realize that's my third cup this morning, right? Some of us don't wait until nearly ten to grace the world with their presence."

I begin to slide the window open and take the lid off his travel mug.

"Whoa, whoa—okay, yes. You're going to the public bathhouse, although for you gals it won't be very public seeing as your mom rented the entire place out for the day. She sounds pretty jazzed about it." He arches an eyebrow at me. "I gather you're not a morning person."

I slide the window closed and slump back in my seat. "Not this morning, I'm not."

"Why's that?" he asks, the concern in his voice tugging at some invisible chain inside me.

"Forget it." I stretch my neck side to side and try to recalibrate. "I'll be fine."

"Feelings inside not expressed."

I twist to look at him. "Excuse me?"

"That's what *fine* stands for. It's a cop-out people use when they want to avoid having a real conversation."

I eye him strangely. "That's a . . . really weird thing to say."

"Maybe, but it's true."

I think on my answer, knowing I can't possibly disclose Chip's findings to him or tell him how I'm planning to break into my sister's laptop after she goes to bed tonight to scope out information on the fired employee. But the way he keeps glancing at me breaks down my good judgment. Before I can stop myself, I ask, "Can I ask you something?"

"Sure."

"If you knew some . . . some potentially critical information that could cause pain to someone you loved, would you confess what you knew immediately, regardless of circumstance? Or do you think there's a right time and place to divulge a painful truth?"

His gaze flares with surprise before he schools his expression into something more pensive. It's as if he's working to read between each one of my chosen words. "I think the answer depends on what you value most."

"How do you mean?"

His face remains contemplative as he navigates the bus toward the exit ramp. "What if you tried flipping the question around on yourself? Would you feel loved if someone waited for the perfect time and place to tell you that same painful truth? Or would you want to know immediately 'regardless of circumstance,' as you put it?"

Guilt chews at my subconscious even after I say, "I'd value the thoughtfulness of how and when I'm told." His silence is causing me to second-guess my stance. "What about you?"

"The truth, regardless of circumstance," he says without missing a beat.

His conviction is a gavel strike to my ribs, and perhaps that's why I can't quite bring myself to meet his eye again. If Micah knew the specifics of what I'm dealing with, would he feel the same? Or would he understand this murky gray area I find myself in now?

We begin to descend into a small city folded inside a valley. Sunshine and mountains surround us, and Micah slowly weaves the bus down multiple streets. A few minutes later, when we turn into a parking lot, I jump as Hattie squeals for everybody to look out the windows. I twist to see a street lined with ornate buildings to my right—bathhouses. I count eight in total. The architecture is breathtaking. Some of them look like they could be photographed in a European history book, while others boast more of a mythical, ethereal vibe. All are as unique as they are intricate.

Micah circles to find a place to park our mammoth tour bus.

"This is a very special place," Mama announces. "Jana has arranged for us all to spend the day here, soaking in the mineral baths that come directly from the town's natural hot spring. Adele, with your new interest in health and wellness, I think you'll find the health benefits to your liking. There's even a steam cave they've opened for us to enjoy at our leisure." Mama's arms swing open wide. "The best part is we'll get to experience it together. They have robes and towels for us inside; just wear your suits."

"Oh, I could cry—you're giving us a spa day, Mama?" Hattie claps her hands together. "This is the best road trip ever."

Apparently, she didn't have the same start to her morning as I did.

"Micah, will you be staying inside the bus?" Adele asks with a quarter of Hattie's enthusiasm. "I need to know how securely I should lock up my personal items."

I glance at Micah who, for some reason, is looking at me when he says, "I was actually planning to hike one of the trails in the Hot Springs National Forest." He picks up his phone and studies the screen, and even from here I can see the flashing red heat advisory.

"You can't go hiking in the forest—it's a billion degree outside." Hattie's brow furrows. "Mama, tell Micah he's invited to come with us."

I feel him trying to catch my eye as if he wants me to weigh in, but I'm currently too busy trying to figure out the best way to forfeit swimwear time so I can engage in espionage.

"Everything I've planned on the road includes you, as well, Micah," Mama confirms. "You're a welcome and honored guest. Plus, you may like to check out the place where your mother once bribed a service attendant to turn their backs so we could break in and have ourselves a decent shower and soak after being on the road for days. For payment, she offered to draw the attendant any picture she requested."

"My mother did that?" He doesn't even try to keep the suspicion from his tone.

"Sure did. On our first road trip together in 1975." Mama winks.

Just as Micah says, "I'll grab my shorts," I'm saying, "I think I'll stay back."

Our eyes lock, and I don't miss the hint of surprise in his.

"Don't be ridiculous, Raegan," Hattie dismisses. "This is *Spa Day*. You can't miss it."

"Really, I'll be fine," I say, feigning a yawn. "Micah can go on ahead, and I'll stay back and have some downtime in the bus. I brought some vacation reads to pass the time. Don't bother locking your stuff up, Adele," I offer, hoping she can't hear the tremble of fear in my voice. "I won't be going anywhere."

"No way, you're not missing out to play security guard for Adele." Hattie narrows her eyes suspiciously and uses her mom-tone. "She can toss her stuff in the bedroom safe like everybody else. Now, go get your suit on. We're not leaving without you."

"I never asked Raegan to stay back for my sake," Adele defends in a semi-calm voice. "I simply asked Micah what his plans entailed."

Hattie turns and cuts her gaze to Adele. "Oh, please, if you're too blind to see that the reason Raegan offered is because you're constantly asking menial tasks of her all the time, then you're in more denial than I thought."

Adele jerks her head back. And so do I. I've never heard Hattie stick up for me like this. At least not in a very long time.

"Oh, *I'm* the one in denial?" Adele prods. "Perhaps we should take a look at your—"

"That's enough, girls," Mama's voice is stern as she swings her gaze from them to me. "Raegan, get your stuff. We'll meet you outside."

Moments later, the lot of us head out into the streets of Hot Springs, Arkansas—one Farrow superstar mama wearing a yellow sunhat and dark glasses, three irritable sisters in swimsuit coverups, and one bus driver in camo board shorts who is watching me like a hawk.

# 9

## Raegan

Our stroll isn't much longer than the length of a block, but the sticky heat outside is an indication of just how efficient the AC is inside our home on wheels. I really wish I was still in it. Even after Hattie's odd defense of me in the bus, it's hard not to feel irritated at her as she prances ahead of me on the sidewalk without a care in the world, wearing a sheer swimsuit cover-up over a bikini that offers little to the imagination. Adele's modest one-piece, on the other hand, might as well be a winter turtleneck. If there are two more opposite personalities in all the world, I don't know them.

I check the knot of my sarong at my waist, wishing for the hundredth time that I'd taken the extra ten minutes to shave my legs prior to leaving home two days ago. I can't say for sure when the last time I shaved was, but I'm positive these legs are not swimsuit ready.

When we approach the front of the street and face the elaborate bathhouses, Mama points to the one with the dome on top—the Quapaw. "This is the one!"

"Oh goodie," I hear Adele mutter under her breath as Hattie cheers. "I can't wait."

Micah reaches out to hold the door for our family parade as we file in by birth order, leaving me to enter in front of him.

"What's wrong?" His voice rumbles low against my ear.

I do my best not to react to the scattering of goosebumps along my neck. "Nothing's wrong."

"Then why did you suggest staying back on the bus?"

"Because I like to read in peace." I glance over my shoulder at him.

If there's a universal face that says liar-liar-pants-on-fire, then he's wearing it proudly. "Or perhaps you were hoping to make a phone call in peace?" Micah's pace slows down, separating us a bit from Mama and my sisters.

"What phone call?" I ask, confused.

But instead of offering clarification, he answers with a question of his own. "How long were you and Tav together?"

Now *this* warrants my full and complete attention. "*What?*" I spin around to face him, misjudging our proximity by nearly six inches when the door closes at his back and bumps him closer.

His voice comes out nearly as serene as whatever wind-chime melody is playing in this foyer. "I'm assuming he's the one you're trying to spare by finding the right time and place to communicate your *potentially critical information* to?"

His word choice is a defibrillator to my memory, zapping me back to our conversation earlier on the drive. *Wait*—Micah thinks my question was related to *Tav*? He thinks the reason I wanted to stay on the bus was to call my ex-boyfriend? It takes me a second to digest this new line of thought, but given my actual reason for wanting to stay behind, this one has to be an easier out . . . right?

"How long were we together?" I repeat his original question in hopes of skipping over his most recent one. I don't want to flat out lie to him. "Um, I guess that depends. Tav and I were close friends before we dated. The timeline kind of runs together."

The slow bob of his chin causes me to zero in on his throat and the pronounced slide of his Adam's apple. And then my gaze slips a notch lower to the raw edge of his T-shirt resting against his collar bone.

"So your breakup was recent?"

"Last fall," I answer before I can stop myself. *How does he keep doing that to me?*

"Only, my guess is Tav doesn't want it to be over, and you're still debating on what it is you want." The conclusion he draws feels too easy. Yet, he's not entirely wrong.

"How did you . . . I mean . . . that's really not any of your . . . " I blow out a hard breath that ripples the fabric of his shirt. "It's more complicated than that."

Needing a reprieve, I twist away from him to catch up with my family. Three attendants dressed in white are already going over the policies and procedures when we step up to the desk.

"Welcome." A smiling woman with gorgeous dark eyes dips her head in greeting when we approach. She hands us each a key for our lockers in the changing room. "We hope you enjoy your soak and your time in the steam cave. Each of you has a slotted massage time, as well."

"Thank you, Shirley," Mama says, shaking her hand. "We appreciate you accommodating us today. Jana said your staff has gone above and beyond."

Shirley dips her head. "It's truly our pleasure, ma'am. The girls and I, well, we're really big fans of your music." The two young ladies at Shirley's side nod vigorously—Katlyn and Carrie. "There were several rounds of rock, paper, scissors to see who would be assisting you and your family today."

Adele steps forward. "Before we partake in any services today, I'd like to verify that Jana sent our standard confidentiality agreement when she rented this . . ." Adele cranes her neck in an arch as if trying to decide what she thinks of today's unconventional destination. ". . . unique establishment."

"Yes, ma'am, she certainly did. All waivers have been signed by our staff. We're ready to accommodate you as discreetly as possible. We're thrilled the Quapaw is a stop on your special trip."

"Well, I, for one, am ready," Hattie says. "I haven't had a spa day since my kids were in diapers and Peter whisked me away to . . ." She stops herself, and suddenly none of us knows where to look.

Thankfully, Shirley knows how to take a cue. She opens her arms, showmanship-style, and addresses our group of five. "Before I have Katlyn and Carrie escort you to the locker rooms for towels and robes and your pre-showers, please allow me to give you a brief overview. The Quapaw is unique because it's the only *public* bathhouse on Bath Row. Our thermal pool room offers four mineral pools at varying temperatures for optimal benefits in circulation and overall wellness. While you relax, our staff will be standing by to assist you. Please let us know if you require any refreshments. We are also here to escort you to our steam cave built over a natural hot spring at your convenience."

"Lovely. I'm certainly ready for a soak." Mama tugs off her sun hat, lets her thick blond curls cascade down her back, and lifts her sunglasses to her head to reveal her perfectly smooth skin and moderately made-up face. All three attendants gawk at her. She starts to follow Carrie, our attendant, when she spins back and says, "At the risk of sounding presumptuous, if there's any staff interested in taking a few selfies while I'm still dry, this would be the time. I promise my drowned-rat look is not nearly as appealing."

"Oh yes, ma'am."

"Thank you, ma'am."

"Thank you, Ms. Farrow!"

Adele stays as attendants from around the bathhouse gather around Mama while Hattie and I follow the pre-shower procedures before entering the thermal pools. My hair looks like a piece of abstract art after walking outside—like tangled arid noodles, hanging every which way. I'm desperate for a deep conditioning treatment.

Hattie and I leave the locker room wrapped in our fluffy white spa robes, and I plead with God to let us be the first inside the pool. The gorgeous solarium boasts several arched, stained-glass skylights and four serene thermal pools. All are close in proximity but not connected to one another. And yet I'm struggling to tear my eyes away from the toned muscular back of the man standing across the room.

Hattie sheds her robe and pageant walks to each pool for a quick toe-dip.

"Oooh, this temperature is fabulous," she calls out, wading in at a pace I wouldn't be caught dead matching while wearing a swimsuit. The quicker I'm in, the less time there is to build an unwanted audience.

When Micah rotates toward us, I have to remind myself that I'm not watching one of those ridiculous pop-up ads where a shirtless guy rakes a hand through his hair and tells the viewer how great his new deodorant is while his abs glisten in the sunlight. Because unlike a commercial, where I can stare unabashedly at the toned torso of a man who can't see me, Micah most certainly can.

Perhaps I'll just take a swim with my robe on.

". . . hook over there."

"What?" I blink. He's talking to me. By the looks of it, he's *been* talking to me.

He ticks his head to the side. "There's a hook for your robe over there."

"Oh, right. Thanks. I'm just"—*waiting for you to walk away first*— "a bit chilled."

"You're kidding, right? It feels like an African rainforest in here. I'm wishing I could take one of those ice baths."

"If you're looking for the coolest temp, it's that one over there, closest to the door," Hattie points to the pool furthest away as she sinks into the water and closes her eyes.

"That's where I'm headed, if you care to join me?" Micah tips his head in invitation, and for a second, I'm tempted to throw my dignity to the wind and be the type of girl I write about in my fiction.

The one who sashays without a care in the world at the side of Hot Deodorant Dude.

But I'm not that girl.

"Nah, you go on ahead. I'm gonna take my time."

He studies me. "You have really cool hair."

My cheeks flame at his joke, and I pat my insufferable mane. "Not all hair types play nice with humidity." Despite the way he seems to scrunch his brows in confusion, I go on. "If left to its own devices, it could easily become a landmark on Mama's road-trip map."

"Every way I've seen you wear it has been beautiful. Including now," he says in a matter-of-fact tone that causes the bottom floor of my stomach to fall out. "It looks like a cute, curly pom-pom."

When he finally turns and strides for the furthest pool, I can't help but stare after him dumbly. Was that a compliment? Did he just call my pom-pom cute? Only, before I can overthink it for another second, I realize I'm about to miss my opportunity to disrobe without his notice. *It's now or never.* With one quick tug at the knot of my belt, I shuck off my robe and toss it onto a chair too far away to be considered "poolside." Then, with the grace of a marble statue, I slip into the middle pool without bothering to test the temperature first. The shock of the boiling lava water engulfing my skin causes me to yelp and splash as soon as I break the surface.

Despite every *Do Not Run* warning sign posted on the walls, Micah does just that until he's crouching at the edge of my pool. "Raegan—what happened? Are you hurt? Did you slip?" He searches my face, but I'm in too much discomfort to form a coherent reply.

Unfortunately, Hattie does it for me.

"I'm pretty sure she jumped in all on her own," Hattie replies unhelpfully. "Not sure why you'd jump into a hot tub that has stairs, Sunny Bear."

With my arms hovering above the water, I propel myself toward said stairs. "I . . . I must have missed those at first glance."

"My pool is the perfect temp, in my opinion, if you want to join me." Hattie slips back down into the water and returns to her Zen-like state.

Micah reaches out to capture my forearm and guide me up the stairs. For multiple reasons, my skin is now liquid fire.

"Watch your step," he instructs as I pray for a tornado to rip through Bathhouse Row before I reach the top.

"Thanks," I mutter. "I think I'll just sit here on the ledge for a while."

Without invitation, he settles beside me, plunging his legs into the lava pool beside mine.

"Yikes," he howls before jerking them right back out. "This *is* hot!"

"What about my flailing squeal caused you to believe otherwise?"

"You should have come with me to the cooler pool."

I don't tell him he's right.

I feel his attention on my profile, but unlike the hours we've spent riding side-by-side together in the cockpit of the tour bus, this feels much, *much* more intimate. There's no center console separating us here, no coffee travel mugs to distract or window ledges to lean against for added protection. I'm acutely aware that there's nothing but an inch of wet concrete between our two bodies clad in swimwear.

"I'm sorry the weather didn't cooperate for your hiking plans today," I extend as some kind of strange diversion tactic.

"Wish I could say I was sorry you didn't get to stay back and make your call to Tav." He quirks a smile at me. "But I'm really not."

My mouth gapes at his forwardness, and he laughs.

"You're oddly open, you know that?"

"If that's supposed to be an insult, you could use some pointers in that area."

"It's not, I just don't know many people who say exactly what they mean as much as you do."

"It's hard to teach healthy communication skills if I'm not willing to live by them."

"Teach?" I scrunch my face. "Are you a teacher?"

"No." Micah plants his hands on the slick pebbled concrete behind him and leans back, saying nothing for a second. This up close and personal, I can see the pulse beat in his neck and the bolt of gold that streaks through the chocolate-brown iris of his right eye. Hattie's wrong. Ryan Reynolds has nothing on Micah Davenport. "I was a licensed specialist in psychology at a school district where I live."

I blink. "What does that mean?"

"I ran emotional disturbance testing, behavioral testing, cognitive testing, and scheduled in-office therapy for students and their families in need of extra assistance."

My mouth gapes slightly as I rehearse his words in my head several times over. "So then, you're not actually a bus driver."

"Not exclusively. I've driven rigs this size a few times with my father and held a class C license since I was twenty-one. School districts always need extra drivers on hand during sports seasons, as does my local church in the summers. It's come in handy more than once."

"A therapist," I muse again. Suddenly so much about him makes sense. His thorough advice and commentary, his listening ear, his astute questions, his willingness to engage in meaningful conversation. *Micah is a therapist.*

"I'm actually taking some extra time this summer to—"

"Hello, darlings," Mama says as she bursts into the pool room with Adele on her heels. They both have bright pink cheeks and skin. "That steam cave is an absolute must. Micah, your mother and I missed that blessed experience when we road-tripped here. We were much too concerned about getting our hair washed with actual shampoo in a stand-up shower and not in a gas station sink. The soak time in the pools was a bonus."

Micah stands to assist my mother in hanging up her robe on one of the hooks and then does the same for Adele. His act of chivalry causes me to speculate what Tav would have done if he were the one present. Would he have hoisted himself out of the warm water to walk across the wet concrete and help a woman he's known since birth? The answer that surfaces is not a becoming one. While Tav has an arsenal of Southern manners at his disposal, he's rarely without the paid staff who've attended his every need for decades—at home and on tour. Charm is far more fleeting than chivalry.

"You never did say what the bath attendant asked my mother to sketch for you both to get in without paying, Luella."

Micah follows a step behind Mama, ready to reach out for her at any moment if she loses her footing on the slick floor. The base of my throat burns as I picture him doing that for his own mother not so long ago. Lynn has only been gone a few months, hardly enough time for Micah to break a lifetime habit.

"The attendant couldn't decide, so she asked Lynn to draw what she drew best." Mama smiles. "So she drew Chickee's house."

"She drew my great-grandmother's house?"

Mama nodded. "She used to draw it often on the road, always made it look like a fairy tale. That house was her favorite place on earth. No matter where we traveled or what landmarks we visited, Chickee's house was what she sketched the most. That's the house you grew up in, correct?"

"Yes, ma'am, it is." The atmosphere changes almost instantaneously as Micah's expression sobers. And I don't even have to wonder about the grief that's captured his thoughts. I know it well. All of us in this room have known it.

While physically he's in the same thermal pool as Mama, his mind appears to be elsewhere. The pool they're in is narrow and long, stretching the length of the other three combined. It's also elevated several feet above the rest.

It's a stage if ever I saw one.

With shaky confidence, I stand and cross the damp floor to the empty pool closest to the door, the one with the coolest temperature. I take the steps into the water and watch as Adele glides into the pool I just vacated. She appears to relax into its heat with ease.

Strangely, my muscles can't seem to find the same reprieve, not when Micah has become so disquieted.

A moment later, the low hum of an old spiritual, the one about praying down at the river that's been sung since the 1800s, warms my ear. It's Mama. On the second time around, she does what she does best and adds lyrics to a melody that never fails to squeeze my heart until it feels like I've been hugged straight from heaven.

Maybe it will do the same for Micah. Three months is both so little and so very long to miss someone who now resides in heaven.

Sure enough, Mama's voice croons the simple words in a solo, and one by one we join her until the four of us Farrow women are singing from four different quadrants inside a room that might as well be a cathedral. When it's my turn, I close my eyes as my heart thunders against my rib cage. Our harmonies anchor to one another the way they have since I was in grade school, each of us building in dynamic as the chorus swells into a blend so achingly right. I wish we could secure this same sense of unity outside of song. Because it's here, with my heart open and my voice lifted, that I feel the most connected to the family God gave me. No matter the differences between us, our frustrations, tensions, offenses, or grief, when the four of us sing together, all the chaos in our world is forced to yield as we merge into one with the music.

I've never desired to charm an audience the way my mother's done for decades, perhaps because the voice I've dreamed of sharing with the world is penned from my imagination. But when the four of us become a single instrument, I can't help but picture the pride I once saw in our daddy's eyes when he used to watch us from his favorite recliner. It's the closest I'll ever come to understanding what God must feel when He looks at His beloved children.

As our volume decreases on the last chorus, and as our final few notes linger into a stillness that feels as reverent as a church meeting on Sunday morning, the whole room suddenly erupts in applause. My eyes open to scan the spa staff lining the walls and clapping with a passion that makes my insides melty, as does the way both my sisters are smiling.

And then my gaze lands on Micah. He's smiling, too, only he's not looking at the staff or at my sisters or even at my Mama.

He's looking right at me.

# 10

## Raegan

The National Park we're staying at tonight in Hot Springs has a noise curfew of ten o'clock, which means everyone in our crew has finally, *finally* stopped stirring inside their bunks. I glance at my phone impatiently for the hundredth time and decide to wait an extra ten minutes . . . just to be safe.

But as I stare into the abyss of my dark cocoon, my mind is not rehearsing my plan to hack into Adele's computer while she sleeps; instead, it's being held hostage by the statement Micah made about Tav and me earlier today.

*"Only, my guess is Tav doesn't want it to be over, and you're still debating on what it is you want."*

It's the reason I couldn't even look at Micah when Tav called after dinner tonight.

I squeeze my eyes closed, wishing it could be as simple as Micah made it sound.

Perhaps that's the danger in dating someone you've known all your life. Cutting them off is like cutting off a part of your own history. Our lives have been entangled since birth, with commonalities too impossible to ignore: both artists in our own rights, both youngest children of prominent families with ties to the music industry, both set on making our own way despite the influence and affluence of our last names. Only, Tav is actually living his dream as the lead singer of a band, and I'm . . . I'm several unpublished manuscripts deep with nothing to show for it.

I think of the magical portal Micah and I discussed on our way to Memphis, and I wish I could change my answer now. If I could, I would go back in time and talk to that head-in-the-clouds teenage girl with the crush on her best friend. I'd tell her that, much like her writing dreams, all the pining and hoping and journal-filling about Tav's every move wouldn't amount to anything but heartache.

Much to that young girl's surprise, Tav wouldn't fall for her in high school like she'd written about. Truth is, our relationship had survived on sporadic texts and phone calls until I was home from college and he was gigging at venues in the outskirts of Tennessee, trying to build a set list Farrow Music would be willing to sign. It was during those late-night road calls when Tav asked for my help with his lyrics. By my senior year, I'd filled three notebooks with song hooks, bridges, and choruses. And his set grew from three to thirty.

Tav had stayed in town for my college graduation party, and I was certain he was about to confess what I'd been feeling since girlhood. Only, when he pulled me aside, it was to tell me he'd been signed with Farrow Music Productions, which would require him to be on the road for a full year. That was when my patience had officially run out. I told him I was in love with him—just blurted it out like a fool, hoping with everything in me that he would say it back.

But instead, Tav claimed he needed space to think, and that he was sorry I'd misunderstood his intentions. Crushed was an understatement to the devastation that followed his rejection.

Our communication dwindled to silence for eight long months until the random June day when a VIP invitation for a small show he'd secured in Denver appeared in my inbox, along with two plane tickets and a note asking me to come. He promised he'd make it worth my time if I trusted him enough to show up. When I'd arrived at the venue, Tav pulled me up on stage and sang a song we'd cowritten together years prior.

He'd kissed me on a spotlighted stage while a bar crowd roared and cheered our names. The grand gesture had gone viral overnight—as views of *Tav Z + Luella Farrow's Daughter's LIVE KISS ON STAGE* ticked north of three million.

In less than a week, my identity had been redefined by two things: my famous last name and my lead-singer boyfriend. I'd tried to convince myself that this was a small price to pay for the happy-ever-after I'd written about for a decade, but there were other factors at play I couldn't ignore. Like how Tav's downloads had skyrocketed across every streaming platform after our kiss went viral. Like how he'd been given the green light at venues that had previously turned him down. Like how the timing for our future plans was never quite right.

*Just one more tour and then we'll settle down* was the line he'd fed me for nearly three years.

We didn't make it to a fourth.

Pulling the emergency brake on my runaway thoughts, I focus once again on the loud static of Adele's white-noise machine and Hattie's heavy, rhythmic breathing. Slowly, I pull back my privacy curtain and stare across the aisle at the closed bunk directly across from mine. I haven't heard a peep from Micah since he turned in after losing a round of Canasta, joking that all the mineral water he'd absorbed at the thermal pools earlier must have weakened his ability to strategize. We'd all laughed—even Adele.

I plant both feet on the cool floor and note the trash from dinner has been taken out. I'd volunteered for the job, but then Tav had called, asking for lyric help again.

When I told him things had been busy, he'd fallen quiet. Tav knew all about life on the road. Only, for Tav, "busyness" on the road had included developing *confusing feelings* for his fill-in keyboardist, and then later alerting me, his girlfriend of three years, that he needed space to "figure out" what he really wanted. Or in this case, *who* he really wanted.

Our breakup last fall had happened in the midst of Hattie's custody trial with Peter and Adele's fight to keep the negative morale at FMP from making headlines—all while Mama's song continued to sweep the charts at number one.

There was little time to mourn a broken heart.

But then Tav called me three and a half weeks ago, asking for my forgiveness and trying his best to assure me he was finally ready to settle down. He claimed his lapse in judgment was a result of being caught up in the loneliness of fame. *"You were right all along, Rae Rae. Our history is special. It's worth too much to throw away. I know we can make this work this time if you give me another chance. Will you at least think about it? We can talk when I'm home."*

I push the nagging conversation aside and creep with stealthy steps toward the darkened dining table. With the shades drawn on every window inside the bus tonight, the tiny green charge light on Adele's laptop is impossible to miss. And much like this morning, adrenaline floods my gut at the thought of what I'm about to do—what I need to do in order to confirm or deny my ex-brother-in-law's involvement in the tell-all against my family. My fingers tremble as I pry open the lid on the table, but the glow of the screen is so blinding I immediately rotate the laptop away from the bunk hall. Suddenly, the dining area feels much too close to the sleeping quarters. If someone were to wake to use the restroom, I might as well be a lighthouse.

Making sure to mute the sound of her keyboard first, I type in Adele's password and then slowly stand and walk backward into the front lounge, shielding the light by lowering the screen. Once I can get to the driver's cockpit, I'll be able to close the privacy curtain and search through Adele's emails for some more information on the fired employee and their relationship with Peter—

"*Raegan, stop.*" A hushed voice lashes out through the darkness, right before my heel collides with something solid near the base of the sofa. In a hellish montage of cause-and-effect, I trip, stumble, and clutch the laptop to my chest, determined to sacrifice every bone in my body if it means avoiding Adele's wrath. But instead of hitting the floor as I expect, two large hands reach into the darkness and pull me upright.

"Don't scream," a familiar tenor says in my ear, arms still secured around my middle. "Not unless you want to wake this entire bus." He waits a beat and then another. "You good?"

I nod but realize he probably can't see the movement in the darkness. Then again, how was it he'd seen me at all? "Other than wondering how it is you're always nearby to catch me at my worst? Sure." I exhale a shaky breath. "It's really too bad for you those Red Cross punch cards aren't a real thing. No doubt yours would be filled by the end of this trip."

I feel the rumble of his chest against my back when he chuckles. "Perhaps I better settle on a prize, then." He releases me, and I turn around to face him in the dark right as he flicks on the headlamp strapped to his forehead. I bite back a cry from the instant attack on my retinas and shield my eyes with my forearm.

"Sorry about that, I thought it was still on the night mode. There. It's safe to come out now."

I peel my arm away and note the dim glow of the space around us.

"What are you doing out here with that thing? Mining for silver?"

Again he laughs, then plants himself on the sofa. "No, I was reading. I turned off my light as soon as I heard the creak of a bunk, figured someone was coming out to use the restroom. Didn't want to startle anyone. Guess you saw how well that worked."

I realize only then that I'm still clutching stolen evidence to my chest. I quickly twist away from Micah and slide Adele's computer under the cushion of the sofa opposite him.

"That's not suspicious at all," he deadpans.

I rotate back to address the crime at hand, but stop short when

I note what he's wearing on his face for the first time. "You wear glasses?"

"Just for reading."

Of course he does, because why wouldn't a guy who doesn't need any extra points on the attraction scale also wear reading glasses? "Right."

Micah tugs his headlamp off and proceeds to sweep the light down the length of my body. "What on earth is printed on your pajamas?"

I glance down at the brown, textured spheres haphazardly placed on my matching top and boxers. "Goo Goo Clusters."

"A what cluster?"

I jerk back a step because this is a personal affront if ever there was one. "How do you *not* know what a Goo Goo Cluster is? That's . . . that's practically sacrilege where I come from."

He sets the headlamp on the arm of the sofa, casting the entire lounge in a soft aura of white. "Well, where I come from, students text each other a brown emoji that looks suspiciously similar to that whenever they—"

"I'll have you know that Goo Goo Clusters are a Nashville novelty—chocolate, caramel, marshmallow, nougat, and peanuts. No taste buds can resist them. Not even snooty ones from up north."

His smile comes slowly. "Then I sincerely hope I'll get the chance to put that to the test. But in the meantime, perhaps we should get back to your ninja activities in question . . ."

I glance at the sofa where I've stuffed Adele's laptop. "It's not what it looks like. I just needed to do some important research."

"On Adele's work computer?"

My eyes flick to the floor for a fraction of a second to gather my thoughts, but that's all it takes to see the workspace he's created on the floor and side table.

There, at Micah's feet, is a stack of journals and what looks to be a handwritten timeline with a stretch of dates, locations, scribbled notes, and a handful of names I recognize. Two of which belong to my parents.

And just like that, I wish I could be plunged back into total darkness. I want to unsee all of this so badly that I'd rather turn myself in to Adele than process the truth in front of me.

Like a movie I can't stop, my mind replays every red flag I chose to ignore since Micah arrived on scene. Every strange circumstance I naïvely labeled as coincidence. Every conversation I blindly participated in. Every pilfered sample chapter I read that included information only a select few from my mama's past would know about.

Somehow, I foolishly managed to convince myself that Micah was interested in me for more than my family name when really he used me as an accomplice to further a plot against us all.

The running narrative in my head continues to shift in real time.

Micah isn't here to fill in the gaps of his mother's timeline; he's here to finish out an entirely different timeline—one Lynn must have started and sold to the highest bidder before she died. A tell-all to end all tell-alls, authored by the scorned ex-best friend of one Luella Farrow.

And we all fell for it. Most of all—my sweet, generous mother.

"*How could you?*" My voice breaks on the question. "How could you keep this from us?"

His lighthearted expression changes in an instant. "Raegan, what are you—?"

Disbelief and hurt pulse up my throat in tandem. "You're him."

"I'm who?"

I shake my head and soon my entire body follows. "All that talk today about open communication and valuing truth above timing, and yet you showed up here thinking you could keep a secret *this huge*?"

Even in the dim light, I see how my words strike him. Yet he doesn't defend himself or even try to explain my accusation away. He simply remains silent.

Hysteria rises inside me like flood waters.

"You're not even going to deny it?" I hiss.

"No."

His admission hurts far more than it should.

Much too aware of our proximity to my sleeping family, I demand my rickety legs to move and take the exit stairs in bare feet. I push out the bus door and into the thick night air, knowing Micah will catch the door before it has the chance to slam. At least I'm right about something when it comes to him.

At first, I have no plan as I march past the picnic table and toward the tree line, I just know I'm not ready to face him yet. Not like this. The deeper I venture down the dusty trail, the less cloudy my thoughts become and the less wounded my pride feels. It's then I do what I do best: plug the facts I have into the blank novel outline stored in my brain, the one currently crafting a backstory and matching scenes in real time until a surprising revelation nearly causes me to stumble.

What if Lynn put Micah up to this on her deathbed? What if Micah is as unwilling a participant in this twisted game of revenge as I am? I remember how sorrowful his face looked today at the pools when Mama spoke about his mother. He's grieving, I'm quick to remind myself. *And grief does strange things to people.* Even therapists, I'd reckon.

Finally, I stop and rotate to face the spy we've been harboring on our bus for days. "I'm not going to ask you why or even how this all came about—God gave me a good enough imagination to fill in those blanks myself. But I do very much care about what happens from this point on. I know you're grieving, Micah. But you must know there's a better way to find closure than this."

"Raegan." Everything about him appears unnervingly steady. "Please believe me when I say I never intended to hurt you or anyone else in your family. I only ever wanted to find the truth—"

"The truth?" I shake my head, completely bewildered by how deceived he must be to believe a stunt like this could lead him to truth. "Micah, this isn't the way. Please, I'm begging you, no matter how deep your mother's issues went with my mama, please break this contract with Willow House and whatever other commitment you made to her ghostwriter regarding this trip." The pinpricks of hives have begun on my forearms, but I don't care. I don't care about anything but the here and now. "I'll help you however I can, I promise. We can do it together." Fat tears climb my throat as I press a hand to my chest. "I know my family is a total mess, but not even the messiest of us deserves to be exposed like this. Let our mother's offenses stay in the past."

For what feels like a year, Micah stares at me, unblinking, and for the first time, I doubt my negotiation skills. Was he expecting me to yell? Fight? Carry on like a lunatic until I alerted the entire campground of his transgressions and betrayal against my family? Maybe he expected me to pull Adele out of bed.

I guarantee she wouldn't have offered him the same deal.

But then he raises his palms as his voice cuts through the silence. "I want to help you, Raegan, but I'm no longer certain of what you're accusing me of. I can say with confidence that other than the nondisclosure agreements I signed for Adele prior to the trip, I've signed nothing else. I've never heard of Willow House, and I'm not even sure what a ghostwriter is, much less why I'd be working with one. I do value honesty, but I also value discernment, which is why I didn't disclose my primary motive for being on this trip with your family because the secret I'm carrying affects more than just me."

The moon is bright overhead, lightly illuminating Micah's features in a silvery blue halo. He appears sincere, earnest. Yet I feel completely ungrounded. If he's lying, then he's an even better liar than Peter San Marco. But if he's not, how can he possibly explain the timeline and sketches and names—

"Raegan, I need you to keep breathing, alright? Nice and slow." He catches my eye and demonstrates the movement of breath with his hand. I wonder if this is how a therapist works their magic on patients, by casting spells that trick them into believing they're calm when really they're a boiling pot of injustice.

"May I continue?" he asks.

Somehow, I nod.

He inhales what appears to be a cleansing breath of his own.

"After Luella sent my mom the award for Song of the Year, my mom reached out to her and told her about her prognosis. As you know, she invited Luella to come while she was in hospice—she was weak but coherent. None of us were in the room with them, but whatever happened in there gave my mom peace, which in turn, gave my family peace. She declined rapidly after that night and died just five days later." He clears his throat. "Unfortunately, the peace we found during her passing didn't last for me. I found something else instead."

Even though it's nearly midnight and the summer air is warm and thick and full of cicadas trying to match the whir of the bus's AC unit, nothing would have kept me from hearing Micah's next words. My gaze is fixed on his mouth, my ears tuned to his voice.

"Frank Davenport is not my father." Other than the clench of his fists, his body is rigid as he speaks. "My brother read me the official paternity test results the day I answered your mom's voicemail about a box of travel journals she found during the bus renovation. It felt like . . . like an answer to a prayer I didn't even know how to pray. And believe me, that's a commodity I don't have much of at the moment." He takes another breath. "I came on this trip with the intention of searching for leads that might ultimately help me discover the identity of my biological father."

The pulse beat in my ears that had been so strong only moments ago seems to sputter out entirely.

"Oh, Micah." It's all I can utter in light of the compounding grief he's faced in such a short period of time. First the loss of his mom, followed by a loss I can't even begin to fathom. "I can't . . . I don't even know what to say." I step toward him. "Did you tell Frank you know?"

"No." Micah shakes his head solemnly. "My brother and I are positive he doesn't know about this. He wouldn't have kept this kind of a secret from me. We're too close. It would have broken his heart."

"So you agreed to drive for us because you think my mama might be able to help in your search? Is that why you've been asking about their last tour in '94?" Pieces are clicking into place. "That's why you were drawing a timeline tonight."

138

He's slower to answer this one, and there's an expression on his face I don't dare try to interpret. "When I determined that I would have been conceived during the end of that summer tour"—he closes his eyes and the moonlight dances over his head, causing his hair to appear nearly copper—"the man who made the most sense at the time, given what I knew, was . . . Russell."

My jaw drops open. "You thought my dad had an affair with your mom?"

"It was only a hypothesis, one that was quickly proven wrong by his detention in Germany."

My eyes nearly bulge out of my head when I realize the other ramifications to such a hypothesis. I squeeze my eyes closed for all of two breaths, surprisingly grateful for Germany.

"I'd hoped my mom's journals might be a help, too, although that was before I started reading them. My mom was definitely not a traditionalist when it came to keeping a journal."

His sudden tone shift makes me curious. "What does that mean?"

"They're half doodle, half words, half scraps of random paper—"

"That's too many halves."

"I never claimed to be a math wizard."

"No, you're just a bus-driving therapist in search of his biological father."

Micah clears his throat again. "Actually, for the sake of full disclosure, I'm an unemployed bus-driving therapist in search of his biological father." He raises that calming palm again. "But that's a story for another time. Right now, I'm hoping you'll explain what it was you were accusing me of originally."

I swallow and nod, feeling weary to my bones. As horrible as it would have been for Micah to be the secret author behind the tell-all, I'm left once again with a key suspect who will be impossible to negotiate with. "Someone with access to my mama's history and personal information has signed a book contract and is currently using a ghostwriter to write a tell-all about my mama and family . . . and I'm the only person who knows."

Micah starts to speak twice before he's able to utter a word. "I swear to you, Raegan, I know nothing about that."

"I believe you." And I realize, in that moment, I do. I trust him.

"I appreciate that," he says. "I'm not a fan of keeping secrets, but since my father is still out on a boat in the middle of the Pacific, I need to be careful what I say and to whom when it comes to my search."

"I can respect that."

He nods. "Thank you. If there's any way I can help you, Raegan, I will."

"At the moment, I'm not even sure how to help myself." The confession is as defeating as it is true.

Micah stuffs his hands in his shorts pockets and tips his head to the bus. "For now, we should probably get some rest. Tomorrow's another long day."

Exhausted after tonight's emotional showdown, I peer up at him and nod. We walk down the path in contemplative silence together.

"If you wouldn't mind, I'd like to get on Adele's laptop for a few minutes. I'm trying to verify something."

"Want me to play lookout? I can read a few more entries in the journals while you search."

"That'd be helpful, thanks."

When we reach the bus, Micah allows me to climb the steps first. "Can I ask what you're researching?"

My fingers grip the cool metal handle as I say, "A suspect who has never shown an ounce of mercy when it mattered most."

---

*August 16, 1975*
*Eugene, Oregon*

*Dear Chickee,*

*I'm writing this from inside the hotel bathroom in Eugene, Oregon, while Luella sleeps. Our bus ride here was long, but we met up with Luella's friend at the university and bought the VW bus. It's lime green and smells of stale potato chips, but it runs! Plus, it will save us on lodging costs now that we can sleep inside it for the remainder of our trip. With our combined savings and the money you gave me, we should be all set once we reach Nashville. Thank you again.*

*I know I put on a brave face when we left your house yesterday morning, but I couldn't talk for nearly two hours for fear of blubbering. I wonder if this is how everyone feels when they leave home for the first time? I hope it gets easier. I also hope Luella is right about Tennessee being a fresh start for big dreams.*

*I'm not sure what my big dream is yet, but Luella assures me hers are big enough to share. I suppose, when I think about it, my most important dreams have already come true.*

*I love you,*
*Lynn*

*August 20, 1975*
*Redwood National Forest*
*California*

*Dear Chickee,*

*I sent you a postcard today from the most beautiful place I've ever seen. I tried to draw it, but I never could get the scale right. The trees here are enormous, even taller than our tallest buildings downtown. I know you'll love the picture on the postcard. Luella took a few with her polaroid, too. I'll show you everything when I can come back and visit.*

*You're probably wondering about the sketch of the bridge on the next page. Luella and I sat right there for nearly eight hours, listening to nature and writing songs. There's one I wrote that I can't wait to play for you. If you look closely, you'll find the lyrics hidden in this sketch.*

*I told Luella about <u>him</u> tonight before bed, the Monster I lived with before you rescued me. She cried, and because she cried, I did, too. She asked if he's the reason I never want to get married or have kids of my own. I told her the Monster doesn't get to be the reason for anything I do or don't do anymore. I'm not sure she believed me, but she did sug–*

*gest we make a pact. So right there atop our sleeping mats, we vowed to never let any man come between us. We promised to protect each other always, not only as best friends, but as sisters.*

*Tomorrow we're going to see the Pacific Ocean because Luella said no sister of hers can go all the way to Nashville without knowing what it feels like to stick her toes in the surf for the first time. I can't even imagine what it will feel like. I don't think I'll sleep a wink tonight.*

*I love you,*
*Lynn*

*August 26, 1975*
*San Francisco, California*

*Dear Chickee,*

*So much has happened since I last wrote. Shortly after we left the Redwoods, we met a van full of new friends from the same area where that big oil spill was last year. They invited us to come with them to San Francisco. Turns out, they all live together in a commune and call them-selves Jesus People. In a way, the place reminded me of Camp Selkirk. They took us to the ocean, and it was even better than anything I could have imagined! I went shoeless the entire day. We've stayed with them for the last three nights, and a part of me doesn't want to leave. We've been working on more songs, and there's something that feels especially inspiring about singing outside.*

*Tonight they asked us to lead the song service. I don't know how many of us there were in total, and that part doesn't really matter anyway, but when we sang tonight, something happened inside me—like the spark of a fire. People were singing and clapping and even dancing to our songs, and I didn't want it to stop. I think I feel it now, the passion Luella speaks about so often.*

*Maybe she doesn't need to share her dream with me anymore, because I think her dream just became mine.*

*I love you,*
*Lynn*

*August 31, 1975*
*Amarillo, Tulsa, Hot Springs, Memphis*

*Dear Chickee,*

*Well, you made me promise to say yes to all the adventures you would say yes to if you could, and boy oh boy have I kept my promise. You wouldn't even believe all the things we've done! I can't write out everything, as it would take a week, but as you can see, I've sketched out some of my best memories (except for the rattlesnake under our tire in Amarillo. That was truly horrifying, and I don't want to give you nightmares).*

*One of the highlights was a bathhouse in Hot Springs, Arkansas. Luella and I were long past ready to wash our hair and smell of something other than stale road food. I never knew clean could feel so good.*

*You'll also find a sketch of a historic ballroom in Tulsa. That's where a radio dance-off contest was held to win two tickets to see Elvis at his concert in Memphis . . . Chickee, I won!!! I don't have the faintest clue what I was doing with my feet, I just told myself to keep on doing it until I fell on the floor in exhaustion. Luella cheered so loud for me that she nearly lost her voice. After I won, we deemed this place our lucky ballroom and promised we'd be back one day, hopefully, to perform songs of our own.*

*We see Elvis tomorrow night. Can you even believe it? Elvis!*

*Thank you for pushing me to do this.*

*We'll be in Nashville in two days.*

> *I love you,*
> *Lynn*

*P.S. I'm working on a map of our epic adventures this summer! I think it will make for a nice keepsake down the road. I'll send you a copy when I send you this journal.*

# 11

## Micah

As much as I desire a follow-up conversation with Raegan after last night, I decline the offer to trail behind the Farrow ladies as they shop in strip-mall stores with names like *Heavens to Betsy Boutique*. I opt instead for some downtime with my mother's journals inside a coffee shop called *Fixin' To Café*. I thumb through several entries of her road trip, as well as multiple sketches, poems, and travel games she created throughout. It feels surreal to read her words from a time long before I ever called her mom.

Once my waitress sets a steaming bowl of grits at my table—a first for me—I switch my focus to another family member. I give the journals a rest and decide it's time to fill my dad in on my summer gig as a bus driver. As I expect, my call goes directly to his voicemail. I leave him a message along with a promise to leave another for him at our next stop. Perhaps these check-ins will make the difficult conversation we'll have after he returns a tad less painful.

Garrett is next on my list. The few texts we've exchanged since I arrived have been transactional at best, so I'm relieved to see his name flash on my screen only a minute after reaching his voicemail. In his line of work, that kind of response time is rare.

"You're where?" he asks again as the hospital intercom crackles in the background.

"Two hours past the Arkansas-Oklahoma border in a town that's three stoplights long."

"Is this when you tell me you're gonna go cow-tipping for fun?"

"Not sure the company I'm with would consider that fun." I smile, imagining Hattie dodging cow patties in her fancy footwear.

"Any discoveries of consequence to report? Or perhaps siblings I should know about?"

I assure him he's still my one and only and ask how life has been back home when an image of Raegan in her Goo Goo Cluster pj's flashes through my mind. I've seen a lot of women cry—most in a professional setting, and a few back before I had any clue what I wanted in a relationship. But thinking, even for a moment, that I could have been the cause behind the visible anguish in her eyes had been wholly unbearable.

I'd lain awake in my bunk long after she returned Adele's laptop to the charging station. But it wasn't her assumption or even her accusation I replayed. It was the empathy she extended to me, the grace. That even though she believed me guilty of hurting her family in such a blatant way, she'd been willing to look past my crime.

She'd actually offered to help me.

As a therapist, I've worked with many types of people. I've seen hurt, betrayal, trauma, and fear manifest themselves in a dozen different ways, but rarely have I seen it look like that. Like compassion. Like mercy.

Like Raegan.

I clear my throat, willing my thoughts to make a U-turn as I answer my brother's questions about the motor coach and our living arrangement on the road.

"Sounds like Southern hospitality isn't a myth, then."

Raegan's sweet smile comes to mind again. "I'd say it's pretty real."

An alarm sounds over the hospital's loudspeaker. "I've gotta run, bro, but Kacy said to tell you you're missed around here. She also wants an autographed vinyl from Luella."

I laugh. "I'll see what I can do. Give the twins a hug from me."

"Only if you promise to send pictures of any tipped cows."

A few minutes after I leave the café and hike back to the air-conditioned bus, the Farrow family climbs aboard. Raegan joins me in the cockpit, and the relief I feel at her presence is odd given how short a time I've known her. A part of me had wondered how things might change for us today—with both our secrets out in the open—but if anything, Raegan seems to have lowered her guard even more.

She glances from me to the jump seat. Or rather, to the small deposit of trust I left for her there. "Is this one of Lynn's journals?"

"I thought you might want to browse through one while we drive," I say easily, though watching her handle it with such care doubles my pulse.

With reverence, she runs her palm across the cover of the green travel journal. "Are you sure? I know what a treasure these must be to you and your family."

"I trust you, Raegan. You're welcome to read them all if you'd like to." A simple offer that's anything but simple.

I reverse out of the parking lot, and soon we're back on the interstate headed west following signs for Tulsa. Traffic is as light as the mood in the back of the bus today. All sister drama has been noticeably low today. Perhaps the shopping excursion was good for them all, most certainly for Luella. Every time I catch sight of her in my mirrors, she's smiling.

From my periphery, I watch Raegan overcome her earlier hesitation as she opens the journal and begins to read. She doesn't lift her head again for thirty minutes.

"These entries are incredible. Mama's talked about Camp Selkirk

146

since I was young—it's where she met my daddy for the first time—but how your mom described their baptisms was . . . beautiful." She shakes her head. "I love all her doodles and sketches about the places they stopped. I didn't realize Lynn was so artistic. Also, this food log and daily spending total is awesome—it's hard to believe a hamburger was ever thirty cents." She taps the penciled graph she's referencing. "There's so much detail on every page."

I encourage Raegan to turn the page and look closely at the sketch of a bridge surrounded by giant redwood trees. Hidden into the grooves of each tree trunk is a treasure you can't see without rotating the journal. As soon as she does, she gasps. "No way. Are these the lyrics for 'Crossing Bridges'?"

I nod, having made that revelation only a few hours ago myself.

"I wish each page came with a key, like on a map," I say. "Sometimes there's so much stuff between the entries that I'm not sure I'm comprehending what's most important. At times, it's like the art is acting as another language."

"I suppose that's exactly what it is." She holds it up. "A creative's love language."

"Well, that particular gene must have skipped me entirely, because my eyes are exhausted after about three or four pages."

Raegan turns abruptly in her seat and reaches for her messenger bag resting against the back of mine. After a minute, she pulls out a notebook I've seen her write in multiple times since the day we left. She opens it up and holds it out so I can see it without having to take my eyes off the road for more than a couple of seconds. She flips to a page and then to another one.

I laugh.

And so does she.

Raegan's journal keeping, though not the same as my mother's, is full of flourishes and scribbles and brainstorming webs with arrows that connect content from one page to another like an insane game of hopscotch.

"Are *you* offering to be my key, Raegan?" I amend half-jokingly.

Her smile holds. "I'm offering to help you however I can. I'd want to know the truth, too, if I were you."

"I appreciate that," I say as she begins to close her notebook. "Wait. What's that?" I reach a hand out to stop hers, only the brush of her skin beneath mine makes it difficult to move it away. The page reveals multiple bubbles filled with random words interconnected with lines.

"It's a plotting web," she says without her usual inflection.

"For your fiction book?"

"Yes, for Birch Grove." There's a touch of dejection in her voice when she answers. "This is how I work a scene when I'm stuck. Sometimes it's easier to dump everything in my brain at once onto paper."

"Is Birch Grove your title?"

"No, it's the name of the mountain town where the story is set. The title is actually *The Sisters of Birch Grove*."

"I like that," I say, changing lanes. "Is that what you were working on yesterday before dinner?"

"No, there's not much for me to work on—as far as my fiction goes, I mean." I don't like the defeat I hear in her voice when she says this, and I'm tempted to press her on it. But before I can voice another question, she says, "I was just messing around with some lyric ideas."

"For Tav?" I ask, though I already know. I couldn't help but overhear their video call after dinner last night when I took out the trash. He must have mentioned those lyrics five times over the course of me walking to and from the camp dumpster. If I was in analyzing mode, I'd say their relationship pulls heavily in one direction. But I'm not in analyzing mode. Technically, I shouldn't even be in therapist mode.

She studies the page filled with strike-through phrases. "I haven't been able to come up with a good chorus hook yet."

I slide my sunglasses on. The cloud cover is gone, and the sun's rays are intense today. When Raegan does the same, I can't help the disappointment I feel at the loss of those brown eyes peering back at me.

"How long have you been his cowriter?"

Instantly, her hands begin to fidget atop the notebook, and I'm confident I know her answer before she speaks it. "Technically, I'm not a cowriter. I just help where I can."

More like he just uses her where he can and then takes the credit for her work. His type is easy to pick out in a crowd. A high-achiever who's hyper-fixated on his own success, even at the expense of those closest to him. I can't picture Raegan with a guy like that. Or maybe I just don't want to picture it. She deserves better.

I glance in the rearview and take note of the various locations and distraction levels of our fellow passengers before broaching an equally sensitive topic, one I've been waiting to ask since she crawled into her bunk with Adele's laptop. "Did you find anything helpful during your search last night?"

Unlike the other subjects we've discussed, this one causes her to take a deep breath. "Not what I was hoping for."

Raegan hasn't told me who she suspects the author of the tell-all to be, but there's no question she has someone in mind. Whether or not she'll confide in me is up to her. I won't press her on that.

I flip the turn indicator, change lanes, and turn off at the next exit in search of a gas station before we risk having to push Old Goldie through an abandoned town. I was hoping she could wait on a fill-up until Tulsa since our food selections would be better there, but I have a feeling it's now or never.

As we pull into the station, my gaze catches on the pair of giant Sasquatches standing guard on either side of the mini-mart doors like the two archangels guarding the entrance to the garden of Eden. I put the bus in park and release the air brakes. Luella grabs her new favorite hat—the one she purchased yesterday with the fake auburn ponytail hanging out the back—and tucks her real hair inside it. Paired with her oversize sunglasses, she looks like an entirely different person.

Within thirty seconds, all my passengers have vacated the bus and made their way to the mini-mart. As soon as I round the side of the rig, pop open the gas cap, and insert the nozzle, I regret not asking Raegan to pick up my favorite energy drink before I die from heatstroke.

"I think it's Cheater Peter."

I rotate in the direction of the familiar voice behind me and hike a curious eyebrow. "That's an unfortunate name."

"But a fitting one. Peter is Hattie's ex."

"The one in Greece?"

"There's only one." When she steps into the pocket of shade between pumps, I don't hesitate to join her. Our proximity is closer than two casual friends who met less than a week ago should be, but it's easily justifiable seeing as this conversation needs to remain private. I keep the mini-mart in my periphery.

"Hattie and Peter were married for ten years and have two kids together—as you know by now. Aiden and Annabelle. He had an affair with a woman half his age who was also Farrow Music's top-producing popstar at the time."

"I think I remember reading something about that. What was that—a year ago?" As much as I try to avoid the clickbait news articles that pop up in my morning news feed, Luella's name has always held more intrigue than other celebrity gossip.

"Almost eighteen months ago now. Adele discovered their affair at the office and it was . . . horrible. For everyone involved." Raegan shudders at whatever memory she's reliving. "There's been so much drama since then, but ultimately, when Adele fired Peter, Francesca broke her contract and pulled her entire catalogue from the label. Peter was the head of the legal department, and Adele claims he altered Francesca's contract right before the news of the affair leaked so that her legal consequences for exiting the label's contract prematurely would be minimal. Honestly, I don't know all the details, but I do know that after Peter filed for wrongful termination, we didn't see Adele for months. She basically lived at the office, and

Hattie was . . ." Raegan shakes her head, and this time she glances down at her feet. "I stayed with her for a while, helped with the kids, cooked meals, checked homework and made school lunches, and was her emotional support during the divorce and custody trial. Not to mention the go-between for her and Adele, as well."

I scan the tension lines in her face. "That all sounds very difficult."

"It was."

"And you think he might also be the one behind this?"

She tips her head back to rest against the concrete structure, and I snap my eyes away from the smooth skin of her neck to the mini-mart windows behind her where I can clearly see Luella and her two daughters walking the snack aisles inside. "For Hattie's sake, I really, really don't want it to be him. But he checks all the boxes. He knows so much about our family history—he married into it. There were dates and details and retellings of events in those early sample chapters my editor friend sent over that only Mama's closest circle would know." I watch as she tugs on her bottom lip and slowly meets my eyes. "That's why I thought maybe your mom could have been . . ."

"I get it." I reach out and squeeze her shoulder before she can apologize. "I would have thought the same thing if the situation were reversed. The circumstantial evidence was pretty condemning."

"I'm wondering if Peter might have been siphoning information from the employee Adele just let go for confidentiality issues. The woman worked with Peter directly for years, but I couldn't find anything more than her name and past position. I was hoping to find something concrete to confirm my theory, but Adele's emails on the subject were pretty cryptic."

"Do you think he was paying this woman for information he could use in the book?"

"Possibly. I don't know. The synopsis I read promised an outline of the poor business decisions Farrow Music Productions made from the beginning, and how the label was founded on fraud." She grips her head with both hands. "He would so do something like that."

From the corner of my eye, I glimpse my other three passengers lining up at the register inside the building and know this conversation will need to wrap up in a matter of minutes.

"Why not tell your family about this?" I ask. "I'm sure Adele would—"

"No." She shakes her head. "I can't do that. Not yet. Hattie is in too fragile a place with her kids gone right now—they're literally *with* Peter for goodness' sake. And Adele is so stressed about Mama's appearance at this festival going perfectly that something like this could completely derail everything she's been working toward at the label." She lowers her voice. "Chip, my editor friend, warned me that even if I could find out who the author behind this is, they're still in contract with the publisher. If it's Peter, then I have no chance of negotiating with him."

"The way you did with me."

She holds my gaze. "Nothing in me wanted it to be you, Micah."

Her admission causes the space between us to shrink, and I'm not sure if it's because I've taken a step toward her or if she's taken one closer to me. Either way, I'm close enough to smell the berry scent of her shampoo and see the luminous shimmer of whatever pixie dust she brushed atop her cheekbones this morning. I like it. I like her.

I stuff my hands into the pockets of my shorts to keep from touching her without invitation. "Would it help to talk through the other suspects you've considered?"

Her face drops. "I wrote out a list of every long-term staff member we've had at the house, along with Mama's closest friends, but none of them make much sense. They've either signed Adele's ironclad nondisclosure agreement or wouldn't know the specific details I read in those early sample chapters."

"What about Tav?" I regret the question as soon as it's out.

"Tav is not the author."

I school my expression to keep it in check. "Why not? You told me he's been a friend of yours for a long time. I'm guessing he would have been given similar access to your family as Hattie's ex."

"Cheater Peter and Tav are not the same. And please don't try to *therapist me* into telling you why."

"*Therapist you?*" I laugh.

"You know what I mean."

"I don't, actually. In case you've forgotten, I'm still unemployed."

"Ha, right. I'm pretty sure the once-a-therapist-always-a-therapist slogan applies to you." She narrows her eyes. "You know, at first I couldn't figure out why I kept sharing so much with a person I just met, but I know now. And I know about your tricks." She crosses her arms over her chest and doubles down. "Tav is not a suspect. Sure, I might have questioned that a few months ago, but his motivations are different now."

"In what way?"

She hikes her eyebrow in an I'm-on-to-you way.

"Listen." I hold up my palms. "I'm just trying to make sure no rock is left unturned here. If you tell me you're confident he's not the one behind this, then I'll support his removal from your proverbial suspect list."

Her gaze drops to her blue-painted toenails. "You guessed right the other day at the bathhouse. Tav wants me to give us another chance."

Despite myself, I feel my competitive edge surge. A full five seconds go by before I'm chill enough to ask, "And what do you want?"

"To stay friends, which is why I haven't given him an answer yet."

"But you're working on his lyrics."

She bristles at my flat tone. "As I told you before, I've been helping Tav with songwriting for ages. It doesn't mean anything."

"To you or to him?"

She opens her mouth, and then her lips twist as she points at my chest. "Ah, *see*? There you go again with your therapist tricks." She tips her head to the side. "How about this: I'll answer more questions about my ex when you're ready to tell me the story behind how you came to be unemployed. Deal?"

"Deal." I can't help but smile at her cheekiness. "Don't look now, but your mom and sisters are headed our way."

A gate lowers over her expression then, and I don't have to wonder where her mind has gone. *The tell-all.* "Are you sure you shouldn't at least pull your mom aside and tell her about—"

"No." The warning in her eyes and the fear in her tone cause me to stand down.

I nod. Understood. I also understand something else in that moment: Raegan's pattern for delaying conflict.

"I'm gonna grab a few snacks from inside." She hitches her thumb toward the mini-mart. "You want me to get that energy drink you like? The purple one?" Her hair blows off her shoulder as she steps into the sunshine, and for what feels like the hundredth time today, I'm struck by her beauty.

Before she can take another step away, I reach for her wrist and gently tug her to a stop. Her look of surprise quickens my pulse as I imagine what I'd do in this moment if she were mine. But instead, I simply say, "I never want you to feel tricked by me. Not ever. You only share what you feel safe enough to share with me and nothing more. Deal?"

She blinks twice, then swallows. "Deal."

I release her wrist, and it takes several seconds before she moves again.

Ten minutes later, once everyone has settled into their seats with their carefully selected road-trip goods, Raegan climbs in beside me and sets my favorite energy drink in the cup holder. I thank her and then note the small plastic bag on her lap as she buckles up.

As soon as I twist the key in the ignition and check my mirrors, she's cupping something between her palms. "I have something for you. Wanna guess?"

I make a show of examining every angle of her hold. "If it's hush money, you should know I only accept crisp hundreds."

She rolls her eyes. "Try again."

"Unless you've hidden a pearl inside that hand clamshell, I'm out of guesses."

She opens her palms, and inside is a white wrapper with the words *Goo Goo Cluster* stamped on top. Her favorite candy.

"Now you can see for yourself how amazing they are," she says.

"You're pretty confident about this."

"What can I say, I have high standards when it comes to my chocolate."

On my first bite, I confirm she isn't wrong. This might be the best treat to ever come out of a gas-station convenience store. On my second bite, I ask her where I can find a matching pair of Goo Goo Cluster pajamas.

# 12

## Raegan

Mama's up to something; I can feel it.

First, it was the weird way she insisted all of us girls purchase coordinating outfits and boots on our outing this morning for whatever she has up her sleeve for us tonight, and second, she's been unusually giddy all day. I tried to get whatever secret she's hiding out of Micah by bribing him with a second Goo Goo Cluster, but he swears he doesn't know anything more than I do. All she told us is that after dinner we're going to an old ballroom called Carter's that she and Lynn sang at back in the day, along with a verbal caution to *"prepare our hearts and our dancing feet for a good time!"*

Perhaps one of us girls might have pressed Mama for more if we hadn't been so enamored with checking in to the fancy Tulsa hotel Micah pulled up to in midtown. The idea of showering in a non-mobile bathroom where shaving my legs doesn't involve advanced-level acrobatic training was all I needed to skip out of that bus with a huge smile on my face. Even Micah looked ready for a break from the road, and he's the diehard among us. I can only imagine how nice it will be for him to stretch his long legs out on a real mattress.

Not that I've thought all that much about his long legs.

The hotel concierge has arranged for a town car and driver to meet our crew at a side exit door at six o'clock sharp to take us to dinner and then to whatever special arrangement Mama has made for us. Our rooms are booked on the top floor in a private hallway bracketing Mama's presidential suite. Before we stepped on the elevator together, I overheard Mama ask Micah if he'd escort her downstairs a few minutes early to discuss a few things with our driver beforehand. Naturally, he agreed.

When I exit my room and step into the hallway at ten minutes to six, Hattie has just done the same. We take in our coordinating outfits and smile at each other. Per Mama's specific instruction, we're both wearing variations of a denim skirt on the bottom, a sleeveless blouse on the top, and a pair of cowgirl boots of our liking. Mama had handed us her credit card and given us full rein of that darling little border-town shop, but up until now, I haven't seen what either of my sisters settled on.

"You need darker lipstick," Hattie says cheerily. "And you're in luck because I happen to have your ideal shade on me."

"What a coincidence," I say, grinning as she comes toward me in her white snakeskin cowgirl boots.

Her own smile is an exaggerated kind of amused, and for one fleeting moment in time, my chronic worry over Hattie vanishes. All I see is the stylish, party-planning, always-up-for-an-adventure sister she used to be before Peter slowly began to isolate her with definitions of *wife* and *mother* that were contrary to anything good or right or true.

"Here, try this one." Hattie whips out a tissue from her clutch purse and instructs me to wipe off the clear gloss I'm currently wearing before handing me the berry lipstick and a mirror. "With your olive undertone and layered, chestnut curls, you need something a bit more dramatic. Plus, this one will look fabulous with your fuchsia top."

I thank her as I apply the lipstick. She's absolutely right; it's a pretty shade. When I hand it all back, I'm momentarily dazzled by my sister's beauty. She's striking.

"You look like a supermodel," I say. Between her summer-tanned skin, shiny snakeskin sleeveless blouse, and stunning figure, she looks ready to walk a runway.

"Oh, please, I'm thirty-seven. I'm old enough to be the *mother* of a supermodel."

I roll my eyes. "You'll never not be gorgeous."

Her light denim mini skirt is roughly a foot shorter in length than mine, as I'd opted for a mermaid fit that draws the eye to the small of my waist and hugs the curve of my hips before flaring out at my mid-calf. The slit in the front seam begins a few inches above my right knee so I can move freely. But my favorite piece of the outfit I chose is the distressed cowgirl boots I found at the thrift store at the end of the block. They add some fun character to the whole ensemble.

"I love the outfit you chose, too," Hattie admires. "That cut is stunning on you." She takes a step back and waves her hand from my head to my toes. "Why don't you dress like this more often?"

"Asks the woman who can literally wear anything from any store," I deadpan while conducting my own comparison between my hippy pear-shape and Hattie's svelte Barbie-shape.

"Oh, please," Hattie dismisses me. "Between that hair and those Greek goddess curves of yours, we'll be batting men off you all night. Your figure is what all the girls want these days—don't you watch reality TV?"

I roll my eyes even harder at that. "I think being newly single has obstructed your pulse on reality."

"Mark my words," she says, pulling her phone out from her pocket. "There will be at least one man giving you a double take the instant he sees you."

My stomach bottoms out at the flirty insinuation in her tone. "What—*who*?"

"You're way too smart to play dumb, Sunny Bear. But you're also way too honest to do anything about it while Tav's still a question mark in your head."

"Hattie, Tav's not a—"

"Nope." She puts out her palm like a stop sign. "I'm self-aware enough to know I do not have the emotional capacity to counsel you or anyone else on their love life at the moment. I was just making an observation is all." She winks at me before glancing down at the time on her home screen. Her eyes startle wide. "We're supposed to meet Mama downstairs in three minutes. Where's Adele? Do you think she went down without us?"

I scrunch my forehead. "I don't think so."

Like a single unit, we move to the door on the opposite side of the presidential suite and knock.

"Adele? You in there?"

Her voice is muffled by the door. "I'm going to skip tonight."

Hattie and I look at each other before we ask in unison, "Are you sick?"

"No."

"Then let us in," Hattie says, pressing her mouth closer to Adele's peephole.

"You two are going to be late for dinner. Go on without me, I'm fine."

But thanks to Micah's *therapisting* I know the use of *fine* in this situation means she is obviously *not fine* at all.

"Let us in, Adele, or we'll camp outside your door and sing Backstreet Boys obnoxiously loud."

When Hattie starts in on the verse of "Quit Playing Games with My Heart," the door swings open, and I actually gasp at the sight of my oldest sister. She looks . . . she looks so young.

"I know, I don't know what I was thinking when I bought this today. I have a kid in college for heaven's sake. I look like an idiot."

"No!" Both Hattie and I shout in unison. "You look great!"

Hattie continues to point out what works about her outfit while I nod in agreement and play a quick mental game of spot the differences. Adele's dark denim skirt is a classic style that stops just above her knee with a short slit on each side. The perfect cut for her shapely legs. I suddenly wish my brother-in-law, Michael, was here to see her like this. She's tucked a teal, sleeveless top into the belted waist of her skirt, which makes the teal accent color in her mid-calf cowgirl boots pop. I study her a second longer, realizing it's not only what she *is* wearing that has me in such befuddlement, but also what she's *not* wearing.

A blazer.

Apart from very rare occasions, Adele is never in a public setting without a blazer. Heck, she's rarely in personal settings without a blazer. If I didn't know better, I'd bet she slept in one, too.

She faces the mirror and tugs at her top. "If my office could see me right now, they'd—"

"You're not at the office, Adele. You're in Tulsa with your sisters and your mama. You don't have to be anyone's CEO tonight. You just get to be a woman on a mom-and-sisters road trip," I conclude.

Her eyes shift to look at me in the mirror, and slowly her shoulders begin to relax.

"Raegan's right, we're all just sisters tonight." Hattie places her hand on Adele's arm, and I'm so moved by the rare affection between the two of them my throat thickens. "However, Mama's gonna have all our hides if we don't get downstairs soon. Let's go."

After a resigned sigh, Adele nods at herself once in the mirror and then turns toward us. "Okay, I'll go. Let me just grab my blazer—"

"No!" Hattie and I both blurt in unison.

To ensure she listens, we each grab an arm and pull Adele to the door. "Sorry, but tonight is a blazer-free zone," I say. "Hattie, grab her purse on the side table."

"On it."

To my surprise, Adele actually chuckles a little when the door slams hard behind us.

"You're bossy," she says with a bit of pride.

I beam at her. "I learned from the best."

This time, Hattie is the one to laugh. All the way down the elevator and into the main lobby where the concierge is waiting to take us to the town car we're ten minutes late for. We hustle to the glass doors to see Mama sitting in the back seat of the black town car alone and Micah standing inside a small hallway with his hands stuffed into his pockets, waiting.

The three of us file into the tight area in birth order: Adele, Hattie, and then myself.

"Look at you, ladies." Micah whistles and then slides into a hilarious attempt at a Southern drawl. "Y'all look way too good for your mama to unleash the scolding she's been threatening ever since the clock struck six." He salutes and then pulls open the exterior door to the parking lot. "Godspeed."

Each of my sisters bids him goodnight as he holds the door for them to join Mama in the car. Only, when it's my turn, it's as if the world pauses . . . with the exception of Micah's gaze, which heats my bloodstream as it slowly drifts down my figure and back up to meet my eyes again.

"Wow, Raegan. You're . . ." He swallows. "You're stunning."

I can't fully register the low swoop in my belly his compliment provides because I'm too confused as to why he's not dressed for an evening out. "Aren't you coming with us?"

"Your mom gave me the night off tonight. I thought I'd catch up on some journal reading."

"Oh, right," I say, failing to mask my disappointment. "Of course. You deserve a break from us."

His lips part but nothing comes out, so I take it as an invitation to continue.

"I'll keep my eyes and ears open for any details you might be interested in while I'm at the club tonight. Mama mentioned our mothers sang there together back in the day."

"*Raegan Lynn*," Mama scolds out her open window in the back seat. "We are going to miss our reservation, and I am not about to deal with three hangry daughters all evening."

I shoot Micah a chagrined smile and dash out the door he's still holding open. "Enjoy your night off."

But as soon as I step off the curb, I feel his hand secure my wrist and soon he's spun me around to face him again. "Raegan . . . *Lynn?*" he says in a husky tone I feel all the way to my toes. "Your middle name is Lynn?"

"Raegan, *please,*" Hattie calls out her window. "My kids are calling me in eleven minutes."

"Yes," I answer as I slip my hand from his and climb into the back seat of the town car. The instant I'm situated, I rotate in my seat to stare out the back window where Micah stands bracing the back of his neck with both hands, watching us drive away.

---

Dinner was chaotic. Not only did we arrive late for our reservation at a five-star steakhouse, but Hattie's only quiet option for a phone call with her kids was in the powder room. Nobody thought twice when she missed the appetizer, but when her sizzling entrée had gone cold, worry began to creep its way into my subconscious. I was just about to go in search of her when she slid back into her seat with puffy, red-rimmed eyes. When I leaned in to ask her what had happened on the call, she shook her head and promptly ordered a glass of red wine.

Despite Mama's many attempts to start a conversation with the three of us regarding something about her future dreams for us as a family, she was interrupted nearly every thirty seconds by a patron kindly asking her for a selfie and telling her how much "Crossing Bridges" has meant to them for some reason or another.

Mama never refuses a fan.

"I told you to wear your wig and hat inside the restaurant," Adele mutters after another round of pictures and fanfare. "You do realize you'll be followed for the rest of the night."

"Oh, don't you worry your pretty little head," Mama says, patting her eldest's hand. "There's sure to be a big crowd at Carter's Ballroom; I'll be able to blend in just fine there."

I meet Adele's gaze from across the table and know we share the same unvoiced opinion. Mama has never "blended in" anywhere in her entire life. It's literally the opposite of who she is.

"*Carter's* is where you want to go tonight?" Adele whispers sharply. "You knew I sent two of our senior talent agents out this way last month. If you would've told me you were interested in a nostalgic visit, I would have made all the necessary arrangements for you. Starting with a security team. That venue has a reputation for getting rowdy." She exhales and sets her napkin on the table with a definitive "I think we should postpone."

Mama chuckles dismissively. "Nonsense. I happen to know the main act tonight, and she's brilliant. Trust me, you won't want to miss it. I'm thinking of recommending her to our label, but I was hoping to get your professional opinion first."

Adele pulls back as if Mama just spoke the magic words to solve all problems: "*I was hoping to get your professional opinion first.*"

"Fine, but you have to swear you'll wear your wig and stay close to us for the duration of the evening. The last thing we need is a mob. You're headlining a festival in just over a week, remember?"

Mama crosses herself. "I solemnly swear to blend in."

Adele sighs. "Just keep your wig on, *please.*"

As soon we stand from the table and Adele's back is turned, Mama makes her hand into a puppet and mimics her oldest daughter's final request.

"Careful what you do behind my back, mother," Adele warns in a low voice. "There are roughly a dozen iPhones filming us at the moment."

Instantly, Mama's puppet mouth morphs into a pageant queen's wave as she pauses to blow kisses to every table on our way out. Whistles and applause follow us.

So much for blending in.

It's not until we're being escorted from the town car for a second time that evening and walking through the back door of a historical music hall that I realize Hattie's despondency hasn't lifted. She hasn't muttered a single word since we left the restaurant.

I allow Mama and Adele to pass me by at the entrance of the venue, then hook my arm through Hattie's. The thumping bass line of a driving melody is already ear-poundingly loud from back here, and I know from experience the volume will be ten times more abrasive once we get on the other side of the speakers.

"Hey." I stop her from passing through the barrier. "What's going on with you?"

She stares at the black curtain in front of us but says nothing.

"Hattie, talk to me." My hold on her tightens as fear seeps in. "We don't even have to go in there. I can order us a rideshare back to the hotel if you want."

Slowly, her eyes focus on mine. "What I want is a night off from my life. Can you give me that, Raegan? Can you give me one night where I can forget all the ways my life is a dumpster fire right now?"

I peer into her face. "Did Peter do some—"

"I don't want to talk about Peter! *Please.*" Her voice breaks on the word. "Just let me be tonight." She begins to walk ahead when she suddenly twists back. "And for once, don't let Adele bully you into babysitting me."

I'm so startled by the accusation I struggle for words. "That's not what—"

"That *is* exactly what happens. I know she's the one who sends you to stay with me on the weekend when my kids are at Peter's, and how she asks you to keep tabs on my every move through the stupid tracking app she insists on. Don't defend her."

"I'm not trying to defend her. She's just worried about you." *We all are,* is what I don't say. "She cares."

Hattie's laugh is cold. "No, she cares about our image, not about us." She pushes through the curtain, leaving me no choice but to follow after her.

It takes a minute for my eyes to adjust to the dim, hazy light of

Carter's Ballroom. Between the glare of the glossy floors and soaring, exposed trusses overhead, I feel dizzy in this shadowy sea of dancing bodies. I spot Mama first, in her black wig and nondescript cowgirl hat. She's chatting it up with a dark-skinned man with a graying beard that brushes his collar. Adele is with them, appearing about as comfortable as a cop in a crowd of freshly released prisoners. I scan the crowd for Hattie and find her a minute later, swaying to the music and sipping an ice water.

Though I've never known my sister to have more than a single glass of wine on any occasion—social or otherwise—her choice in beverage allows me to take a full breath. If it's space she needs tonight, I can give her that.

With my anxiety slowly ebbing, I face the stage, watching two men and a female banjo player exit as the emcee stirs up the crowd by throwing out meaningless trivia to gain participation before the main act. I've seen it all before—the circus that is life in the spotlight, although my mama hasn't played in a venue like this for decades. And it's then my mind recalls what it's been fighting against ever since we pulled out of the hotel parking lot: Micah's face when he heard my middle name.

A strange longing brews inside me at the thought of not seeing him again until the morning. The way he examined my face as he said my full name was as if I were a clue in his quest for answers. If only that were true. But I'm as lost in my own quest for answers as he is in his.

The drumroll coming from the front pulls my focus back to the stage.

". . . so please put your hands together for tonight's honored guest and our spotlight talent for the evening. Straight from the heart of Nashville, here's Miss Cheyenne Avery!"

The crowd roars, and my jaw slacks. *Cheyenne Avery?* Surely it can't be. . . .

I twist to find Mama cheering at the top of her lungs while Adele looks positively stricken. I rush toward where they stand on the sidelines as my gorgeous niece takes the stage with the Martin guitar Mama gave her for her fifteenth birthday.

She greets more than a thousand people with a hearty, "How y'all doing tonight?"

The crowd's response for her is deafening.

"What in the . . ." Adele grips my arm to steady herself and blinks up at the stage, bewildered. Her only child strums her guitar and speaks to the audience with the ease and confidence of a performer twice her age.

"Surprise!" Mama squeals. "Didn't I tell y'all you wouldn't want to miss this?"

"But how . . ." Adele, clearly dumbfounded, shakes her head. "How is she here? Her classes aren't over yet; neither is her internship."

"Don't worry, Jana and I worked out all the logistics. Bruce was kind to book her during our trip. The best part is she's all ours for the next twenty-four hours!" Mama hollers proudly.

Cheyenne's background strumming changes to an intricate finger-picking pattern, and my eyes instantly flood with tears at the way her talent has advanced since last I heard her play.

"I'd like to dedicate this first song to my mama." She peers into the crowd. "We don't always see eye-to-eye, but it's her tenacity and dogged determination that beats like a drum in my chest. She's been my guiding light when I've felt lost, and she's been my champion since the first time I poured a bowl of cereal without spilling the milk." A collective laugh and *awww* fills the room. "So thank you, Mama. Thank you for teaching me to stand up, speak out, and sing with my whole soul. I love you."

I watch as my sister's expression melts into a look so full of maternal love and admiration, I can't help the sob that rises and breaks from my chest. I haven't seen my oldest sister cry since the day we laid our daddy to rest in a private cemetery east of Nashville. But these tears are different tonight. Not tears of grief, but of pride.

And then my niece, the first newborn I ever cradled in my arms at the ripe old age of seven, opens her mouth and bares her soul, one perfectly sung note at a time.

*September 3, 1975*
*Nashville, TN*

*Dear Chickee,*

*The three of us made it to Nashville in one piece: Luella, me, and our ever-faithful Lima Bean. We decided she deserved a name since she made it all the way here without a single complaint (other than the jam that prevents us from opening the back hatch).*

*We rented our first hotel room since Oregon last night and took extra time on our hair and makeup before going to our first meeting at TriplePlay Records. Luella had held out the phone so I could hear Russell Farrow's reaction when she called him last night, and his elation at us being here, in his city, made us feel pretty elated, too.*

*When we got there, the three partners had ordered us lunch in their meeting room where they asked us all sorts of questions about our travels. When Luella told them about our rattlesnake incident in Amarillo, they were howling, especially when she reenacted our reactions to it. Between you and me, I'm still not quite ready to laugh at that story yet.*

*Dorian is the funny one of the three. He spent a year in Vietnam and seems to find humor in things most people would cringe at, but his jokes helped calm our nerves. Troy seems to know the most about the music industry and drives the kind of fancy sports car we've only seen in movies—he let us both sit in it, too! Russell is exactly as Luella described: intelligent, confident, kind, and eager to please, at least when it comes to her. I caught him watching her every time she turned her attention to something else.*

*When they finally asked us to play for them, we were ready. Our voices blended perfectly, and I didn't miss a single chord on the guitar. When it was over, the three men were quiet. I'd be lying if I said I wasn't hoping for the same kind of response we received in San Francisco. But there was no applause or cheering, just a lot of staring at us and intense whispering among themselves until we were asked to leave the room. When we were called back inside, they told us they were "optimistic about our potential but that we weren't quite ready for the stage yet." We assured them we were willing to work hard and do whatever they ask of us. That seemed to be the answer they were looking for.*

*Russell has a lead on an affordable apartment for us, and Dorian has a connection for a job at a downtown lounge popular with industry professionals. We'll be waitressing. I hope you won't be mad when I tell you this next part, but we have to lie about our age in order to work there. Luella is nearly twenty so it's not as far of a stretch for her, but when I told them I was still eighteen, Dorian sang me three rounds of Happy Birthday and then gave me a new ID card.*

*I love you,*
*Lynn*

March 14, 1976
Nashville, TN

Dear Chickee,

*I'm sorry I haven't been writing. Truth is, I've never felt so tired. Between waitressing in the evenings, writing and rehearsing new songs in the afternoon, and playing gigs on the weekend that are mostly to empty bars, all I want to do is sleep. Troy gave me some pills from a doctor friend that will help me stay more alert and decrease my appetite. Troy says it would be better if my weight matched Luella's. I suppose he's right, I could stand to lose some pudge around my middle. Guess I should probably cut back on the grilled-cheese sandwiches we take home from The Lounge, too.*

*Russell hasn't missed a single gig we've played. Once he was our only audience member. He called out song requests and yelled* encore *after we walked offstage. We had a good laugh, even though I could tell both Luella and I wanted to cry.*

*In many ways, this dream is much harder than I thought it would be, but I'm happy. Tired, but happy. I love our tiny apartment and driving Lima Bean to work every night with my best friend. Oh, and you'll be thrilled to know, we found a church to attend every Sunday (as long as we get home at a decent hour on Saturday night). I'm planning to call you tomorrow. I miss your voice. Why do phone calls have to cost so much?*

*I love you,*
*Lynn*

*P.S. I got your birthday package in the mail. I'm saving it till Friday. Luella is baking me your famous lemon cake, and all our friends will be over to celebrate. No dieting on birthdays.*

*October 3, 1977*
*Nashville, TN*

*Dear Chickee,*

*I decided a while back that unless something really big happens, I'm not going to write it down. There are too many almosts and too many disappointments to rehash them all. The guys say "that's just life in Music City" and "we can either take it or leave it." Well, we took it all right, and you know what? We got our first big out-of-state show! We're playing a whole set, too. The owner is connected to other venues, and we might have enough bookings to be on the road for several weeks. I'm working hard to shed a few more pounds before Luella coordinates our stage outfits. Troy assured me that these are the same pills fashion models take to stay trim, and seeing as he dates so many beautiful women, I'm sure he knows what he's talking about.*

*He also says that if we keep working hard, we might be ready to cut our first album this time next year. Can you believe it?*

*One more thing, and this one is top secret, but Luella and Russell are in love, and I'm the only one who knows. Our contract with TriplePlay Records states that Luella and I are to remain unattached for the purposes of building our public personas and creating widespread appeal. Luella promised me she'd never break our pact or put Russell over our dream. I trust her.*

*I miss you,*
*Lynn*

# 13

## Micah

I've read the contents of nearly two of my mother's journals at this point, and all the while my mind has continuously jumped from the past to the present. More specifically, to the moment right before Luella's town car left the parking lot and she spoke her daughter's full name for the first time. *Raegan Lynn.* While most of my questions about my mother's life as a rising star remain unanswered, that is the one I keep coming back to tonight. Raegan was born more than a year after our mothers' friendship and careers blew up, so why would Luella choose to name her baby after her?

When I stand up from the bed to stretch my back, the sudden shift of the mattress catapults the journal closest to the bed's edge to the floor. With an agitated sigh, I bend to pick it up, only to see the drawing I'd flipped past yesterday while at the coffee shop. At the time, the charcoal sketch of a building I had no reference for didn't stand out as anything of interest. But tonight, when I read the words *Carter's Ballroom* scripted across the bottom under the date 1977, the spinning in my head comes to an abrupt stop.

And suddenly, I know exactly what I need to do. And better yet, where I need to be.

The Uber ride to Carter's is short, but I run into a jam when the box office out front is closed and all the exterior doors are locked. The red signage states: *No Reentry.* I'm just about to sleuth my way around the perimeter in search of another way in when a young couple stumbles out the main entrance, too busy groping each other to have a care in the world about me or anyone else for that matter. I don't hesitate to slip in behind them.

It takes several seconds to orient myself in the room. The lights are low, but the stimulus is high. There's a full bar surrounded by a massive crowd. My eyes scan the dance floor in front of the stage while music pumps in from somewhere unseen. The vaulted ceiling is about the only antidote for the claustrophobic setting.

Right when I'm beginning to doubt my ability to locate even one Farrow woman in this overstuffed space—much less all four—I spot Raegan in a group of familiar faces, and for nearly a minute I'm too awestruck to take my eyes off her. Every movement she makes is captivating. The way she leans into a conversation when someone is speaking, the way she finger-combs her curls over one shoulder only to have them spring back in disobedience, the way she sways in time to the music as if in a private dance no one else is invited to. Only, I want to be invited.

I stretch my neck from side to side and remind myself why I'm here. And then I'm on the move. Luella's wig choice this evening is nearly black, the darkest one I've seen her wear so far. I don't know much about hair, but the shocking shade is anything but natural looking.

A song has just ended onstage, but the applause is so loud Luella is all but shouting across the small circle gathered around her. Her hands are as animated as the expression on her face. It's then I notice Adele's arm looped around the waist of a young woman who favors her in nearly every way.

"Mind if I join you?" I break into the circle at Raegan's side.

She whips around so quickly, I shoot out a steadying hand at her middle back.

"Micah?" Raegan gasps. "I thought you were taking the night off."

"I thought I was, too," I say simply as the background music fades out and the only sound in the ballroom is the low hum of patrons' voices. My eardrums appreciate the break, and I use the timing to introduce myself, given Raegan's confused expression.

"I'm Micah," I say to the one unfamiliar face among us. "I'm guessing you must be associated with this raucous crew somehow."

"Only when they're on their best behavior," the young blonde says as she shakes my outstretched hand. "I'm Cheyenne." She tips her head to the right. "And this is my mom, Adele."

"Micah's quite familiar with who I am, sweetheart. He's been the bus driver for our trip," Adele states without a trace of her usual aggression. It doesn't take a clinical analysis to see how motherhood affects her.

"He's also a family friend," Luella pipes in happily. "Micah, my granddaughter here just knocked our socks off on that stage tonight. She surprised her mama with an original song and made her whole family proud!"

"Congratulations," I say. "I'm sorry I missed it."

"It was an incredible performance," Raegan concurs.

"Cheyenne will be with us overnight at the hotel, and then we'll drop her at the airport in Amarillo tomorrow afternoon," Luella chirps. "Perhaps we can convince her to share more of her talents with us on the road."

"Only if you promise to join in, Nonnie. I wouldn't be here without you, after all," Cheyenne says.

I notice the slight shift in Adele's posture and the way her arm slips from her daughter's waist. She rotates to look her child in the eye. "I'm still curious as to how you were able to make this trip happen on such short notice in the middle of your summer internship with Union Capitol and Associates?"

Cheyenne glances at Luella before focusing on her mother again. "Because I . . . I decided not to take the internship."

Adele doesn't so much as blink as the all-male cover band is announced onstage. Obviously, this is brand-new information. "That is hardly a decision you should be making on your own at nineteen, Cheyenne. Your father and I worked hard to get you that position."

"I know you did, and I appreciate it, but music is what I want to do, Mom. I've told you that. I don't want to go into business management and work for the family label. Nonnie said—"

"I told her we're only blessed with one life," Luella interjects, "and as I've said before, she should get a choice in how she wants to live it."

Adele's expression is raw when she looks from her mother to her daughter, as if she's too disoriented to formulate a reply. She's been blindsided, and I can't help but feel for the blow she's been dealt.

When Luella starts in with another speech, Adele's voice is tight with hurt. "I can't do this here, Mother. This is neither the time nor the place."

For what might be the first time, I agree with Adele.

Raegan gives me a look that says, *Let's get out of here.* Only, I feel a strange sense of duty to follow up with this potentially disastrous conversation—maybe even offer my assistance to mediate between the three of them if needed. From the expression on Luella's face, something tells me it will be needed.

Raegan loops her arm through mine and leads me toward a walled-off area at the far side of the room. The thumping volume lessens the closer we get to the enclosed area, and my bones will be grateful for the relief from the vibration. Before we're through, she presses in close and asks, "What are you really doing here?"

"I found something in my mother's journals about this place. A drawing—summer of 1977. Know anything about it?"

She shakes her head and points to the arched doorway beyond. "I don't, but I know where we might be able to find out." Her gaze holds a mesmerizing sparkle. "But first, can you help me get eyes on Hattie? Is she still out on the dance floor?"

*Oh, right. Hattie.* I chide myself for playing into the stereotypical fear of a middle child—being forgotten—and search the room from where we stand on the sidelines. I scan the sea of gyrating bodies.

"She's wearing a white snakeskin tank top," Raegan says, gripping my forearm and lifting up on her tiptoes. The heat of her hand searing into my skin is far more distracting than anything else in this dance hall.

"Over there! Near the front. Is that her?" She squints and points. "She knows every word of this song; it's one of her favorites."

I watch the woman she's pointing at sway like seagrass on a stormy riverbank. She's right, it's Hattie. Only, she's certainly not in the condition I last saw her in at the hotel.

"How many drinks do you think she's thrown back?" I ask just as the kick drum picks up again.

"What?" Raegan yells.

I bend so my lips are practically pressed against the shell of her ear. It's an effort not to think of how close her mouth is. "Drinks. How many has she had?"

Raegan startles back. "She had a glass of wine at dinner, and I've only seen her drink water since we've been here."

I watch as Hattie sloshes back some clear liquid from a plastic cup. "I'm thinking she's been enjoying something a bit stronger than water."

Raegan groans. "Wonderful. I'll go grab her as soon as I show you the wall."

"What wall?"

She tips her head for me to follow. "I saw it on my way to the restroom earlier. Took some pictures of it to show you, but now you can see it for yourself."

The second we're tucked behind the protection of the shadowed alcove, the volume in the ballroom is cut in half. The next moment the lit wall of art steals my full attention.

"What is this?"

Raegan leads me to the far end of what looks like a painted timeline that begins in 1968 and runs the entire length of the wall to present day. The painted images of music celebrities and bands are wildly realistic, and there are plaques with information interspersed throughout, along with framed articles and memorabilia.

"Do you see them?" Raegan points to the arrow at 1977, where our two mothers have been illustrated, standing side-by-side in bell-bottoms and tie-dye. They both flash peace signs. The metal plaque underneath them reads: "Lynn Hershel and Luella Farrow on October 3, 1977. The knock-out songwriting duo from north Idaho played a full set with our house band. The first of many magical nights to come, and the beginning of a long and beneficial relationship with Carter's."

I feel an inexplicable surge of pride, thinking back to my mother's entry after her win of the Elvis dance-off. "So they made it back just like they'd hoped."

"We did indeed." To my surprise, the voice belongs to Luella, not Raegan. "This was the first big venue we played—a full set. Bruce, the owner, saw something in the two of us nobody in Nashville would take the time to see. The industry was male-dominated back then, full of solo artists like Waylon Jennings, Willie Nelson, George Jones, John Denver. And here we were, a female duet with a single guitar. But Bruce took Russell's call and gave us a chance. And in return, your mom and I ended up saving his place from demolition." Luella saddles up beside me. "This building meant a lot to us back in the day." Her smile is sad when she adds, "It's one of the last places we played just for us. For those two girls who fought as hard for each other as they did for their dreams."

"How long did you two stay with TriplePlay Records before Russell founded Farrow Music Productions?"

"Too long, if you ask me." Luella makes a scoffing sound. "The split was in the works for quite a while as there were personal and legal ramifications to consider, but Farrow Music Productions was officially founded at the end of 1993. Russell and I risked everything to start that label, but it was time. My husband was too principled to stay in a partnership that wasn't."

I'm about to comment on this when Raegan hollers at us from further down the timeline. "Here's an article about your fundraising efforts to save Carter's in the '80s, Mama." She taps on a plexiglass frame bolted to the cement wall under 1990 and waves us on.

Together, we move down the mural and meet Raegan at the article. I study the black-and-white photo attached to the top of the newsprint. A five-member ensemble—three suited gentlemen who stand directly behind my mother and Luella, who together hold a giant pair of scissors, posed to cut a thick ribbon out front of this very building. I skim the details of how, after years of a struggling economy and slow business, the city was set to bulldoze the building to make room for a popular hotel chain. But the duo, along with the help of TriplePlay Records, organized enough charity fundraising concerts to save the historic building from its untimely death. They even found sponsors from surrounding areas who agreed to foot the bill for specific renovation projects within. This article commemorated the grand reopening of Carter's at the end of 1990.

I stare into my mother's eyes before scanning the three gentlemen dressed in suits behind them. Russell is the easiest to spot as he stands directly behind his wife, his hands resting lightly on her shoulders. "These other two men with Russell are . . ." I try to recall their names from the journals. "Troy and Dorian?"

"That's correct," Luella says. "I know this photo isn't the best quality, but Troy Rigger is the taller, thinner one with the round glasses, and Dorian Zuckerman is the goofy looking one there in the middle with a cigarette bobbing out the side of his mouth. I don't think he ever took a single straight-faced picture in all our time together—God rest his soul."

"He died?" I ask, turning to face her.

"Sadly, yes. Not long before my Russell. Lung cancer. My husband was a pallbearer at his funeral, and Raegan wrote a gorgeous poem she dedicated to their family during the service." She smiles in the direction of her youngest daughter, but I'm stuck on a detail I hadn't considered until then.

"Are you saying the three partners remained close even after Russell started his own label?"

"Not all three." Luella hesitates, seeming to choose her words carefully. "But eventually, Dorian came to work for Farrow Music Productions, and those two remained close friends for the rest of their lives. Our families have stayed close for many years."

My pulse thuds harder at this new tidbit of information. "If Dorian worked for Farrow Music, does that mean he and Russell were together in Germany while you and my mother toured in 1994?"

"No." She shook her head. "While Russell was away securing what would have been our first international tour, Dorian opted to stay back. After Vietnam, he had no interest in leaving the States again. He became our manager for the domestic tour. Without him, we would have been forced to cancel." She remains quiet for a long moment, her gaze growing distant as she says, "Sometimes I wonder how different things would have been if we'd all just stayed home that summer."

There are so many more things I need to ask, but the photo of Dorian Zuckerman doesn't let me go, nor does the question of his involvement with my mother the summer I was conceived.

I feel Raegan move to my side just as a deep, husky cough alerts us to someone behind us.

"It took the artist over a year to map this timeline and paint it for us, but we'd be nothing without our history." A man with bohemian-style dreadlocks and a white beard appears behind Luella and stretches his hand out to me. He introduces himself as Bruce before he drapes an arm around Luella's shoulders.

"It's lovely, Bruce." Luella's admiration for him is tangible.

"Not as lovely as you. Even with that crazy black wig you're trying to pull off." He tsks. "That thing looks about as out of place as a dolphin in the desert, if you ask me." He chuckles, then returns his gaze to the mural again. "I sure wish your Russell was here to see this mural. You both were an integral part of why this place is still standing." Bruce is quiet a moment before continuing. "You two were that rare, fairy-tale romance only soulmates get to experience. It's why the public couldn't get enough of the two of you. You were his queen."

Luella laughs. "Not sure you'd call us a fairy tale if you saw the way I got after him for leaving his socks under the coffee table night after night. The man couldn't walk to the dirty hamper to save his life."

As the last country song fades out in the background, a familiar melody plays over the loudspeakers, and surprisingly, the crowd hoots and hollers at the abrupt change of genre. "How Deep Is Your Love" by the Bee Gees blares over the speakers, and Bruce begins to sway his hips as he quirks an eyebrow at Luella, who laughs all the harder.

"Don't you even try to pretend that's coincidental, Bruce."

"I think we owe it to your Russell to cut a rug in his honor."

He extends a hand to her, and both Raegan and I are impressed by the rhythm he keeps while grooving to the song. The man has to be close to eighty, and yet he could "cut a rug" better than most people a quarter of his age.

"You know I can never say no to his song." Luella trails behind him to the dance floor.

I turn to ask Raegan if we should collect Hattie from the dance floor, but Raegan seems to have fallen through another portal. I wave my hand in front of her trance-like expression.

"Raegan?"

Her focus snaps to mine, and her mouth opens and closes twice before sound follows. "What if . . . what if my mama's real story was published before Peter's lies are released?"

It takes a minute for me to track what she's asking since she's jumped multiple topic hurdles to get here, but as soon as I'm able, I want to know more. "What do you have in mind?"

"You heard Bruce, my parents' love story is compelling—it covers so many romantic tropes and stretches over a long period of time: love at first sight, friends-to-lovers, forced proximity, forbidden romance. There's even a secret wedding ceremony they managed to keep hidden from the public. These are the bedtime stories I grew up with, Micah. I know them by heart." Her eyes are wild now as if she can't quite believe what she's about to say. "When Chip confirmed the tell-all was more than a rumor, he said the best we could hope for would be for the tell-all to be overshadowed by something far more deserving at the time of release. What if I could write that something?"

I recall what Raegan told me about the fiction book she wrote—the one about struggling individuals who fight for what they want. "I think you're plenty qualified."

She drops her gaze. "For credibility, I'd have to write it under my own name."

"Is that an issue?"

"Writing is the only thing in my life that's truly mine. No pressure, no expectation, no fear that my mistakes or failures will have any ill effect on my family. I always imagined if I was ever to get published, I'd do so under a different name."

I know this particular conversation is far more nuanced than what she's told me. I also know I should be professional enough to help her explore the pressures she's mentioned as a Farrow—and the root cause to her aversion for conflict—but I don't do any of that. Because right now, as the music slips into something slow and melodic, I don't want to be a therapist. I want to be a man, one who acts on the all-consuming attraction I've felt for Raegan since the first time she smiled at me.

I step toward her to ask her to dance, and when we lock eyes it nearly sends my pulse into an arrhythmic episode. Whatever this is between us—I don't want to suppress it any longer.

But the instant I start to speak, a short, shrill scream breaks through the dance hall. And then a second one, followed by a third, until an entire chorus is chanting a singular name that has been shouted in concert venues worldwide for decades.

As if in slow motion, the two of us rotate toward the mushroom cloud of patrons rising from the dance floor. And before I can even spot the way Luella's black wig has been yanked from her head, exposing her signature blonde curls underneath, my adrenaline has kicked into action.

There's no time to form an escape plan, nor enough security detail to create a proper barricade, but even still, I charge toward the chaos with a single instruction for Raegan.

"Get to the town car!"

"What?" she yells back.

"The town car!" I holler again over my shoulder. "Tell the driver to wait by the back door!"

And then I'm smashing through a mob of bodies in order to retrieve a woman I've come to care for with an intensity that doesn't make sense for the short time I've known her. And yet, she's not the only Farrow who's made her mark on me in record time.

# 14

## Raegan

The whirlwind of the last twenty minutes has stolen twenty years off my life. I'm sure of it. Between screaming for Adele and Cheyenne to follow me through the pandemonium of the dance floor, collecting my niece's guitar and gear from behind the stage, and watching Micah barrel through the back door with my petite, wig-less mother in his arms like Kevin Costner in *The Bodyguard*, I've nearly hyperventilated a dozen times. As if that wasn't bad enough, the irritated skin on the inside of my left wrist has erupted in stress hives.

By the time our town car slams to a stop at our hotel, the driver has already called for the security team to escort us to our floor via a staff elevator.

The instant the elevator doors open to reveal our quiet hallway, an out-of-breath Adele whirls on Mama. "Did I or did I not warn against something like this happening without a proper security detail?"

"We're all fine, darling. There's no need to overreact."

"*Overreact?*" Adele scoffs. "You could have been *trampled*—or worse!"

"Yet instead I was saved by a bus driver in shining armor." Mama beams up at Micah and pats his arm. "Thank you again, Micah dear. I just knew those beefy biceps of yours would come in handy."

I close my eyes, wishing I could evaporate along with the sweat that's prickling at the back of my neck. Moments like these are when I wish I could slip away into a different life. Preferably a fictional one.

"*Mother.*" Adele's voice is low and controlled when she speaks again. "Do you not realize how your recklessness put all of us at risk tonight, my daughter included? Safety is not something we have the luxury to take lightly."

"Adele," I begin, "I don't think Mama was intentionally being reckless. I think—"

"Did you know about this, Raegan?" Her gaze spears me through. "Were you involved in advocating for my daughter to quit school?"

"No, I didn't know anything about tonight." I glance at my niece. "But Cheyenne is an adult, and she's—"

"Mother." Cheyenne steps in front of me. "If you need to blame someone for what happened tonight, then blame me. I'm the one who called Nonnie. She was only trying to help make my dreams come true."

"Dreams are what children speak of, not mature and responsible adults. I will not support you throwing away every opportunity we've worked so hard for just because your last name hands you a golden ticket. The second that ticket is no longer shiny, you'll be crumpled up and thrown away, just like every other girl your age who thinks she has what it takes to make it in this industry." She pinches the bridge of her nose. "This is not the future we planned for you."

My sister's targeted words throw me back into a memory so vivid my entire body rocks off-center. Adele, sitting across from me at Mama's kitchen table where Daddy once sat with his morning coffee and Bible, sifting through the contract pages I'd just received from a renowned literary agent offering me and my novel representation just over a year ago.

*She sets it down and lets out a heavy sigh. "I'm sorry, Raegan. But I can't support you signing this right now."*

"What?" *Shock vibrates my vocal chords.* "Why not?"

*"Because it's clear this woman is only interested in representing your last name, not your talent. And unfortunately, those things can't ever be separated. Even if you're half as good of a writer as she's said you are, you'll forever be Luella Farrow's daughter first. You'll be judged differently than your peers—every move you make, every book you write, every interview you give." She lays her palm on the stack of freshly printed papers. "Fame has a price tag, and all of us have paid a portion of it in our own way. A literary agent will never have your best interest in mind, and certainly not your family's. I need you to put this on hold for now, especially in the wake of everything that's happened. It's not the right time."*

Cheyenne's heated debate launches my mind out of the past and back to the present. "What if I don't want the future you've planned for me? Nonnie has had a fifty-year career in music. Her success is the only reason you have a job—"

"My *job* is based on the cruel understanding that this industry has far less to do with talent and far more to do with how much you're willing to let it suck from your soul." Adele refocuses her gaze on Mama. "If you've led her to believe that you've somehow arrived at this place of stardom unscathed, then you should be ashamed of yourself. Because none of us have."

Adele stares at our mama for so long that my lungs burn from the charge in the air. And then, without another word, my oldest sister stalks down the hallway. Alone. It's so quiet when she makes it to her room that the swipe and click of her access key card doesn't prepare me for the sharp rattle in my chest when the door slams shut behind her.

Nobody speaks for close to a minute. "Looks like I'll be bunking with you tonight, Nonnie," Cheyenne says, resigned.

Mama nods, but her gaze remains fixed on Adele's closed door. "She'll come around, sweetheart. Don't you worry."

But worry is exactly what I hear in Mama's faint voice.

With her University of San Francisco duffel bag flung over her shoulder and her guitar case in hand, Cheyenne kisses me good-night before she follows Mama down the hall to her suite. I'm just about to head to my own room, as I desperately need to locate my emergency supply of antihistamines in my travel kit, when a sickening thud of realization hits my gut at what appears to be the same time it hits Micah's.

We whirl around to face each other, our eyes panicked.

"Where's Hattie?" We both demand in unison.

We point at each other. "I thought *you* had her."

"Me?" He points the finger at himself. "Why would I have her?"

"Because *you* were the one on the dance floor."

"Right," he remarks slowly, "only you seem to be forgetting the part where I was busy rescuing your mother from being mowed down by a mob. Forgive me for assuming you conducted a head count of the members in your immediate family before our getaway car left the premises."

"I *did* conduct a head count," I sputter back. "There were five of us in that car. . . ." But my argument cools as soon as I recall *why* there were five of us in that car. *Cheyenne.* I slap my hand to my mouth and feel my eyes bulge in horror as I speak around my trembling fingers. "I forgot my sister."

"No, we all forgot your sister," Micah says, gripping my arm and tugging me toward the elevator. "The important thing is we remembered her. We'll simply order a rideshare and pick her up. She'll be fine."

"Don't say *fine*," I nearly cry as the elevator door closes us inside again. "You've ruined that word for me forever."

For once, Micah has no response, and I'm ninety-nine percent sure we're both better off for it.

By the time we're inside the rideshare—an electric blue four-door hatchback, driven by a kid who can't be much older than eighteen, given his backward ball cap and baby-face grin—I've panic-dialed my sister five times without an answer. I can feel the hive vine snaking up my forearm and settling into the crook of my elbow, but I don't have the time or the mental capacity to care. If something happens to Hattie because of me, I'll—

"Do you have a tracking app on her phone?" Micah's question feels like a divine intervention.

I gasp. "Yes! Oh my gosh! You're a genius!"

"I was hoping you'd finally recognize that." He reaches over and squeezes my kneecap. "Breathe, Raegan. We'll find her."

As quickly as my fumbling fingers can move, I tap into our shared family app and spot Hattie's location on the map. She's not at Carter's. It looks like she's now across the street at someplace called Ye Ol' Western Bar and Grill. I provide the address to our driver, and within a few minutes, we've pulled up, jumped out, and rushed inside a bar that looks like it could be a set in a Louis L'Amour novel.

"There she is," Micah says, barreling ahead to where Hattie's slumped on a stool, her head down on the glossy bar top. Alone.

"She belong to you, mister?" the barkeep asks.

"To us, yes." Micah moves his finger between him and me, and a warm floaty feeling is suddenly at war with my surge of adrenaline.

"Lady came in about twenty minutes ago with a no-good crowd. They all moved on after her credit card was declined."

I shiver at the idea of anyone trying to take advantage of my sister and set a protective hand on her back. She barely makes the effort to lift her head. "Hattie? Honey, are you alright? We're here to take you back to the hotel."

"Just leave me," she slurs. "I'm a terrible person."

"We're not leaving you." Not for a second time, anyway.

"Afraid she can't leave without paying off her balance. I ran her card twice," the barkeep states. "Receipt says non-sufficient funds."

"Here." Micah hands his Visa over to the guy with three piercings in his bottom lip, and I assure him I'll reimburse the total as soon as we get back to the hotel. He shakes his head. "Don't worry about it."

So instead, I worry about how to get my sister into a standing position, which is much harder than it looks in the movies. It doesn't matter how petite a person is when they literally can't lift their own legs to save their soul. When Micah grabs her opposite arm and slings it around his neck, our walking speed triples. That is, until it's time to brainstorm the best way to get her into the back of a sedan while our young driver offers us his pro tips on transporting intoxicated passengers. I'm wondering if he's learned these best practices from the college stamped across his backward hat or from this side hustle he looks in no way old enough to have.

"I'd scoot her to the middle seat," he says. "That way she's propped up between the two of you like the tomato plants in Mom's garden cages."

"Good advice," Micah says, shooting me an amused look as he hands me the other end of Hattie's buckle. Immediately after I click her in, her head lolls back against the seat.

Micah thanks our driver again for agreeing to wait for us while we took care of business inside the bar and has just started to ask him questions about his life when Hattie begins to groan and clutch at her abdomen.

With lightning-speed reflexes, Micah flicks the ball cap off our young driver's head and apologizes profusely as Hattie lurches forward, proceeding to empty the contents of her stomach into the offering Micah holds between his hands. The entire production is over in less than five seconds, and yet I know it will scar the majority of us for life.

Our driver laughs and thankfully rolls down the windows. "Bruh! Sick catch! And don't worry about the hat. It's not mine. I stole it from my brother after he kissed my girlfriend last week. Poetic justice, right?" He signals a turn. "There's a trash can at the end of this street. I'll pull up so you can toss it. But I think I'll snap a pic first—ya know, to offer Dillan some closure."

Horrified at, well, everything that's transpired up to this point, I eye Micah, who is obviously trying his hardest not to gag at the smell wafting in the back seat despite the added airflow.

"That's not how closure works," Micah says in a decidedly puny voice.

"What's that?" our driver asks as he pulls up to the curb and hands back a stack of McDonald's napkins to clean Hattie's face.

"Nothing," Micah replies as I reach across Hattie and drop the used napkins into said closure cap.

"I'm so, so sorry about this, Micah," I whisper.

His nod is subtle yet concentrated as our driver opens his door for him to make a smooth exit and transfer to the garbage can.

The minute we're driving again, Hattie pushes up to a sitting position and rests her head on my shoulder.

"Sunny Bear? Do you think I'm a b-b-b-ad mom?" Her question is so slurred and pained, my stomach cramps.

"Of course I don't. You're a wonderful mother."

"But what if . . . what if my kids choose Fran-chessa?" It takes me a second to interpret her brutal pronunciation of Francesca's name.

"That won't happen. Your kids adore you."

"They adore her, too. Just like they adore her big Greek family and her big Greek house, and soon they'll love her big Greek wedding, too." A sob breaks from her throat. "He's marrying her, Raegan. He asked a twenty-four-year-old to marry him in front of my kids."

My insides scream with outrage. "Oh, Hattie. No."

"What if . . . what if he takes them from me forever?"

Fear grips me in its talons the same way it did two months after my nephew Aiden was born and I found Hattie catatonic on the bathroom floor while he screamed in his crib and Anabelle walked through the house with a half-eaten bowl of sliced strawberries, most of which were smeared on the front of her mermaid nightgown. And then I think of how hard Hattie fought to get well again, how hard we all fought to wage war against the cloud of postpartum depression that stole her from us for nearly a year.

I can't let her go back to that dark place again.

And the truth is, she's been teetering on the edge since the day Adele caught Peter alone with Francesca in the recording studio.

Our driver is pulling into the hotel's unloading zone when I start in with a plethora of panicked assurances in Hattie's ear.

Micah reaches behind her back and clasps my shoulder, his expression both kind and sympathetic when he says, "She can't hear reason in this state, Raegan. Why don't I help you get her inside and cleaned up, and then we can assess what should happen next."

I nod because there's simply nothing else I can do.

It's the same response I give him when he suggests we take her back to my room for the cleanup portion of our plan. And again when he suggests I help her into some more comfortable attire before we prop her on my sofa so she can hydrate before sleeping off her intoxication. And then again when he offers to come back and check on us after he showers.

Of all the plans he's suggested tonight, that one is by far my favorite.

# 15

## Raegan

I've just taken a half dose of the prescription antihistamine I keep in my travel bag to stop the hive vine on my forearm when Micah knocks at my door. I answer in my sweats and my favorite sleep tee filled with Jane Austen quotes, but take care to keep the ugly red bumps hidden from view. If he saw them earlier while we cared for Hattie, he didn't mention it.

As he stands in the empty hallway with a stack of journals in his arms and reading glasses on his face, I'm wondering at the advanced math formula involved in taking an already attractive man and making him ten times more attractive with such a minor change.

"I figured since we don't know how much Hattie had to drink tonight, it might be good to have something to do while we keep an eye on her."

Every cell in my body swoons at his suggestion.

"You don't have to stay up with me, really." I'd planned on it, of course, hence my half dose of meds, but Micah has a bus to drive tomorrow. "I'll be fine." I scrunch my nose as I catch my slip. "I mean, I don't expect you to—"

"What if I told you I'd like to stay up and keep you company? Would you be good with that?"

I nod, willing the butterflies inside me to stay in their respective cocoons. They don't.

He stops and scans my hotel suite, noting Hattie asleep on the far sofa where we'd propped her on pillows. "I'm glad she's resting."

"Me too."

As we each take in the ransacked suitcases, hastily discarded clothing, damp towels, half-drank water bottles, and toiletries scattered about the sofa opposite Hattie's, Micah starts to make his way over to it as it's the only other place in the room to sit outside of the bed. Only, I have no energy left for cleaning tonight, and I'm certain he doesn't, either.

"I'm not opposed to sharing the bed with you," I say two seconds before my brain catches up to my mouth.

Micah turns slowly, smirking. "I'm flattered, Raegan, but I'm afraid I'm not that kind of guy."

I ignore the heat engulfing my neck and point to the mess in the tiny living room area. "Then by all means, please feel free to pick up the trail of soggy laundry and towels on the sofa so we can—"

"On second thought, the bed sounds swell, as long as you're sure you can keep your hands to yourself."

I roll my eyes. "I'll do my best."

I perch at the foot of the king-size bed where he tosses me a couple of pillows before taking two for himself and stretching out horizontally across the head of the mattress. I don't hesitate to follow his lead. It's been a long night.

He sets the journals between us once we're settled, and I smile at him over the stack.

"Thank you," I start, knowing the sentiment is nowhere near enough to cover my gratitude for what he did for my family tonight. "You were . . . tonight was . . ."

"Gross?" he supplies helpfully.

"No doubt about that." I grimace. "But I really do appreciate your help with my sister tonight. There's no way I could have done all that on my own."

He holds my gaze, and I don't even try to swat the flutters away this time. "I think the two of us make a pretty good team."

Of all the things he could have said, this hits with unexpected warmth. He can't possibly know how un-team-like my world often feels. "I do, too."

"There is something I'm going to need an answer to, though, before we can go any further in this new partnership of ours."

My stomach clenches as I think of all the possible topics my family drama provided him tonight. No doubt he has lots of questions. I would, too. "What do you want to know?"

"Why on earth are you called *Sunny Bear*?"

I'm barely able to stifle my laugh to keep from waking Hattie. "It's really silly, actually. My dad used to call me his *little Rae of sunshine*, emphasis on the Rae. But *Rae* never really stuck, so then they started calling me variations of Sunny. Then one infamous day when I was about seven, Sunny morphed its way to Sunny Bear, which makes absolutely no sense at all, but that is the origin story of my nickname. It's ridiculous."

"I think it's pretty cute." His oversize smile causes his glasses to slip a tad on the bridge of his nose, which I think is *pretty cute*.

"I'm twenty-six. Sunny Bear's life-span should have ended before I entered middle school."

"We'll have to agree to disagree, Sunny Bear." When he makes no effort to look away, I'm suddenly grateful for Lynn's journal-keeping. It's clear I'm going to need a distraction from Micah's glasses tonight.

I reach for the pile of hardbacks between us.

"Have you been reading these?" I find the one I flipped through on the bus and locate the last entry I read—when Lynn and my mother were making their first album with TriplePlay Records and my parents were secretly dating to keep the guise of Mama being a young, eligible, blonde bombshell.

"I've read through two of them. She jumps months and even years in the coming entries. I don't think journaling was as much of a priority to her when they weren't on the road."

"So you're saying I have a lot of catching up to do?"

"Be my guest." He slides over the second journal with the date range of 1976–1979. My parents' unofficial wedding was in '80, though their marriage the public knew about was in '82. Adele was born two years later, and I've always wondered about those years leading up to it—what Lynn and my mama's relationship was like back then, and how their slow but steady rise to fame affected it. I'm about to say this very thing when Micah's voice cuts through my thoughts.

"Why did your mother name you after mine?"

Unlike before, this beat of silence that passes between us is thick and palpable.

I swallow. "I've often wondered that myself."

"You've never asked her?"

"Not directly, no." When I think back to the days before Mama's final visit with Lynn, it's difficult to recall the closed-off way she once spoke about her old friend, or about the time period before Luella Farrow was a standalone act on stage. I used to interpret Mama's tight-lipped responses of the *before* era as a lack of affection for a woman who had so obviously wronged her.

But as of late, I'm not sure I interpreted much about my mother's past friendship with Lynn correctly at all.

I splay my fingers over one of Lynn's hand-drawn crosswords near an entry in '77 and think of how sad it is that her creative design was never completed.

"Honestly, Micah," I say with extra care, "discussing some of the details of our mothers' pasts might be a bit . . . awkward."

"You mean because we believed them to be mortal enemies once upon a time?"

My lips pull to one side. "Something like that, yeah."

Gingerly, he rotates the journal from beneath my palm so that the clues of the crossword can be read by us both. We each take a second to scan through them, but my gaze halts at the clue given for four across. The only clue Lynn wrote was: *Us.*

The simplicity of it is distracting. I've just started to puzzle it out when Micah says, "I'm willing to lean in to the awkward if you are."

I look up from the crossword. "What?"

"Lean in to the awkward. It's something I use to say a lot in my school office. We're trained from an early age to retreat from anything that makes us feel uncomfortable, but comfort never pushes us to grow or even view things from a different perspective. So, if given the choice, I lean in to it."

I want to say something intelligent in response, but my insides are too rattled by the truth bomb he's detonated. Everything he said sounds right, and yet I pretty much do the opposite. Maybe it's not too late to try.

I prop my head in my hand. "Then I'll lean in with you."

"Deal." He nods earnestly.

"I didn't realize how close our mothers were all those years ago until recently. I knew they were teenage friends who became bandmates, and enough about the mess that followed their split and broken contracts to assume my mother avoided conversations about Lynn out of resentment. But I don't think that anymore. Now, I think she avoided talking about those times out of pain. My mama was different after she came home from seeing Lynn in Idaho. . . ." I purse my lips, remembering her tears, her vulnerability, her return to attending weekly church services even though it meant a three-ring circus of security detail and disguises. But mostly, I think about her desire to talk late into the evenings about things she's never spoken about with me before. "I think whatever bond was broken between them all those years ago began to heal as soon as that old song of theirs went viral."

Micah's eyes are soft on my face. "I don't know what shocked my family more—having that prestigious award show up at my parents' house, engraved to my mother, or opening the door to Luella herself standing there only a month later at my mom's request."

From the sofa behind us, Hattie releases a soft snore. We both freeze and then slowly twist to find her burrowing deeper into one of the extra blankets Micah requested at the front desk.

I return my gaze to the open journal between us and trace the seven-letter blank for the clue on three across once again. *Us.* I count out the letters for *friends*, but it doesn't fit with the answers for the vertical clues. And then—

"Sisters." A raw sensation crawls up my throat and seems to confirm my timely hypothesis. I tap the blank row. "That's what they were to each other once, just like your mom wrote in her journal. An old friend you can live without after a time, but a sister . . ." I shake my head. "That's different. My sisters can infuriate me like no one else in this world, and because of that, I suppose we can hurt each other like no one else in the world, too. But no matter what offense comes between us, I'd never be able to cut them off completely." A new conviction surges within me. "I think Mama gave me Lynn's name out of hope. Hope that one day, despite all the brokenness between them, things might be restored."

Micah sets his hand on the page next to mine. His palm covers entries written before either of us were born, treasured words that hold mystery and truth, joy and sorrow. And I imagine, for Micah, a fair amount of heartache, too.

"Can you tell me what happened between them?" he asks.

"I don't know all the details that led up to their fight, but I do know it was your mama's decision to leave it all behind—their music, their tour plans, their new record, their friendship." I take a breath, wanting to take care in how I say this next part. "Farrow Music Productions was still so new at that time that when Lynn backed out, it cost my parents every cent of collateral they put down on the company, and eventually, it bankrupted them. They lost their home and had to move with my sisters into my grandparents' house while my dad worked to rebuild the label from the ground up. The way my mama tells it, she thought she was done with music forever after all that. She didn't step foot on stage again until I was three years old, after much encouragement from my daddy."

"I didn't know any of that." Micah says, rolling on his side to thread a hand through his hair. "I never knew it was my mother who initiated the decision to leave." I can hear the grief in his long exhale. "It's hard not to think of all the questions I wish I could ask her now, starting with the motivation behind why she would choose to keep so many secrets from us."

I nod to the journals. "Maybe the more you read, the more you'll understand. Your mother expresses herself well through her writing. She obviously had a way with words."

"I have it on good authority she's not the only one with that gift." This time when his gaze fixes on mine, the query in his voice transports me back to the mural in Carter's Ballroom, to a conversation that feels as foreign now as it does impossible.

Had I actually suggested I write my mama's love story for publication?

I barely have time to answer the first question due to the one that comes directly behind it: *Would I actually write under my real name?*

"You're panicking," Micah notes calmly. "Why?"

I try to sit up, but the mattress is like quicksand, and it takes two attempts to push myself into a cross-legged position.

"I misspoke before—at the mural. I can't write a book like that. I wasn't thinking clearly."

His expression doesn't budge even a fraction of an inch, and the patience rolling off him is almost irritating.

"Micah," I start again, this time bolder. "I don't know how to write nonfiction. Obviously, there's a Raegan Farrow doppelgänger on the loose who says stupid things when she's stressed out."

His lips quirk. "I can vouch for the fact that it was most definitely

195

you back at that mural: jean skirt, purple top, curls for days, and a face I've enjoyed looking at from every angle since the day we met." He hikes an eyebrow, and all the fluttering I'd managed to contain to my abdomen is now roaming free in every nook and cranny of my body.

"You know their stories by heart, Raegan. You said so yourself. So take the next step and write them down." He readjusts his position on the mattress to mirror my own and then reaches for my hand. I offer him the one that isn't marred by signs of stress and slip the other behind my back. It's easy to melt into the sensation of his touch. "Don't sell yourself short just because you're afraid to lean in to something new."

"What if I lean so far I fall flat on my face and fail my whole family?" I whisper in the hollow space between us.

"And what if it's the best thing you ever do for your family?" he asks. "What if what you write does exactly what we hope and it knocks Cheater Peter's book right off the shelves?" He clasps my hand a little tighter. "What if this is the timing you've been waiting for?"

I close my eyes and focus on the feel of Micah's hand on mine until I can process it all over again. Only, this time, when I plug the details into my own story narrative, I don't give fear a plot point. Because if anyone in our circle is qualified to write my mama and daddy's love story, it's me. Adele's version would read like a business exposition of dates and facts, and Hattie's idea of writing was to bribe her sorority sisters to finish her term papers with VIP concert tickets to any show Mama's team could get their hands on. And Mama? Well, she's an orator by nature. I've rarely seen her put pen to paper.

It's strange to think how little I knew about the personal life of Lynn Davenport prior to opening her journal for the first time, when now I can hear her voice inside my head, telling me a story I'm inspired to follow. Perhaps nonfiction isn't as different as I fear.

The idea sprouts chill bumps down my arms.

"I'll call and talk to Chip tomorrow," I say. "Ultimately, it's his decision to make or break."

"And your family's." I don't miss his not-too-subtle hint.

I gesture to the couch where my sister is snoring off her booze and hike an eyebrow. "Would you like me to wake Hattie to ask her now or . . . ?"

"Raegan," he says gently. "It's easy to fool ourselves into thinking secrets are the best way to protect the ones we love, when it's really ourselves we want to protect."

His words knock hard against my chest. "That's not what's happening here, Micah." I disconnect my gaze from this intense staring match, only to realize our hands are still entwined. "I know my family. News like this will throw everyone into chaos." I gesture again to Hattie. "It will be best if I have a prepared solution at the ready when I tell them. I need to be certain."

"Is that the same logic you apply to Tav—that you need to be certain before you discuss your relationship?"

He must anticipate my reaction because he loosens his grip a second before I pull my hand away.

"That's . . . that's not the same thing at all."

"Okay," he says simply. *Too* simply.

"What do you mean by *okay*?"

"Exactly what it sounds like." He smiles annoyingly. "If you say it's not the same, then it's not."

I study him suspiciously, and he leans back, planting his palms on the mattress behind him while his biceps put on a show that is not appropriate for the moment. "You think I'm avoiding a conversation with him because I don't know how I feel?"

"It doesn't matter what I think. What do you think?"

"For not working as a therapist right now, that sounds like a very *therapisty* thing for you to ask. For your information, I was the one who ended things between us."

Something indecipherable crosses over his face. "And yet you're the one who said things are still complicated between the two of you."

"Aren't all breakups complicated at some level?" I ask in earnest. "I've known Tav all my life; I can't just flip a switch and pretend all the history we've shared doesn't matter or that I don't care about his future. I'm not that kind of person."

"You're right," Micah says. "You're not that kind of person. I do know that." There's a dull ache in my lower belly when he looks away from me. "I'll make sure you get the privacy you need for that phone call tomorrow with Chip."

I'm not sure what I've done wrong, but I want things to go back to how they were five minutes ago. "Thank you," I say, my throat suddenly tight. "I appreciate that."

I scramble to think of a way to get us back to a better place and reach for his mother's journals when—

"What's that?"

He captures my left arm mid-reach, and I silently chastise myself for killing the atmosphere even further with the ugly hive vine that is still present despite my half dose of medicine. I open my mouth to dismiss his concern when he strokes his finger from the underside of my wrist to the middle of my forearm. His eyes narrow with concern. I try to pull my arm back. Only, this time, his hold tightens.

"It's nothing, it's just—"

"Hives," he says knowingly. "What are you allergic to?"

"Stress." I try to say this with casual indifference, but somehow it makes the crease between his eyebrows intensify. "Believe it or not, they actually look better now than they did earlier. I only took a half dose of my antihistamines since I wasn't sure how Hattie was going to do tonight. They usually take a couple of hours to disappear."

"How long has this been happening? How often?" he asks in a decidedly doctoral tone.

"A few years. The first time was in the months following my dad's heart attack."

Without warning, he releases my arm, stands from the bed, and walks to the bathroom sink. He's back an instant later with a washcloth. There are no words exchanged as he settles beside me again and presses the cool, damp cloth to my sensitive skin. Technically, I'm the baby in my family, yet given our unique dynamics, I'm rarely the one being looked after in a physical sense.

"Should I call you Dr. Davenport now?" The tease in my voice is thicker than I intend, and though I want to blame it on the antihistamines floating in my bloodstream, I know not even a medically induced coma could mimic the way I feel every time Micah comes close.

"My brother, Garrett, is actually our resident family doctor," he says, while applying pressure to my arm. "A dermatologist. Any medical tips or tricks I've managed to pick up over the years are from him."

"Are you saying I owe your brother a thank you for his past advice?"

Micah's gaze pierces me. "Depends on which advice, I suppose. If I'd taken his most recent advice, I never would have met you."

I wrinkle my eyebrows. "He didn't support you coming here?"

"He worries I'm becoming too impulsive."

My breathing shallows as I contemplate the possibility of never having met Micah, and there's no doubt in my mind how not-a-fan I am of that equation. "I'm glad you didn't listen to him. You were meant to be here. With us. With me."

The compress stills on my arm, but Micah doesn't meet my gaze this time. And maybe that's the reason I find the courage to say more. "Maybe being impulsive isn't the worst thing a person can be."

He's slow to lift his head, but when he does, his eyes are dialed in on my mouth. "Maybe not."

Every thought in my head evaporates with the exception of one: *lean in to this.*

And so I do.

And then, after only a second of hesitation, so does he.

Our lips are a fraction of an inch apart when a loud moan erupts from the opposite side of the room, breaking the heated spell between us. I propel myself off the mattress and toward my sister, rushing her to the bathroom in a blurred frenzy.

There is absolutely nothing charming or romantic about the thirty minutes I spend tending to my sister.

After I've helped Hattie back to the sofa and Micah's finished yet another round of cleanup, he settles back on the bed, this time engrossing himself in his mother's journals. Tentatively, I resume my place at the far end of the mattress and pick up the journal nearest me. I sneak a glance at him again, and it's as if those few heartbeats we shared earlier were nothing more than a fleeting, confusing moment of temptation. Perhaps that's all they were for him.

But as I flip the page to start reading, I know they were way more than that for me.

*September 13, 1979*
*Idaho bound!*

*Dear Chickee,*

*I can't stop smiling! Ever since Luella surprised me with a plane ticket home to see you, I've been a mixture of every emotion imaginable. She knew how badly I wanted to show you our first album in person—I just can't quite believe she made it happen. She must have saved every tip she made for over six months. I'll be on a plane in three days! I can't wait to hug you and show you and tell you everything. Four years is way too long.*

*See you soon,*
*Lynn*

*February 6, 1980*
*Nashville*

*Dear Chickee,*

*Today started out like every other day. After practice, Luella and I drove Lima Bean to The Lounge on Broadway and were busy bussing tables during the dinner hour when Troy and Dorian and Russell burst through the front doors and started hollering our names and drawing all sorts of attention. At first, Luella grabbed my arm because we both thought something must be terribly wrong, but then they shouted for the barkeep to turn on the radio right then. If they didn't do so much business there, I'm sure Mr. Buchanan would have turned them out on the street as he reminds us often how genteel his establishment is. But about two min-utes later, the DJ announced our song on the radio! Luella and I nearly collapsed with joy. We were jumping and crying and laughing and hugging all at the same time. Five years in and over a hundred live performances under our belts and none of them compared to this moment. The best part was they were playing your favorite song: "No Clouds Overhead."*

*I love you,*
*Lynn*

May 10, 1981
On the road!

Dear Chickee,

It's official! We're on tour! Troy sat us down last Christmas and told us once we had three songs in the top forty in a three-month period, he'd personally rent us a bus and set up a summer tour. Well, we currently have four songs in the top twenty and one that hit number one! Luella and I keep pinching ourselves that this is our lives. We quit The Lounge a few months back to spend more time in the studio, but we're there so often with the guys it kind of feels like we still work there, only now we don't bus our own dishes.

In other news, Troy tried to arrange for Luella to attend a movie premier with a big-time Hollywood actor for some added publicity be-fore our tour, but Russell was strongly opposed. The conversation got so heated between the two men that at one point Dorian had to step in and keep them from coming to blows right there at table eight in The Lounge. Luella and I weren't present when Russell confessed what only I've known since last fall (their courthouse wedding), but the mood around the studio has plummeted from bad to worse.

Russell and Troy haven't spoken to each other in weeks, and there were many times Luella and I wondered if the tour would be canceled over it, but Dorian reassured us that they will work things out eventually and that we should stay focused on what we do best. So that's exactly what we're going to do.

I love you,
Lynn

December 19, 1981

Dear Chickee,

For months we've listened to Troy's lectures about the importance of protecting Luella's public image from the press. There are all sorts of rules we follow to ensure she's perceived as single and desirable even though she's been married to his business partner for over a year. So far, it's been easy to trick the world as people believe whatever story we tell them from the stage about us being two regular chicks who chased a dream all the way from Idaho. But it's when we're all back home that I realize just how different things have become.

Since we'd agreed it would be best for us to continue living as roommates, I didn't expect much to change other than the size of the house we purchased together with the private backyard, patio, and pool. But being single and having a married best friend and being single and having a single best friend are two different things. I try to explain this to Luella on the nights Russell doesn't sneak over and we can actually talk the way we used to, but I don't think she quite understands what I'm saying.

Tonight, when I found the National Enquirer shoved in the kitchen trash featuring an unflattering picture of me next to the stunning Luella with a caption that read: Life in Luella's Shadow, all I wanted was to run to my best friend for comfort. But her husband was over and her door was locked, so instead, I sat on the sofa alone and ate a bowl of pistachio ice cream.

I love you,
Lynn

# 16

## Micah

Three synchronized vibrations startle me from a dead sleep. Delirious, I shield my eyes against the amber haze slicing between the drapes and the wall and work to place where I am and why I'm lying on top of a mattress fully dressed. But my line of questioning halts the instant I eye the sleeping beauty at the foot of the bed.

*Raegan.*

At the sight of her dark curls cascading over the white pillowcase, the events of the last night flash through my mind like the flipped pages of a graphic novel: The nightclub. The mural. The mob. The bar rescue. The vomit hat. The cleanup. The intoxicated sister asleep on the sofa. The hours Raegan and I spent talking and reading journal entries and nearly . . . I swallow.

I'd almost kissed her. In truth, I don't think it's possible to be any more kissable than Raegan Farrow. But unlike Sleeping Beauty, a kiss is not what she needs most right now.

I scrub a hand down my face and remind myself *once again* why it's imperative to implement boundaries. First, she's barely one foot out of a complicated relationship with her ex. Second, we're only hours away from being stuffed back into a tin can with her family, where there is hardly enough privacy to breathe much less figure out what this is between us. And third, and perhaps most important, she doesn't value open communication. The secrets Raegan is keeping are living on borrowed time, and seeing as I represent the collateral damage of such a secret-keeper, I can't affirm the stance she's taken.

Yet at the same time, I also can't ignore the way my blood turns molten whenever she's near.

The three phones go off again on the desk like an SOS, and I'm careful to navigate around her adorable socked feet without disturbing her and quickly silence each device. It's not until I swipe to unlock my phone that I read the red-lettered warning affixed to my home screen: Severe Storm Alert. There's a straight-line windstorm headed through Texas and Oklahoma, with winds upwards of seventy miles per hour and hail.

Adrenaline swamps my insides as I click into the report and then to the weather radar, which confirms our worst-case scenario for today's driving itinerary. According to this, chances are good Cheyenne's flight in Amarillo will be canceled, and whatever else Luella had planned there simply isn't worth the risk. We'll need to head north. I grip the back of my neck and track the oncoming hailstorm's predicted arrival time.

We need to get on the road. *Soon.*

But as I begin to calculate a new route for us, the logistics involved in rousing the troops for such an early travel time begin to read like a bad math story problem in my head: If it's currently 5:15 a.m. and there are five Farrow women asleep in three different hotel rooms, how long will it take to load a tour bus? Special considerations of note: one Farrow is a country music legend, another Farrow is furious at said country music legend, and still another Farrow smells like she spent the night hugging the toilet.

Answer: I'm screwed.

I glance over at Hattie on the sofa and recall the numerous times Raegan woke to assist her in the night any time she coughed or moaned or lost her blanket to the floor. Sometime around three, when Hattie had yet another retching episode in the restroom, I proposed we tag-team any future wake-ups. Too exhausted to argue with me, Raegan accepted my help the next two times her sister needed attention. I look between the two sleeping women now, torn at whom to wake first. Ultimately, I choose Hattie. A few extra minutes of sleep won't make much of a difference in her condition, and it will likely take her twice as long as the others to perform the basic function of walking to the lobby. At this rate, she'll need close to a day to recover, as well as a few gallons of water to drink. I had a college roommate who taught me all I needed to know about the cruelty of hangovers my freshman year.

I crouch down in front of her and repeat her name numerous times in a low voice until she makes a sound that's almost human.

"Hey, Hattie. We need to get on the road soon. Can you open your eyes?"

She pries her eyelids open and studies me for several seconds. "Micah?"

"Morning." I smile, careful to keep my volume low. "Did you hear me? You're gonna have to walk down to the bus in a few minutes." She starts to push up on her elbow, and I grip her arm to assist. "Not too fast," I caution. "When you can, place both your feet on the floor to ground yourself. It will help with your equilibrium and balance."

I wait for her to adjust her T-shirt and uncurl her legs from the sofa cushion. The instant her feet hit the floor, her hands fly to her head and she sways forward. I catch her shoulders and help her lean against the backrest.

"My head is pounding," she complains.

"Do you have any more of those crackers Raegan gave you last night?"

"I think so."

I search the table and hand her a few before giving her a couple of ibuprofen. "Take these with a full glass of water. Slowly." She sways again, and I realize moving her is going to be much more difficult than I anticipated. "Where's your room key? I'll grab the rest of your bags and come back here after I wake the others. How 'bout you just focus on drinking your water, okay?"

She blinks at me several times without answering, and I'm afraid I'm going to have to repeat myself all over again when she shocks me with "You're like her, you know?"

"Who?"

"Your mom. She was my favorite person when I was a kid."

I'm rarely without a response, but Hattie's groggy comment stuns me. "You remember my mother?"

She closes her eyes as if to pull up something in the recesses of her mind. "She used to read to me on the bus, and whenever she stayed over at the house, too. She called me 'Wild Thing.' That was my favorite book."

"*Where the Wild Things Are*?" I ask. I know the book well. Mom kept it in her music room.

A tiny smile plays on Hattie's ultra-chapped lips, and she takes another small sip of water. "I cried myself to sleep for weeks after she left us, and I kept our special book under my pillow until we had to move out of that house."

The surprising revelation tangles with my own raw grief, and it takes me a moment to secure my composure. Never once had I imagined how the two Farrow sisters would have felt at the sudden abandonment of an adult who'd been a huge part of their lives, never to be seen again. I've counseled students and families on how to heal from this kind of traumatic event more times than I can count. Parents, friends, favorite aunts and uncles, etc. Absence by death is one thing, but the absence of someone we love by choice is a different kind of pain. A different kind of heartache.

"She sent me a postcard once, on my tenth birthday. It was the last time I heard from her." The curve in her lips is slight. "It was of a river someplace in Idaho. I . . . I can't remember what it was called. I think it had a man's name."

"The Saint Joe." It was my mom's favorite river near our home and the place where my brother and I have fished with our dad since we were boys. It's also where we were baptized as young adults.

Her eyes pop open. "Yeah, that's the one."

"Do you remember what the card said?" I ask, careful to keep my voice hushed for the sake of her hangover and the sleeping sister on the bed behind me.

"It was only two words." Hattie exhales slowly. "*Stay Wild*. I still have it in my jewelry box at home."

With her head resting against the wall, her eyelids close again, and I rise to look for her room key on the desk when her groggy voice says, "She'd be so disappointed in the way my life turned out."

I rotate to see Hattie's features pinch with a distinctly different variety of pain. Not from the aftereffects of a night spent trying to escape by way of a beverage that can only numb for so long, but from a far more insidious kind of torture. The kind that weaves its way around every tendon and fiber in a person's body.

"No, she wouldn't," I contend. "She'd empathize with your struggles, and then she'd look you in the eye and say something along the lines of: 'Nights always feel the darkest right before you switch on the light.'"

Hattie blinks. "Did she used to say that to you?"

"Often."

"Why?"

"Because the idea of walking across my dark bedroom in search of the light felt scarier than staying awake, fearful of all the things I couldn't see. Until I did it." I smile at her. "You'll get there, Hattie. Maybe not today or tomorrow. But you will."

I can feel her gaze trail after me as I swipe her key card off the side table and stride out the door into the hallway beyond.

The answer to the day's math story problem of how long it takes to load five Farrow women and their luggage into a bus: twenty-four minutes. Not too shabby.

Once parked at the side exit of the hotel, I race down the bus steps with an energy that shouldn't be possible after so few hours of broken sleep. But by the bedraggled look of my passengers this morning, it would appear none of us got our recommended amount of beauty sleep last night. The collective energy level of all five women combined can't be much higher than that of a geriatric sloth.

As Luella's recently knighted bus driver, I feel it's part of my duty to remedy this. I stand near the bus entrance like an overenthusiastic church greeter and welcome each of the ladies by name as they step aboard Old Goldie with a clap. "Great way to hustle this morning. Should be a smooth drive once we head north."

When not one woman responds to my encouragement, barring a slight smile from Luella, I observe their limited interactions with one another and realize that perhaps the high-wind warnings aren't the only issue we'll be up against today. I may have rerouted one storm only to have taken another along for the ride.

Luella is uncharacteristically withdrawn when she steps aboard, and it's clear from the wide berth Adele gives her that the tension from last night hasn't thawed between them. Cheyenne, on the other hand, might as well be sleepwalking. Thankfully I don't require her help to confirm her flight out of Amarillo back to California has been canceled due to the weather. I suggest she try to rebook from Denver this evening, even though I know the chances of her getting a flight out west today are slim. She might be delayed until tomorrow. Her barely perceptible nod is followed by a downward tug of her pink baseball cap.

Hattie, whose arm is looped through Raegan's, takes a bit longer to reach the bus. Her movements are slow, and her sunglasses are affixed to her face. When I offer her the same cheery greeting as the others, she slaps her hands over her ears, which knocks her dark sunglasses to the ground. "Please. Stop. Clapping."

"Sorry." I bend and retrieve her sunglasses before guiding her to the top of the stairs where she promptly collapses onto the sofa with a groan.

Raegan climbs the steps after me into the front lounge and yawns. "If you're looking to change career paths, I think you'd make a good cheerleader."

I take her in with a smile and find that she's changed into fresh travel clothes, but I also notice the dark half-moons under her eyes. "You should try and get some sleep while we drive this morning. There shouldn't be too many curves in the road. We'll be on the interstate for a while."

She shakes her head. "I already offered my bunk to Cheyenne today."

Surprised by my lack of foresight at the number of bunks versus the number of passengers, I ask, "So where will that leave you until she can secure a flight out?"

"I'll be fine on the couch."

"No way," I counter. "You can take my bunk. If she ends up staying with us overnight, I'll take the couch."

"Micah, your sleep is far more valuable than mine—no one else can drive this thing, remember?"

"*Shhhh.*" Hattie says draping an arm over her eyes. "Can you two fight over sleep later, please? You sound like new parents."

Raegan shrugs as if to say, *Guess that solves that,* only it absolutely does not solve anything. There's no way I'm sleeping in a bunk while she takes the couch in the living area. Not happening.

She touches my arm, and my skin ignites. "I'll make us some coffee."

"Then consider yourself my new favorite person."

"Shhhh," hisses Hattie again. "It feels like a woodpecker is breaking through my skull."

"What happened to you?" Adele asks in a tone that reflects no grace.

Hattie groans and flops an arm over her eyes. "Too many vodka tonics happened to me."

On her way back to the bunk hall, Cheyenne places her hand on Hattie's head. "You should drink a Pedialyte and eat some saltines, Aunt Hattie. It's the best cure for a hangover."

"And you would know that how?" Adele chirps. "Last I checked you were still nineteen."

Cheyenne's eyes are definitely wide awake now. "I'm in college, Mom."

"Oh? Are you back in college again? I can't keep track of your ever-evolving future."

Cheyenne huffs a frustrated sigh and keeps walking. "I need more sleep before we start this up again."

"You know who else sleeps during the day, darling?" Adele calls to her daughter while Hattie cups her hands to her ears. "People who drop out of college and have to work the graveyard shift just to pay their electricity bill."

"*Everyone. Please. Stop. Talking.*"

I look to the back bedroom door where Luella has unceremoniously closed herself inside and wait to see if she'll come out and offer to pray for the day the way she's done every time we've started on the road, but she stays put. Perhaps Raegan comes by her avoidance tendencies naturally.

I scan the rest of the passengers in the lounge and wonder if they all do. "Mind if I say a prayer for our drive? I'll make it quick, Hattie."

Raegan stops fiddling with the coffeemaker and bows her head. I do the same and then offer up a prayer for the safety of those traveling in the direction of the oncoming windstorm. It's not until after I say *amen* and take my seat behind the wheel that I realize I should have prayed for the safety of those in the eye of the storm brewing inside this rig, as well.

# 17

## Raegan

Despite the short night and early start, I'm thankful for Micah's quick thinking to get us out of harm's way when he did. He seems to have a knack for that. Red Cross should really make him their volunteer of the month.

In addition to his navigational app anchored to the dash, I have the weather app open on my phone, feeling safer with every mile we travel north—so safe I doze off more than once, waking each time my head bangs against the passenger side window.

"Go take my bunk, Raegan," Micah says for the tenth time. "Please."

I straighten in my seat and then pivot the AC vent closest to me so it blasts cold air directly into my eyeballs. "I'm staying up here for moral support."

He laughs. "Hate to break it to you, but your moral support could use some work." He taps the digital map with his pointer finger. "According to this, we'll be in Wichita in two hours. Should be a good place for you to make your phone call, which is yet another reason for you to consider taking a nap now."

If I wasn't so exhausted, I'd argue that my motion sickness might keep me up in the back while we drive, but I don't think that will be the case today. I can barely keep my head upright on my neck. And he's right, if I have any hope of having a coherent conversation with Chip, then I need my thoughts to be clear. "You promise you'll be okay up here?"

He lifts his coffee. "I'm good, although I'll miss the entertainment of watching you fight against sleep. And here I thought my two-year-old niece Hannah was bad."

"Is that your brother's daughter?"

"Yes. Hannah will stand straight up in her bed as soon as Garrett and Kacy put her and her twin sister, Lainey, down for the night. The rule is that they can't get out of their bed once the lights go out, so instead she sings and dances and tosses all the toys she ferreted away during the day at her sister to get out of sleeping." He shakes his head. "Little stinker."

"I hope I get to meet them someday," I say without realizing how presumptuous it sounds until it's out. Micah and I are only friends. Sure, we're friends who almost kissed and spent the night together on the same mattress while reading his mother's old journals until dawn, but yeah . . . only friends.

What are his thoughts on all that this morning? I can't get a read on him.

"I'm sure they'd like you—all of them." He pulls his gaze to the road again. "I'll wake you when we stop."

"All right." I push to standing and begin my climb over the driver's cockpit toward the back when I remember the other wake-up he assisted with this morning. I pause and twist to crouch near his ear so as not to be overheard. "Thank you for what you said to Hattie this morning."

His brow crimps in confusion. "When?"

"When you told her to find the light switch."

"I thought you were asleep."

"I'm glad I wasn't," I admit softly.

He doesn't take his eyes off the road, but I see the way the cords in his neck tense and release on his next exhale. "What she's going through right now . . . it's tough. I've sat with a lot of hurting parents in her position. I don't envy her pain."

Quite an observation coming from a man I know is carrying around a considerable load of his own pain right now. Grief. Betrayal. Secrets still unanswered.

I can't help but reach out and touch his shoulder, wishing he wasn't behind a steering wheel right now so I could give him a hug. "You're a good guy, Micah."

As his beautiful eyes flick to mine in the rearview mirror, my insides liquefy. "Get some rest, Sunshine."

On my way through the lounge, I pass an unconscious Hattie splayed out on the sofa and take a moment to cover her bare legs with a light throw blanket. The inside of the bus is chilly with the AC on full blast.

When I straighten, I notice Adele sitting at the dining table. Her laptop is propped open in front of her, but her distant stare is directed out the window. The stress lines around her eyes have softened into a reflective expression that looks . . . sad. The occasions I've witnessed this side of my sister have been so few and far between in the last handful of years that I can't bring myself to look away. I'm suddenly struck by an onslaught of memories. Me sitting with her at her kitchen table while Cheyenne was off at elementary school. Though our age gap has always felt vast, as a teenager, I valued my alone time with Adele differently than I did with Hattie.

Hattie took me shopping for new clothes and talked about the latest décor trends and brainstormed the big events she had upcoming at the label, while Adele fed me smoothies with hidden veggies and quizzed me on my schoolwork with Jana. History, politics, math, and even for a short time my Bible lessons and Scripture memorization. But there was always this moment at the end of our time together when she'd step down from playing the role of Strong Older Sister to simply be my friend. We'd discuss the artists she enjoyed at the label and those she could barely tolerate. She'd show me recipes she was saving for rainy days that rarely came and ask me to weigh in on family vacation plans we rarely took due to Daddy's obligation to the label. We'd laugh at Mama's eccentricities and shake our heads at Daddy's lack of work-life balance.

As I matured, so did our talks at her kitchen table. The most memorable of them all having to do with Tav. While the whole of my family rooted for the moody musician I'd been infatuated with since childhood, Adele cautioned me about his intentions.

Somehow my big sister had called the end of our love story before the first chapter had ever been written.

My throat tightens as I think of what I'd give to go back to the days where honest conversation flowed easily between us and trust went both ways. But just as quickly as the thought comes, so does a sickening wave of realization: I can't ask her for what I haven't been willing to give myself.

Maybe Micah was right last night in the hotel room. Maybe I've been fooling myself into believing this secret I'm keeping about Peter is for their protection, when really it's me I'm trying to protect. If I want Adele to confide in me, then don't I have to be willing to do the same with her?

I offer up a silent prayer and take a seat across from my sister. Her expression goes from mild confusion at my presence to resignation.

"If this is about what happened with Cheyenne last night, I'm really not—"

"It's not," I say quickly. "But I can understand why you'd be upset."

Her tired eyes rove my face, but she says nothing more.

I will my mouth to open, but it takes several tries until the courage shows up. "I was hoping to talk to you about something else." I rub my lips together and again plead with God to give me the right words. It's been a long time since I've tried to engage in a conversation with Adele of this depth. "The day Mama showed up in the driveway with Old Goldie, I had a meeting with an editor friend of mine, and he mentioned a—"

"You met with an editor?" Adele's posture stiffens. "For what reason? I thought you agreed to put your hobby on hold for now, Raegan. There's too much going on."

On second thought, I probably should have jumped ahead to the phone call when Chip confirmed the tell-all. "He was giving me feedback on a manuscript, but that's not actually what I—"

"Raegan." She drops her head into her hands and kneads her temples. "I don't have the capacity to talk about your fiction when so much in our real world is hanging by a thread. It's not a good time."

Her disparaging tone sparks a fire in my belly. "I'm not asking you to discuss my fiction with me. I haven't asked that of you since the last time you shot it down and told me I needed to put the family first."

She lifts her head slowly, her eyes narrowing on me. "I'm sorry if putting your family first is such a burden on you, but not all of us get to do what we *want* in life. If that makes me your personal villain, I'm sure you can find others on this bus who will commiserate with you."

I bite the inside of my cheeks and try to remember why I sat down in the first place. "There's something in the works you should know about."

She puts up her palm and shakes her head. "Unless it's directly related to Mama's performance at Watershed, it can wait until after the show. I cannot handle one more distraction. I never should have allowed Mama to convince me this trip was a good idea. It was a mistake."

"I know you have a lot on your plate right now, but—"

"You don't even know the half of it."

"You're right, I don't. And whose fault is that?" I challenge, meeting her gaze straight on in the silence that follows. "I can't remember the last time you've shared anything of importance with me that didn't involve me running an errand or organizing a schedule or checking up on a family member to avoid a potential crisis." I glance around at the quiet bus. "But Mama's in her room, and Hattie and Cheyenne are both asleep, and I'm sitting right here." I feel the tears climbing and fight to push them back down. "I'm asking you to treat me like a sister. To talk to me."

For a split second, when the weariness returns to her features, I think she might actually take me up on my offer—that this might actually be the first step in a whole new direction for us as sisters. But then I see her gaze flick to where Hattie lies asleep on the sofa. "Were you with Hattie last night?"

I nod. "She stayed in my room. She . . . was up most of the night."

Again she rubs at her temples. "I need you to keep a closer eye on her. That can't happen again. There are too many distractions right now as it is, and I need Mama to stay focused on this festival—it's imperative." Her eyes tick back to me again. "Can you manage that?"

*When haven't I managed that?* is what I want to argue back. "If that's what you want."

"No, it's what *we need*," she corrects. "There's a difference, Raegan. The burdens I carry are for the well-being of our whole family. Despite what my daughter chooses to believe about life, not all of us get to live how we want."

She turns her attention back to her laptop. It's a clear and final dismissal. With heavy limbs and an even heavier heart, I push away from the dining table and into the hall.

After toeing off my shoes, I crawl into Micah's bunk as my mind goes to battle. Why should I feel an ounce of guilt over keeping something from Adele when she routinely shuts me out and asks me to put my life and goals on hold? Last year her reasoning was Hattie's divorce, now it's the festival, and chances are high that a month from now Adele will have a new excuse as to why I should keep my hobby hidden away from the world. Her instincts might have been right about Tav, but that doesn't mean they're right about everything.

As I press my face into the cool cotton of Micah's pillowcase, I'm enveloped by his scent, and soon my thoughts have shifted back to him. There is much I wish I could change about my present circumstance, but Micah is without a doubt the one thing I wouldn't change. I meant what I told him last night—I couldn't imagine him not being here with us. With me.

As exhaustion tugs at the corner of my mind, I lift him up in a silent prayer, asking God to guide our next steps and, most importantly, to help Micah on his quest to discover his birth father.

"We're here, Raegan."

I blink my eyes open and stare into the face of the man I fell asleep praying for. "Where's here again?"

He rests his folded arms on the bunk frame. I roll onto my side, noting how our height difference is nearly obsolete in this position.

"Wichita," he says with a smile. "Good nap?"

"Yes." I yawn and sit up to stretch my neck, careful not to bonk my head on the top of the bunk. "Thanks again for loaning me your bed."

"I would say my bed is your bed, but I don't think that has the same connotation as '*mi casa es su casa.*'"

I laugh. "I don't think it does."

Micah tips his head toward the street-facing window. "Hattie is upright, sitting on a bench in the shade eating saltines and drinking some electrolytes we stopped for a few minutes ago, and the others are out picking up some lunch orders to go."

"Together?" I ask, confused. "Are they all speaking to each other again?"

"Not unless they were speaking in a silent language." He tugs on his ear. "Do these Farrow family showdowns typically last this long?"

"Longer. And I have a feeling Adele will wait to address what happened last night with Cheyenne and Mama until after the festival."

Micah's eyes grow so wide it's comical. "You're kidding, right? That's nearly a week away. Surely the stonewalling can't last that long."

"Oh, it can. Hattie and Adele went nearly six weeks without speaking after Peter won the lawsuit. I was their go-between." I shrug. "Adele told me herself in no uncertain terms that she doesn't want to deal with any distractions unrelated to the festival."

"Distractions as in . . . having important conversations?"

"Correct."

The puzzled look he gives me lingers. "And you think that applies to the tell-all?" When I give no indication either way, he sighs and presses his palms against the top of the bunk frame. "Raegan, I understand your family dynamics are less than ideal, but please think through this logically for a minute. What happens if news of the tell-all leaks to the public soon? Don't you want your family to be prepared? Adele will need to be ready with a statement from the label."

Just the mention of her name shoots a bolt of indignation through my core. "Do you have any idea how often I've submitted to my sister's preoccupation with preparing our family for the worst, Micah? How often I've done or not done something based on *her* judgment of what's best for *the Farrow name*? So often I'd be mortified to say the number out loud if I knew it." I want to ease the tension I've created with a laugh, but the sudden constriction of my vocal chords prevents it.

When I look away, he touches my chin and draws my gaze back to his. "I'm sorry."

I pick at the raw hem of my shorts, planning to tell him that it's fine, that I usually reserve these pent-up moments of familial

218

tension for my fiction, when the thought triggers an unprompted confession. "Two weeks ago I walked away from a book contract with my favorite publisher for *The Sisters of Birch Grove* because I wouldn't agree to write under my given name."

His face goes slack. "*What?* Why?"

"Because I believed publishing under a pen name would allow me the autonomy I rarely feel in my real life, as well as the ability to succeed or fail on my own merit." Tears crack my voice. "Because I know the minute I publish as Luella Farrow's daughter, I sacrifice all that."

Understanding dawns on Micah's features, and I'm guessing he's replaying our conversation in the hotel room through a different filter.

"Your sister doesn't know about the offer?"

"Adele hopes my writing will stay a hobby—there's less risk involved to the family that way." The raw admission burns in my chest. "So yeah, maybe I'm taking the coward's way out by thinking I can solve this crisis without her involvement, but I promise you, there's a cost to both options."

"Raegan."

I pat my pockets in search of my phone. I must have left it up front. "I should probably leave so I can call Chip before everybody comes back." I shift to jump off Micah's bunk to the floor below when he takes my hand and assists me down.

If ever I've contemplated the tight quarters back here before, I have an entirely new frame of reference now. There's barely enough room for one person to stand in this small pass-through, much less two. My instincts scream to twist away, to shelter myself the way I've always done, but without a word, Micah pulls me to him, and soon my cheek is pressed against his chest. The steady rhythm I find there calms my rapid-fire thoughts.

"You're more than a hobbyist. Wanna know how I know?" he asks with a voice I could listen to all day. "You care too much. A hobby you can pick up and put down without a second thought, but a calling is part of who you are. Part of a purpose God made you to fulfill."

Tears fill my eyes as validation sings through me.

"Thank you." Slowly, I wipe the dampness from under my eyes. "You have a real gift in making people feel seen and heard. You're obviously in the right profession."

I expect his face to lift into a humble grin, but he remains stoic. "Afraid the jury's still out on that." Before I can ask him to explain, he reaches into his pocket and pulls out my phone. "You left this on the jump seat so I plugged it in for you."

"Oh, thanks."

"You had a few missed calls."

I tap on the home screen and find Tav's name in my notifications. He's probably wondering about his unfinished lyrics. When I look up, Micah's watching me intently, and the shift in his demeanor is enough for me to take note.

"What's wrong?" I ask.

"Nothing that can't wait until later. You should go make your call."

"Micah," I say, my concern growing. "What is it?"

"Tav's last name is Zuckerman."

"Yes." I furrow my brow. "That's right."

"Which means his father is Dorian Zuckerman, one of the business partners your dad worked with at TriplePlay Records and then later at Farrow Music?"

I nod, wracking my brain for relevance. "Yes, that's right, but—"

"He's mentioned all throughout my mom's journal entries, Raegan. Her mentions of him are . . . favorable." His voice is hushed, and yet the emotion behind it causes a seed of nausea to sprout in my belly. "Your mom confirmed he was with them the summer of '94. He stayed back to manage the tour while your dad was away in Germany."

"No." My mouth forms the word, and yet it's barely audible as it passes my lips. "Dorian couldn't be your . . . he can't be."

His next question is so quiet, and yet it echoes through my bones. "Tell me why not?"

*Because you can't be related to my ex,* I think. *Because that kind of freakish irony is only reserved for soap operas and manufactured reality TV shows.* "Because—because Dorian was already married to Donna by then. He was an honorable man," I say instead.

"Even honorable people make mistakes, Raegan," he says. "It's clear from my mom's entries that she was struggling with loneliness, and as for Dorian, I can't imagine being away from home for months at a time is easy on any marriage. The possibility of two people acting out of weakness seems like a viable option I shouldn't overlook."

I search his face, hating how logical he sounds about something so insufferable.

"But if he is your father, that would make Tav your . . ." I can't say it. I can hardly even think it.

"I know what it would make him." His voice is resolute as he stares off into the distance. "I didn't realize how connected Tav's family was—is—to yours."

"I told you I've known him all my life."

He nods and drops a pained gaze to my face, to my mouth. "You did."

I shake my head, hoping to shake off this entire subject. "Let's keep in mind that this is only speculation at this point. An educated guess. Nothing is confirmed yet. You need to talk to Mama."

"I know." He pushes a hand through his hair. "It just feels wrong talking to her before I get the chance to sit down with my dad."

"I know, but you're doing your best to navigate a difficult situation. There's grace for that." I give his arm a light squeeze before I take a step into the hallway. "I should go."

I'm halfway down the aisle when he says, "We should exchange numbers. Just in case."

"In case of what?" I smile and turn back. "We've barely been more than a bunk away from each other all week."

His only answer is a smile, so I rattle off the digits to him before I step from the bus to a busy sidewalk in what looks to be the heart of downtown Wichita. My good humor quickly fades as soon as I duck into the nearest coffee shop and begin to mentally prepare for the conversation ahead. After I order myself an iced white mocha, I pull up the cryptic email I'd sent Chip late last night, informing him I'd be calling with news today.

My nerves take a nose dive. Am I really going to do this? As I study Chip's simple reply of *Call me anytime, I'll answer,* my phone chimes with an incoming text from my newest contact.

Micah D., bus-driving ex-therapist:

I believe in you, Sunshine. You've got this.

I read his text over three times and can't help but bite the smile from my bottom lip in response to his encouragement. I give his text a thumbs-up in reply and secure a corner table. The second I'm seated, I tap Chip's contact.

Chip's phone rings twice.

"Raegan?"

"Hey, Chip. How are you?"

"More than a little curious at your email, to say the least. Hang on just a minute; let me close my office door." I hear the distinct sound of a door closing in the background and then, "Did you figure out who's behind it?"

"I believe so, unfortunately," I say. Cheater Peter's smug grin comes into focus.

"And by that response, I take it it's not someone you can negotiate with?" he asks.

"I'm afraid not."

"I'm sorry, I wish there was more I could do to help you."

I take a deep breath and feel my palms grow slick around the cold disposable cup. Am I actually doing this? I could still back out, still pretend not to know a thing about a secret tell-all when it all hits the fan. And then what? Cower as I watch my already fractured family deal with the aftermath of a scandal I could have assuaged with the mere stroke of my pen? And then I think of Micah's text: *I believe in you. You've got this.*

"Actually, I think you can help me, Chip." I wait two heartbeats and then push the rest of the words out. "What if we published a book about my family before the other one hits the shelves?"

There's a beat of silence before Chips asks, "We as in *you* and *me*?"

"Yes," I confirm. "*We* as in I write a book with exclusive content and eyewitness accounts regarding my mama's early romance with music and with my father when she met him in the mid '70s. He was the love of her life, and they were married for forty years when he passed away. I've never written nonfiction, but I know romance. It's what I read and what I love to write. If you think that's something Fog Harbor would be interested in acquiring, then I'd love for you to be my editor."

There's such a long silence that I pull the phone away from my ear to check the connection.

"I'm sorry, I'm just . . . wow." He laughs then, big and full and bright. "I don't think I could be more shocked if you told me a pterodactyl was about to fly through my office window and deliver the sub sandwich I ordered for lunch." He clears his throat. "Am I right to assume you've reconsidered your position on using a pen name? Because it will be your name as Luella's daughter that will be the selling point on something like this."

"That's correct," I say, trying to shove the clickbait headlines of every viral video of me kissing Tav from my mind. Here we go again. "I'm willing to use my own name as long as you think it will create the diversion we need to undermine the tell-all."

"I absolutely think it will." I hear the click of computer keys in the background. "By cross-referencing a few publishing data sites online, my best guess is the tell-all is slotted to release within the first quarter of next year. I'm going to shoot straight with you, the turnaround time on your first draft will be tight. If you can send me a paragraph or two on your basic premise, and whatever supporting documents or extras you might be willing to include—old letters, pictures, etc.—then I'll work up a proposal over the weekend and set a meeting with the board on Monday for emergency approval. If they sign off like I think they will, I could have a contract to you by early next week. But, Raegan." His pause has me pressing the phone even closer to my ear. "I'll need at least the first fifty pages in-house by the end of the month and likely the finished first draft no later than the end of October. We'll have to move on this exceedingly fast to get it all the way through production in time for publication. Are you positive you have the capacity to take on a project of this caliber?"

My eyes widen as the weight of such a task sinks in. Three months to write a book about my family that they know nothing about. I try to push the guilt down to embrace Adele's words at face value. I'll tell them all after the concert. And then I think of how much writing I'll need to do over the course of the next week and just how little I know about structuring a book like this. And how the minute I get off this phone I'll need to search for the closest Apple Store and buy myself a new laptop. "I'm positive."

"Okay," Chips says, a whisper of disbelief still in his tone. I recognize the reaction, seeing as it's looping through my own brain at this very moment. "Then I suppose I better clear my schedule and start on that proposal."

"Thank you," I say, hoping he can't hear the way my voice trembles. "I'll do my best to get you a basic outline by the end of the day."

"Don't hesitate to text if you have any questions—day or night." His excitement is unmistakable, and I smile to think of what a book deal like this might mean for a young editor as deserving as Chip Stanton.

"Will do," I confirm.

"And Raegan, if we can pull this off and it's even a fraction of the success I think it can be, then I have every hope those readers will follow you anywhere you want to take them, even if that road leads to some of the best fiction I've read in years."

Tears flood my eyes as I work to swallow the thickness in my throat. This certainly isn't the road less traveled I'd imagined for myself as I hid in my mama's house, writing as a means of escape. Or the road I hoped would keep me anonymous to critics who will only see me as a product of nepotism. But perhaps the road less traveled wasn't the road meant for me. Perhaps this was always the path I was meant to take.

The road that follows a journey my mama paved for me decades before I was born.

A road that led me right here to this very moment.

# 18

## Micah

Several years ago, I was "volunteered" by a member of the school board to drive a group of theater kids in a fifteen-passenger van for five hours across the state after the re-cruited parent came down with the stomach flu. I'd prepared myself for random outbursts in song and the occasional misquote of an epic movie line. But what I hadn't prepared for was the depth of drama I'd be dragged through after an argument about the cast of *Wicked* divided my passengers. After an extended two-hour freeze-out period, in which there were only hand gestures used, the students had given me no other choice but to pull the van over.

I'm about five minutes away from doing the same thing with the Farrow women.

We've been back on the road for three hours, and in that time, Cheyenne has attempted—and failed—to engage her mother in a productive conversation about school while Luella has been a rare sighting for the majority of the trip. Her avoidance of conflict has certainly passed its way down her family line.

I glance over at Raegan sitting in the jump seat next to me, typing away on the shiny new laptop we stopped to pick up after what appeared to be a positive phone call with Chip, the editor. Due to our mixed company, she couldn't provide me with much information, which in and of itself only furthers my point. When was the last time this family talked through anything of significance with one another? More importantly, do they even know how?

To be fair, my perception of my own family's openness wasn't exactly accurate. The mere fact I'm driving through the Midwest on a quest for my unknown father is proof enough the Davenports were missing a few vital conversational tools in their toolbox, too.

The image of Tav Zuckerman's full name flashes through my mind again, and I clench my molars until my jaw aches and stare out at the nothingness that is the US-40 detour we're on due to the brutal construction traffic on I-70. It will take another four hours to get from here to the Denver airport for Cheyenne's rebooked flight tonight, but with any luck, I'll be able to get us back on Luella's original course by tomorrow afternoon.

I tug at my damp shirt collar and tap the AC arrow lower as I direct my thoughts to the conversation I'll need to have with Luella soon. I calculate the risk/reward ratio of involving yet another person in the details of a sordid past I only recently accepted as my own. I might hold some skills in the art of mediating hard conversations, but it's rare I have to mediate myself.

Raegan stretches out her hand toward the air vents. "Did you turn the heater on?"

My eyes snap to hers and then to the vents, which are indeed blowing out warm air. I smash the down AC arrow again and again to no avail. *No, no . . .* this cannot be happening.

"Whoa. Chill out, Micah," Raegan reprimands. "It probably just needs a break. It's been running nonstop since we started out today."

But *chill out* is a luxury I no longer have access to, which is perhaps the only reason I've been able to manage on three hours of broken sleep as well as I have. *It's hot.* I check the interior thermostat on the wall behind Raegan's head, and sure enough, the perfect sixty-nine-degree temperature I've had it set to all week despite multiple protests from my frostbitten passengers has crept to a brutal seventy-nine. Make that eighty.

A slow-rising panic begins to congeal my insides. I've barely begun a diagnostic check of each gauge on the dash when I'm interrupted by Raegan announcing, "We'll just crack the windows. Don't worry, Kansas isn't humid like Arkansas or Oklahoma. It's dry heat." But as soon as she follows through with her mastermind plan, a wind tunnel of arid air fills the cab. She sticks her hand into the fiery furnace. "On second thought, it's pretty warm out."

"*Please,*" I say with what feels like the last shred of patience I'll ever possess. "Close your window."

Her eyebrows pinch together, and she looks ready to unleash an arsenal of snark when my attention pulls to my side mirror where a giant white cloud has engulfed the back of the bus. I bite back a choice word or five and bang my palm against the steering wheel. Raegan unbuckles in order to lean over my shoulder long enough to see the nightmare unfolding behind us in real time.

"That's dust, right?" she asks feebly.

"Not unless dust comes out of a radiator." My eyes dart from the billowing steam to the water temperature gauge. Sure enough, it's maxed out. We're overheating in the middle of Nowhere Kansas. Perfect. "Crank the heater as high as it goes."

"What?" Raegan's neck whips back in my direction. "But you just told me to roll—"

"As high as it goes," I repeat as I engage the emergency flashers. I decelerate and pull off to the old country highway.

"Hey," Hattie hollers from the back. "It's stifling back here. Can you turn up the AC, Micah?"

Raegan's eyes go wide. "Wait—why are we pulling over here? There's nothing but cows and wheat for like a hundred miles."

"Because every minute I drive on is another minute we risk blowing up the engine." Sweat dampens my shirt front and back and seems to pool from every pore on my face. I maneuver Old Goldie into park and turn off the engine, plunging us into an eerie silence.

Suddenly, every Farrow woman on the bus is crowding around the cockpit, demanding answers to a million questions at once. It would appear the emotional freeze-out phase of the last three hours has come to an abrupt end. However, this wasn't exactly the kind of pull-the-bus-over situation I'd had in mind.

Slowly I stand and turn to face them, my hands raised so as not to poke the bear any further. *Bears,* I mentally correct. "First, I'd appreciate it if everybody remains calm. It would appear we've over-heated the radiator. I'll give the engine a fifteen-minute cooldown before I decide if I should try and limp us along to the nearest service station, but that would be a best-case scenario."

"And what's the worst-case scenario?" Adele asks, waving her phone. "Besides being stuck in the middle of nowhere without air conditioning or cell coverage?"

I fan my shirt, which does absolutely nothing. "Worst case, we'll have to walk to the nearest town. The last sign I saw was for Scarecrow, five miles to the west."

"Scarecrow, Kansas?" Cheyenne blurts. "That can't be a real town name."

"Darlin', I can tell you from experience that Scarecrow doesn't even make the top ten for craziest town names I've come across in my career." After a moment, Luella grants me a nod and says, "We trust your judgment, Micah. If we have to walk, then we'll count it as part of the adventure."

Grateful for her sudden optimism, I give her a courteous smile. I much prefer this version of Luella to the one who's been hibernating for the better part of the day.

"Speak for yourself, Mama. I've only recently stopped seeing double." Hattie groans and then ducks her head to look out the window. "Anyone know if a cow can be ridden bareback?"

I don't know Hattie well enough to determine if she's joking or not, but the sweat dripping from my chin as I cut through them for the exit must convey I'm not in much of a joking mood. An inch from the exit, I turn back. "In the meantime, you should all prepare the items you'd want to carry with you before it gets too hot to remain inside."

And with that, I push out the door, only to be trailed by my favorite Farrow.

"I'm sorry," Raegan says, shuffling behind me in the dirt.

"Why, did you break the radiator?"

"No, but I feel bad that you're having to—"

I spin in the dirt and face her. "You did nothing wrong, so there's nothing for you to apologize for. I, on the other hand, will likely be apologizing for several offenses once my brain is no longer set to broil."

She bites the smile of her bottom lip. "Can I at least help you with something out here? Hold the tools or . . . I don't know, read you an instruction manual?"

I yank my sweat-soaked shirt over my head and wipe my face with it, before sitting on the shaded back bumper and patting the open spot next to me. "No need. We'll be walking in about ten minutes."

Her mouth falls open, but I have no idea which of my offenses she's deemed gape-worthy. "But you said we're only walking if it's worst-case scenario."

"It is worst-case scenario. That acrid smell is not just antifreeze. Most likely we've burned through a hose or two."

"Then why did you even give us both options?"

"Because offering even a modicum of hope creates a far better psychological outcome than starting from a place of despair. Hope, even at the smallest level, builds a quiet resilience, whereas forcing a hard decision on them would only create resistance and resentment."

Her eyes go round.

"It's basic psychology," I say as genuinely as I can. "This way, they have time to prepare mentally and physically while also working toward a common goal with one another. And if your family needs anything right now, it's that: a common goal."

After a hard sigh, she plops next to me and drops her head in her hands. "You must think my family is an absolute mess."

"All families are messy."

"Mine especially."

I nudge her shoulder and then huff a hard sigh. "Come on, we should probably go break the bad news to them. It has to be stifling inside that bus by now."

"Wait." She lifts her head, and I don't miss the way her gaze snaps from my bare chest to my face. Or the blush that creeps up her neck. "You should probably prepare yourself, too."

"Okay." I quirk an eyebrow in interest. "Enlighten me."

"A hundred bucks says Hattie will complain the entire way. Even when she's not recovering from an epic hangover, she *hates* all forms of exercise and always finds excuses out of it."

I laugh. "Noted."

"And Adele always has to be in front. Mark my words, she'll take the lead within the first two minutes."

"Also noted."

"And Cheyenne won't leave her guitar behind—nor should she. The heat will warp the body and hurt the sound. She has a backpack case with her, but maybe we can volunteer to share the load if it gets too heavy. Five miles will be long in this heat."

I nod. "Agreed. Good plan."

"And then there's Mama . . ." Raegan gives a little shake of her head. "She's off today. I think the tiff between her and Adele is bothering her a lot more than she'll admit."

"I think so, too." I stand and offer Raegan my hand. I pull her to her feet but can't quite get myself to release the hold. The feel of her delicate fingers in mine is almost reward enough to make a walk down a hot Kansas highway in hundred-degree weather worth it. I swipe my thumb across her soft skin. "You should know, I'm planning to talk to your mom about Dorian as soon as I can get a free moment with her."

Raegan's curious gaze trails my face, and it takes every bit of willpower in me to recall my reasons for not kissing her. "Are you prepared for what you might find out?"

"No, but I'd rather know one way or the other."

She's just about to respond to that when the bus door flies open and four more Farrows burst out.

Raegan and I drop hands before we round the corner to find mother, daughters, and granddaughter all outfitted in appropriate walking gear and whatever personal belongings they've deemed worthy for the trek to Scarecrow.

"Are we walking?" Adele asks in her no-nonsense tone. "If we're going to be hot, we might as well be getting our steps in for the day. I'm guessing if we're needing a tow to a service station, we'll be looking for overnight accommodations. Let's hope Scarecrow has something decent."

"I can help search as soon as we're back in coverage," Cheyenne says. "I'm guessing we're not going to make my flight."

"At this point," I say, looking around at the farmlands, "I'd say it's not looking good."

"Thank you, everyone," Luella chimes in, looking from her daughter to her granddaughter. "I appreciate your flexibility. I'm sure Micah will see to it that Old Goldie gets patched up in no time."

I slide my gaze to Raegan, hoping my earlier point about hope building resilience has been proven when Hattie harrumphs and shuffles to the front bumper, holding out her thumb to the dead highway.

"You put that thumb down right now, Harriet Josephine," Luella scolds. "No child of mine is going to hitchhike."

"Then I hope you're fine with me stealing a cow."

# 19

## Raegan

Despite Cheyenne's offer to search for "decent accommodations" in Scarecrow, Kansas, after 4.6 miles of walking in the blistering heat, none of our cell phones show even a single bar of signal strength. At the risk of sounding like a completely ignorant American, I didn't even realize there were still places in the US without cell coverage. Or people who would voluntarily choose to live in those places. But as we stand at the entrance to a gravel driveway arched by a wooden sign with the words *No Place Like Home Inn* carved into it . . . it looks like we're about to introduce ourselves to some such people.

Outside of a silo and two equipment barns, this is literally the first sign of civilization we've seen. And we're all too tired, thirsty, and hot to debate the poor manners of knocking on a stranger's door. Even Mama, who under normal circumstances would throw a fit about dropping by unannounced, is far too flushed to care. Micah expressed his concern over her exertion level several times in the last hour, but without shade or alternative transportation, there's been little choice for us but to keep walking. At one point, he soaked his T-shirt with water from his water bottle and draped it around her neck. Naturally, she protested him fussing over her so much, but she didn't take it off. Unfortunately, his selfless act didn't come without a cost. His shoulders and upper back are going to remind him of his sacrifice for at least a day until the redness fades into his established tan.

"I'll do the talking for us," Adele says as soon as we approach the *inn*. "It will be less overwhelming if only one of us explains our situation to the owner."

Micah gives me the side-eye I've come to expect, and I raise him an eye roll. Just like I'd warned earlier, Adele had commanded our troop of six like we were a military operation. I study the older two-story farmhouse, which from the outside looks to be at least a hundred years old, though well-loved and equally well-maintained. The closer we get to the front door, the larger the dwelling becomes. Even the charming wrap-around front porch, which looked tiny from the road, now seems anything but as I count six empty rocking chairs. I sweep my gaze over the interesting choice of emerald-green shutters surrounded by dusty white shiplap siding. Even if this isn't an actual inn that houses traveling strangers like us, I'm hoping whoever lives here can spare a few glasses of sweet tea and will be able to point us in the right direction. Or be a mechanic who can work magic on Old Goldie.

"You should probably take this back," Mama says, handing the damp, wrinkled shirt back to Micah. "I'm not sure I'd open the door if I saw a shirtless man standing on the other side of it."

"I would. Especially if he looked like that," Hattie says under her breath, and I elbow her in the ribs as Micah pulls the shirt back over his head. And though I'd never admit it to my older sister, I'm ninety-nine percent sure I'd answer that door, too.

Adele reaches for the ornate bronze knocker in the middle of the door, and it's only then I recognize it's shaped in the face of the cowardly lion . . . from *The Wizard of Oz*. She pulls back the bottom half of his beard and knocks it against the wood.

A moment later the door opens to reveal a middle-aged woman with peppery hair pulled back in a loose braid, wearing a blue checkered apron and holding a wooden spoon . . . which is currently dripping something whipped onto her canvas shoe. "Oh, goodness. Well, hello there!" she greets us with a broad smile, looking from Adele to the rest of our sweaty crew. "I should probably save you nice folks some time. If you're here to try and sell me something, I probably already own it. And if you're here to try and sell me *someone*, I definitely already know Him. I've been trusting in Jesus since before I knew how to make a decent pie. And I don't much like to think about life before pie." She shudders.

Once again, Micah and I share a glance.

Adele appears so off-guard that she actually stutters, "N-no, ma'am, we're not here to sell anything or anyone for that matter. We're sorry to bother you, but our bus broke down a few miles back, and we're hoping you might have a phone we could use to call a tow truck."

She steps further out onto her porch and glances left and right. "Where did you break down?"

Hattie points exaggeratedly. "Exactly four-point-six miles that way."

"But there's nothing but wheat farms out that way." The woman gasps. "Did you walk all the way here in this heat?" When her gaze falls on Mama's flushed cheeks, I'm worried she's recognized her, but then she exclaims, "Please, please, come inside where it's cool. I'm happy to help. Nobody should be out in this heat—not even if it's Jesus you're selling. I've just finished up a French silk pie, and I have some iced tea in the fridge to share."

"Thank you, ma'am. We appreciate your help," I say just as Mama teeters on her feet.

"Nonnie?" Cheyenne calls out. On sheer instinct, I open my arms to catch Mama's frail, fainting frame just as Micah swoops in to lift her from me as if she weighs no more than a paper doll.

"Mother!" Adele cries as Hattie calls out, "She needs water!"

I'm completely mute as fear sweeps through me.

"Good gracious, bring her inside to the sofa." The woman waves us through an entryway so plastered in knickknacks it would take more than ten minutes to process everything in this space. But one thing's for certain: I can definitely understand why she said she didn't need anything we might be selling. It would appear she has one of everything already, especially if it's in any way related to Dorothy's magical journey to Oz.

"The green velvet one there is fine. I'll get some ice water and some cool washcloths. Poor thing's probably got heatstroke."

Cheyenne follows after the woman to help while Micah lays Mama down.

The three of us sisters crowd around her, and thankfully in a matter of a few seconds Mama opens her eyes and blinks up at us. Her brow rumples as much as it can, given she's had every fountain-of-youth facial treatment imaginable. But even though my mama might look forty, she's nearly seventy. And something about that revelation punches me through the heart. And by the looks of it, Micah is having a similar reaction. His brows are furrowed as he watches her every movement.

"Oh, phooey," Mama says, coming to. "Did I make a dramatic entrance I hadn't planned on?"

"Mama." I drop to my knees in front of her and take her hand. "That was really scary. How are you feeling now? Are you dizzy?"

"Just a bit parched is all," Mama amends.

"Well, I don't want you leaving this couch until we're certain you're okay," Adele says in her usual take-charge way.

"I'll be just fine after a sip of water and a decent sit-down." She smiles and pushes herself up to a seated position.

Micah plants a hand on Mama's shoulder. "I agree with Adele, Luella. You should take it easy while we figure out a plan for the bus."

There's a protest brewing in Mama's gaze when we're interrupted by our gracious host.

"Oh good, you're awake." She hands Mama a giant glass of ice water, and Cheyenne folds a damp wash cloth to blot Mama's forehead with. "That was quite a scare."

"I'm feeling fine now, thank you." Mama takes a few ladylike sips of water. "We'd like to repay you, Ms. . . ."

"I go by Dottie. And there's no repayment necessary. Hospitality shouldn't be the exception but the rule. At least, that's been my motto ever since I opened my home as an inn."

"You have a beautiful home," I comment, noticing the life-size statue of Scarecrow standing guard next to the staircase. I'd hate to run into him in the middle of the night. "You must be quite a fan of *The Wizard of Oz*."

"Fan is putting it mildly, sweetheart, but yes. I'm a strong believer that there's no place like home." She winks as Micah steps forward.

"Dottie, may I trouble you for your house phone and a . . . phone book?" The look on Micah's face is so iconic I nearly laugh. I'd bet money my niece has never seen a phone book in her young life.

Dottie waves her hand in the air and starts for the kitchen. "Of course, but I'll save you the trouble of calling around. There's a large service station about two hours east, but my brother Billy owns the local mechanic shop just ten minutes up the road. You would have run straight into it if you could have kept on driving."

"You've got to be kidding me," Hattie mutters as she collapses into a winged-back chair across from Mama, one with tiny ruby slippers printed all over it.

"I'm sure Billy can help get a tow figured out for your rig, too."

Micah follows Dottie into the kitchen, but not before he sends a pleading look in my direction.

I situate myself next to Mama and waggle my eyebrows at him. *Good luck*, I mouth an instant before he disappears into Oz.

I've never bought into the superstition that bad news comes in threes . . . until today. Not only did our bus break down in the middle of nowhere, forcing Cheyenne to miss her second flight back to California, but after hours of waiting to hear from Micah after he left for town with a man who could be Harrison Ford's twin brother, the part we need replaced on the bus will take a minimum of twenty-four hours to get to Billy's shop. And that's with paying all the expedited fees to rush it. Bottom line: without transportation and working phones, we're stuck in Scarecrow, Kansas, for at least a full day.

Thankfully, good news also seems to come in threes, or at least that's how I'm choosing to look at it. After feeding us all generous slices of French silk pie, Dottie kindly offered us lodging in her six-bedroom inn for however long we need. And to no one's surprise, Dottie's impressive Oz collection doesn't stop downstairs. Nope, each of the six rooms is themed. According to our host, the inn has fallen on hard times due to the economy, but with some minimal dusting and a few quick linen changes, I'm happy to report our group managed to reset the place for guests in no time at all.

We set Mama up in the Glinda the Good Witch room, which is everything tulle and sparkly and pink, like Mama. Adele and Cheyenne—despite the unresolved issues between them—agreed to take the lofted Tin Man Suite that holds two queen beds and hosts a large en suite bathroom. Hattie took the Wizard's room, decorated in an elaborate landscape of the Emerald City. She's documented every square inch of the inn to show her kids once she's able to find WiFi. And I set up camp in the Cowardly Lion's quarters, the only room with a desk suitable for working on a secret writing project.

I made sure to save the best accommodations for Micah, though.

Sometime after seven, he pounds on my door and steps inside with horror-filled eyes. "Do you happen to know why there are creepy, oversize bats hanging from my ceiling?"

I lean back in my chair and stifle a laugh behind my hand. "Those aren't bats; they're flying monkeys."

He stares at me as if I'm a flying monkey. "Raegan, I realize we didn't grow up in the same part of the country, but I've never seen

238

anything close to that in a zoo." He slips off the backpack he's wearing and opens it to reveal his mother's journals for me to reference in my writing endeavors. It was beyond considerate of him to anticipate my need for them. Lynn's date-keeping will come in handy in these early chapters.

"Micah, thank you, that was incredibly nice of you to—"

But Micah is not ready to move on yet. "What is with all the weird stuff in this house? Did you see the stuffed dog in the dining room?" He drops his voice. "I've never been so disturbed while eating pie in my life. I kept waiting for him to leap up on the table and rip out my throat."

"Relax," I laugh. "Dottie's allergic to animals. That Toto dog was never a real dog. She found a perfect replica in Japan and had it shipped."

"Is that supposed to make me feel better about the mental state of our hostess? Do you forget what I do for a living?"

"She's an avid collector," I defend.

"Of what?" He throws up his arms. "The things night terrors are made of?"

"No, of *The Wizard of Oz*." I narrow my eyes at him. "Wait—have you never seen it?"

"No, and I have to admit, she's not really selling me on it, either."

I gape at him. "You've never seen Judy Garland sing 'Somewhere Over the Rainbow' or skip down the yellow brick road with Tin Man, Scarecrow, and the Cowardly Lion?"

"If I didn't know you better, I'd request a drug test."

"Micah, that movie is considered an American *classic*."

"Technically speaking, my first car was also considered an American classic," he deadpans, "and the heater only worked when the radio was tuned to AM."

I laugh like I haven't laughed in years, and it feels so undeniably good after the last few days we've survived together.

He waits till I've recovered from wiping my eyes before asking, "How's your mom doing tonight?"

"She seems back to her normal spunky self—which you know is hardly normal at all."

"That's good." His chuckle falls flat, and I see the tension on his face for the first time.

"Hey," I say gently. "You alright?"

"Yeah, I've just been worried about her."

And it's then I realize how close to home my mama's fainting spell must have hit for him. "Oh, Micah, I'm sorry. She's okay now, really."

He nods and clears his throat, then points to the open document on my laptop. "And how's that going?"

"Slow, but having your mom's journals to reference for the time-line of events will be so helpful. Thanks for bringing them. I have to figure out a way to send this off to Chip tomorrow morning somehow. I'm already late on it."

"We'll get it figured out." He plops onto my bed, then positions himself so that his back rests against my headboard. With a yawn, he scans my entire room. "Hey, why don't you have any demon creatures hanging from your ceiling?"

"Because not all of us can be as lucky as you." I study the tired lines of his face. He looks more than tired, really. He looks exhausted. Thinking back over the last twenty-four hours, I honestly don't know how he's still upright.

"You should get some sleep, Micah. You've been going nonstop since the hotel this morning."

"I will. I just need a minute to work up the courage to return to my room first. I know what would help, though."

"What's that?"

"If you read me what you have so far."

"What? No." I laugh nervously. "It's not even edited yet, and I barely know what I'm doing—"

"I don't care, I just want to hear you read." His shoes drop to my floor in a tandem thud, and he closes his eyes. "Consider it my bedtime story."

My cheeks heat. "You're ridiculous."

"So you've mentioned a time or two."

Realizing he's serious about not exiting my room until he gets his way, I twist back to my screen and scroll up to the first of the six pages I managed to write after dinner. The quiet of this house has been a timely gift, and I'm planning to take full advantage of the private quarters for as long as we're here. Not having to worry as much about my sisters accidentally barging in on a writing session has lowered my anxiety by half.

I clear my throat and start to read the first chapter. I'm only three pages in when I hear the deep throaty exhale that defines the unconscious. I turn to find Micah slumped on a stack of pillows and fast asleep on top of my bed.

I debate waking him and forcing his return to the Flying Monkey room, but then I recall all the selfless things he's done for my family today and decide to let him rest peacefully a while longer. Besides, it's not like I'm going to need my bed tonight. My afternoon nap gave me a second wind, and at the rate this manuscript is coming along, I might not sleep again until deadline day. An unexplainable exhilaration zips through me at the thought: *I'm going to be a published author.*

I stand and pull the quilt off the end of the bed, unfold it, and tuck it around Micah using the traditional burrito-style technique my mama always used on me. The blanket's edge barely extends over his long legs. But even with a few accidental knee bumps to the mattress and the fumbling of my under-practiced tucking skills, Micah doesn't stir.

Yet something inside my chest most definitely does.

***

*April 10, 1982*
*Nashville*

*Dear Chickee,*

*I wish there weren't so many miles between us. I know you tell me not to worry about you, but I can't help it. I suppose it's similar to how you must worry about me even though I try my best to convince you I couldn't possibly be better. On many fronts, this is true. We have sold-out shows booked through the end of the year and a southern state tour we're getting ready to start next month, but I'm lonely. I haven't actually said that out loud to anyone for fear of sounding ungrateful, which is the same reason I keep so many thoughts to myself these days.*

*A few weeks ago, I felt brave enough to address the increasing number of tabloids featuring either my perceived jealousy of Luella, my lack of suitors, or my undesirable figure to our label, hoping they might step in or at least offer a solution. Instead, Dorian did his best to convince me that any publicity is good no matter the topic. But who exactly is it good for? I can't imagine how unflattering pictures of my backside increase sales.*

*Luella is often featured in the rags, only the articles written about her are either about her impeccable style or which celebrity she's rumored to have flirted with. How is it our fans find Luella's singleness mysterious while they find mine matronly?*

*I miss you,*
*Lynn*

*November 17, 1982*
*Nashville*

*Dear Chickee,*

*I moved into my own home two weeks ago. I took pictures of it today so I can bring an album with me before I fly out to see you next month. The house has everything I asked for, even a guest room I named after you. I had it painted your favorite shade of blue, and it has tall bookshelves, a television, and a large window overlooking a grove of red and black maples. There's even a Bible on the nightstand. It makes me feel closer to you. I miss hearing you pray. And I miss the prayer rocks you used to write on and have me scatter in the garden out back. How many rocks do you think you've written on by now? Thousands, probably. Maybe someday I'll start a prayer garden just like yours. Of course, that would mean I'd need to start praying regularly again. It's been a while.*

*Do you ever get tired of the quiet, Chickee? I thought this transition would be easier than living in a house where I often felt more like an accessory rather than a best friend. But that was before I knew how this much silence would remind me of the Monster.*

*Saturday is Luella and Russell's "official wedding," and just like Troy predicted, the world has gone absolutely mad for it. For a man obsessed with Luella's public perception, Troy was the mastermind behind Russell's onstage proposal last summer at our Dallas concert. Do you know what the press calls them? Nashville's Fairy-Tale Couple.*

*It makes me wonder if all fairy tales start off as a lie.*

*It makes me wonder if I might be living one, too.*

*Lynn*

*September 2, 1983*

*Dear Chickee,*

*Luella and Russell are having a baby! With as off as things have felt between us all since their official wedding ceremony, this news brought so much joy to my heart. I'm going to be an auntie! As you know, I've never seen myself having kids, so Luella's children will be as close as I come to experiencing "maternal bliss."*

*Baby Farrow is all anyone can talk about on the media—which is both a relief and a blessing. No more awful backside pictures of me to report. Just pictures of Luella's rounding tummy. Perhaps this baby will be what sets all things right again. I hope so.*

*Lynn*

*P.S. I've already sent you this in a letter, so you better start working on a blanket now. Luella's due in late February.*

243

*August 27, 1987*

*My heart refuses to believe you're gone.*

*Jan 1, 1989*
*Nashville*

*Dear Chickee,*

   *I made a New Year's resolution three years ago that I'd start these up again—for you. I bought this blue journal days after your funeral, but it's done a better job of collecting dust than thoughts.*

   *I spent Christmas at the Farrows' this year. Little Adele offered to share her Strawberry Shortcake bed with me, and I must have read* Where the Wild Things Are *to Hattie at least a dozen times. I envy her energy and spunk, although the new prescription Troy ordered me is helping, despite what Luella says. It's hard to take advice from someone whose life has always been next to perfect.*

*Lynn*

*June 14, 1991*
*Portland, Oregon*

*Dear Chickee,*

   *Luella and I realized over dinner that neither of us has been back to this part of the country since our first road trip in Lima Bean, God rest her soul. I'm embarrassed to say I sobbed the day she refused to start up for me. In a way, she felt like the last piece of the girl I was when I still believed dreams could be shared forever.*

   *Franklin invited me to go stargazing with him tonight outside the city. I've mentioned him to you before, haven't I? He's our driver. He's not nearly as polished as the trio, and I think that's why I like him so much. He says what he thinks and doesn't much care about what others think of him. At least, not in the way I've been trained to. He's an odd mix of rugged and gentle, and he talks about fishing and camping the*

*way I used to talk about music and God with Luella in the early days.
I hope he's our driver again next year.*

*Missing you always,*
*Lynn*

July 5, 1993
Austin, Texas

*Dear Chickee,*

*We played a huge show last night on our Patriot tour, and I
couldn't help but feel the growing tension between Troy and Russell.
I asked Luella about it backstage, but she refused to break Russell's
confidence. I reminded her that Russell is not only her husband but
also our shared manager and that I have a right to know what's going
on. Once upon a time, it was my secrets she cared about keeping most,
but those loyalties seem long gone now. She's a wife and a mother,
not to mention the original sweetheart of country music. It's hard
to know where I fit in that equation anymore. Even after all these
years, I'm still living in her shadow. I said as much to her after the
show, but she was too focused on saying goodnight to her girls to
respond back to me.*

*I started riding in the jump seat next to Franklin at the start of this
summer tour rather than in the back with the Farrows. At first, Franklin
didn't say much about the change, but he can't seem to keep his thoughts
in his head for too long. He asked me why I never sleep more than a
few hours at night and why I only pick at my food during meals. I was
surprised he'd noticed, but he told me he's noticed a lot more than that
when it comes to me. Sometimes I can't decide if I'm insulted by his
honesty or intrigued by it.*

*Today he asked about the pills I take. I explained to him that they are
prescription and that I've taken them for well over a decade now. He
said prescriptions can be wrong. I told him bus drivers can be wrong, too.*

*Lynn*

*September 16, 1993*
*Nashville*

Dear Chickee,

The mounting tension I've felt for months between the trio was revealed when Russell finally announced he was breaking away from TriplePlay Records to start his own label, Farrow Music Productions. To say the least, the meeting where it all came to a head was explosive. First, Russell accused Troy of cheating the company, then Troy retaliated by threatening Russell with a lawsuit if he even thinks of pulling Luella and me off his label. But Russell stood his ground like a sentinel, flashing a folder of receipts and telling Troy that if he so much as parks his sports car near our homes, he'll be subpoenaed.

I wish I could say I understood the reasons why Luella and Russell kept their discoveries a secret, but by the time they brought me into the loop, the decisions had already been made, and it's difficult to feel much of anything but hurt. Luella says leaving TriplePlay will be the best thing for all of us as Troy is nothing more than a wolf in sheep's clothing. Only, Troy isn't the one who kept me in the dark for months and made plans on my behalf without my knowledge. In a way, I can empathize with the betrayal I read on Troy's face during that meeting. I feel it, too.

Dorian left with Russell to become a partner of Farrow Music shortly after the split. I am grateful to have a familiar face at the studio. He still makes me laugh, even on the days I want to cry.

Because of all the changes, there was no tour scheduled this summer. I didn't realize how much I would miss seeing Franklin until June rolled into July. There's so much about this year that has felt off, but not sitting next to him, talking through the night the way we used to, has felt especially so. I wondered if he might have been feeling the same way since I got a letter from him out of the blue. I read it over four times before I replied. I hope he writes again. It will help the time pass before he's driving us around on tour again next summer.

Lynn

*August 8, 1994*

*It's our last night of driving before we're back home in Nashville, and Franklin has just told me he loves me. It's both the best and worst thing he could have done. I told him I'm not the marrying type of gal and that if he knew what was good for him, he'd choose to love someone else. Someone less damaged, less lost. He refuted every one of my arguments and told me he won't change his mind, but he'll pray I change mine. He's so stubborn!*

*Even if I could allow myself to feel the same way about him, I know it would never work between us. Franklin would hate living under a microscope here in Tennessee, and I'm bound by my contract with Farrow Music for another five years. Russell's been in Germany working out the details for our first international tour next year, and Luella's been so focused on his homecoming that it feels like the only time we see each other is when we're on stage performing.*

*But friendship isn't meant to be a performance.*

*Friendship is meant to be communicating and sharing and connecting and commiserating. Together.*

*I've been so desperate to talk to someone who understands this push-pull tension I feel, and yet when I had Franklin right there in front of me, I pushed him away.*

*Lynn*

# 20

## Micah

It's been a long time since I snuck around in a dark house, but I'm having major flashbacks of my teenage years as I move to shut Raegan's door behind me while clutching my shoes to my chest. I do a triple-check in the dim hallway for any early rising Farrows. Thankfully the coast is clear.

After a speedy shower—which smarted far less on my scorched shoulders than I feared—I finally took a moment to assess the other fear lurking in my mind. The one that shook me from a dead sleep. The one that would make me Tav Zuckerman's half brother.

I read the last few entries of my mom's journals this morning searching for clues, yet they ended as unresolved as I feel right now. What had happened after my mom pushed my father away? Where did she go? Who did she see?

I follow the smell of strong coffee down the stairs, mindful of every creak and groan. I don't know who's up at this hour, but I pray at least one of them is Luella. I'm only two steps into the kitchen when it's clear my prayer has been answered.

"Good morning, handsome," she says in her honeyed tone, wearing an apron that has the state of Kansas traced in glitter on the front. She holds out her arms for a hug I gladly accept. Somewhere between rescuing her from a nightclub and stripping off my T-shirt for her to wear like a scarf yesterday, hugging became natural.

"How did you sleep?" she asks, pouring me a mug of coffee as if she's the hostess and I'm her guest.

I take the mug she offers and appreciate the fact that she doesn't bother to offer cream. She knows I take it black. "Uh, I slept great, thanks." I don't bother to conclude that the reason for such great sleep was likely *where* I'd slept. It certainly didn't hurt my feelings to wake up to the sight of Raegan sleeping at her desk ten feet away. It took every ounce of my willpower not to plant a kiss on her head as I tucked the quilt around her shoulders before I left her room.

"What about you?" I consider Luella through filtered eyes after yesterday's fainting spell. "You feeling okay this morning?"

"I guarantee I'm feeling better than those crispy shoulders of yours." She grimaces. "I do feel terrible about that. I asked Dottie to pick up some aloe vera for you at the grocery store. She should be back in a bit, but she told us to make ourselves at home. She left us some options for breakfast, too." Luella lifts the egg carton as if it's a foreign object she's never before beheld and says, "Perhaps I'll whip up some eggs for us right quick." And something about her innocence is so endearing I can't help but laugh. Perhaps the conversation I need to have with her will be much easier than I thought.

As she turns toward the stove, I'm about to ask if she's considering ditching the festival to become Dottie's second-in-command at the inn when Adele breezes in with a mug already in hand. Apparently, she's been up for a while. And apparently, she hasn't been keeping company with her mother this morning. The bus breakdown had definitely thawed a few layers of their freeze-out, but given Luella's sudden look of uncertainty and Adele's robotic posture, there's obviously still work to be done here.

"Can I get you a refill, Adele?" I ask, gripping the coffee pot before she has a chance to.

"Sure," she says, looking about as comfortable as my shoulders feel every time I lift my arms ninety degrees. "Thank you."

I keep my pour slow while I make a mental switch to the order of my priorities for the day.

"Your mom just offered to make us some breakfast," I say.

Adele lifts her gaze from the stream of dark liquid to her mother at the stove. "*You're* going to cook, Mother?"

My lips quirk at the surprised tone in Adele's voice, and I realize my hypothesis was correct. I don't think Luella has spent nearly as much time in a kitchen as she has in a studio.

"Every Southern woman knows how to scramble an egg or two, darlin'," Luella declares, cracking one into a bowl where more shell than yolk end up.

Adele and I share a knowing look.

"What can we help with, Luella?" I ask, emphasizing the *we*. Adele doesn't miss it. "Is that pancake mix on the counter there beside you?"

Luella stops fishing for shells long enough to look to her left and read the blue bag beside her. "Affirmative."

"How are you at pancake flipping, Adele?" I ask the eldest Farrow daughter. "Because I admit, I'm pretty lousy. I'm much better at slicing fruit." I grab a handful of apples from the basket on Dottie's table and then go on a hunt for a knife.

"Oh, Adele has always been a wonderful cook," Luella chimes in. "I always told Russell he should have let her go to culinary school. That girl loved experimenting with all sorts of recipes. She even taught Jana a few of her signature dishes."

"Oh yeah? I could use some tips in the kitchen. Did you take any culinary classes?"

"No," Adele answers simply, wasting no time in finding a mixing bowl and spoon.

"Russell said brains like Adele's would be wasted in the kitchen. He used to tell her she was—what was it, Adele?"

"'Built to sit at the head of a boardroom,'" Adele answers in what might be the most reticent voice I've heard her use. Soon, she's collecting the ingredients she needs from the pantry and fridge, and its only then I notice how she leaves the store-bought mix unopened. She's making pancakes from scratch, from memory.

For a woman who brought her own prepackaged meals aboard the bus, I'm more than a little surprised to find out she's a foodie at heart.

I slice a few apples on a cutting board I find next to the fridge. "How long have you been CEO of Farrow Music?"

"Just shy of five years." She stirs the batter, adding in milk a little at a time.

"And she's done a fabulous job taking over after Russell died. It's a hard gig, but we're hoping it will get lighter. Aren't we, darlin'?" Luella says, and I don't miss the way Adele's gaze flicks to hers.

"That's the hope, yes."

"I would imagine it's tough to balance work and home life." I leave an intentional pause. "Cheyenne seems like a really great kid."

"She is," both women say in unison and then look at each other once again.

"There's a special place in a grandmother's heart for her first grandchild," Luella says as she plops a giant brick of butter into her frying pan to make way for her egg mixture. "Adele and Michael did a wonderful job raising her—they were very involved parents right from the start. She has her mother's tenacity and confidence and Michael's open-mindedness and charisma. He's a physical therapist."

I'm careful to keep my tone light and my hands distracted with the apples when I say, "I've worked with a lot of young adults her age, and it's rare to find such support and love shown to them in a family."

Adele says nothing, but as she pours the batter onto the griddle, the stiffness in her back and shoulders disappears.

"I do love her," Luella says, turning away from her scramble to stare at her daughter. "So very much."

"No one doubts that, Mama," Adele says, staring at her bubbling pancakes. "But love doesn't mean encouraging a nineteen-year-old to quit school just because it's not as fun as when she's playing her guitar. I know that she's talented and beautiful and can write a song hook like she's been doing it for decades, but it's important to us that she has a degree to fall back on. She made a commitment. That means something to her father and me." She quickly flips several pancakes in a row with ease. "You and Daddy would have hunted me down if I would have dropped out of Cornell halfway through to pursue cooking."

I glance up at Luella, who seems to have forgotten all about the eggs on the burner. I leave the apple station and step in to turn the stove off so Dottie doesn't come home to a fire drill in her front yard.

"You're right." Luella doesn't hesitate to inch her way closer to her daughter at the griddle. I can barely hear her when she says, "We expected a lot from you—too much."

Adele angles her head.

"I've been thinking about what you said at the hotel, about how none of us have been unscathed by my fame—"

Adele closes her eyes. "I was angry when I said that, Mother."

"But you weren't wrong. I know your father gave you very little agency over your future at the label. I should have been more present to challenge some of his expectations. He was the love of my life, but he struggled to let go, to rest."

Adele is quiet for so long I'm not sure she's going to respond at all, but then she says, "I don't regret my degree or the time I got to spend working side by side with Dad, but perhaps he could have given me space for . . . balance."

I can't help but feel grateful when Luella touches her daughter's shoulder. "Then maybe that's what we can help Cheyenne discover, too."

The freeze-out between mother and daughter appeared to be fully thawed by the time Cheyenne and Hattie joined us for breakfast. With the help of a few well-placed questions here and there, the conversation between the women flowed naturally throughout our meal. Even when Dottie showed up with armloads of groceries, the warm atmosphere remained stable. Several people questioned Raegan's uncharacteristic sleep-in this morning, to which I did my best to cover by suggesting she was likely still recovering from our long and tenuous day yesterday. Hattie seconded my statement with the raise of her coffee mug.

Once the chatter at the table dies down and the dishes are cleared and washed, I overhear Adele inviting Cheyenne to sit with her out front. Cheyenne nods easily and then reaches for her mom's hand. I see Adele give it a squeeze as they walk out the front door.

It's another step in the right direction.

And now it's time for me to take a step of my own.

⬥

I track Luella through the living room and watch as she steps onto the back patio. She's holding an iced tea in one hand and a book—no, a Bible—in the other, and though I know I'm intruding, I can't wait. Not another day or even another hour. I ask God to be with me in this, come what may, and then I step out as soon as she settles into a rocking chair.

"Mind if I join you?" I point to the matching chair beside hers.

Luella's expression holds no sign of irritation at the interruption. Instead, a light seems to turn on inside her. It's easy to see where Raegan gets her infectious smile from. And just like that, my steady pulse trips over itself.

"I'd love nothing more than your company. Please, sit." She gestures to the empty rocking chair, and I comply. "I watched the sunrise out here with Dottie this morning. It came up just over that wheat farm out there." She points to the field beyond Dottie's fenced yard. "Who knew Kansas was so lovely? I think God planned this stop for us on purpose. Thank you for picking up on His cues."

"A smoking radiator is pretty hard to miss."

"I'm not just talking about the radiator." She rocks back in the chair, her hands resting on the Bible in her lap. "I know what you did for Adele and me today. Consider me in your debt."

I dip my head and chuckle humorously. "I think I might be calling in that debt sooner than you think."

"That right?" She quirks an eyebrow. "What's on your mind?"

My knee bounces on its own accord as I meet her gaze. There are at least ten different ways I've thought about approaching this conversation with Luella, but I push them to the side now as I work to reconcile the woman beside me with the one I spent reading about through the eyes of my mother in the wee hours of the morning. "I finished reading the journals."

Immediately, her face sobers. "Ah. I'm sure you have questions."

She can't possibly imagine how many questions I have. "Have you read them?"

"Yes." A simple answer, yet her tone is anything but.

"I figured so," I say with an exhale, "seeing as this road trip is a mirror image of the one you took with my mother in 1975."

"Until Kansas," she amends with a thoughtful smile.

"Right. Until Kansas."

A pang radiates from behind my rib cage as an image of Luella stepping out of my mother's music room in April materializes in my mind. "Was this road trip something you discussed with my mother the night you came to see her in hospice?"

"It was certainly inspired by her, but no, we didn't discuss it. I didn't even realize I had her journals until after I started the renovation of the bus." Her face turns contemplative. "As you know, it was a challenge for her to speak when I saw her, but forgiveness is in our hearts more than it's in our words."

"Forgiveness," I repeat. "Is that what was happening behind that closed door?"

Luella takes a minute as she rubs her palm over the cover of the Bible. "Both given and received. It's meant to come in a perfect pair, no matter how pride may tell us otherwise."

Her admission is stirring, yet I'm still struggling to understand how an estranged friend for more than three decades would be granted forgiveness when the truth my mom held surrounding her son's conception was buried with her.

"Would you tell me what happened between the two of you after that tour? It seems, from my mother's journals, like there was a slow but steady decline in communication between the two of you, as well as some differing expectations as time went on. Which I suppose is understandable after a twenty-year partnership."

Luella flashes me a knowing grin. "Are you always this diplomatic, Micah?"

"It's always my goal, ma'am, but not always a reality." Especially when the subject hits closer to home.

She takes a cleansing breath as she rocks back. "As you know, that summer was especially stressful, not only because Russell was caught in the red tape of the American embassy, but also because we'd used our life savings as collateral for booking that first international tour, seeing as our label was too new to secure a loan. Your mom had written a few songs to record for our new album, and the sound was raw and emotive and like nothing we'd ever created before. Russell and Dorian were excited to promote it."

"But that album never happened," I supply.

"No, it didn't."

Luella picks up her iced tea from a glass side table and takes a sip. "I used to say two bad fights is what ended us, but as I've reflected and prayed and read your mother's journal entries, it's just as you said: a slow decline of poor communication and unmet expectations. The fights simply revealed what was already broken." She turns her glass and watches the ice cubes collide. "The first argument happened the morning after we pulled Old Goldie into Nashville. Ending a tour is always chaotic, and that one was no exception. Everybody was exhausted as we unloaded—our band, our crew, my girls, Lynn, and myself. The tension in the bus had been high, but I figured it would sort itself out once everyone was back home on a regular schedule again. But that next morning, just as I'd set the phone down after talking with Russell at the embassy, Lynn stormed into my kitchen soaked from head to toe from the rain, gripping a magazine. She demanded I tell her what Russell and I were really up to with her. I had no idea what she was talking about.

"I remember having to tell my girls to stay upstairs while the two of us went out on the patio in the storm. I'd never seen her so enraged. She accused me of going behind her back with Russell and trying to steal her songs while slowly edging her out. The suggestion was so ludicrous to me I laughed, but then she threw the magazine at my feet. She told me someone had alerted her to an article in *Country America* magazine. In it was a statement supposedly quoted by Russell alluding to some big changes with our upcoming album, changes that would make Lynn little more than a backup vocalist instead of an equal partner in our band." Luella shakes her head. "It's what your mom feared most, and it was right there, printed in black-and-white. Even our picture looked distorted, me in the front, her pushed off to the side. I swore to her I knew nothing about it and that there was no way Russell would ever say anything of the sort—he loved her like family. But she refused to believe me, and why wouldn't she? I was the wife of the man she'd accused of breaking the foundation of our friendship."

Luella takes a deep breath and seems to center herself again. "I told her I would get ahold of Dorian and figure out how this botched quote made it into such a reputable magazine in the first place and get it retracted."

Dorian's name strikes a match in my gut, and it's an effort in self-control not to cut in with more burning questions that need answers, but I take a breath and coach myself to wait. "I'm guessing the retraction wasn't as easy as you thought," I conclude.

"No," she says. "Three days later, I heard a rumor from a reliable source that Lynn was seen at a bar downtown we used to frequent with an old associate of ours, discussing the legalities of breaking her contract with Farrow Music so she could go out on her own—as a solo act. I'd never felt so betrayed."

"Wait, you're saying my mom wanted to break her contract with you to secure a new one?" My brows furrow at this. "That doesn't seem right. She became a music teacher at a private elementary school in her hometown the year after I was born. I never knew her to have any ambition toward fame. She wouldn't even join the church choir."

"Yes, but remember: you have the gift of hindsight now. Back then this was fresh, and I was fueled by stress and betrayal—two dangerous factors. When I went to her house to confront her on the rumor, she was gone and nobody seemed to know where she'd went or with whom. My anger grew by the day, and with Russell still detained, the entire world felt like it was crashing down around me. The idea of her leaving us high and dry with no explanation enraged me. Then one day, about a month later, I saw the tabloids in the supermarket. The front page was a picture exposing Lynn and Franklin's secret Las Vegas wedding."

The match strike catches on fire as I contemplate the dates she's referring to now, knowing that sometime between their initial fight and my mother's Vegas wedding was a conception date with a man that wasn't her husband.

I'm just about to say this when Luella hits me with "I told her for years that Frank would be a man who would treat her right, a man nothing like her own father. But she was adamant she'd never marry, so to realize she'd married him without even telling me they were involved was . . . extremely difficult. We'd kept so many secrets for each other. For heaven's sake, she was the only person I'd trusted with my own secret marriage to Russell, and yet she hadn't confided any of this to me."

"Is that what your second fight was about then?" I ask. "Their wedding?"

"You know as well as I do that a fight is never really about the subject we claim it to be."

"Very true," I say.

"When your mom finally showed up in Nashville in a large moving van with her new husband, I was ready for her. There are few things I regret more than the ugly words we exchanged that day. I threatened to sue her for breach of contract, while she threw all our lyric books off the shelves and told me she was done. She wanted nothing more to do with anything we'd created together. At one point, your dad stepped between us and pleaded for us to stop and consider our history instead of throwing away twenty years of friendship. But our pride proved stronger than our loyalty. By the time we settled out of court, Lynn agreed to sign over all her rights to our songs—even the ones she wrote under our shared name. She also signed over any and all royalties those songs might accrue in the future." Luella lifts her head. "We signed a no-contact agreement with our lawyers, and that was it. Our songs were the first and last connection we shared."

"Until you sent the award to their home last spring."

Her nod is solemn. "Yes."

For several minutes, the only sound on the patio is the whir of the overhead fan.

"I'm sorry, Luella," I say. "I know you had to file for bankruptcy to cover the cost of that canceled tour and that Russell had to start the label from the ground up again. My mom was wrong to leave you like that."

"We were both wrong." Her voice is watery and thick. "And it cost us both dearly. I would pay back the money we lost on that tour twenty times over if it meant getting to have Lynn in my life these past thirty years. To have stayed close with Franklin and been able to watch their two sons grow up."

As her last words stab into my subconscious, I lean forward and stake my elbows on my knees. This is going to be harder than I thought. For a moment, I can't decide if Luella being able to provide the answer I need will hurt more or less than her not being able to. In theory, I know how I should feel. But theories are often proven wrong because people aren't theories.

"Luella, I wish there was an easier way to say this, but part of why I agreed to drive the bus for you this summer is because . . . I'm searching for my biological father."

There's a long pause followed by a look of denial and then, "But Franklin—"

I shake my head. "Is my dad in all the ways that matter, but we don't share blood. My brother ran the paternity test at the hospital himself, twice. Just to be sure."

"I don't . . . I don't understand. When? Who?"

I lift my head and meet her stunned gaze. "By all my calculations, I would have been conceived sometime by the end of the tour and before their wedding date in Vegas. I know this is a lot to take in. I'm sorry."

"Don't you dare apologize to me. I'm—I'm the one who's sorry. You just found this out?" Her eyes soften and leak at my confirmation with a sympathy that shreds through the top layer of my composure. "You were hoping I might know who? Oh, sweet boy." She shakes her head several times. "I wish I could give you that." She covers her mouth then, her eyes growing round. "You're saying she was pregnant with you the day we fought at her house?" I give her a moment to process these events again through the lens of this new filter. I've had weeks to think on it, yet it still feels like a foreign object being shoved into my brain.

I scrub a hand down my face as a sticky breeze causes a sheen of sweat to dot my brow. Luella's skin appears flushed, as well. "I do have a working hypothesis that it could be Dorian Zuckerman."

"*Dorian?*" Luella's protective pushback is stronger than I anticipated. "No, it's not him."

Obviously, I've hit a nerve. I approach with caution, knowing she's still close to Dorian's family. "I know he was your friend and that he was married at the time of the tour, but affairs often occur when—"

"It's not that." She sounds flustered, and I'm about to tell her we can take a break from this for now, that maybe getting a refill on her iced tea and moving inside where it's cooler would be better, when she says, "Dorian was injured in Vietnam. It left him unable to father children. They struggled for years trying to have a family of their own, undergoing dozens of tests and procedures back east."

I sit up straighter. "You're saying Tav was adopted?"

"No," Luella says patiently, "I'm saying Dorian and Donna did in vitro and used a sperm donor to become pregnant with Octavian. In vitro had quite a stigma back in the '90s so they rarely volunteered that information. Honestly, with as close as Tav and Raegan are, I'm not even sure if she knows."

The present tense of their combined names in Luella's sentence is like three shots of espresso hitting my nervous system all at once. Somewhere a voice of reason tells me to leave it alone, to move on with this conversation, but that voice doesn't have a chance now that every neuron is firing in the same direction. "It sounds like your two families have meant a lot to each other?"

Luella nods absently. "The older girls were always a bit annoyed with Tav—he was the stereotypical only child, and they weren't used to having a little boy around the house. But Raegan." Luella clucks her tongue. "That sweet girl of mine has been smitten with him since the day she learned to say all four syllables of his first name, *Oc-tav-i-an*," she emphasizes with a smile. "I'm rarely surprised when it comes to my youngest daughter, as she's always been my easiest child to please, but she about shocked my curls straight the day she broke off their engagement last fall."

*Engagement.* The word is a freaking neon sign shorting out my frontal lobe, zapping weak brain cells left and right before I can even process what Luella's just said.

The opportunity doesn't come.

The patio door slides open, and Billy, Dottie's brother, steps out. He removes his ball cap and dips his head toward our table.

"I apologize for the interruption," Billy says in a relaxed timbre I could easily mimic after spending hours with him yesterday. "But I'm afraid I have some bad news about the bus."

"Oh no." Luella sits up straighter. "Are we not good to leave later this evening?"

"I'm afraid not, ma'am." Billy looks to me. "There's been a shipping mishap at the warehouse. Part we need is currently en route to Florida."

"Florida?" Luella shrills.

"That's right, ma'am." He nods again. "I've secured us a new replacement part. Only, thing is, we have to drive west of Denver to pick it up. At this point, it's an overnight trip. They close in a couple of hours. But once I have the part in hand, I should be able to fix you folks right as rain in roughly a work day. Best case, I can get you back on the road within forty-eight hours."

"I'll go." I'm so desperate for fresh air and a fresh perspective that I practically jump out of my chair. "If you can help me secure a rental car in town, I'll pick up the part in Denver and bring it back to your shop."

"No need for a rental, son. I'm happy to take you myself, though according to Dot, I'm not as good with night driving as I use to be." He winks. "Might need you to be my eyes come nightfall."

"I'll grab my bag."

# 21

## Raegan

Pulling an all-nighter on a writing deadline must take some practice because mine ended with twenty pages' worth of the letter g and a stiff neck. How on earth can it be after noon? I yawn and stretch my torso side to side in the hard desk chair, careful not to knock the open journals to the floor, and wonder at what point in my delirium I decided my keyboard would make for a decent pillow. I drag my cursor through the manuscript and highlight the evidence of my failed attempt to work till dawn and delete it back to the ten pages I managed to write before my forehead crashed into the middle of the alphabet. I blow out a frustrated sigh at the words that remain. Something's off with the story, and I don't know what. I used a template to create a digital timeline, inserted every important date I came across in Lynn's journals that pertained to my mama, and even drew out a plot web to get the creative juices flowing. And still, what's here isn't as compelling as I want it to be—*need* it to be.

The remnants of a dream linger in my subconscious, but it's not until I push the chair back in search of my morning caffeine fix that I feel the quilt slip from my shoulders and fall to the floor. The same quilt I'd used to cover Micah with last night.

*Micah.*

I spin and stare at the rumpled comforter where he'd slept as my mind replays the dream as if it's being streamed on a device with poor WiFi: Micah and Tav in the same room together, making uncomfortable small talk, all while Tav loops an arm around my waist and Micah refuses to meet my gaze.

I shake my head. It was just a dream. A nightmare is more like it, one that could easily become a reality if Micah's newest hypothesis is true. *Where is he now?*

After a quick stop to freshen up in the bathroom, I follow the lingering aromas of breakfast in search of coffee, but Dottie is the only person I find, and soon I'm locked in a discussion about the wonders of technicolor cinema. The woman is so gracious and hospitable, but after three attempts to escape in the name of a much-needed shower, my only hope is a one-for-one exchange: me for Hattie. When my sister comes down the stairs freshly showered and asking if she can hitch a ride into town to find some WiFi to call her children, I don't hesitate to slip away and return to my room.

Only when I do, I'm not alone.

I freeze in the doorframe of my bedroom, my mind short-circuiting in my verbal command center at the sight of my niece bent at the waist reading my secret project. And she's apparently so engrossed in the chapter she can't hear the alarm bells ringing inside my skull. I close the door behind me, and she jolts upright, whirling around with a hand pressed to her chest. Her smile comes instantaneously, as if the sight of me brings sweet relief. I wish I could say the same about her in this moment.

"Good morning, Auntie Rae. I was coming to brainstorm some lyrics with you"—she points to her Martin on my bed—"but when I saw *Chapter One* on your computer, I got completely sidetracked. I was hoping it was the sequel for Birch Grove." Her smile brightens.

"How come you didn't tell me you were working on something new?"

I take a quick swig of my piping-hot coffee to lubricate my brain and hope I have enough esophagus left to speak. "It's nothing."

She laughs as if I'm trying to be modest. "Hardly. I was so sucked in. I didn't even realize until halfway through the first chapter how little I knew about Nonnie's early days in Idaho at that camp. Are you helping her write her memoir or something?" Her tone is innocent as she lifts one of the open journals on the desk. "I thought these old journals must be Nonnie's at first, but the handwriting is too different to be hers." She twists back. "Who's Lynn?"

An unexpected protectiveness rises in me at the thought of Lynn's journals being out in the open for anyone to read. I should have been more careful. I've grown as attached to her raw and honest reflections as I have to her son. "Those are private, Chey. All of that is."

She sets the journal down and backs away. Her cheeks bloom pink, and instantly I feel like my title of favorite auntie should be revoked.

"Oh gosh," she says. "I'm sorry. How rude of me, I should have asked you before I read something on your laptop, it's just I've always read your books, and I was excited and—"

"No, no." I exhale a shaky breath and set my coffee mug down. "It's okay."

Cheyenne and I have always been close. Of course she thought it was okay; she's been my unofficial beta reader for years. How was she supposed to know I'd be hiding a secret from literally everyone in my life outside of Micah and Chip?

"I was just surprised," I admit with a sigh.

Her uncertainty at my cryptic response is humbling, and I do my best to reassure her with a hug. Thankfully, she doesn't hesitate when she presses her clean curls to my shoulder. I don't know how she got my hair—yet another genetic mystery in the Farrow tree— but it's just one more connection to bond us.

"I really am sorry," she says. "I shouldn't have assumed it was okay."

When she pulls back, I study her, asking a silent question I already know the answer to. *Can I trust you?* Yes, I can.

"I'm writing something I haven't told anyone in our family about yet, but it's something I hope will help protect them from a true invasion of privacy in the future."

Her eyes grow round, and I nod toward the bed and then reclaim my coffee. She props her Martin against the desk, and together we settle onto the mattress, the way we used to when she was a preteen and I was visiting home for a weekend from college. It's strange to think that once upon a time this was her mother and me, just reversed. I can so easily picture Adele, coming into my room and asking if I needed any extra help with my math workbook. I was forever needing extra help with my math. But magically, when Adele explained fractions to me, I understood them. After I worked a few problems on my own, she'd reward me with a watermelon-flavored sucker, the kind with bubble gum inside. She'd eat one, too, and whoever could blow the biggest bubble at the end would get to choose the day's reward activity. If I won, I chose the bookstore with the biggest selection of children's books in the city, and if she won, she always chose some elaborate baking endeavor I was in no way qualified to assist with. I was probably the only fifth grader who knew how to make the perfect crème brûlée. The memory pricks me with bittersweet nostalgia, and for a moment I wish for nothing more than to go back to when things were less . . . like how they are now.

I stare into Cheyenne's dark brown eyes and fill her in on everything that's happened with the tell-all up to this point, including my diversion tactic. Her shock is short-lived as indignation quickly takes the lead. The flash of injustice in her eyes is her mother's. "I've never wanted to hate someone more than Uncle Peter."

"I know." I grab her hand. "But hate speaks to what's in *our* heart more than his. That's something I have to remember, too."

She nods solemnly.

"You can't tell anyone about this, Chey. Not even Allie. I still need to get Nonnie's approval before I submit anything to Chip, and I can't do that until I have a few chapters in hand to show her. And I need them to be right."

Cheyenne ponders this. "What's not right about what you have now?"

I shrug and rub my forehead. "I'm not sure yet."

"May I?" Cheyenne gestures toward the desk and I nod, thinking she's going to read through my first draft again for critique. Instead, she picks up the open journal beside it, and I realize I never answered her earlier question.

"Those old travel journals belonged to Lynn Hershel before she became Lynn Davenport. She was Nonnie's original music partner and childhood best friend before the two went their separate ways in the early '90s. She was around long before Nonnie became Luella Farrow as the world knows her now." I pause, careful not to reveal more than what's mine to share. "She's also Micah's mother. She passed away a few months ago."

Her eyes snap to mine. "Micah as in *your* Micah?"

"Cheyenne," I chide.

"Sorry, but it's obvious he thinks you're like the best thing ever."

Her words create a spark I don't want to stamp out.

She flips through the journal, her interest seeming to grow with each page. "I always thought Nonnie and Papa met in Nashville."

"No, they actually met in Idaho at a summer camp the girls worked at when they were your age. Papa was on a national scouting trip when he heard Nonnie sing at a little chapel, then invited the girls to come to Nashville to meet with his label. Nonnie's loyalty and love for Lynn, for music, and for Papa were once an inseparable trio."

The mug stills and hovers in front of my lips as I hear those words repeat in my mind for a second and then third time.

"Auntie Rae?" Cheyenne asks, dipping her gaze to meet mine.

"I think I know what I need to add," I say on the back end of a whisper.

She peers at me quizzically.

"The thing that's felt off—the reason the story hasn't felt full enough to me yet." A terrifying elation swells in my core. "I can't tell Nonnie and Papa's love story without including Lynn. Her part is too important to the early narrative of, well, pretty much everything Nonnie wanted and worked for in those early years. And it's never been told before."

"I barely even know her name," my niece admits perfectly on cue.

"Which is precisely why her perspective will be valuable. She disappeared from the public eye for thirty years, and yet she helped shape Mama's entire future." I swallow. "She's still shaping it even now."

My fingers itch to get started with the revision of the first chapter, and I can't wait to talk to Micah about it.

"When do you hope to show Nonnie your book?"

"As soon as the festival weekend is over. I should have the contract in hand by then."

Cheyenne stands to retrieve her guitar and slides the strap over her shoulder. Some people have comfort blankets; Cheyenne has her music. She perches on the edge of the hard desk chair and forms chords but doesn't play them. "Mama asked me to stay on the trip through Watershed."

"She did? When did that happen?"

"After breakfast. Honestly, if I hadn't been there to witness it myself, I would have sworn Micah had hypnotized the whole family." She forms another chord and then strums. The low resonance of a minor chord fills the room, but I have half a mind to take the instrument away and demand her full attention. "Micah was in the kitchen with Mama and Nonnie when I got down there, and I'm not sure what happened, but they were both in good spirits. Like nothing was awkward. And then Aunt Hattie joined us, and Micah started asking some questions about our different kinds of communication styles, and soon everybody was chiming in with their thoughts and it was all so . . . normal." Cheyenne lifts her head. "For like an hour there I felt like I was in a completely different family."

My heart swells to five times the size. Once again, Micah to the rescue.

"And then Mama asked me to talk to her on the patio, and she asked if I'd stay on this trip so we can talk more about what I want for the future. I said I would."

"Chey, do you really want to drop out of school?" I ask softly.

She stops strumming and pats the strings. "I told Nonnie last night that I don't want to work in finances or business—I loathe numbers. Music is my passion. Why would God give me a talent He didn't want me to use? Some days it seems like the only reason I keep going to those classes and working at the internship program is because I'm afraid to disappoint my family—my mother, especially. But fear can't be the reason I do or don't do something."

My chest thuds with resounding empathy. "Did Micah tell you that?"

She shakes her head. "I told myself that."

Whoever says this next generation doesn't have a clue about life should meet my niece. "It's wise."

"I'm open to hearing what my mama has to say, but I don't want to be in my thirties and feel obligated to a life I didn't choose and never wanted."

*That* I feel. So much so that I sink back into the mattress several inches while a sharp pain wiggles it's way under my ribs. How different would things be today if I'd asked God to show me how to use the talents He gave me when I was Cheyenne's age? And how different would things be if I'd learned to balance those plans with the needs of my family through real communication?

If Lynn's journals have taught me anything, it's that. I wonder how much of Lynn and my mother's friendship could have been saved if they'd talked to each other sooner. If they had believed the best about each other. If they had shared their hurts and fears and rejections before it was too late. There's a thundering of conviction in my chest that's impossible to ignore.

Despite Lynn's faults, she raised a son who thrives on the very thing she struggled with most, so much so that he was willing to step into my family's mess even while in the midst of his own.

"Do you know where I can find Micah?" I ask Cheyenne as she strums a melody as beautiful as her soul.

"Last I saw, he was out back, talking to Nonnie."

# 22

## Raegan

I'm on my way to the stairs in search of Micah when I hear movement in his room. The door is cracked, so I knock as I enter. I'm fully anticipating the jabs he'll make about me sleeping in past noon as soon as he sees me, but when I step inside the strange flying-monkey quarters, I barely recognize him. He's the same gorgeously handsome man I saw last night, yes, but his movements are uncharacteristically erratic.

And he's stuffing a sweatshirt into a backpack.

"Micah?" I say. "Hey, what are you—"

My question drops off when his gaze collides with mine. It's at that exact moment Cheyenne's words register in a totally new way. Micah was out back with Mama. Talking to her. *About Dorian.* Suddenly, that dizzy sensation I get when looking too far over a railing roils through me.

"You talked to Mama about Dorian?" I confirm gently.

"Yep." His short reply ratchets my nerves even higher. My nightmare this morning feels far too much like a bad premonition now. I fight every instinct I have not to think of him and Tav as half brothers and instead try to funnel my energy into the support he needs most.

He's reaching for his deodorant and toothbrush on his side table as I move toward him and touch his arm. His entire body goes rigid.

"It will be okay, Micah, you're not alone in this. You should take your time, there's no need to rush into anything."

I watch the constriction of his back muscles on his next inhale and exhale exchange and try not to imagine how to navigate the introductions between—

"Dorian's not my father."

His words release a pressure valve in the center of my chest that allows all my oxygen to whoosh out at once. I remove my hand from his arm and press my palm to my anxious heart. "Oh, thank God. How do you know for sure?"

But when he turns to face me, his expression is not one of gratitude at all. "He's unable to have biological children."

"Then what about Tav?"

He turns away again. "I'm sure your mom will fill you in on everything. But right now, I have to go."

"Go where? What are you talking about?" I try to get a better read on him even though my every internal alarm bell is ringing.

"To an auto-parts store in Denver with Billy. We'll be gone overnight." He drops his reading glasses into a case and zips it into the front pouch of his backpack before slinging the strap over his shoulder.

I reach for him and gently tug his arm. "Stop, please."

He drops his gaze to his feet.

"Were you really just going to leave without . . . without even telling me what's going on with you?" My voice is dangerously close to slipping into a new octave.

This time when his eyes find mine, there's something new there. *Hurt.* "Well, you didn't bother to tell me you were engaged."

I rock back a step, mind reeling, but I manage to hold up my left hand and show him my empty ring finger. "I broke things off last fall, just like I told you I did. I'm *not* engaged to Tav."

The intensity of his hooded gaze makes it feel as if he's memorizing every line and curve of my face. He cycles a painfully slow breath before he says, "He seems to be confused about that, and honestly, Raegan . . ." He studies my mouth for three impossibly long heartbeats. "I wonder if you might be a little confused, too."

"No, Micah, that's not—"

He holds up his hand and drops his chin to his chest. "Look, I like you, Raegan, a lot, and I wanted to believe we were on the same page, but the whole reason I'm on this trip is because someone I cared about held back the truth from me. It's probably best we take a step back and give each other space to think things through."

"I don't need to think things through. I know what I want and it's not Tav."

"And yet you're still taking his calls."

His sharp words puncture through me as he moves to stand in the doorway without a backward glance. "I've gotta go. We'll be here for a couple more days. I hope you accomplish everything you need to with the extra time."

And then he's gone, leaving me to wonder if I've just ruined one of the best things to ever happen to me.

Two days in a big quiet house where all the inhabitants are occupied in various ways should have felt like an answer to prayer; after all, time was what I needed to finish these chapters before the festival. But time was also a reminder of the chasm that had opened up between Micah and me. Which made the hours move ever so slowly.

At least Hattie had filled the hours with one-on-one pie-making and life lessons with fellow divorcée, Dottie, while Adele took advantage of uninterrupted office time at the local coffee shop down the road. Cheyenne became Mama's accompanist in the family room, going over her song set for Watershed—per Adele's request—while I struggled to put words on the page. But try as I might, my mind continually drifted back to Micah standing in his bedroom, accusing me of lying to him by omission. The same way his mother had done to him.

And every time I replay it over in my mind, I wish I would have said something back—something to better explain myself. But then again, he'd probably dismiss any explanation I offered as an excuse. Micah had made his point clear many times over now. He doesn't agree with how I'm handling my family situation or with how I handled Tav. And maybe he's right. Maybe I have been stalling in more ways than one.

In the few hours he wasn't on the road with Billy or working alongside him at the shop, I'd offered him a wide berth, even though that's not what I want. But seeing how he hasn't sought me out, I'll continue to give him the space he's asked for.

As we sat down for a final dinner at Dottie's house last night, I could have sworn I felt his gaze on me as Billy told riveting tales about the unsolved mysteries of what car mechanics discover during routine services, but every time I looked up, Micah was looking down at his plate.

We opted to leave the morning after the bus was given a clean bill of health from Billy so we'd have a full day of drive time ahead of us. Dottie's tearful good-bye was bittersweet as she sent us away with more pies than our tiny RV fridge could hold. Apparently, Micah had saved Adele's premade meals from certain death when Old Goldie was without electricity for days by loading them into a cooler at the shop, which scored him points where my big sister was concerned.

Due to our extended stay in Kansas, Mama decided to skip the photo op she'd been hoping for at Four Corners Monument. As documented in the journals, she and Lynn stopped there on their original road trip. But it was too far south and ultimately not worth the delay.

I finished reading Lynn's journals on my own last night. Micah had left them in my room, and I needed to understand the rest of the story, unfinished as it was. I'd sat at my computer for nearly two hours afterward, riding a wave of creative inspiration. Her angst and emotion were palpable, stirring my own creative juices, but even still, her final entries haunted me.

I wonder if they'd haunted Micah the same way.

I wonder if they are still haunting him even now.

While Cheyenne plays Adele the new song she and Mama wrote yesterday at the house, I opt to sit at the dining table, facing forward, as it will be easier for me to work from here. The tug to go back to my book is strong, and in only a few minutes, I'm sucked in again. It writes like a novel, and yet the story is true—as real as the woman singing a duet with her granddaughter only a few feet away.

As soon as we cross back into cell range, I'm grateful to finally send off the updated proposal to Chip, documenting the new changes I'd made on the original file he'd sent me.

His reply email comes quickly.

Raegan,

The changes in your outline look great—thanks! Looks like I'm set to pitch this to the publishing team tomorrow. It's quicker than we normally do things, but it's not every day we have a project of this caliber on the table. On that note, if you happen to have a couple of finished chapters, I'd love to use them during my pitch.

If things go the way I suspect they will, I should have a contract worked up within seventy-two hours for negotiations. As I've mentioned previously, it's always a wise practice to have a trusted legal advisor look over the details for you. I want you to be as comfortable with the terms as we are. The author is our number-one priority.

Looking forward to the future,

Chip Stanton
Acquisition Editor
Fog Harbor Books

I write Chip back, relaying to him that the timeline sounds good so far and that I'm hoping to have something for him after the festival. If all goes well, there shouldn't be much lag time for either one of us. Despite the sour notes between Micah and me, I hope he'll love what I've written about his mother as much as I love what I've written about mine. I'm just not sure when to give it to him.

Purposed energy fuels me as I continue to write. I'm careful to keep the light on my screen set to dim and my font size small. The last thing I need is to get so absorbed I miss someone peeking over my shoulder. Only one more chapter to go before I meet my first deadline.

Just as I start, Hattie plops down opposite me at the table and bites into a juicy apple. "Do we get to know what you've been working on? I'm guessing it's something romantic." She waggles her eyebrows. "And possibly inspired by recent events?"

Obviously, Hattie hasn't paid much attention to the most recent events.

Cheyenne immediately stops strumming her guitar, which alerts the other passengers to our conversation, and since I'm facing the front of the bus, I can see that Micah has been alerted, as well, when our eyes connect in his interior mirror.

"Raegan's a fantastic writer." Cheyenne prematurely jumps to my defense, and I wish I knew Morse code so I could tell her to change the subject altogether. "I hope you all can read her novel one day. It's my favorite story of hers."

"Your favorite?" Hattie asks. "How many of her stories have you read?"

"All of them," Cheyenne says a bit slower, as if she's only just now realizing that this is dangerous territory.

"And how many is that?" Hattie persists, looking at me now.

"Six," I admit. "Though most of them would be considered short stories. Only one has been properly edited."

"Oooh, can I read it?" Hattie asks. "Is that what you're working on now—the novel?"

When Cheyenne looks my way this time, her expression is a mix of *oh crap!* and *what do we do now?*

"No, this one isn't finished. I don't have much written on it yet." I glance down at my keyboard, hoping that will be the end of the discussion. But soon Hattie's fingers do a tap dance at the back of my laptop screen.

"I vote you read us an excerpt. Come on, we could all use some fun entertainment. We've been driving for hours, and Micah said there are no more stops planned until we reach the RV park for the night." Hattie leans in close and whispers, "Also, I think we're headed to a nice mountain resort tomorrow. I heard Micah asking Mama if he could take us on a special twenty-four-hour detour. She agreed."

"The reason there are no more stops is because last time you took thirty minutes to pick out a single bag of mini Oreos," Adele replies loudly, to which Hattie rolls her eyes. "Mama said the park we're stopping at is first come, first served. We don't have time to waste on more of your junk-food scavenger-hunt games."

Hattie ignores her and smiles at me good-naturedly. "Then at least tell us what this one's about." She pulls up her knees and props her chin on her arms.

I can already feel the perspiration gathering on my lower back and under my arms. I don't dare look at the insides of my wrists where I can already feel an all-too-familiar rash starting to populate.

"Um . . . well, let's see . . ." I glance up from my laptop and catch Micah's laser-focused eyes on me, as if he can hear every word. Or perhaps he's waiting for a told-you-so moment. Perhaps that's what he thinks a liar by omission like me deserves. "It's about a talented woman from a very small town up north who meets a generous businessman who promises to make her dreams come true."

"What's her talent in?" Hattie asks.

"Who?" I ask in a voice pitched so high my vocal chords strain.

"The woman—your main character, I presume? What does she do?"

"Music." The minute it's out, I want to retract it. Why couldn't I have said she was a local delicatessen who specializes in French pastries?

Adele looks up then, confused. "That sounds similar to our parents' story."

Sweat drips down my spine as I open my mouth like a caught fish. I feel Micah's gaze boring into me from the front of the bus as if he's expecting me to confess right here and now, but I can't.

Instead, I throw him the most pathetic, pleading look I've ever concocted in my life.

Micah flicks his gaze from the road to me one last time before he gives a final disappointed shake of his head. One I'm sure I deserve. But mercifully he announces, "Pit stop in two."

In a matter of seconds, he swerves the bus for the rest-stop exit while everybody does their best to remain in their seats.

"A little more warning next time would be nice!" Adele hollers before muttering, "So much for no more stops."

Cheyenne peers out the window. "Looks like it's just a scenic stop and some restrooms. No mini-mart to tempt Aunt Hattie." She turns back to me and mouths a silent apology in my direction, but this was in no way her fault. I'm the one writing in plain sight.

I try to catch Micah's eye once more so I can gauge where his head is at, but he doesn't glance into the mirror again after he parks the bus at an overlook at the base of the Rockies.

We all file out of Old Goldie. Some of my family head to the stone facility that resembles something that could be found in a life-size fairy garden, while others stop to take photos of the scenery at the lookout.

But I'm too busy watching Micah to notice.

He's resting against the stony overlook, his elbows firmly planted while he takes in the epic view of the mountains surrounding us at the base of the Rockies. I know he's asked for space, but how can I possibly ignore what he just did for me? I owe him a thank you. Truth is, I owe him more than that.

He turns and straightens to face me, as if he's sensed me behind him, and for a moment, I wish we could go back in time. Because I want to be near him, maybe even need to be near him. If there is anything these last two days have shown me, it's that.

It's such a simple revelation, and yet it's one hundred percent the truth.

A few days ago, Micah was the easiest and best part of this whole trip, and now . . . now here we are. Distant. Awkward. Insecure. "Thank you," I begin. "For what you did back there."

He blows out a hard breath and then tugs on his neck the same way he did in that bedroom. "You had the perfect opportunity to tell them, Raegan, and you chickened out."

"I'm going to tell them," I blurt before I can stop myself. "After the festival, once I have Mama's blessing."

"Life very rarely follows our plans."

"It's only a few more days."

"And if it all blows up before that? Then what? I'm living proof that things don't always go the way we want them to."

My heart twists at the pain I hear behind his statement and what I did to contribute to it. I can only hope that the steps I've taken to finalize things with Tav will give me the opportunity to build a bridge across this chasm.

"I'm sorry you found out about my engagement the way you did. I can see how that felt unfair, but I have thought about what you said, and I'm waiting on a—"

"Raegan! Come take a group photo with us—the lighting is perfect! My kids will love these mountains," Hattie calls from farther down the rock wall where my family is posed in front of the Rockies. A tourist in a big tweed hat is waiting patiently as the stand-in photographer.

I force a practiced smile on my face and steer my gaze in their direction. "Okay, sure, I'll be right over."

But when I turn back to Micah, he's already halfway to the bus.

# 23

## Micah

Raegan hasn't sat in the jump seat for two days. She's offered it to each of her sisters, to Cheyenne, and even to her mom, but she hasn't come within three feet of me since our talk at the rest stop yesterday. In fact, for the majority of this day, she's been in the back bedroom with the door closed.

And it's probably for the best because whenever she's in my line of sight, she's all I can focus on.

I cannot wait to be outside—trekking through the woods, fishing in the lake, inhaling mountain air that isn't tainted by the sweet smell of Raegan's hair. What do they put in shampoo these days, anyway?

Thankfully, I'll have the next twenty-four hours in my favorite natural habitat to think about nothing but nature.

I'm self-aware enough to know when I'm reaching my boiling point, and usually by now I would have hiked or swam or biked and then called my dad to process it all over an afternoon of fishing.

Right on cue, the single-lane gravel byway appears, which places our bus front and center to the Ruby Mountains. This final stretch of road is one of my favorites because it marks the last twelve miles before we reach our destination. After the epic sights of the Rockies and national forests, the Rubies are a totally different breed of beauty. Yet, they require no special introduction or fanfare. I've made this trip with my dad and brother multiple times, just the three of us. It's probably why I feel bonded to it the way I do. I wonder if that's how this whole road trip has felt for Luella, revisiting the places she once shared with my mom.

The midday sun breaks over the tallest, grass-covered peak to illuminate the lush valley below, exposing every shadowed crevice, canyon, and glittering lake and creek. Whoever said Nevada was nothing but high desert and casinos hasn't traveled much outside of Vegas. No towns, no people, no cell-phone towers in view, no distractions. Just natural beauty upon natural beauty. And much like it did when I was a teenage boy, my chest constricts with the evidence that I am not here by chance. And neither are any of my passengers.

Hattie stretches awake from the jump seat beside me and gasps as she presses her face to the window. One by one, I hear the awestruck exclamations from each of the Farrows in the lounge behind the driver's cockpit.

"This is so beautiful! I can't wait to see where you're taking us," Hattie exclaims. "You've been here before, Micah?"

Grateful for the distraction from Raegan finally emerging from the back bedroom with a vaguely sheepish look on her face, I nod at my passenger. "Yes, I was seventeen the first time I was on this road with my dad and brother."

"You came often?"

"Every few summers." As I say it, a memory surfaces of my dad dropping his arms around our shoulders as we looked out at the mountains from the top of camp. *"Boys, there will be times when you're tempted to doubt the hand of God in your life, and when that happens, I want you both to remember this right here. The same God*

*who spoke these mountains and valleys into existence is the same God
who knew your name before you were even a sparkle in your mother's
eye."* Fourteen years later, his words resonate in a profoundly new
way than they did back then.

I blink away the swell of emotion as the dust plumes behind us
and the mountains continue to beckon us forward with a welcome
I need more than my next breath. We could all use more space than
Old Goldie can afford us.

Once we arrive at the main gate of the grounds, I do a quick
check-in with the retreat host I've known for decades, Kent Spar-
ton, and then hop back into the bus with a renewed vision to make
every hour here count. I want the Farrows to enjoy this place as
much as I have.

"Got our keys, ladies!" I dangle two sets of keys before pocketing
them both. Due to the openness of our accommodations, privacy is
more difficult to come by than in our past lodging situations.

"Wait, are all of us women sharing one large suite?" Hattie
presses her face to the window and peers out toward the ridge
we're temporarily parked at. She can't see anything from here, which
I'm happy about. I've been hauling hard to get us here these past
two days, and I want them to be surprised. Despite the long hours
behind the wheel and the cramped leg space, this nine-thousand-
feet-above-sea-level dream destination will be worth it.

"That's correct, Hattie. The vacancies are limited this time of year,
but Kent made some adjustments to my reservation so that all of you
can sleep comfortably in the same space." I hop in the driver's seat
and begin to pull into the spot Kent indicated on the map. Due to
the mammoth size of our bus, we'll have to take our luggage down
the dirt trail in a wheelbarrow ourselves.

"I've always wanted to stay at a mountain resort." Hattie states
with an eager grin. "I started making a list with my kids of the things

we want to do together once they're back—Aiden's first pick was to go camping and make real s'mores. Maybe I can practice here if they have one of those propane fire grills."

Unsure if she's making a joke or not, I twist my head in her direction. "You've never been camping before?"

She shakes her head. "My ex wasn't outdoorsy."

Once I'm parked, I stand to take a quick survey of the rest of my passengers. "Have *any* of you been camping before?"

"I went boat camping with some friends in California once last summer," Cheyenne offers with a shrug.

I sort through her explanation for hidden meaning. "As in, you were anchored overnight in a lake and slept inside the cabin with the use of full electricity and facilities?"

She nods.

I look to Adele and Raegan, who eye each other as if one of them might suddenly remember something that could suffice as "camping" in a pinch. They come up with nothing.

"I'm afraid I raised a group of Tennessee pansies, Micah." Luella laughs. "But rest assured, I've been camping many times in my youth."

Awesome. So one out of five.

"Okay," I say with slightly less bravado than before. "Well, the good news is these accommodations are a giant leap above camping."

Adele clutches her chest. "Oh, thank God, I was starting to panic you were putting us in a tent on the ground."

"You can relax, there are no tents or sleeping bags required. As long as you're up for a unique adventure and keep an open mind, you're all going to have a great time." As I scan the group, I do my best not to linger more than half a second on the face of the youngest Farrow daughter. "Be sure to grab your most sensible shoes for trail walking and whatever else you might need for the night. Also, don't forget to pack something warm for our campfire. It will get into the low forties overnight. Drop your supplies in the luggage wheelbarrow outside, and I'll push it down."

"A luggage what?" several Farrows ask in unison.

"You'll see."

After I talk everyone into tossing most of their belongings into the wheelbarrow, we begin the stroll down the dirt path as the ladies follow after me.

"You kind of look like you're leading a harem," Hattie quips as I steer the wheelbarrow to where the wooden signs are posted with arrows indicating which way to turn for lodging.

Five minutes in the fresh air and I almost feel like myself again.

"Kent said there's a beaver dam not too far off the trail over there. Might be a nice nature walk for some of you later. There's also a beautiful stream for fishing if you keep going in this direction, which is where I plan to be this afternoon. There's plenty of gear if anyone wants to join me. Hope you like trout; it's what's for dinner. There's also a mini-mart back near the check-in, but the pickings are slim." *And likely expired*, is what I don't add.

Nobody remarks on that, but it's probably because they're too busy staring at my surprise.

I plant the hefty wheelbarrow of luggage and face my harem. "Welcome home. This is our little slice of paradise for the next twenty-four hours. Yurt One is yours; Yurt Two is mine."

They stare at the accommodations behind me and then at each other. When not one of them says a word, I twist back to double-check that neither yurt has blown away in the last ten seconds. But the two circular structures covered in thick, waterproof fabric are still there.

"Don't get too excited now," I joke. "I wouldn't want anyone to strain something."

Hattie sets off to the far side of Yurt One while the others linger in the grass out front.

"Feel free to go inside and check it out," I encourage. "Kent says they've done a lot of upgrades."

A reserved Raegan pulls even with me.

"You may need to explain to everyone what these are," she says with noticeable hesitation.

"They're yurts." I glance at her blank expression. "Have you never seen one before?"

But just as I ask, Hattie jogs around to the front. "Micah, please tell me this wooden box is not our only option for a restroom." She points her finger to the private outhouse about five steps from the back of Yurt One. "And why are there signs posted about bears and snakes?"

I hold out my palms. "Listen, as long as you pay attention to your surroundings, you'll be just fine. Besides, there's also a pit toilet inside the yurt. Kent assured me everything is sanitized and ready for use."

"A *pit* toilet?"

"It's not an actual pit, Hattie, it's a—"

I'm cut off by a high-pitched complaint bellowing through the yurt's opening. Adele. "*This* is where he wants the five of us to sleep tonight? Mama, please go talk some sense into him. We are not camping people."

Beside me, Raegan groans and closes her eyes. "On second thought, you might want to give them time to acclimate before you—"

But I'm already trudging toward the entrance. I hear her follow.

"Is there a problem I can help with, Adele?" I ask with a level of diplomacy that would have made my psychology professor proud. I take a second to survey the inside of the yurt. It's a perfect match to the pictures I reviewed on Kent's updated website. Light-years more luxurious than when I last stayed here with Dad and Garrett.

Five twin beds with plaid quilts line the circular interior walls, leaving plenty of room in the center to stretch and walk around. The floor rugs inside are plush and clean, and there is a functional mini kitchen with a pump sink and two chairs and a small sofa on the farthest side.

"The problem is that this is a tent," Adele explains. "Albeit, it's more of a tall, oddly shaped circus variety than something you'd see pitched in the wilderness, but still, it's camping outside with nothing but canvas to protect us from whatever creatures are roaming about at night."

"According to the outhouse, that would be bears and snakes," Hattie provides unhelpfully.

"Now, girls, let's not be dramatic about this," Luella pipes in. "Micah has given us an adventure and—"

"Did you say *snakes*, Aunt Hattie?" Cheyenne's voice wavers. "I don't do snakes." A visible shiver wracks her body before she turns to Raegan. But whatever she finds on her aunt's face makes her clear her throat and paste on a smile. "Um, but the décor in here is totally charming, very . . . rustic."

"*Rustic* is the appropriate word for it," Adele adds, "which is why I'll be spending the night in my snake-free bunk on the bus." Adele holds out her hand to me, and it takes every ounce of my restraint not to toss the keys out the open door into the snake-ridden bushes.

I cast a glance between the lot of them. "*This* is *not* camping. Camping doesn't involve indoor stoves or filtered drinking water that pours through a tap, much less furniture to sit on and utensils to eat with and an electric space heater to keep you warm through the night. Last I checked, nobody here is being asked to chop wood or sleep on the ground or bathe in the snow runoff. *This is not camping.*"

"Okay, sure," Hattie says slowly. "But this is also not the type of accommodations we're used to staying at. I suppose I expected something . . . different. No offense, Micah."

"That's it exactly," Adele agrees with a nod. "This is a simple matter of unmet expectations."

And it's right then that all the irritation I've been pushing down—the stress, frustration, indignation, fear, and rejection—reaches its peak.

"That's an interesting point," I say, focusing my attention on the middle sister first. "Because I can honestly say I never expected I'd be in the position to hold your warm vomit in a hat while riding in the back seat of a sedan, Hattie. But I did it because your safety was more important than my comfort." I face off with the oldest

Farrow sibling next. "I also wasn't expecting to tote your specialty foods back and forth from the bus to the cooler outside Billy's auto shop to keep them from spoiling in the heat, Adele. But I did that, too. Why? Because I knew it mattered to you. And this—" I fling my arms out wide—"this place right here matters to me. So much so that I drove the extra miles while everyone slept and set up the arrangements in order to share it with you." I shove my hands through my hair. "Even a few hours in nature, of breathing in fresh mountain air, is proven to improve our mental clarity, energy, mood, sleep, and stress."

I reach into my back pocket and fist the bus keys in my palm. "So, no, this place is not a resort. There's no spa or five-star restaurant to dine at, but there are mountains and trees and trails and streams and beauty everywhere you look if you're willing to adjust your expectations and open your eyes." The instant my gaze falls on Raegan, at the shocked way she's watching me, my chest is seized by a pain I don't want to name. "It's your choice: stay and give nature a try, or go back to the bus and lock yourself away for the night." I drop the bus keys on the small table in the center of the room. "But I'm going fishing."

# 24

## Raegan

I snap my family out of our stunned silence and point toward the door Micah just exited. "Uh, I should probably . . ."

"Yes, go!" Mama says with a swishing hand motion. "Go."

"Did we just break Micah?" I hear Hattie ask as I rush to dig through my overnight bag for my checkered Vans—the only closed-toe shoes I brought suitable for a trek through the woods. As soon as they're double-knotted, I'm out the door and jogging down the fishing path Micah pointed out earlier. Adrenaline spikes my blood as I call out to him. He's walking at a brisk pace while carrying a fly rod, net, and some kind of woven purse bag in the other hand. Even if I hadn't witnessed him coming unraveled at the seams inside that yurt, I'd know by his cadence alone that he's not okay. I just don't know if he'll even accept my help.

When there's no indication he's heard me, I quicken my pace, dodging rocks and roots and trying not to think about what else could be lurking in the bushes along this trail. "Micah—wait!"

He stops this time, but he doesn't turn around. And it's this, more than the distance we've kept from each other since Kansas, that hurts the most.

Fear churns into a muddy mixture inside my core as I near him. Unlike the last man I pursued for nearly two decades, this man is worth the chase, even if I've only known him less than two weeks. I have to fix this.

I'm a couple of strides away from him when I stop completely, my lungs desperate for air. He barely twists his neck, as if he's trying to keep me out of his peripheral vision altogether. "You should go back, Raegan. I'm not in the best place right now."

"So maybe you shouldn't be alone," I push. "Maybe you should talk to someone."

On an exasperated sigh, he tips his gaze to the sky, and I watch the muscles in his back expand and contract. "What is it you think we should talk about?"

I take a breath and prepare my heart to initiate a conversation that requires a hundred percent vulnerability. "I made a phone call today. To Tav."

He places his gear on the ground, turns, and pins me with such a devastating stare my knees nearly give out. "And?"

"Whatever you thought you knew about my past relationship— you don't. Tav doesn't *want* me now. And the truth is he never has. I chased him, I pursued him, I wanted him, and I was totally fine with whatever crumbs he threw my way for years because I thought it would be enough. I thought I could love him enough for the both of us." Micah winces as my words break from my throat. "He didn't even have the decency to break off our engagement. He made me do it for him, so he could do what he wanted without a guilty conscience. Which was to choose between me and his keyboardist." Tears threaten to spill onto my cheeks at the humiliating admission. "I'm convinced the only reason he asked me to marry him was because my name and industry connections look better for him on paper, but I've never been the one he loved. I never should have said yes to his proposal. The reason I don't talk about it is not because I'm trying to hide it, but because I'm ashamed." A sob escapes me. "It's been complicated trying to deal with the fallout without hurting either of our families in the process or triggering the media. And you were right; I didn't want to have that conversation with him again. It sucked the first time, and it sucked again today. But I did it." I swipe at my cheeks. "There's no possibility of confusion now. It's over."

So many emotions cross his features at once, and I'm certain I've never felt more naked or exposed than I do right now.

"He's the one who should be ashamed, Raegan." His voice is gravelly when he speaks, and I feel every letter scrape against my unprotected heart. "Not you."

As I meet his gaze again, I press my lips closed, barely able to trap my feelings for him inside.

"I need to apologize to you," he says. "I've been too pushy when it comes to the tell-all."

"No, you haven't," I whisper. "I know I've been a coward, and I'm trying to change that."

"I can see that." The conviction in his tone draws my eyes back to him. "I'm sorry."

I don't quite succeed at biting the tremble from my bottom lip. "I'm sorry, too."

I focus on him again, at the crease in his forehead, at the hint of sleeplessness under his eyes, at the aching disappointment etched in every line of his face. "I'm sorry your mother hid this part of her story—*your story*—from you."

The cords in his throat constrict, and it's his turn to look away. "Raegan—"

"And I'm sorry it wasn't Dorian. Not because I wanted it to be him, but because at least you would have had an answer. And you deserve an answer." I take a step closer to him, and then another. "And I'm sorry I didn't deal with Tav a long time ago, because I know you really needed someone these last few days."

"Not just *someone*, Raegan." His throat works again as he looks down at me with an intensity that sends fire sparking through each of my limbs. "I needed you. I *need* you."

"I need you, too."

When he moves in close and brings his hands up to my face, I'm as overwhelmed by the rightness of his touch as I am by a familiarity I can't explain. Logic says I hardly know him, and yet I've had a knowing sense about him since the moment we met. As his thumbs graze my jaw and his fingers push into my hair, I lean in to his caress.

"You're so, so beautiful," he breathes. "Every part of you."

And then his lips are on mine, soft and coaxing, confident and secure. We couldn't possibly be more exposed to our environment, locked in an intimate embrace in the middle of a high desert. As birds caw overhead and bushes rustle with unseen life, the two of us are the only thing that exists in the world. He cradles my face to take our kiss deeper, and I follow his lead willingly. His chest is solid beneath my fingertips, sending a flush of heat throughout my body along with the realization that this, *this* is what a kiss should feel like.

When we break apart, Micah tips his forehead down to mine, and for a moment, neither of us moves nor speaks. My lips feel as blissfully swollen as my heart, and then Micah slides his fingers down my arm and captures my hand in his. "I think I'm in deep trouble with you, Raegan Farrow."

I don't even try to fight the smile that overtakes my face as he threads our fingers together and looks at the trail before us and then back at the gear he abandoned on the ground.

"What can I carry for you?" I break away to move toward the gear.

He collects his fly rod and the basket thing from the ground. "You want to come fishing with me?"

"That depends."

He spins around. "Oh? On what?"

"If you're planning to kiss me like that again before the day's over."

And then everything he's collected is back in the dirt, and his arms are around me, and his lips are on mine, and I'm smiling and laughing and wishing I had the ability to stretch this moment into forever.

"See?" he says, when he finally pulls back. "You're trouble. We're nowhere near the water yet, and I promised trout for dinner."

"Alright, so no more kissing until after we catch some fish. Deal?"

I reach for the net, but Micah doesn't move. When I glance over my shoulder, he simply says, "I'm trying to decide if that deal is worth it or not."

"Come on," I laugh, bumping his arm playfully. "Rewards are meant to be motivating. Let's go."

For the first time on the trail, I take in the mountains hemming us in. Though most of the foliage is lower to the ground, there are groves of pine and juniper trees dotting the edge of the trail leading us to the lake. The air is dry, and the sun is high and hot, but surprisingly, Micah hasn't complained about it once. "So tell me what it is you enjoy most about this high-desert mountain paradise."

He strokes his thumb across the back of my hand. "Right now? You. Definitely you." He winks. "But the fishing and hiking are pretty phenomenal, too. The only thing that compares are the trails near Camp Selkirk close to where I live." He looks down at my Vans. "I'm glad to see you changed out of your sandals first, but those are a sad excuse for hiking boots."

"How much of a deal-breaker will it be if I admit I've never owned a pair of hiking boots?"

He makes a sound like I've just knocked the wind out of him. "That hurts, Raegan. But compared to other issues we're facing, that's a fairly easy problem to solve." He squeezes my hand, and I squeeze back.

I watch him out of the corner of my eye, noting his contentedness. "So you're a big nature guy."

"Guilty as charged." His laugh is weak when he says, "My mom used to say my dad passed his love on to me. Guess she was speaking figuratively."

"The truth is out there somewhere, Micah. We'll find it."

When he falls quiet, I decide not to push him anymore on that topic for now. It's far too nuanced of a conversation for flippant sentimentalities or false promises. Instead, I begin to think about another conversation he put off last week.

"Watch yourself. These stickers are a beast if they get into your skin." He moves to stamp down a gnarly piece of brush on the trail with the bottom of his boot. "Also, the trail is going to get a bit steeper in the next half mile or so. Kent cut in some steps down to the brook, but I have no idea what shape they'll be in now."

"Got it. Thanks."

I press my lips together and hum as I allow my mind to wander into a territory I've yet to explore with him until now. "So were you the guy who left an egg-salad sandwich in the breakroom fridge to spoil? Or maybe you got caught making too many inspirational quote printouts at the copy machine? Or maybe you used the school bus for your personal recreation and that was an automatic pink slip."

"What are you doing?" He gives me his classic side-eye. "If this is what heatstroke looks like on you, I am not medically trained for it."

"Brainstorming possibilities of why you're unemployed."

"Ah, then please continue. Your storytelling is better than mine." I jab him in the ribs. "You owe me."

"Brace yourself: it's short and depressing."

"Well, I happen to love writing happy endings, so maybe *you* should brace *yourself*."

His chuckle fades into a sigh. "I was hired by the school district shortly after I graduated. I was all blind ambition and ego—certain I could make a difference in a job that has one of the highest turn-over rates in education. But after five years, the red tape of dos and don'ts became a noose around my neck, and I saw more paperwork within the four cement walls I sat in every day than people. And I was miserable."

"I can't imagine you trapped inside an office every day." Micah is a goer, a doer.

"That's pretty close to what my mom said to me, too."

This turns my head. "What did she say?"

"'Life's too short to be questioning what you're doing with your time every day.'"

Once again, Lynn's words carve a mark on my heart. "Wow."

"Exactly. That kind of life advice hits differently coming from a person who is literally signing papers for their hospice care."

I wait for the sting in my throat to subside before I ask, "What did you do?"

"I stayed up most of that night—I prayed hard, took a walk, read through Philippians, and then prayed some more. And in the morning, I submitted my leave of absence."

When I say nothing, Micah peers down at me. "Garrett thought I was impulsive and acting out of grief. He was sure I'd regret it."

"Do you?"

He doesn't answer me for several strides until we're standing under the shade of a pine tree. "I regret not knowing if I made an actual difference during the time I had there. But I don't regret the time I spent with my mom in her final days—even knowing what I know now. Maybe even especially so. And I don't regret forcing myself to take a long, hard look at my own mental health the way I was paid to do for others nearly sixty hours a week."

His words push my thoughts back to those difficult months after my dad died. How I sold my little condo outside the bustle of the city to move in with my heartbroken mama. How Adele became an instant CEO, managing everything and everyone in sight, and how Hattie crawled inside herself and rarely left her home. I was so desperate back then for our fractured family to feel whole again. No cost felt too high, no sacrifice too much. Until one day it did. Until the cost felt like it was suffocating me from the inside out. I don't even know how to relate to the freedom he so freely lives in.

"I think you're incredibly brave," I say after a minute.

"How much do I need to pay you to say that in front of my brother when you meet him?"

"I'm serious." I tug his hand to a stop. "And I'm also absolutely certain you made a difference in your five years at the school. Look at what you've done in the short time you've been with us." My eyes mist again. "You have a gift, Micah. And wherever you go, I have no doubt God will use it to help people. It's who you are."

His expression softens on me. "Thank you."

"You're welcome." I pull him forward again. "So tell me what you would do if you could do anything."

"Anything?" He cranes his neck from left to right, staring up at the hills above us. "This. I've always known there's something healing about being outside in God's creation. Something that challenges and rewards us in ways sitting inside a therapist's office can't compete with. The most life-changing moments I've experienced didn't happen in a classroom or in a counselor's office. They were usually out on a lake with my dad or driving through the Cascades on a road trip or hiking a new trail with my brother. There's a divine intimacy in nature that can't be duplicated. I want to help people find that."

Despite not having a whole lot of personal experience with outdoor life myself, I trust his conviction and ponder it for the next few minutes.

By the time we reach the brook, we've fallen into a companionable quiet, as if this world is one we've navigated together forever. But maybe I only feel that way because Micah is at my side and he seems at home in a way I'm not sure I've ever experienced myself. He instructs me to tread lightly as we make our way down to a fishing spot that looks like an illustration straight out of a children's fairy-tale book. It's maybe ten feet wide with boulders on either side and wildflowers intermixed throughout the bank. I half expect a clan of friendly gnomes to peek out from the forest beyond and invite us to a potluck.

He keeps his voice to a low murmur to keep from scaring the trout that are visible even from several paces away. He told me that his dad's best fishing advice is to take the time to observe everything you can about your spot before you set up your rod. Apparently, the best fishermen are also the best students of nature. By the looks of it, Micah is near the top of his class.

As Micah studies his surroundings on shore, I study him. I've never fished a day in my life, but he's selling me on it pretty hard, and he hasn't spoken a single word since he last cast his line. The sky above us is blue, the weather ideal, and I'm suddenly overcome with the kind of peace that stirs my heart to pray.

I'm attuned to the expert way Micah positions his rod. Both his right and left hands have a job to do, and there's an intricate dance between keeping slack and holding tension. Fishing, I suppose, is a lot like life. No wonder Micah is so skilled at it.

When a trout bumps the fly without biting, Micah eyes me. "You're probably bored out of your mind. I should have turned back to grab a rod for you, too."

"I'm happy to observe. It's fascinating. One day, when I'm back to writing fiction, I might have to draft you into a story." Heat crawls up my neck as my words replay themselves to my ears. "Not *you*, per se, but this." I gesture to his line in the stream. "The fishing stuff."

"Ah, yes, it's the fishing stuff that has you all fascinated and flustered for certain." His grin is so cocky and absurd it's laughable, but before I have time to come up with a reply, he says, "I think it's time for the quiet observer to have a private lesson. You know, for the sake of inspiration."

He tells me to anchor my feet on the shore as he positions himself behind me and places the fly rod in my hands.

"I couldn't write this scene in a book, ya know."

"Why not?"

"The whole man-tutoring-a-woman thing is too cliché," I say with exactly none of the nonchalance I'm trying for as my body hums to life at the feel of his embrace. His arms lock mine in place as his hands fold over my fingers to hug the rod.

"I have faith your imagination could do it justice." His breath sweeps the sensitive spot directly below my right ear, and all I can think about is how close his lips are to my skin.

"Relax your shoulders," he instructs gently. "There you go. Now hold the rod steady. Your eyes should sweep the water from left to right. Good, now find your own rhythm." We remain this way for several minutes as he works the slack in the line, instructing me on how to do the same while I actively work to keep the fire in my core contained.

I tangle the line several times, and it's an effort to right my mistakes, but Micah is never impatient with me. He simply tells me to try again, and I do.

And then, we get a bite. A big one.

All at once, the slow rhythm of casting and waiting is turned up to maximum speed. I start to duck away and allow him to take the lead, not wanting to forfeit our catch because of my clumsy handling, but Micah won't have it. He talks me through every step, and though there's a struggle going on between fish and fisherwoman, Micah is a calm, focused, and steady teacher.

When the fight is over and the victory is ours, Micah turns to me with a wink and says, "Cliché or not, you just caught us our first trout for dinner, Raegan Lynn."

I squirm a bit when he makes me hold the twelve-inch trout for a picture because "All fishermen need proof of their catches."

And then Micah squishes his cheek to mine, holds the fish up between us, and tells me to take the selfie on the count of three. The picture is absolutely ridiculous, and yet I adore everything about it. I'm pretty sure, in time, I could easily adore everything about Micah, too.

"Perfect," he says right before he pockets the phone and begins to prep the fish near the water. "We'll need a few more fish to feed our crew. That is, if there's anybody left at camp when we return."

"Honestly"—I shrug—"your guess on that is as good as mine."

For the next hour, I watch from a boulder in the shade on the water's edge as Micah manages to catch us another three trout, and once again I have that feeling like I wish I could freeze time and come back here again. I reflect on his mother's wise words and ask myself some hard questions regarding the time I've been given. Not just on this road trip or even in regard to the book I'm currently writing, but with the people I've been given, too.

Once he's finished cleaning the catches, Micah places the flayed trout inside the basket thing he calls a creel, then squats near the water to scrub at his hands in the moving stream until his fingertips blanch white from the cold. When he rises and stalks toward me, sunlight threads through his cinnamon-brown hair and glistens off his tanned skin. Every muscle in his arms and legs is flexed, and it feels every bit like a fictional scene coming to life.

Only this is not fiction.

When he's close enough to reach for my hand, he pulls me up from the boulder and steadies me at my waist. His eyes are focused on my mouth. "Is it okay with you if I collect my reward now?"

With the nature soundtrack of a babbling brook behind us and the beauty of this hidden valley on our every side, our lips find each other as if this exact spot was mapped out for us long ago.

We kiss until our lips feel tender with the kind of idyllic delirium only achieved by true connection. We kiss like it's the beginning of a story we've barely begun to write and have no intention to rush. We kiss like two people who were destined to meet despite the generation of regret that kept them apart.

The temperature has already begun to drop as we make our way back to the campsite just after six. Micah's grip on my hand remains firm as we approach the cutoff at the path, and I feel his gaze skim my profile. I wonder if he, like me, is already counting down until our next private moment. If Adele has managed to convince our entire crew to join her on the bus overnight, then perhaps the wait won't be as long as I fear.

I nudge him gently. "You can't keep looking at me like that, Micah."

"Like what?" He feigns innocence.

"Like you're two seconds away from kissing me senseless behind Yurt Two."

"Huh," he chuckles. "And here I thought my poker face was among the best in the world."

"Let me assure you, it's not." My laugh is cut short by the change in the wind. *Smoke.* "Do you smell that?"

"Kent probably has a campfire going up at his place."

But the closer we get to the yurts, the more intense the scent becomes. And then we hear the voices—all female and all familiar.

"Shhh . . . I think they're coming," an unidentifiable relative announces.

We both eye each other questioningly.

As soon as he drops his gear off at his yurt and we've rounded the other side of it, the crackle and glow of an impressive campfire beckons us close. I can hardly believe what I'm seeing: each and every woman in my family standing next to a circle of camping chairs.

"We're sorry, Micah," Hattie blurts out, which seems to prompt others in the group.

"We made some sides for dinner." My niece points to a tree stump outside the circle with a hodgepodge of interesting food selections. "We did our best with what we could find at Kent's minimart. It's mostly Pop-Tarts, pork rinds, sunflower seeds, and baked beans from a can. Oh, and Mama bartered with Kent for some fresh s'mores stuff for dessert."

Adele is slow to meet our gaze, but when she does, she steadies it on Micah. "I may have overreacted earlier."

Mama hikes an eyebrow and crosses her arms over her chest, saying nothing but everything all at the same time.

"I'm sorry," Adele says. "I . . . didn't realize how sentimental this place was to you. And I can see now why you love it so much."

The look on Micah's face is one of befuddlement. "I appreciate that. Thank you."

Mama rounds the fire. "Kent came down when he heard all the

fussin' and carrying on down here. He told us how you and your brother would come for trips with Frank in the summers. Sounds like Kent's boys followed you around everywhere you went when they were younger."

Micah chuckles at whatever memory flashes through his mind. "They were good kids, although neither lacked for energy."

"Kent still marvels at the level of patience you had for them, taking them on excursions and fishing trips so he could get things done around the busy months," she says. "He said you're a huge part of why they're both working with him now."

"Are they really?" Micah asks with awe in his voice, and I can't help but think that even as a teenager Micah had a gift for nature and people. The thought fuels me with pride.

"The three of them did a full critter check of the yurt for us," Hattie explains. "They told us to holler if there was anything else we needed tonight. Nice people."

"They are," Micah agrees.

"What do you have in the cooler, son?" Mama asks. "We're hoping it's something that will go with cherry Pop-Tarts and charred beans." Her laugh is light, but I can see the way her term of endearment touches Micah.

He clears his throat, then slings an arm around my shoulders, pulling me close to his side. "Our Raegan caught us a trout."

There's a chorus of surprised cheers and claps, but the delight I feel in this moment has little to do with my part of the catch and everything to do with the people I'm about to share it with.

# 25

## Raegan

After we said good-bye to the yurts, I spent the long driving day that followed writing from the jump seat of the bus while Micah played lookout for any approaching family members via his interior mirror. Thankfully, I'd managed to complete and polish the first three chapters of the memoir due to Chip after the festival—barring Mama's approval, that is.

As soon as we'd parked in Crescent City, California, last night, I'd mapped a rideshare to the nearest office-supply store to print out a hard copy for Mama since she loathes reading on screens, and I covered up the errand by offering to make a grocery run for fresh produce and snacks. My family was more than happy to provide me with their shopping lists. And despite his road weariness, Micah had volunteered to escort me.

Which meant he was with me when Chip's email came through in the checkout line.

Raegan,

As expected, the publication board was thrilled with our proposal. Attached is the first draft of your contract. We can discuss specifics once you have a chance to review it in detail. Does tomorrow work for a call? I'd like to get a writing update from you, as well.

Chip Stanton
Acquisition Editor
Fog Harbor Books

Now a beautiful new day has dawned. And I'm blessedly alone as I comb through each section of the contract, awaiting my phone call with Chip. I'm struck by how surreal this moment is. Three weeks ago, I'd been convinced a partnership with Fog Harbor Books wasn't in the cards for me. And yet here I am, sitting on a bench overlooking the Pacific Ocean and planning to sign an author contract under my real name. My initial review did clarify one thing: the shocking offer Fog Harbor is willing to advance me for this book will eventually need the attention of a lawyer as long as Mama gives me her blessing. Perhaps Adele's cautious thinking has influenced me more than I realized.

I snuggle into the oversize sweatshirt I borrowed this morning that still smells faintly of campfire, and as if sensing the action from afar, the owner of said sweatshirt texts me an update of his beach excursion with my family.

Micah D., bus-driving ex-therapist:

We're still out collecting shells. Should be headed back your way by eleven. Does that give you enough time, or do I need to stall? Your mom wants to be at the Redwoods by early afternoon.

Raegan:

Timing is great. Thanks again for escorting them to the beach this morning. I owe you. My call is in five minutes. I have my list of questions ready.

It's almost two minutes before Micah texts back, and when he does, I analyze the five words as if they were five paragraphs.

Micah D., bus-driving ex-therapist:

Wish you were with us.

On the surface his sentiment is sweet and endearing, but I saw the reservation in his eyes last night when the contract came through to my phone. I know he's concerned that the cart is way too far ahead of the horse, but this is still my best option. If I only get one chance to win Mama's blessing on this project, then it's vital I understand everything involved—including the proposed publishing contract. I've gone through it line by line three times now, and after some extensive Googling in my bunk, I feel fairly confident.

At least, until I think about everything I've kept from my family.

As quickly as the guilt moves in, I remind myself that I only have a couple more days to keep this secret. And didn't Adele ask me to keep the peace and limit all distractions until after the festival?

My decision is for the greater good. Mama will see that; I know she will. And her vote is the one that will matter most.

When Chip calls, we spend the first fifteen minutes rehashing the meeting he had with the Fog Harbor executives in greater detail— their elation over the exclusive proposal, the specific deal points of the contract, the marketing plans they'll put into motion as soon as the contract is executed. Through it all, Chip's enthusiasm over this project is impossible to miss.

"Raegan, I don't want to add any pressure to your plate, but is the timeline we discussed still on track?"

I rub my lips together, thinking through the agenda for the next few days. Per Mama's request, we'll spend the afternoon at the Redwoods, then do another long stretch of driving tonight in order to get her to the outdoor amphitheater in George, Washington, a full twenty-four hours before her first performance. Adele had spent the majority of the bus ride yesterday confirming rundowns and makeup and backstage-interview schedules. Since Daddy's passing, she doesn't trust the details to anyone else. Not even the talent managers on her payroll.

"Yes, as soon as my mother is able to read and approve the sample chapters, I plan to send the signed contract back to you. My hope would be after the weekend."

Chip is quiet for a moment. "And what do you think the chances are of her not approving it?"

I inhale a fresh pull of ocean air and fill my lungs. The truth: I can't imagine Mama protesting after she reads what I've written, especially since her heart has been so open with us after Lynn's passing. "Slim."

"That's good to hear." He sounds relieved. "I hope it will be a productive and positive conversation for you both."

"I appreciate that. And I appreciate everything else you've done for me and my family."

"It's been my honor. Who knew when Allie introduced me to her roommate's aunt at the Christmas party last year that this would be happening now?" He's quiet for a moment. "Celebrity memoirs are popular for a variety of reasons—but I think what you're working on has the potential to reach past our basic fascination with fame. One of the things we discussed in the meeting was your use of the word *legacy* in the proposal. Few people take the time to reflect on the legacy that's been left for them, much less the one they're leaving for the next generation. I hope you'll continue to explore that as you work. It's the perfect union to some of the themes you wrote about in your fiction. "

I watch a wave break against a giant rock formation fifty feet or so away from the shore and ponder the weight of his words. "I don't think I've thought of it like that before."

"The editor I used to work with, Ingrid, always said, 'Perspective is the most powerful tool in a storyteller's arsenal.' It's how she sold me on Allie's fantasy series."

I smile, thinking of the tall, quirky brunette who'd become a treasured friend over the last year. "How is Allie? Is her first book still slotted for next year?" My niece is already planning to preorder at least a hundred copies for everyone she knows. When the girl supports someone she cares about, she goes all out. I have been a recipient of such love for some time now. I only hope I can return her generosity of spirit in equal measure one day.

"Allie is . . ." The hesitation in Chip's voice catches my notice. The same way the memory of him escorting her to the Christmas party did last December. Only, Chip has a girlfriend now. And despite what I hoped, that girlfriend is not Allie.

"Allie's like a sunflower in a forest of pine trees," he finally concludes.

"Wow, that almost sounds poetic."

"Not if you realize how stubborn sunflowers can be," he says with mock jest. "They just pop up wherever and whenever they want."

"And yet they're still stunning wherever they grow."

"Right, well—" he clears his throat—"we'll touch base soon, Raegan. Safe travels."

After we end the call, I search the heavens overhead and ponder the connection between legacies and life, and one question circles my heart and mind: *Will the book I'm writing play a part in my own legacy one day?*

My family came back to the bus from their time at the ocean with salty, mussed hair and wind-chapped cheeks. But even more than that, their postures spoke of the kind of peace nature invokes. A peace I was only just now beginning to recognize thanks to Micah's passionate insight. Even Adele seemed uncharacteristically calm, despite the list of last-minute details she was confirming with Mama's bandmates, production team, and styling crew.

The drive to Redwood National Forest was less than an hour away, and I'd been more than a little surprised when Adele had offered me the only other nausea-proof seat on the bus—which also happened to double as the best workspace on the bus, as well—since I'd given the jump seat to Mama. Instead, Adele set up her office in the back bedroom for the day. The thoughtful gesture made a ripple of affection course through me, which was immediately followed by a ripple of anxiety. *Would she understand why I'm doing this?*

"Once we see the park signs, I believe we take the second entrance into the park," Mama speculates from up front. She's been a chatty navigator on this short stretch of coastal highway, and Micah's amused gaze has flickered to find mine in the rearview several times. "Although, hmm, on second thought, perhaps I better reference the pictures in this map book again. Things look a smidge different now than they did in the seventies."

"I hate to break it to you, Luella, but this beast isn't exactly known for its tight turning radius. We may only get one shot at finding the location you're after once we get into the park."

"Don't you worry your handsome head about that. I'll find it. I just need to make sure this map matches my memory is all." Mama goes back to studying the guidebook she picked up, and Micah gives me a wink in the rearview.

Cheyenne plunks down beside me and sets a spiral seashell as big as my palm on the table between us. "Aunt Hattie and I went shell hunting this morning. She found a few treasures for Anabelle and Aiden, and I found this one for you. It didn't seem fair you were stuck in your bunk while we got to experience the ocean."

The guilt is creeping in again. Cheyenne knows nothing about my call with Chip. The tangled web of omissions is more difficult to manage while stuck on a three-hundred-square-foot bus. "Ah, that was sweet of you." I tip my head to hers. "I love it." I run my finger over the cool inside of the pink shell while Cheyenne hums a chorus she came up with during her beach walk. She's only strung a few words together as of yet, but her melody is so addictive I can't help but harmonize.

Mama flips around from her jump seat. "Bring your guitar along with us today, sweetheart. We're going to need it."

Cheyenne's eyebrows scrunch into a V. "On the hike, Nonnie?"

"We won't be walking too far," Mama says before she turns to face front again.

"Okay, I'll bring it." My niece looks to me, but I can only shrug. I have no idea what Mama has planned.

Hattie joins us at the table, showing us the videos she took for her kids at the ocean, and then the videos they've sent to her from Greece so far. A stone balcony with a view of a jewel-tone coast-line and a sky at sunset linger in the background like a tempting visitor. I know I shouldn't be awed by it, but it's stunning. The kids are goofy and giddy, and even though they appear happy and well cared for, I watch my sister's chin quiver just before she shuts it off.

I wish I had the words to soothe her heart, but I touch her hand instead, hoping to remind her I'm here just the same.

A second after Mama scares us all to death with a shriek over her discovery of the spot she's been searching for on the map, Adele cracks the back bedroom door open with her laptop in hand.

"Mother," she hollers to be heard, "did you know Travis Knight was asked to replace Jim Labarro at the festival?"

Mama twists back and frowns. "I heard that was a possibility, seeing as Jim's been in and out of the hospital."

"It's official now." Adele groans and comes out to plop on the sofa. "Here's hoping his agent has finally retired—or better yet, been blacklisted from the industry."

"The Gorge is a ginormous venue, darling. It will be easy to keep our distance."

"That's much easier for you to say when I'm the one who will be stuck with him behind the scenes while he ogles and comments about every young female in proximity." Adele gives a full-body shiver, and I don't know whether to be alarmed or intrigued by her comments. I'm not often privy to shop talk when it comes to the music label, but this conversation feels more personal than professional.

"Who's Travis's agent?" I ask.

"Troy Rigger," Adele provides with an eye roll. "He's an old ex-business partner of Daddy's and a real piece of work. I don't know how he still has clients willing to be represented by him." Her eyes flit from me to her daughter. "Actually, now that I think of it, I want you to steer clear of him, Cheyenne. There's some bad history between Papa and Troy, and it would be best for you to keep your distance."

The familiarity of his name surfaces quickly. Two weeks ago, the only thing I knew about Daddy's life as a talent agent in the '70s and '80s was the name of the label he once represented at TriplePlay Records. But Lynn's journal entries had painted the once gray-scale history of their past in vivid color. This man was the one supplying diet pills to Lynn for nearly two decades, the same one obsessed with keeping my mother's sex appeal and desirability first and foremost, even after she was married to my dad.

"There it is!" Mama exclaims. "That's the entrance for the trail we need."

Adele closes her laptop and perches on the sofa as Micah traverses the tight curves and slows for the speed bumps. It's only been minutes since we were on the highway, yet I feel as if we've been transplanted inside another universe altogether. It's as if each of us has shrunk to the size of one of Mama's woodland figurines and been placed inside a garden bed. Only, it's not that any of us have shrank, but that the nature around us has been magnified by a factor of ten or twenty. Even from the outskirts of the forest, the massive size of these tree trunks makes it seem like we've entered a fantasy set in a land of giants.

Minutes after parking, we trail after Mama, gobsmacked by our surroundings. Cheyenne has her guitar strapped to her back, and my sisters seem to be doing exactly what I'm doing: straining our necks to glimpse the top of the redwood trees. It's not possible. I stumble over roots and debris more times than I can count, but thankfully, Micah's arm is always in the right place at the right time for me to steady myself on.

"Incredible, isn't it?" His voice is hushed as we circle a fallen tree trunk wider than the length of my SUV. Maybe even the length of our tour bus.

"You've been here before?"

"About a decade ago. It was my mom's idea, actually. Unusual since she was such a homebody. She didn't often accompany us on the road," he says. "We set up camp not too far from here." He slows and glances around the forest. "She went off on a long walk one afternoon. We were afraid she must have gotten turned around out here, as much of the forest looks the same. The three of us split up to search the area. I remember it well because I was the one to find her." He stops and points to the place where my mama has stopped. "Right there."

Near the base of a small wooden bridge arched over a slow but steady stream of water is Mama. For close to a minute, we watch her . . . until one by one, the five of us gather behind her in anticipation of what's to come.

When she finally rotates to face us, her cheeks are damp, and her voice tender. "Forgive me, I didn't realize how I would feel seeing it again after all this time." Her gaze sweeps over my sisters until it lands on Micah. "Lynn and I cowrote our first song together while sitting right here, on this bridge. There were many choices for us in those early days and years, some we took, others we skipped. It's what 'Crossing Bridges' is all about: friends who love each other enough to cross them together or not at all."

"My family will always cherish the award you sent her, Luella," Micah says quietly.

Mama shakes her head. "She deserved so much more than that trophy. I wish I would have taken that step decades sooner."

I look between the two of them, at the unspoken truths no one says out loud.

Because the truth is, their reunion was little more than a short-lived good-bye.

"It meant the world to her," Micah confirms.

Mama's eyes swim with tears, and it pains me to watch her grieve. "And your mama meant a great deal to me." Her chin quivers. "Out of respect for your family and town, I chose not to attend her memorial service. It didn't seem right after missing so many years of her life." She takes in a shuddered breath. "But with your blessing, Micah, I'd like to pay your mother a tribute in the best way I know how, in a place that was special to us both."

I watch Micah swallow twice before he manages to speak again. "You have it, Luella."

My mama nods to him gratefully as Cheyenne positions her guitar. She doesn't wait to be cued, she simply begins to fingerpick the chorus of a song the whole world seems to have memorized. And by the somber expression on all our faces, it's not lost on any of us that the same song that once began the journey of two best friends in search of their dreams is the same song dedicated to the end of their dreams. A final benediction echoed from the treetops in the same place they'd once plotted their futures together.

Though tears glisten on my mother's cheeks from the splashes of sunlight cutting through the thick branches above us, the original melody of "Crossing Bridges" never wavers. Neither does her voice. There's not a note, a breath, a single word sung out of sync or off-key. There are far too many years of practice for Mama to choke under the strain and weight of emotion, and yet it's the emotion inside her that pours out in every lift and swell of her gift. On the rise and build of the chorus, it's as if we've all disappeared, as if the only person who really matters is the one person who isn't here.

Cheyenne's accompaniment is flawless, and just like her Nonnie, her eyes are closed as if in prayer, tears trickling down her cheeks. My niece never knew this woman her grandmother once referred to as *sister*, and yet her sorrow is real. Hattie's lips tremble as she silently mouths the lyrics while Adele stares into a distance beyond what our human eyes can see. On the last time through the chorus, Micah folds my hand into his, and it's then my tears spill over. Not only for the woman whose name I bear, but for the children, the husband, the friends, the life she left behind.

> This bridge can hold us both / Our comings and our goings
> It's steady and secure / Where water's always flowing
> We can take it on together / The way we've always done
> Not afraid of looking back / Not afraid of what's to come
> There's more for us to find / Let go of what's been lost
> As long as we're together / This bridge is ours to cross

It's quiet for nearly a minute after Mama stops singing, and I can't find the off switch to the overflow of emotion welling inside me. My heart thuds inside my chest, and my palms grow damp. I can't seem to pinpoint the source of this new ache inside me. All I know is that I want it to stop.

I sense Mama is about to say something to conclude our time together when, instead, Adele turns toward her daughter. "I never thought I would enjoy listening to that song again after all the cover bands and remixes I've been forced to hear this last year. But you two—you and Mama together—you have something special."

With muted approvals, the rest of us concur.

"I also think," Adele goes on, "if it's okay with your Nonnie, you two should consider performing this song together onstage at the festival."

Cheyenne's eyebrows lift in question as she looks from her mother to her grandmother, who smiles through her sorrow.

"I'd be honored, darling girl. And I think if Lynn were here to ask, she would feel the same."

Cheyenne moves a trembling hand to her mouth, obviously too overcome for words.

"I remember your mother well, Micah," Adele says as she faces him. "She smelled like lavender and honey. I always thought it was such a comforting scent. It's the same one I use in my home."

I catch sight of Cheyenne's soft smile. "I never knew that's why you bought it."

"I never told you," Adele admits softly. "Lynn was my first experience with loss as a child, and I missed her very much after she left."

"Me too," Hattie says, wiping under her eyes. "I can still remember the last time she tucked me into bed. It was the last time she read to me, too. I can't believe it's almost been thirty years since that night."

"I don't believe love and loss are limited by the boundaries of time," Mama says. "Scripture says that in heaven we'll know love in full, but loss we'll never know again."

At this uncharacteristically open conversation between my family members, I press in closer to Micah, hoping to share in his steadiness and slow this incessant rhythm in my chest. But instead, the ache I felt at the ending of Mama's song has seeped into my bones. As much as I'd want to label it as grief, the tension inside me is different than with loss. Yet somehow it feels just as dire.

Micah's face remains stoic as the breeze picks up and skitters pine needles along the dirt trails beside us.

"Thank you all for sharing your memories of her with me," he says. "I won't forget this."

"It's us who should be thanking you for sharing her with us." Mama steps forward and wraps her arms around him. "You've brought the best parts of her with you."

# 26

## Raegan

Mama and Cheyenne have been practicing harmonies in the back bedroom of the bus with Adele while we've been winding our way up Highway 101. They've been going over Mama's song set to get my niece up to speed on everything she needs to know in the coming days. But as the day rolls to night and darkness descends over the road, a prickly unease begins to weave its way through my ribs. The honesty and vulnerability we experienced at the Redwoods has lingered on the bus, shifting the atmosphere to one of warmth and levity, and yet I can't seem to fight this internal chill.

Hattie's shriek in response to whatever movie she's watching with headphones nearly has me coming out of my seat, which in turn alarms the man driving beside me. Apparently I wasn't the only one lost in thought. He reaches across the gap between our seats and stills my fidgeting hands.

"I think I need to give my mom the chapters to read tonight," I blurt, as if I can't get it out fast enough.

"What?" Micah whips his head in my direction. "What brought that on?"

"I don't know, I just feel . . ."

"You just feel what?" he presses.

"Uncomfortable." *Convicted*, I mentally correct myself.

I can easily visualize the crisp white computer paper I slid underneath Micah's pillow earlier today and try to imagine what it will feel like to hand those first three chapters over to my mother.

"Where do you think that discomfort is coming from?"

"I'm not sure." Or perhaps I don't want to be sure.

"Where are the chapters now?"

"Under your pillow."

Again his eyebrows shoot up. "Is that because you want me to go down as your accomplice?" When I feel the blood drain from my face, he grips my shoulder and shakes me. "That was a joke, Sunshine. A bad one, obviously. Sorry." He glances my way again. "Why are they there?"

"I thought you might want to read them." Though he'd given me his blessing to reference his mother during our fishing excursion, I wanted his eyes on it. On all of it.

He reaches for my hand again. "I do, very much. Thank you. I've been waiting for a chance to redeem myself after falling asleep that night in Kansas mid-chapter."

I smile, though I'm certain he can tell it's a preoccupied one.

He gives my hand a squeeze. "Would it help to talk through your plan?"

There's no doubt in my mind that it would, and so I do.

Using coded words that can't be easily interpreted by Hattie, in case her movie finishes early, I tell Micah what I've been contemplating since the moment we left the Redwoods. I tell him my idea to read Mama the sample chapters in her room tonight as soon as Cheyenne exits. I tell him that I don't want to wait until after the festival and that I'll let Mama decide what should happen next.

When I finish, Micah's expression is unreadable.

"What are you thinking?" I ask.

"That you're panicking."

"Maybe a little, but aren't you the one who says we should lean in to the uncomfortable feelings when they come? Well, that's what I'm trying to do. I'm trying to do the right thing."

I rub at the inside of my wrist, and without warning, Micah rotates my arm to inspect it under the light of the rising moon. He scowls disapprovingly before bringing my irritated skin to his lips. A shiver runs through me at his sweetness.

"At some point, we need to brainstorm new ways for your body to manage stress."

As wonderful as a cure for my stress hives would be, the *we* in that sentence is definitely the most appealing part. He tips his head to the icy water bottle he retrieved from the freezer at our last pit stop. It's one of his tricks for staying alert during the longer evening stretches of driving. If he feels sleepy, he places the frozen bottle between the back of the headrest and the nape of his neck.

"Use it," he urges. "You need it more than I do."

I lay it across the irritated skin, thankful for the instant relief and the distraction it offers from my obsession of watching Mama's door.

"Did you pray about this decision, Raegan?" he asks in a low tenor.

I don't have to wonder what he means by *this decision*.

"I'm too afraid to," I practically whisper.

His voice gentles. "If the timing is right tonight, then God will give you the opportunity and the words."

Despite his diplomacy, I hear what he's not saying. Probably because it's the same fear I've been wrestling with for hours. "You think I missed my window to tell her before the festival, don't you?"

In true Micah fashion, he takes his time in answering. "I don't think that's a question I should answer for you. But at this point, I do think you need to evaluate the motives at play for why you'd be doing it tonight." He sighs. "I know you want to do the right thing, but I think you need to ask God what that is."

As hard as it is to hear, I know he's right. I also know he's likely been right all along. "How much longer do we have on the road until we stop for the night?"

We'd passed the California-Oregon border only a few hours after leaving the Redwoods, and Micah's goal for the night is to make it just over the halfway point so we can get an early start in the morning and pull into the festival by noon tomorrow.

"Maybe an hour or so more. We're getting closer to my neck of the woods now."

I wish our itinerary could have included his stomping grounds. But there's a comfort in knowing we'll be close. "How far from your home are we now?"

"From here? Probably eight hours. From the outdoor amphitheater we're headed to—five, max."

I peer out the darkened windows, wishing it was still light enough for me to make out the Pacific on the other side of the cliff.

Micah returns both hands to the steering wheel. "I've been thinking about something, too. Since the Redwoods."

The change in his tone puts me on alert. "About what?"

"I'm going to let the search go."

"*What*? But why?"

"Because I can't stop thinking about what Luella told me in Kansas—how my mom disappeared for an entire month. It could literally be anyone, Raegan. I can't let this secret consume my life."

"Okay," I say, trying to understand this drastic shift in plans. "So what if you turn it over to someone else, then? A private investigator? If you need help with the financial side of—"

"No." The word is a full stop. "I want to let it go. I felt peace today in that forest, and so much gratitude for what I do have. I think that needs to be enough."

In the quiet that follows, I resolve to meet him in this new place as long as he, too, is making this decision for the right reasons. "And have you prayed about this?"

"I have. And I have peace." He brings my wrist to his lips once more, and the sweetness of his kiss awakens every sleepy cell in my body. "Thank you for asking."

The commotion in the lounge behind us has me straining against my seatbelt to see Cheyenne cradling her guitar as my oldest sister holds the bedroom door open for her before shutting it behind them both. *God, please give me the words.*

Bolstered by Micah's hushed assurances that he'll keep them plenty distracted for me to have the alone time I need with Mama, I unclick my seatbelt and gingerly step over the center console, passing Hattie's rapid texting session on the sofa before I reach Adele and my niece near the bunks. The winding motion of the bus, combined with the mounting pressure of the moment ahead, does little to combat the rising nausea inside me. I can only hope sitting with Mama will ease it.

"Everything go well?" I ask my niece.

"Great! We even went over her duet she's doing on day two with Keith Urban. She sang his part and I did hers, it was so much fun. I still can't believe I get to sing at Watershed with her on Friday night," Cheyenne whisper-yells. "When Nonnie was describing her memory of singing on that stage with Lynn on their last tour, I was seriously getting goosebumps. I really hope I don't pass out from nerves. I wanted to keep practicing, but Nonnie said if we didn't stop for the night, she was going to require toothpicks to hold her eyelids open."

Cheyenne hugs me before passing through the lounge to put her guitar away.

"Mama's exhausted," Adele confirms, edging by me in the tight space to slide her bunk curtain open. She pulls out a fresh pair of satin pj's. "The day was more emotionally taxing than I realized. Sleep will be good for her."

"But Mama never goes to bed this early."

Adele furrows her brow. "This was hardly a typical day, Raegan. Honestly, it would be good for us to tuck in early tonight. The next few days will be packed. The energy of twenty thousand people in one space will be draining, to say the least."

"I'm sure that's true," I say, eyeing Micah's bunk where the chapters are hidden. "I'll just give her a hug good night, then."

Only as I'm about to push toward her door, I realize the headboard of Adele's bunk shares a wall with Mama's bedroom. Adele *cannot* go to bed right now. Every sensical thought in my head begins to unravel.

"Oh, I think Micah was hoping to talk to you." The words tumble out of my mouth despite the fact that I don't have the necessary logic to support them. "The jump seat's open now." I smile.

Suspicion masks her face. "What would Micah want to talk to me about?"

"Not sure." I panic-laugh, knowing that unlike me, Micah could pull this off with Oscar-worthy talent. "You never quite know with him."

Her frown deepens, and she lowers her voice. "Does this have to do with the two of you?" She peers at me in question. "I like him, Raegan, I do. Far more than I ever liked Tav. But the two of you getting involved right now would be detrimental to—"

"Whoa, what? No." I'm so caught off-guard by her assumption I can barely form words. "I can assure you Micah won't be talking to you about our relationship status."

"Then allow me to talk to *you* about it. Despite what you may believe about yourself, you are a terrible secret-keeper. It's been obvious that something's going on between the two of you since the first hour of this road trip." She rests her hand on my arm. "I can see how much he cares for you, but the last thing our family needs right now is to be targeted in yet another media frenzy. We agreed you would keep your broken engagement to Tav on the down-low, and I need it to stay that way a little longer. Luella Farrow's youngest daughter showing up at a three-day country music festival filled with twenty thousand die-hard fans, hanging all over Lynn Davenport's son, won't go unnoticed. That is clickbait material. For the next few days, our family will be watched by everyone with a social media page, not to mention all the media that's been invited to cover the event." She pats my shoulder twice and smiles. "He shouldn't be too hard for you to avoid at the venue, seeing as I'm going to need you to act as my liaison during rehearsals. It's going to be all hands on deck." She gives me a conspiratorial look. "Which also means you'll need to keep a close eye on Hattie, too."

She must think my dumbstruck expression is the equivalent of being one hundred percent on board with this plan, because she straightens and adds, "As far as Micah goes, if the two of you are still interested in each other after a few months off the road, I'd be happy to discuss what a future could look like between the two of you then."

When she turns and moseys down the hall into the restroom, I'm left reeling, yet I only have a moment to shake off my befuddlement before I lose this opportunity. I slip the manuscript from under Micah's pillow and rotate toward Mama's door. I slip inside the small but well-furnished bedroom and close the door behind me. Due to the blackout curtains, I can't see her, but I can hear her deep, rhythmic breathing. I fumble around her mattress to her bedside. She doesn't stir.

But with an impending book contract and unsanctioned tell-all on the horizon, I push myself out of compassionate daughter mode and into confession mode.

I rub her back until her breathing hitches.

"Mama?" I whisper. "It's me. Raegan."

"Hey, sugar," she answers, groggily. She rotates slightly and places a hand on mine. "I'm sorry I didn't say good night." She yawns. "You're sweet to check on me."

My heart pounds. "Mama, I . . . I was hoping to talk to you about something important."

"Are you okay?" Her grip on me tightens. "Is this about Micah?"

"No, it's not about Micah." *It's about you,* I want to cry. *It's about our family. And I'm so, so sorry I didn't tell you sooner.*

"I'm afraid my mind is mush tonight, sweetheart. Is it something that can wait until tomorrow?"

I think of the reading time required for three chapters, and the explanation I'll need to share with her on how I came to learn about the fraudulent book in the first place. And I think about the time it will take to list all the reasons why I'm certain Peter is the author behind it and how I was inspired to write something of my own to cushion the blow.

But more than all of that, I think about Micah's caution to check my motives and rely on God for the words and the timing. *Why did I wait so long?*

As I hold the comforting hand of my sleepy mama, tears gather in the corner of my eyes and leak down my cheeks in the darkened room. And instead of God providing me the words to speak, I'm overwhelmed by one thought: this isn't the way.

My desperate need for relief at the eleventh hour can't come at the expense of someone else's peace—certainly not my mama's.

I'm too late.

"Sure." A repentant tear drips off my chin onto her blanket. "It can wait until after the festival."

# 27

## Micah

There were many *oohs* and *awws* from Cheyenne and Hattie as we drove up the Pacific coastline early this morning, and then again after we turned off at Aberdeen and passed through Seattle on I-90, but the drastic scenery changes of the Columbia River Gorge in central Washington, with its yawning canyons and mammoth bluffs dotted with wind turbines and a river that cuts between it all, had them up on their feet. Everyone crowded around the windows in the front lounge to gawk and remark at the epic view. Everyone except for Raegan. She's been beside me all morning, and yet she's so lost inside her own head I'm not even sure a meteor strike could get her attention at this point.

"It kind of reminds me of the Grand Canyon," Hattie observes with awe.

"Just wait till you get on the grounds," Luella says. "They may have updated the sound system and plastered those mega screens to the side of the stage since I was last here thirty years ago, but God's creation will never need an upgrade. It's perfection."

When I pull through the main gate and show the first security guard Luella's pass, he radios our clearance to several other guards, and soon we're being ushered through a series of private gates and into a reserved parking area between the back of the main stage and a canyon with a killer view of the Columbia River. There are temporary trailers set up in a horseshoe with names of each head-lining band on the doors—the one nearest us is reserved for Luella Farrow herself.

Cheyenne slaps her cheeks and squeals. "Nonnie, can you even believe it? You're headlining *at Watershed*! You're the coolest grand-mother in the whole wide world!"

"Guess that makes you the coolest granddaughter since you're singing with me, baby girl."

The whole bus seems to buzz with her joy, sans one, whose head is tipped against her window, eyes staring out but not seeing. I sensed Raegan was struggling last night, but when her reaction to my glowing review of her first three chapters at our coffee stop this morning was little more than mild indifference, I knew she was spiraling out. Regardless of the situation surrounding this memoir, what she's written is a treasure. I have no doubt her mother will be honored by the words she's penned. I know mine would have been. Her tone is respectful, honest, vulnerable, and completely captivat-ing. It made me want more. *She* made me want more.

As soon as we're all unloaded and standing outside Old Goldie behind the massive stage of the amphitheater, Adele wastes no time in securing her family manager hat. She spends the first five minutes reciting the order of events from whatever app she's typed them on, and then she dictates every person's role *in* those events. I can't help but notice how often Raegan's name is read, while Hattie's name is mentioned only once. I have a feeling, given the way Adele eyes Raegan when she says it, that there's been a side conversation in regard to the middle sister that has ended up on Raegan's plate.

When Adele finally turns to lead her parade across the lot to meet up with their first contact, I clasp Raegan's arm and drag her around to Old Goldie's shaded side.

"*Micah*," Raegan hisses, which as far as I'm concerned is a huge step up from comatose. "What on earth are you—"

"I'm worried about you."

She looks beyond me toward the bluffs as several runaway curls blow around her face in the ever-constant wind of the Gorge. They've fallen out of whatever twisty knot she's secured on her head today, and I find the look completely irresistible. Then again, I find pretty much all of Raegan's looks irresistible. "I'm fine."

I stare harder.

"Okay, I'm not fine, but what does that matter? Either way, I have to figure out how to live with myself for the next two days and then who knows how much longer after that."

At the sound of her rapid breathing, I gentle my voice and demonstrate what I need her to stop and do. "Take a breath, Raegan."

"I don't have time to take a breath," she snaps. "Did you not hear Adele's list of to-dos for me? *This*, right here, is my actual life. The road trip has been a dream, a piece of fiction in which I get to borrow the life I always wanted under false pretenses. But at least for now, I'm back on duty."

And something about the way she says it pricks an awareness in me that wasn't there until now. "You hate this."

Even through the thin armor she's put up, I see her flinch at my words. "This is my job."

"No, this is your *family*. Those are two separate entities."

"Well, very soon I may not have either one." The uncertainty in her voice melds to something on the verge of hysterics, and soon her words are rushing out in one long stream of consciousness. "Adele will never forgive me when I tell her the truth, Micah. How could I have been so stupid to have convinced myself that I could take this on alone? You were right, I should have come out with it right away and not—"

"*Stop.*" I push in close, until her back is touching the wall of the bus and my palms are on either side of her head. I need her to see me. "Look at me, Raegan. Look at me." She's trembling all over now, and I wish we were inside this bus and not exposed to the world, but I do my best to shield her with my body from anyone milling about this part of the grounds. "You love your family—through all their quirks and faults and idiosyncrasies, you love them. I see that in you as clearly as I see the amber flecks in your green eyes right now. I don't know how they'll respond when you tell them the truth, and it would be reckless of me to speculate, but I do know that you would do anything to keep your family from harm. I've had a front-row seat to that since the day we met." Her body stills, and I bend to speak directly in her ear. "But what I don't see . . . is you accepting the same gift of compassion for yourself that you offer everyone else."

The way she presses her lips together as if to fight off a sob undoes me, and I'm seconds away from demanding she let me take her place as Adele's lackey when Adele herself rounds the bumper of the bus.

"There you—*oh.*"

I barely register the sleeve of Adele's linen blazer before I've flattened my body against Raegan's and pressed my mouth to hers, blocking her current state from her older sister's view. There's not a doubt in my mind which scenario Raegan would rather be caught in.

Adele clears her throat, and I push off the bus and straighten as if just realizing we have company, which gives Raegan the opportunity she needs to turn and wipe any remaining tears from her cheeks.

When I don't offer the oldest Farrow sister an apology for what she interrupted, it seems to throw her off balance for a minute.

"I'm pretty sure we discussed this last night, Raegan." Adele speaks to her sister's back. "Please fill Micah in."

Raegan rotates, but before she can verbalize a response, I get to it first. "Fill me in on what?"

Adele looks more than a little uncomfortable, and I'm more than okay with that. "It would be best if you two didn't show any displays of affection this weekend, given the interesting dynamics of your personal histories. There are too many eyes and ears around. We don't need any misunderstandings."

I look between the two sisters and then loop my arm around Raegan's waist. She doesn't hesitate to lean in to me. "No worries, there are no misunderstandings here."

I know I'm ruffling feathers, but the idea that Adele thinks she has this much power over her sister's love life is ludicrous.

"Unfortunately, Micah, that's not the way it works in our world," she replies curtly, to which I'm about to remind her that I'm not *in* her world and that maybe her sister shouldn't be either if she's going to continue to treat her like a glorified errand runner. But before I can start, she tosses each of us a neon-green rubber bracelet. We break apart to catch them.

"Those are your VIP access passes for your seats and backstage. They also allow you back to the private lot and into the artists' tent. Security won't let you through without it, so don't take them off."

Raegan, the peacekeeper, slips hers on and twists to face me. "How about I text you and we can meet up later?"

I study her for a moment, noting the rosy color in her cheeks has returned, as well as her steadied breaths and focused gaze. I acquiesce with a reluctant nod. "Sounds good."

When the two are several paces away, I call out to them and ask Adele if she can give us just one more minute since I have a feeling time with Raegan will be scarce until the festival starts tomorrow.

Raegan walks toward me and mouths, *What are you doing?*

"I want to read your book," I say without preamble.

Her eyes widen, then narrow into slits. "I thought you said you read it last night—"

"Not that one." I shake my head. "I have an entire day where I won't be sitting behind a steering wheel, and I'm in one of the most beautiful places on earth. I'd like to grab a chair and sit in the shade by the river and read a brilliant piece of fiction until the concert starts."

"Micah, I don't even—"

"Can you access the file from your phone?"

This stops whatever excuse she was about to give me. She nods.

"Will you send it to me? *Please?*"

She twists back to check on her impatient sister. "Only if you promise to be honest with me."

"Do you know me at all?"

She rolls her eyes, and the smile she offers is enough to ease the pinch in my chest from earlier. "Fine, I'll send it to you."

As she jogs to catch up with Adele, I watch her slip her phone from the pocket of her floral shorts. Exactly thirty seconds later, I'm holding a digital piece of Raegan's heart in my hands. If I can't be with her for the next twenty-four hours, this has to be the next best thing.

Turns out, I was right about two things. The first: Adele kept Raegan working at such a breakneck pace that apart from our texting and a brief walk of the grounds last night before we all turned in, I've barely seen her. The second: *The Sisters of Birch Grove* surpassed even my most optimistic expectations. It's exquisite. Even as misting tents went up and sound checks blared and thousands upon thousands of boot-and-hat-wearing country-music lovers entered the main gates and danced in the grass as the opening bands came out to rev up the crowds, I couldn't pull myself away from reading. Raegan's story about a family's struggle to reclaim their connection after a life-altering event sent them spinning in different directions is as provoking as it is profound.

I search for her face in the VIP section of the amphitheater as the sixth band of the day finally exits the stage. It's nearly sunset, which means the temperature will be dropping soon and the arid breeze will feel nearly as cool as the river. I see Hattie first. She waves at me with an exuberance that has me matching her infectious grin. I make my way over to her, noting the empty seat between us.

"Can you believe this?" Hattie yells, twisting from our VIP seats near the front of the stage to the impossibly huge crowd stretched out above us. "It's unreal, right?"

As I follow her gaze, the massive bowl of people sitting and standing as far as the eye can see under a rapidly changing horizon is more than my feeble mind can comprehend. It's no wonder Luella wanted to come back here or why some of the biggest stage names have called it their favorite venue, returning tens of times. I get it now. Impressive is an understatement.

She holds up her phone, capturing a video I have no doubt she will be sending to her kids.

"Did you see the amusement park rides on the back side of the grounds?"

"The what?" I yell.

"Amusement rides." She makes a circle gesture with her fingers and then pulls out her phone to show me the pictures she took of the rides she sent to her kids. "I used to love thrill rides, but Raegan loves the Ferris wheel. She used to ride that thing over and over while Mama performed at state fairs."

Warmth blooms in my chest at the thought of young Raegan. "Where is she now?"

"Adele asked her to sit with Cheyenne while Mama does her backstage meet-and-greets with fans." Hattie shrugs. "She trusts few people in our industry. There are some real creepers."

The statement bothers me—as much for the truth of it as for the questions it stirs. Questions I've vowed to put to rest, I remind myself. Hattie fills our wait time by pointing out every industry professional she knows—on stage and off, providing nuggets of backstory on each of the headliners and those up-and-coming on the country-music scene. And a small part of me can't help but feel vindicated that Tav Zuckerman's band didn't make the cut for such a festival this year.

As soon as the lights change, the roar of the crowd becomes deafening. And when Luella is announced and she struts on to the stage, I can't help but gawk at her outfit.

"It's great, right?" Hattie squeals in my ear. "I picked it out for her!"

"It's . . ." I laugh, unsure if I even have the vocabulary for what it is. "It's so *her*."

Luella's silver jumpsuit looks like she fell into a cave of diamonds and got to keep whatever she could glue to herself. Every time she shimmies across the stage in her white cowgirl boots or monologues about something or other to her fans, the crowd stands and cheers. I've seen Luella perform on YouTube clips taken by fans, I've seen her give acceptance speeches at award shows, and I've watched her sing with her daughters on multiple occasions now, but I've never seen her like this. This is Luella the Music Legend. In between old fan favorites, she's funny and charismatic and entertaining as all get-out, and I have a sudden flashback of my mother's early journals. Of those first entries where she describes Luella's natural charm that won friends over quickly—a trait that couldn't be more opposite of my mother's personality. She was always slow to trust and open up, but once she did, she hung on tight. It's no stretch of the imagination to visualize how Raegan's mother and mine would have made a good match in music and as friends. Yet ultimately, I can't imagine my mother's journey continuing on the way Luella's did. My mother lived the life she wanted—a quiet life in Chickee's house, teaching children music, serving at her church, working in her garden, loving on her husband and her two sons.

A hand grasps mine, and soon I'm staring into the eyes I've been dreaming about seeing again since we last parted ways. Raegan's curls are soft around her face, and her makeup is fresh. And I swear my heart bucks in my chest at her beauty. She says something, but it's impossible to hear over the acoustics. She tries again, lifting up on her tiptoes this time as the fabric of her long, indigo sundress swishes against my calves.

"I missed you."

Her voice has been the narrative in my head all day, telling me a story I didn't want to put down until after the final page was turned. But these words, *these words* I hear differently. I don't care about the setting or the crowd or whatever displays of affection Adele warned against. I care about Raegan. More and more with every minute we share.

I reach for her face and tilt her chin to mine and say the same to her without the use of any words at all.

When Luella introduces Cheyenne a moment later and invites her on stage with the rest of her band, the three of us lose our minds, along with the sold-out festival all around us. While Cheyenne sways beside her grandma and fingerpicks the intro to "Crossing Bridges," Luella dedicates the song to my mother and to the early years that shaped her—the good and the painful. She talks about choices and mistakes and heartache and redemption. And when she looks at her granddaughter, she talks about legacy.

Raegan and I reach for each other's hands at the same time and hold on throughout the entire tribute. The horizon behind the stage explodes into a vivid display of neon orange and pink, and as their harmonies layer and swell, I truly hope my mother can hear this from heaven.

The standing ovation goes on for so long, the sound and energy of it is like nothing I've ever experienced. I don't know how many minutes pass before Raegan tugs my hand and indicates for Hattie and me to follow her out of our row, but we do. Not even sixty seconds after we exit out the side gate and flash our wristbands to step inside the large, air-conditioned VIP tent filled with industry professionals and headliners does the applause in the amphitheater finally die.

"You've done that a time or two before," I tease.

She shrugs. "I've learned to read my mama's signals to the band. When she's getting close to walking off stage, she always moves her palm to rest over her heart. She and Cheyenne will join us here afterward for the interviews."

I scan the tent, my gaze catching briefly on the back of a man in a flashy aqua shirt telling jokes I can't hear at one of the opening bands I saw this afternoon. His guffaw sounds showy and forced, and even from here, I wish I could mute him.

There are gobs of refreshments provided, all lining the perimeter of the tent. Fresh fruit on ice, meats and cheeses, cookies and candy, and an assortment of individually packaged snacks. I note several familiar faces, thanks to Hattie pointing them out to me earlier.

In less than five minutes, Luella and Cheyenne join us in the tent, and instantly, Hattie and Raegan are all over their niece, hugging and congratulating her.

"You were incredible out there," I tell Luella as a woman in an apron asks if we'd like anything from the bar. We both order ice waters.

As Luella answers my questions about what it was like to be on that stage in comparison to other venues, a grating timbre assaults us from behind.

"Been a long time since I've seen you sing a duet, Luella. Brings back memories, although I can't say they're especially good ones."

The man behind us looks to be around Luella's age. He screams of old money and smells of imported cologne. His thick brown hair is styled in a way I'd bet is a lot to keep up at his age, as is the way his tanned skin is pulled taut everywhere but the creases around his eyes. Yet not even the best antiaging treatments can erase the reddish undertones in his neck and cheeks likely caused by the same hard liquor he's nursing now.

Despite our proximity, he doesn't seem to notice me . . . yet I can't seem to look away from him.

"Wish I could say it's a pleasure to run into you here, Troy," Luella says flatly. "But we both know that's not true."

The name I've read dozens of times over in the pages of my mother's journals surfaces, along with twenty years of her memories. *Troy Rigger.*

"Ah, come now. I just wanted to compliment your beautiful granddaughter for a job well done tonight. As far as music partners go, you've certainly upgraded since your last one." His eyes trail to Cheyenne and linger on her backside in a way that makes me want to rip that drink from his hand and shove him to the ground. "Although I suppose I shouldn't complain too much." A smirk alights his face. "Not every woman in my past played as hard to get as you did. Although, I suppose second best is better than nothing."

Every nerve ending in my body feels raw at what he could be alluding to.

Though she stands at least six inches shorter than him, Luella steps in close and drops her voice to an unfamiliar register. "If I so much as see you breathe in the same direction as my granddaughter this weekend, I will personally see to it that you lose what little standing you have left in this industry."

"Grudges are so unbecoming in a woman your age, Luella." He takes a slow sip of his drink. "Don't you think it's time the two of us called a truce?"

Luella opens her mouth to retort just as Adele taps her mother on the shoulder to inform her the interviewer is ready to roll. I don't miss the way Adele refuses to make eye contact with Troy Rigger or the way he slips out of the tent without so much as a backward glance.

And I certainly don't miss the way dread pools in my gut at the knowing sense that the answers I seek might be closer than I realized.

# 28

## Raegan

Mama and Cheyenne are seated at their last interview inside the media tent as Adele, Hattie, and I watch from the sidelines. The gal interviewing them—Tonya, with CMT—is around my age and has mentioned multiple times that this is her first time at Watershed and how she's done all sorts of extra homework on the headliners to ensure she gets an invite back. Though my mama is all smiles for the camera, I can tell by the way she stretches her calf by lifting the toe of her boot that she's ready to call it a night. She hasn't done such a high-energy show like this in ages. She must be exhausted. And she still has a couple of song collaborations set for tomorrow. My phone vibrates against my palm, and I find a text from Micah.

Micah D., bus-driving ex-therapist:

> Hey, can we take a walk? I need to process some information with you.

I can feel my brow rumple at the odd expression. Process some information?

Raegan:

Of course. We're just finishing up here. I can meet you at the bus in a few. Are you okay?

Micah D., bus-driving ex-therapist:

Not sure.

I'm still distracted by his text when I overhear the interviewer start her wrap-up.

"What our audience can't see here is what an incredible support system Luella has in her three daughters. They're all standing off camera here, waiting to dote on their mother"—she leans forward— "and likely on you, too, Cheyenne. I saw the hug your mama and aunties gave you when you came off that stage. They're proud of you."

Cheyenne grins at us. "I'm proud of them, too."

Tonya twists back to Mama. "I'm sure in a family like yours, there must be all sorts of stories, which is why I was thrilled when my producer stumbled across news of a book in the works written by your daughter. I'm a huge book nerd, and I just love a juicy origin story." She waggles her eyebrows. "Is it too early to give us a teaser?"

A sickening hush falls over the tent as my pulse slams to a stop. Mama lifts her head to scan the three of us while Cheyenne's panicked gaze darts straight to me. I feel the millisecond Adele tracks it, and every second thereafter when her gaze drills a hole through my temple.

*No. No, no, no, no, no . . .*

My mama's practiced smile holds, but there's a hesitation in her speech. "Sorry, but I'm afraid I can't say much about it."

Tonya bobs her head and glances down at her notes. "Oh, of course, well, we'll be sure to check back before it releases next year, but I know I won't be the only one adding it to my shelf."

I don't know if the interview lasts another hour or another minute because every sound mushes together to form one ugly mosh pit of noise inside my skull. I'm aware of everything and nothing and then it's over. Only, before I can utter a word in explanation, Adele cuts me off with a hard shake of her head. "Save it for the bus."

Our silent walk across the dark and dusty parking lot feels like a death march, but try as I might, I cannot make sense of how this is happening. I haven't even signed a contract yet!

The instant the five of us Farrows are closed inside the stuffy bus, Adele speaks calmly from the bottom of the inside steps. "Tell me it's not true, Raegan."

I was expecting anger—*rage*, even—but the pinch of pain in her voice momentarily freezes my own.

"Tell me the secret meeting you had with that editor wasn't you going behind your family's back. Tell me you didn't sell your mother out just so you could finally see your name printed on a book cover."

"You've been talking to an editor?" Hattie's face looks as if I just struck her across the cheek.

The tiny bag of pretzels I consumed before the show threatens to come up, and my heart is beating so violently inside my chest that it's a battle to hear myself think. "No, I mean, yes, I did meet with an editor a few weeks ago, but that meeting wasn't—"

Adele pushes away from the closed door and takes each step into the lounge at an excruciatingly slow pace. "What did you do, Raegan?"

"*Adele*," Mama admonishes. "Stop this madness right now. You know your sister would never do anything without asking my permission first. That interviewer was obviously mistaken."

Her defense of my character slices so deeply I wonder if a person can die from internal bleeding caused by shame.

"Mama," I whisper shakily, as sweat gathers as the back of my neck from lack of air circulation. "I was going to tell you everything after the festival. I've only written three chapters so far, and

I'd never sign a contract without your approval first. But my book isn't the only—"

"If you didn't sign anything, then how do you explain the media?" Adele presses. "How do you explain your name being attached to a book we knew nothing about?"

"Adele, *please*." I swing around to face her. "I was going to tell you after we left Tulsa, that day on the bus when I sat with you at the table and you told me you didn't want any more distractions—"

She jerks back. "Is that your defense? To blame *me* for your disloyalty?"

"Stop." Cheyenne pushes forward. "Auntie Rae is writing this book because she's trying to help us—listen to her."

Adele's mouth smacks open, and for a full three seconds her gaze drags between my niece and me. The gutted look on her face sears into my conscience. "You confided your secret book to my *daughter*?"

Mama's eyes are glassy when she lowers herself onto the sofa. "Help us understand what you've done, sweetheart."

Heat builds behind my eyes. "The week before we left, I found out from a trusted friend who works in publishing that there's a book being released about Mama. The book deal was signed this spring, and the author has gone to great lengths to protect their anonymity, including using a ghostwriter. I read their sample chapters."

Hattie plops down on the arm of the sofa Mama's seated on with an expression I've seen far too many times over the last year. The same expression I've feared ever since Chip confirmed the unsanctioned book was likely the work of someone harboring a vendetta against our family.

I fight to speak with a confidence I don't feel. "From the little I was able to read, the proposed book synopsis includes some unflattering history about Mama and the label that has never been shared publicly. Including . . ." I hesitate. "A claim to fraud and the mismanagement of company finances. That's the reason I'm writing a book in my own words—to create a diversion by offering fans a credible narrative to distract from the fake one. Something real and true that honors Mama and our family history at the label."

"Let me read them," Adele demands.

"What?"

She holds out her hand. "Let me read the sample chapters so I can figure out who's behind this. There can't be too many options considering ninety-nine percent of the people with access to our family have signed NDAs. I'll figure it out and put a stop to it."

"I don't have them," I admit.

The furrow in her brow deepens. "What do you mean you don't have them?"

"They were sent to me in confidence, and I promised to delete them as soon as I read them. My editor friend could lose his job if—"

"You're worried about an editor losing his job? *Raegan, wake up!*" Adele grips her head. "Do you have any clue how damaging something like this could be to everything we've worked so hard for? No, of course you don't. Because you aren't the one burdened with the financial future of the company."

"Adele," Mama cuts in. "You need to calm down and think about your blood pressure."

Adele rips off her blazer and tosses it on the chair. "My blood pressure is low on the priority list at the moment. If I don't squash these rumors immediately, our deal could be off."

Hattie leans forward uneasily. "What deal?"

Adele and Mama exchange a look. But it's clear from Adele's tight-lipped expression that's all we're getting from her.

Mama turns to us. "Sit down, girls."

"No. Do not sit down." Adele stubbornly remains standing while Cheyenne and I take a seat on the opposite sofa. "Mother, you *cannot* talk about this. We are still in negotiations. You signed paperwork."

Mama ignores the warning. "Two years ago, I asked your sister to pursue partnering with an investment firm for the label." At our shocked faces, she raises a palm. "It was my decision, and I would make the same decision again if given the chance. The load is too much for Adele to carry on her own. She found a private investor about eighteen months ago, but sadly we lost them due to . . . family matters."

"Due to *Peter*," Adele corrects sharply, and she seems to miss the way Hattie winces. "Don't protect him. His actions were reprehensible, and he put the company and our family in a precarious position for far too long. No business or company would touch us with our tanking ratings and our top-selling artists pulling out left and right, thanks to Francesca. The label was on the verge of bankruptcy, and losing that deal almost forfeited everything Daddy worked so hard for. If not for the resurrection of 'Crossing Bridges,' we would have lost it . . . and likely more. Those royalties have paid off a massive amount of debt and will float us for now, but not forever. Which is why we're still in negotiation with a new partner." She turns back to me. "So, no, we don't need a diversion, Raegan. What we need is to destroy whoever is stupid enough to think they can go up against us and win. This could likely be our last chance at securing a partner willing to agree to our terms and keep the label in our family name."

It takes everything in me to force the words past my shame. "I know who's behind it."

"You do?" Hattie asks, her voice as thin as my own.

I don't want to face my family. I don't even want to face myself.

Adele zeroes in on me. "You've *known* who it is, and you said nothing?"

Tears climb my throat. "I was only trying to protect . . . people." *Hattie* is who I don't say.

"*Who is it?*" Adele demands in a voice that sounds dangerously close to breaking.

I swallow back my tears, knowing that once it's out, everything will change.

I look at Hattie, and despite the stuffy air inside this bus, she's wrapped her arms around herself in anticipation. She's always been so much smarter than she's given credit for. Of course she's figured it out by now.

"I'm so sorry, Hattie." I say keeping my gaze locked on my middle sister. "But I believe it's . . . Peter."

The silence that follows is so isolating that when I finally dare a glance at Adele, it's the first time I see more fear in her eyes than anger. Whatever relief I hoped would come once the truth was finally out and all my secrets were revealed was a myth. This feeling is ten times worse.

"Why do you think it's him?" Mama's question warbles.

"Because he's the only one who makes sense with what I read. I didn't want it to be him, but who knows your stories of the early years well enough to write them? It started at your camp days with Lynn, and by the third chapter, it was the story of your real wedding date with Daddy and how we celebrated every year with hot chicken and a family pool party that ended with Daddy reciting his wedding vows to you. It was both specific and personal. Peter had access, and he has motive."

Hattie bursts up from the sofa and runs down the steps and out the bus before any of us can stop her. I stand to go after her, but Adele holds up her palm and tells Cheyenne to go after her instead.

The minute my niece is out the door, Adele looks at me as if she doesn't even know who I am.

"How could you keep something like this a secret from us for weeks? Do you really have such low regard for our family—for *me*?"

"No, I—"

"You should have told us the second you caught wind of this."

"I should have, you're right, and I'm sorry, but I'm not the only one who's been keeping secrets," I push. "I had no idea about a partner acquisition."

"The difference, Raegan, is that the secrets I keep are for the betterment of the whole family, while yours are only to better yourself."

Pain radiates through my chest as her words puncture and burrow.

Mama won't look at me, and Adele won't look anywhere else.

"I thought I could help," I try one last time. "I still think what I'm

writing can help. Peter is estranged, his word is tainted and marred."
I press a hand to my heart. "But I'm Mama's daughter."

"And yet for weeks that daughter has been sneaking around behind our backs, spending her free time writing a book while she
knows our true enemy is out there plotting an attack with his own."
She straightens and shakes her head. "Well, congratulations, Raegan. I hope your dream was worth it, because it likely just cost the
family thirty years in the recording business."

# 29

## Micah

I've spent the last thirty minutes in recon mode—tracking Troy through the grounds, taking note of where his trailer is located and where his tour bus is parked, and trying not to be sick at the thought of what could be true. I'm finally on the way back to the tour bus to find Raegan when I see her bolt in the opposite direction.

The odd sight causes me to hustle, and soon I'm jogging through the moonlit grounds, following Raegan outside the private gate behind the stage and uphill to the main area. There are still hordes of people gathered everywhere I look, dancing and laughing and carrying on as if it's still early in the evening when it's after eleven. I can barely make out the shape of the phone pressed to her ear, and I have no clue who she'd be talking to at this hour or who would even be able to hear her in all of the commotion.

When I finally catch up on the back side of the grounds, she's inside a misting tent that's now a shelter from the wind. Her blotchy, tear-stained face sets off an internal alarm, and I stand to the side and watch her pace while the tent canvas beats against the metal poles. Her hair has fallen from its twisted glory, and she swipes at the curls that stick to her damp cheeks as she speaks to whomever is on the other end of that conversation. Within five seconds I realize it's Chip.

Concern heightens my senses as I put two and two together. Her family must know about the tell-all.

When she sees me, her pacing stops, and less than a minute later her call with Chip ends and her face crumples.

"You told your family?"

"No." Her voice is strained, stressed. "The interviewer told them. Some producer got wind of my book deal with Fog Harbor and asked my mother about it tonight, in front of my whole family and whatever viewers and fans will tune in."

"Wait, how did the media get wind of it?" I'm struggling to understand. "You haven't even signed a contract yet."

"I don't know." She lifts up her phone. "Chip swears it didn't come from his publishing team. He said they're all rock-solid individuals he'd bank his career on." She releases an exasperated cry. "I only needed *one* more day!"

Raegan continues to speak, but due to the raucous diehards who've begun a conga line to some twangy '90s song blaring from a personal stereo system, I haven't a clue what she's saying. The line grows in popularity rapidly, and soon people are grabbing onto strangers.

I twist to scan the massive grounds for a better place for us to converse when I see the rotating neon lights of the Ferris wheel and the empty passenger cars.

"Come on." I grab her hand and haul her through the admissions gate.

"Really, Micah? My family just imploded. The last thing I want to do is ride a Ferris wheel."

"It's this or being forced against our will to join the conga-line people. You choose."

She jerks her head toward the ride, and a few seconds later I lift our joined hands to flash our green wristbands at the operating attendant. We climb into the passenger car without delay and secure the lap bar. We're nearly twenty feet off the ground when the sound below fades enough for her to speak again in a normal volume.

"It was horrible, Micah. Adele is . . . " She shivers in her dress, and I pull off my sweatshirt and drape it across her bare shoulders. "I've only ever seen her this mad one other time—at Peter."

I think back to all the stories I've heard about Peter's transgressions against the Farrow family and the label and try to guess at which one caused the biggest stir for Adele specifically. "When he won the lawsuit against Farrow Music?"

"No, when Hattie spiraled after he chose to stay with Francesca and moved out of their house. His betrayal was so traumatic—it rippled through our entire family." Raegan drops her head in her hands. "And now I'm the betrayer."

I study her profile in the moonlight. "That's a strong word. You don't actually believe that, do you?"

"Who cares what I believe—*they* believe it." She twists in the car, and I notice then we're almost at the top of our first rotation. "Adele accused me of putting my dreams above the family and jeopardizing a business transaction that could cost the future of the company, and Hattie couldn't even face me once I told them how I'd determined Peter was the author behind the tell-all. And Mama . . . " Her chin quivers violently. "She was actually defending me until—until the ugly truth came out." A stiff breeze rocks the passenger car as we halt near the top of the wheel. Raegan reaches out to grip the safety bar. "I have no idea how to fix this."

When we first embarked on this road trip, I might have been inclined to believe that was true—that Raegan didn't have the communication tools she needed to assert herself into the polarizing dynamics and circumstances of her family. But I don't believe that now.

Because I spent an entire day reading the secret inner workings of her mind and heart.

"Yes, you do," I speak the words with a gentle conviction that gets her attention.

As the Ferris wheel begins its descent back down, she swipes her hair back and narrows her eyes at me. "I'm not up for a therapy session tonight."

"I'm not the therapist here. You are." I reach into my pocket, pull out my phone, and tap on the screen until a title page for *The Sisters of Birch Grove* appears. "You know exactly what to do with your family. You wrote it all in your book."

She looks from the screen to me. Twice. "That's fiction, Micah."

"And yet it's real, too." I hold up the phone, her words shinning as bright as the stars above us. "These words are *inspired*, Raegan. In that last scene with the sisters—after all they went through in those hard years—you wrote what living in truth is supposed to look like." I tick them off one by one. "You spoke of establishing healthy boundaries, of open communication, of keeping short accounts, of setting honest and appropriate expectations, of having hard conversations with the hope of reconciliation."

"The truth is already out," she pushes back, her tone desperate, "and now we're more fractured than ever."

"That's hardly the only truth you've been holding back."

She flinches at my statement. "You've known me for two weeks."

"Yes, but I'm an observer. The same as you."

"Fine." She crosses her arms. "Tell me what you think I've been holding back."

I take a breath and allow her to do the same. And then, I tell her the truth she's asked for even if she doesn't want it. "You cower around Adele as if you have no stake or voice inside your own family. And you practically shape-shift in order to placate Hattie, and you treat your mother as if she's a child in need of validation and guidance when it's actually the other way around. You've taken on the role of peacekeeper in your family, and yet I'm thoroughly convinced that none of you actually has much peace at all. Especially you."

She falls back against her seat, swinging our car as we rock above the shadowy outlines of bluffs and canyons. But she says nothing.

"Peace isn't passive, Raegan. It's proactive. The way I see it, you've been a passive character in your own story for far too long."

"That's not fair."

"I agree, it's not fair." I tap my phone screen and illuminate her book in my palm again. "Because God doesn't give us talents He doesn't intend for us to use with Him and *for* Him. You reminded me of the same just three days ago in the Ruby Mountains. You're a writer, and yet you've spent far more energy wishing you could hide behind a pen name than realizing that you are exactly who God intended you to be. He not only knew your name and the family you were going to be born into, but all the atypical logistics in between. And even still, He saw fit to give you a storyteller's imagination." I pause and wait till she meets my gaze. "Freedom and peace work in tandem. And you won't experience either until you're finally willing to be transparent with yourself and others."

She turns her face away from me, but not before I catch the glint of tears on her cheeks. We remain in silence for the rest of the ride down, and by the time the attendant unlocks our safety bar and opens the door for us, the conga line has moved on.

As I walk Raegan back to Old Goldie, she tracks each location of her family members on her app. Hattie is the only one aboard the bus; the others appear to be staying in Luella's trailer. As much as I want to shoulder her pain and ease the burden she carries, I'd be doing her no favors to remove it completely. Raegan has avoided the hard truths for so long that her only real option now is to face them head-on.

I spot the VIP tent in the middle of our lot, where I'll likely be facing my own hard truths very soon.

"You're not coming inside?" Raegan asks.

"Not quite yet." I step in to brush a kiss on her cheek. "I think you and Hattie could use some privacy tonight." I can see the protest in her eyes, but she says nothing. Perhaps she knows what I do: that some battles need to be fought alone. "Don't wait up."

My eyes focus on the back of my target as I cross the dusty lot to a bar that will likely remain open until the last VIP has decided to call it a night. In this case, Troy Rigger. It's such a sad cliché that the same obnoxiously loud man I observed in this tent after the concert—the one surrounded by newbies looking for validation—is now here alone, staring into the half-drunk glass of a dirty martini.

The arrogant way he taps the bar to ask for another from the unlucky barkeep on duty speaks of a man who has rarely been told no. And given the long list of A-list artists he's signed over the years—including Luella and my mother—he hasn't. The fist in my gut clenches hard as I stand outside the opening, roll my shoulders back, and exhale a prayer for a kind of help I can't even name but also know I need.

When I take the stool at the end of the short bar, I don't make eye contact with him. Instead, I order a drink and wait. The worst thing I can do is appear desperate for his company. The only thing more promising to start up a conversation than flattery is curiosity. And seeing as he mentioned how much he enjoys the hard-to-get types, perhaps this will be my angle, too. I keep my eyes straight ahead on the plastic window, avoiding the distraction of a cell phone or small talk with the barkeep. I just sip on my gin and tonic and feel the burn all the way down to my gut.

Not thirty seconds later, Troy bites.

"First time at Watershed?" he asks.

Slowly, I slip out of my self-induced coma and look at him as if I've just noticed there was another human being here. "Oh, uh, yeah. You too?"

He frowns like he doesn't quite know if he should take offense to that or not. *Good.* "I've been taking artists here every year since it started." He holds out his hand to me, and I oblige him. "Troy Rigger."

"Oh, are you a bus driver, then?" I ask without any of the irony I feel.

He blinks. "No. I own a recording label in Nashville. Rigger Records."

I nod as if that might ring a bell, then turn back to my drink.

"What do you do?"

"Therapist," I say. "Here with some clients."

"A traveling shrink, really?" He sounds genuinely surprised and leans in. "Anybody I know?"

"Probably." I take another sip of my drink, wishing I could have ordered a tonic minus the gin, and shrug. "Confidentiality."

"Of course." He bobs his head as if he's the picture of integrity. Doubtful. "After all my time in the industry, I could be an honorary therapist." He barks a laugh, and I offer him the tiniest smile in return. It's all he needs. "I have more dirt on most of these headliners than they have in their gardens." He points at the tent wall to indicate the tour buses and trailers on the other side of it. "I'm a steel trap, though. If there's one thing I've learned, it's how interconnected everyone is in this industry. I swear, that whole six degrees of separation statistic doesn't apply to musicians in Nashville. Everybody is related to somebody."

Every thought in my head empties to make room for a series of new ones I don't want to accept.

I force myself to rotate in my stool just enough for him to feel validated by my hard-won approval and so I can look him in the eye. It's quite possibly the most difficult eye contact I've ever made. Because I see it. Even without a proper DNA test. I have his eye shape and his nose and even the widow's peak my brother always teased me about growing up.

Turns out, it's hereditary.

"Do you live in Nashville?" I ask.

He tips his head and grins with pride. "Born and raised."

346

"Is there a family waiting for you back home?"

It's the first time he's hesitated, and I wonder if it's because he's trying to find the right answer, the one that will impress me. Only, that's impossible.

"Bachelor." He forces another harsh chuckle and lifts his glass to tap mine. "By choice," he adds. "You?"

"Currently, but I hope that's not the case for long." Raegan wrapped in my hoodie before she climbed the bus steps is the most welcome image in my mind.

"May I give the therapist some free advice?"

"Please do."

"Women bring more problems than they're worth." He tips back the end of his martini, then sucks off the olive to bite on the toothpick. "Especially in my industry."

"You never married?" I ask, as if he's the most interesting person I've come across.

"Could have, maybe even thought about it once or twice, but ultimately, I've always been more of a test driver than a car owner, if you get my drift." His smile is repulsive. "When I was your age, the only days my bed wasn't warmed by a woman of my choosing was when I agreed to go to her place."

It takes everything in me to look impressed by this abhorrent brag. "Maybe it's the line of work I'm in," I start, "but I can rarely find time to take a woman out to dinner."

He leans in close and examines my face. "You're a sharp-looking guy. Stop worrying about dinner dates and start asking yourself what you can provide that nobody else can." At my look of confusion, he breaks it down for me. "For me, it was often women who were decent singers who needed some insider tips. Vocal coaching recs, exclusive invites to private clubs, extra hours in the recording studio, even a little chemical pick-me-up from time to time, if you know what I mean."

"What? Like drugs?" The question comes out like a reflex I can't control.

"It was no big deal back in the day." He shrugs. "Uppers were easy to snag. Every chick I knew was on a little speed to keep skinny. You know how it is with women. Times haven't changed too much, really."

Rage flashes hot in my periphery, and it takes every shred of willpower to keep a rein on my impulses as the realization sets in. This man supplied my mother with black-market diet pills for twenty years. Twenty years that caused irreversible damage to her kidneys. Kidneys that were too far gone to be saved by the time she entered into renal failure six months before she died.

Troy spits his toothpicks onto the bar napkin in front of him and claps me on the arm as he pushes away from the bar. "Figure out what you can offer a woman, and you'll enjoy all the perks of a relationship without the hassle of being tied down."

I force myself not to go after him, to stay seated and count to a hundred. Two hundred. Three hundred. All the while, I can't erase the mental image of my mother as an innocent young woman starting out in this industry. The same way Cheyenne Farrow is doing now. Why hadn't someone warned her about men like Troy? She needed a father in her life.

Only, my mother's father was a monster.

And as it turns out, so is mine.

# 30

## Raegan

I bolt upright in my bunk at the pounding on the bus door. I expect Micah to intercept before I can get there first, but his bunk curtain is open, his bed empty. My pulse kicks up speed as the insistent pounding continues. My sleepy morning brain is too foggy to glance through the window first, but even if I had, I would have been just as surprised to see Adele waiting on the other side of it. Given the state of things between us, I figured I was months out from being summoned by her directly.

I've barely unlatched the door when she pushes herself inside. "Where's Hattie?"

"Asleep." What other answer could there be at this hour? Hattie's been in her bunk since I got in from the Ferris wheel with Micah last night. And to my knowledge, she hasn't come out.

Adele wastes no time in striding back to Hattie's bunk and rousing her, demanding she join us in the front lounge immediately. She stumbles toward us a moment later, tightening her robe around her waist and shielding her eyes.

"Mama and Micah are gone," Adele announces.

It's such a strange combination of words to be strung together that they don't feel real. "Gone where?"

She shakes the paper in her fist. "According to the note she left, to Idaho."

"*What?*" Hattie and I screech in unison.

"Apparently our mother was on the phone arranging all sorts of plans with Jana last night while I slept on the sofa in her trailer." She thrusts the paper in our direction. "Here."

I take it as Hattie and I push together to read.

*To my darling daughters three:*

*In light of last night, I've expedited our final destination to today. While I imagined momentary tensions flaring up here and there, I see now how blind I've been to the much deeper issues among us. And for that, I surely share some blame.*

*As much as I've desired to leave a legacy to the world through my music, it is nothing compared to the legacy I've desired to leave to my daughters. It's for this reason I'm asking you to meet me in a special place I pray will outlast my greatest hit.*

*Micah has graciously agreed to be my driver for the day, and I've arranged for Cheyenne to stay back and rehearse with the band in my place until I'm back for the 8:00 p.m. call time tonight. Her daddy will be arriving to the Gorge by lunchtime to see her in concert and to watch over her in our absence. You'll find a blue Jeep waiting for the three of you girls in the VIP lot. Cheyenne has the keys for you. It will take you approximately three hours to arrive.*

*See you soon.*

*I love each of you dearly,*
*Mama*

There's an address penned at the bottom of her letter, but even after I read the whole thing through a second time, it makes little sense.

"She just . . . left us here?" Hattie asks, sounding as bewildered as I feel.

"Obviously, she's still reeling from Raegan's forced confession last night," Adele expresses with a notable lack of eye contact. "I've already tried to call their phones. No answer."

I ignore her jab and immediately close myself into the bathroom to freshen up and do a quick change of clothes. When I emerge, both my sisters are still discussing what to do, as if the letter hadn't been clear.

"I'm ready," I say, swiping my sunglasses and purse off the counter and a fruit smoothie from the fridge. I haven't had time to analyze much this morning, but I'm certainly not going to stay here and wallow in the bus all day while Mama and Micah are out somewhere waiting for us. "I'll get the keys and meet you both at the rental."

They both turn to look at me as if my suggestion is nothing short of outrageous, which is why I decide to make another one. "I can drive us unless one of you would rather—"

"I'll drive," Adele cuts in, just as I knew she would. "Hattie, meet us out there in ten. The sooner we get to the end of whatever this is, the sooner I can fly myself and my daughter back home to Tennessee."

To no one's surprise, there is zero conversation in the Jeep between us girls as Adele drives this unfamiliar stretch of highway into an equally unfamiliar state. Given the sibling pecking order, Hattie's riding shotgun while I'm in the back seat, and since the only sound in the vehicle is a radio station that's primarily static, my mind has plenty of time to replay the events of last night and plot them into a story—the whole of it.

Though I'm tempted to stop my mental outline at Adele's fury and Hattie's refusal to look at me after I revealed Peter's latest scheme, I continue onward. I replay the scene in my mind, watching myself

351

load into a passenger car on a Ferris wheel with Micah and hearing the convicting words he spoke loop around my heart:

*"You know exactly what to do with your family. You wrote it all in your book."*

*"You've been a passive character in your own story for far too long."*

*"Freedom and peace work in tandem. And you won't experience either until you're finally willing to be transparent with yourself and others."*

Tears burn behind my eyes as I surrender my heart to this difficult truth and to the God who is not afraid of the secrets I've kept, or the masks I've hidden behind for years.

Unbidden, I picture the conclusion of my fiction novel: three sisters hugging it out under a night sky full of stars, vowing to fight *for* each other and not against. It's an ending that seems so unrealistic compared to where my own siblings and I are currently at with one another, and yet *The Sisters of Birch Grove* is not the only ending I've read recently. There's another story with eerily similar themes about the complexities of sisterhood. One with a bittersweet ending that didn't come until after thirty years of silence and regret.

When we veer off the highway onto an old country road, I stare out the window to see a patchwork of green—from trees, to grass, to forested mountains and lush valleys. It's passing by me in such a blur, but the longing I feel to stop and set up camp here is nothing short of overwhelming. To know the kind of freedom Micah speaks about at a soul-deep level feels impossible, and yet I want to believe it can be mine, too.

If I'm willing to be honest.

"Please pull over, Adele," I say, leaving no time to second-guess.

Hattie's head swings around the passenger seat, and Adele flicks her gaze to me in the rearview mirror.

"We only have an hour to go," she refutes. "I'd rather wait until we're—"

"It's an emergency." I don't know how my voice doesn't tremble at these words or what will happen after I step outside this Jeep, but I do know this is where the hiding has to end for me. And, I can only hope, for all of us.

Adele pulls off to the side and taps her emergency flashers. When I step onto a patch of lush green grass and wildflowers, I face the Jeep and study the two of them through the windshield.

*Please help me, God. Meet us here.*

Adele and Hattie glance at each other and then crack their windows.

"Raegan, what on earth are you doing?" Adele asks.

"I want to talk."

"Then why did you get out of the car?"

"Because I want to talk out here, the three of us."

She must see I'm willing to wait her stubbornness out, because Adele is the first to unclick her seatbelt.

"This is ridiculous," I hear her mutter to Hattie from behind the protection of the glass.

Begrudgingly, they step out of the car and assess me. Adele does, anyway. Hattie hasn't made more than 2.3 seconds' worth of eye contact with me since last night.

I meet them halfway. "I haven't been honest with either of you."

Adele narrows her eyes at me as if I left my frontal lobe back on the tour bus. "We're aware."

I shake my head. "You're not, actually; there's a lot more to it than the events of the last two weeks."

Adele holds out her palms and begins to head back to the Jeep. "I can't do this again, Raegan. I physically cannot do another big round of—"

"I screwed up by not telling you what I found out as soon as I heard it. I was wrong. And I was scared. And I'm truly, deeply sorry for everything my actions may have jeopardized for you personally and for the label you've worked so hard to save since Daddy died. I know you're furious with me, but I hope, in time, you can forgive me."

The raw apology hangs between us, and it must be enough to make her reconsider going back to the Jeep because she turns around.

I look at my middle sister. "And I'm sorry, Hattie, for convincing myself I was protecting you from more hurt when really I was protecting myself by avoiding a conversation I was too afraid to have with you."

I gesture to them both. "I don't want this to be where our sisterhood fractures beyond repair. And it could be, if things continue on like this." I expect some pushback from Adele, but she only stares at me. "I always believed some big scandal was the reason for Mama and Lynn's breakup." I shake my head. "But I read her journals. Twenty years of friendship and music were destroyed due to unresolved resentments."

I press my lips together and draw from a strength that is not my own. "The truth is, I've been carrying around a lot of unspoken resentments, too. I've resented being a full-time employee of the family, where every boundary line seems blurred. I've resented that my relationship with my oldest sister is only defined by her role as my boss. I resent the lack of autonomy I have over my schedule—that how I spend my time, and who I spend that time with, and what I spend that time on has been dictated for me in the name of *the family business*. And I resent that I've been asked to minimize the thing I'm most passionate about by the person whose opinion I've always respected most." I purse my lips. "But not nearly as much as I resent myself for not speaking up sooner.

"I've spent far more time worrying about how you see me, Adele, than asking God what He sees. I convinced myself that my usefulness to this family was synonymous with my value. And I actually believed that creating a secret identity and writing under a pen name would be a better alternative than standing my ground." I search the unsettled expression on my sister's face. "Sometime in the years since Daddy died, I've lost the ability to separate what it means to be a daughter and sister from what it means to be a Farrow." A tear slips out from the corner of my eye. "And I desperately want to find that again, which is why I won't be working for the family any longer." My lips quiver. "I'm quitting, effective immediately."

I expect Adele to meet my statement with a rebuke—tell me how immature and self-centered I am to bail on the family after all the heartache I caused last night—only, Adele doesn't look ready for a fight. She looks . . . tired. Weary. Broken.

"You may not believe this, and I suppose I've given you little reason to," Adele says in a voice that hardly sounds like her own, "but I've never envied you more than I do right now. And I've envied your life for decades." She meets my stunned gaze. "I've resented your freedom as the youngest child, as well as the differences in our responsibilities to the family. Perhaps that's why I felt justified in pushing you as hard as I did once you moved back home." She swallows and rubs her lips together as if uncertain where to go next. "That separation you speak of, between family life and work life, that's felt like a fantasy to me since Daddy gave me a desk at the label." When her voice trembles, she clears her throat. "I thought it might finally be possible when this investor opened negotiations with us, but I never counted on it. Not in the same way Michael and Mama did."

Guilt presses down on me at the repercussions my actions have had on our family. "Adele, I'm—"

"No, listen." She cuts me off. "I'm not saying you weren't wrong for keeping the book a secret, but I was equally as wrong for how I handled it. I took my stress and disappointment out on you last night, the same way I've been doing since Peter showed his true colors." She hesitates. "I'm sorry. It's something I need to change. My cardiologist has made that plenty clear."

"Your cardiologist?" Hattie's distress over the word mirrors my own.

Adele blows out a deep exhale and then stretches her neck side to side. "Michael's the only one who knows this, mostly because I couldn't risk it getting out during our search for an investor, but also because he was the one to drive me to the hospital after I collapsed in our home office. The doctors ruled the episode as a minor heart attack, but I'm at risk for another one if I don't make some changes."

"Adele!" Hattie slaps a hand to her mouth, her eyes filled with horror. "When was this?"

"Shortly after Peter won the lawsuit and we were losing artists left and right. I was up almost every night, crunching numbers and trying to figure out a way to save the label from bankruptcy for a second time. Michael's been on me to step down, constantly telling me to think of Cheyenne and Mama and you girls—and I do! But Daddy trusted *me* to manage his legacy. I don't want to fail him." She swallows whatever emotion is trying to rise. "So I've added natural supplements, prepackaged, nutrient-dense meals, and a watch with a step tracker, hoping it will be enough to offset the burden until we find the right partner. *If* we find them."

"And Mama doesn't know?"

Adele nods gravely. "She knows I'm concerned about my blood pressure—but I haven't told her why. Not after what happened to Daddy."

Icy fingers of fear walk my spine. I desperately wish I could offer her a solution, but before I can even ask her another question about the investor, Hattie starts crying. At first, it's a few tears, and then it's an onslaught.

Adele and I look from her to each other.

"Hattie, I see my cardiologist every other month, you don't—"

"No." She sobs before she buries her face in her hands. "That's not . . . why I'm . . . upset."

"Okay," Adele says, patting her on the shoulder awkwardly.

"I'm the author!" she wails. "The one working with the ghost-writer. It's not Peter, it's me." She slaps a hand to her chest. "I'm the reason the partnership is at risk, Adele, not Raegan. She didn't know."

The sun seems to make a full revolution around the earth with how long it takes me to comprehend what she's saying. *Hattie's the anonymous author of the tell-all?*

"But why? Why would you ever agree to write something like that?"

"Because I can't lose my kids!" She swipes under her eyes with the hem of her cotton shirt. "After Peter won the wrongful termination case, he threatened to take my kids away from me permanently. He said he has all sorts of ammunition he can use against me when the time is right, including my struggle with depression. I was scared— *I'm still scared.*" The tears come again. "He left me with the mountain of debt he was incurring long before his affair came out." She wipes her face on her sleeve. "I have nothing to my name outside of what's left in my trust from Mama, and most of that is what I used to buy Peter out of half of every asset we owned together. I've sold jewelry, clothing, shoes, furniture, designer luggage. I even mortgaged the house three months ago to pay down the lines of credit he took out before he filed for divorce."

"Oh, Hattie," I say as a sudden memory of her declined credit card that night in Tulsa surfaces to mind. "I had no idea things were so bad."

She blows out a shaky breath. "Peter's story was everywhere, and for a long time I took Adele's advice and ignored the reporters. But not long after he threatened to fight me for full custody of the kids, an editor from Willow House emailed. She convinced me to call her back and take advantage of this rare opportunity to piggyback on Mama's recent resurgence in the spotlight. The advance they offered more than covered what I needed for a retainer to secure a new team of divorce lawyers who specialized in custody cases. After they agreed to take my case, I agreed to the book deal. The editor assured me it would be easy since I would just be recounting the memories and stories Mama always told us to a ghostwriter. She told me she'd just need a few exclusive details and a few family secrets—true or not—in order to get the book to sell. I never imagined they would spin it as a tell-all or how much they'd hound me for more and more personal information. At one point they told me I didn't have enough content to fill the word count we negotiated, and if I didn't provide them with more, I would be in breach of contract. That's when I told them the stories Peter told me about the history Daddy had once confided in him about the label—both with Farrow Music and TriplePlay."

Her confession hovers like a cloud above us, and neither Adele nor I speak for several seconds. Adele turns and paces in the gravel silently. It's clear she's struggling. I am, too.

"Why didn't you tell us Peter was threatening to take the kids?" I ask.

"Because I knew what he'd already cost the label. I couldn't go back to Adele and ask for more money when I knew the only reason we were in this mess was because I pushed Daddy to hire him in the first place." Hattie waits for Adele to turn and face her. "You were right about him from the start, and I didn't listen. You were always the one getting special attention for being smart and wise and savvy while I've been the one causing problems. For once, I wanted to feel chosen. Peter made me feel that way . . . at least, he did at first." Her face is pained, and she sucks in a breath. "I'm so sorry. I tried to get out of this contract—I called Willow House as soon as we left the Redwoods that day and told her I wanted out of the deal, and that I'd find a way to repay the advance even if I have to make payments for the next five years. But she said it's binding. No matter what move I make, the people I love suffer for it."

"Oh, Hattie." Adele's voice trembles, her expression chastened. "Do you really believe I hold you accountable for Peter's transgressions against us?"

My sister doesn't look up as she answers. "I don't know why you wouldn't."

I watch Adele's face crumple at that, her eyes glassy and her voice broken. "Then I'm an even bigger failure than I realized. I don't blame you, Hattie. And I'm sorry if I've made you believe otherwise." It's several seconds before she can compose herself long enough to speak again. "I'd cash out every asset I own before I'd let Peter take your kids away from you."

"Me too," I say. "You're not alone in this, Hattie. You have us and you have Mama."

I wrap my arms around Hattie at the same time Adele moves in. When her arms enfold over top of mine, I openly cry at the realization that this is the first sisterly embrace I can remember since the three of us stood at our Daddy's graveside. And with everything in me, I hope that what started here on this road will be the first chapter of a new story together.

# 31

## Micah

Of all the ways I could have imagined starting this day, it wouldn't have been opening the bus door to find Luella dressed and ready for the day before the sun had so much as winked a hello, saying, *"You up for an adventure, handsome?"* And yet here I am, driving her to my hometown in a rental car to the center of Idaho's panhandle without any clue as to why I'm taking her there other than she asked me to.

The car has been quiet for some time now, but not for lack of words—rather, because of them. Despite the abruptness of my wake-up this morning, I had the presence of mind to grab Raegan's sample chapters of the memoir. Even if nothing came of them in the end, her beautiful prose deserved to be read by the person who inspired it.

Out of my peripherals, I monitor the hand Luella keeps moving between her heart and mouth as if she can't decide if she's more touched than she is speechless. She's on the third chapter now, and I know the exact moment she reaches the part about Russell's proposal to marry him in secret because her eyes start leaking faster than she can swipe them. I hand her the unused napkin from our coffee run at oh-dark-thirty and she blots, blots, blots until it's soaked and shredded. When she finally lowers the pages to her lap, it takes her a good two minutes to compose herself enough to speak.

"I didn't realize how . . . how incredibly talented my daughter is," she says. "She captured the stories I've told her with such vivid detail and care. And considering how Raegan never met your mother, I swear I could feel Lynn's presence every time Raegan included her in a scene." She lifts the pages again and holds them out as if they're found treasure. "For fear of sounding vain, I wish I could keep reading."

"You should tell her that," I say, careful not to overspeak. "I feel the same way about her writing. She has a gift." She *is* a gift.

Luella's gaze remains on me. "You care for her."

"I do," I admit without hesitation. "She's a special person."

Luella nods, considering me. "I see a similar specialness in you, young man."

Despite the lingering heaviness in my chest from last night's encounter, I do my best to offer her a polite smile.

"Although you're not as good an actor as you think you are. Something is up with you."

I monitor the road ahead for signs of wildlife as the part of me that wants to tell her about my discovery last night wars with the part that still wants to pretend it never happened. That part loses.

"I'm ninety-nine percent sure I found my biological father last night."

Luella's sudden loss for words plays out through her big, rounded eyes, but I don't allow time for questions. Mostly because I never want his name to be an answer for anything more than a single, isolated moment in history.

"Troy Rigger."

I can feel the pained and whispered *no* she speaks reverberate inside my chest.

Neither of us speaks for several minutes, but unlike me, Luella seems to be sifting and sorting for clues in a mental database I have no access to. And whatever she finds has her twisting in her seat. She stares at my profile. "That night in August, after our tour bus returned back to Nashville and your mother and I fought over that stupid magazine article, she went to The Lounge."

"The bar you two worked at in Nashville?"

"That's right. Industry professionals were always there, either to impress a potential client or to hold dinner meetings with established artists. I received a call a few days later from a mutual acquaintance, informing me Lynn was seen discussing her contract with another label. But," she closes her eyes, "that other label was Troy's. She was with him that night and possibly longer. When I heard, it felt as if Lynn had just poured vinegar on a fresh wound, especially considering I'd told her to stay away from him after our split with TriplePlay. But men like Troy aren't impulsive. They're willing to stalk their prey and wait for a moment of weakness."

"You think he was after my mother for a long time—waiting for an opportunity?"

Her hesitation has me glancing over at her. "I think he was waiting for a moment to get back at Russell and me."

"He's disturbed," I say, realizing only then that our speed is almost twenty over the limit. I lift my foot and set the cruise control.

"Something I ignored for too long in the early years of our career."

As the scenery becomes more and more familiar, I decide to take the back roads. "Did you know what he was like when you signed at TriplePlay Records?"

"Not at first," she says. "But then one night after a long day of recording, he propositioned me. I told him I was interested in his friendship and didn't see him like that, thinking my explanation would resolve whatever mixed signals I must have given off without knowing. But it happened numerous times, always when Russell wasn't around. I hoped if I ignored him long enough, he would eventually lose interest in me, but it seemed to do the opposite. I made sure I was never alone with him, and I told no one, not even your mother. I was too fearful it would cost us the album we had worked so hard for. I didn't even tell Russell until after we were married in secret. As you can imagine, he was furious, and things were never the same. Russell was ready to walk then, even before we found the receipts of how Troy was cheating us financially, but I wouldn't let him. It wasn't only my career at stake, but your mother's, too. Knowing her history with her father, I wanted to protect her by keeping the details private, but really—" She cuts herself off, and it's nearly a minute before she finishes her thought. "Really I put her in harm's way."

My jaw is clenched so tight my molars vibrate. Is that what he'd done to my mother? Propositioned her in a low moment, when she was in need of comfort and a familiar face? The thought makes me want to pull off the road and retch.

"That man is not your father, Micah," Luella says with such calming conviction I'm almost convinced I missed part of her story. She touches my shoulder. "I'm not saying she was right to keep it from you, but as a mother myself, I can understand her reasons. I can also understand now why she married Frank as quickly and as quietly as she did." Luella's words root in deep. "She may have struggled to believe that she could ever receive the love of a husband, but the woman I knew would never deny her unborn child the love of a father. And she gave you one of the very best."

It's an effort not to break down while behind this wheel, and perhaps the only reason I don't is because we're less than forty miles out from our destination now and the roads are as narrow here as they are windy. But I nod my appreciation to Luella, and for the next several minutes, she allows me to reflect on the insight and perspective she's provided before she graciously moves our conversation to talk of new subjects.

We take turns asking each other questions, never once lacking for answers—that is, until I ask her the one question she's avoided since she woke me up this morning and told me she wanted to get a head start on her girls: What are we actually doing?

I know every curve and ridge of the surrounding snow-tipped mountain ranges, every river, lake, and fishable stream within a two-hundred-mile radius, every burger joint and hiking trail and ski slope. I could stock the aisle of the grocery store, and I've memorized the coffee menus of the three drive-ups we have in town. The same way I've sat in every seat at my home church. I don't need a map to follow where these roads lead, because this is my home. It's the only one I've ever known, and even after traveling across the nation, it's the only home I hope to have. And yet . . . I have no idea why Luella wanted to come back.

"Just keep driving," she says. "We're almost there."

As soon as we round the bend on the narrow, two-lane highway, Luella sits up and points at the river. "There it is."

I follow her finger to the open acres of ponderosa pines and spruce trees just past the edge of town, and suddenly I know where we're headed even if I don't know why. I've been a camper and cabin leader at Camp Selkirk more times than I can count. And even though their doors of operation closed a few years back due to low funding, it hasn't kept my dad and brother and me from boating up to it from the other side of the bank to hike and fish. The significance this place has played in my faith journey is incomparable.

Perhaps Luella needs to see this part of her history again, where she and my mother first met. Perhaps that's why we're here, to finish off a road trip that began nearly fifty years ago.

So I ignore the closed entry gate at the front and drive to the open one a quarter mile around the back. I hope the Farrow sisters will do the same when they arrive. Some rules are worth breaking for the people you love. And Luella is hardly the only Farrow I've fallen for this summer.

# 32

## Raegan

Adele holds up her cell phone near the locked camp gate where we've parked the Jeep, searching for a signal, while Hattie and I peer through the trees into the legendary Camp Selkirk. A rush of nostalgia floods my system, even though I've never stepped foot on this soil before. Instead, I'm recollecting the vivid descriptions from Lynn's journals. If I squint hard enough, I can almost make out the river in the background.

"The cell service is too spotty, but Mama's last location as of thirty minutes ago shows she's here," Adele says, pocketing the phone. "Maybe we should keep driving to look for another way in?"

"Or we can hop this gate," I suggest as I pull myself up and over. I land with an *oomph*.

Hattie, whose eyes are still puffy and red, moves to follow my lead. "That's my vote, too."

Dust plumes up from her feet after she lands.

We both look to Adele, the rule-follower among us.

"Over the gate it is, then." She might be the oldest, but she's quite possibly the nimblest. She drops to the other side with ease and brushes off her hands. "Let's just pray we don't get taken out by a wild animal before we find them."

We trudge our way down a trail covered in branches and pine needles toward a large firepit that ignites the images Lynn's early journal entries created. I'm instantly covered in goosebumps as I think of the nights Mama and Lynn must have spent together, writing songs and talking about their dreams. There are several buildings in view now, and I can hear the river just beyond the sloped tree line.

I can hear something else, too.

Singing.

We follow the sound to the white-steepled chapel, where Mama is sitting inside on the steps of a platform a fraction of the one she performed on last night, shadowed under the large arms of an old wooden cross. Then I see Micah, sitting in the back pew, his gaze ever-watchful and curious as we find each other in this sacred space. It's all I can do not to run to him first and tell him everything that happened on the road.

But when Mama stands and moves toward us, whatever she sees in our faces causes her stride to falter. Hattie rushes ahead and falls to her knees. Sobs wrack her body all over again as she confesses what Adele and I have already forgiven her for.

"I'm so sorry, Mama," she weeps. "Please forgive me."

Mama kneels to meet Hattie on the floor, wrapping her arms around her until all my sister's shame and regret are cried out where they belong: at the foot of a cross.

"Oh, sweet girl," Mama coos. "How could I ever deny you what I was given so many years ago right here in this chapel?"

Once Hattie has taken several calming breaths in Mama's arms, Adele and I help them both to their feet again. Mama hugs each of my older sisters first, and then she reaches for me. She holds my face between her palms and speaks with such unbridled love and pride. "Promise me you'll finish the memoir you started, Raegan.

*Please*. It's one of the most beautiful tributes I've ever read, and I'm not even to the births of my three daughters yet. You brought so many of my memories to life, memories I never want to forget—even the painful ones that have caused me to grow despite myself."

At first, I'm confused. How had she—

"Micah had the forethought to bring your chapters along with him this morning," she answers without prompt. "It's why I have no mascara left on these sad natural lashes. I cried it all off."

Once again, I find Micah. He dips his chin, and I mouth *thank you* through a watery smile.

Mama's expression remains tender. "I never want you to stop writing. I want to support you in stewarding that gift however I can. Agreed?" I nod as she hugs me. "Good."

After Mama releases me, she seems to take a moment to collect her thoughts before addressing the three of us.

"This," Mama says, "this right here is what I was praying would happen between you girls while we were on the road. That you'd learn to fight *for* each other and not *with* each other. I was on my knees most of the night, asking God to intervene today so you wouldn't have to walk the same path I did. I don't know what all happened on your drive today, but I can clearly see my prayers are being answered.

"As you know, I once had a sister I loved and swore to protect. I never could have imagined a future without her. And yet, somehow I lived thirty years without Lynn." She pauses. "If I could go back in time, I would have done so many things differently, starting with choosing humility over my pride." Her gaze scans over each one of us.

Mama steps out of our circle and walks down the altar steps into the sanctuary, taking in the stained-glass windows and running her fingers along the back of the wooden pews.

"As Raegan wrote about in her chapters, this is the church where I first heard the Gospel. I met Lynn at the firepit down the path, and only a week later we were singing up here together on this stage.

Back then, the only legacy I ever desired to pass down to my future children was the hope we'd found inside these walls. It consumed us back then, this idea that God had plans to use us despite our faults and broken childhoods. But as I've grown older and my life became more and more cluttered with the debris of fame, I've questioned the real legacy I'm leaving behind to my children." She turns to face us again. "I hope what I give you today can be something that lasts for generations to come."

She continues weaving through the rows of pews, her sparkly shirt and boots glinting in the sunlight through the window panes.

"After I reconciled with Lynn last April and we said our final good-byes, I drove through this town for the first time in decades and ended up right back here. I walked through this abandoned campground alone, stood at the waters I was baptized in, and sat outside these chapel doors and repented. I prayed and wept for the sister I lost and for the sister I found again only days before she went to meet her Savior. I asked God to show me how I could honor her life, and immediately, my thoughts went to you, my darling daughters three. The idea for this road trip came as a way to reconnect us again, as my memories of that first road trip with Lynn are some of my most precious. But I was wrong in thinking I could force you to choose each other. That choice is yours alone to make."

The three of us are openly wiping tears from our cheeks now, and once again, Mama approaches the platform.

"Jana helped me with the logistics of the road trip—but I'd always planned for us to end right here, at Camp Selkirk." Mama shifts her focus to the back of the chapel. "Micah, can you join us down here, please?"

"Yes, ma'am." It's only when he starts toward the stage that I can see how glassy his eyes are. He joins our half circle at my side, and I can't help but reach for his hand. He squeezes it lightly.

Mama stands before us now. "I purchased this campground the week after your mama passed away, Micah. I couldn't stand the idea of such an important piece of our shared histories remaining closed to those who need it most, the way we once did." Our collective gasps ring throughout the chapel, but Mama continues, undeterred. "And I recently altered the deed to include five names—all equal shares in a living inheritance. My three daughters: Adele, Harriet, and Raegan. And Lynn's two sons: Micah and Garrett Davenport."

Micah's jaw hinges open as his gaze searches Mama's. "Luella, that's . . . we couldn't possibly—"

"You can. It's what's right, and I won't be convinced otherwise. I missed out on so much when it came to your mother's life and family. And the truth is, I wish I could have known you as a boy so that I could have witnessed your transformation into the incredible man you are today. I can't thank you enough for what you've done for us these last two weeks, so I hope you and your brother will accept this gift and continue to be a part of our lives and family for generations to come. In addition, I'm also hoping you'll accept the undefined job description of camp director. Seems fitting after what we discussed in the car today, doesn't it? I could barely keep the words in when you shared your heart about bringing therapy to the outdoors." She winks.

Micah clears his throat twice but still can't seem to get any words out. By the shocked looks around our circle, none of us can.

"I figure we can do a bit of vision casting on our drive back to Nashville. Ideally, my hope would be to have this place up and running by this time next summer. Think that could be possible?"

Clearly flustered, he rubs at the back of his neck. "I truly don't even know what to say to all this, Luella—"

"Say yes!" Hattie beams. "You're perfect for this."

"I'm not sure I have the qualifications or credentials to manage something—"

"Nonsense," Mama laughs. "Nobody is ever fully qualified for anything. It's why we need Jesus."

"She's right," Adele adds. "You're the one for such a job, Micah."

"Thank you. All of you." He clears his throat. "This means a great deal to me, and I know it will mean so much to Garrett, too.

The hospital he works at is always looking for nonprofits to support inside our community. I'm willing to bet Camp Selkirk will be a top contender, considering how well-loved it is."

"I'm excited to bring my kids here," Hattie says. "We'll help however we can, especially if s'mores are a reward."

"Cheap labor." Micah chuckles.

"Michael will be all over this project," Adele adds. "And as long as you can assure Cheyenne she won't have to deal with snakes, I'm sure she'd be up for a family work trip."

Micah chuckles. "Not many snakes around here, but there is some wildlife we'll need to prepare her for."

"Fair enough."

I move to thread my fingers through his, though I can't yet think about how far this camp is from home. "I'll help too, of course, however I can."

His soft gaze roams my face as a divine peace sweeps over me.

It's then I hear Mama hum the first note of a hymn we've sung together a hundred times over, one fitting for a moment like this. By the fourth note of the melody, every sister has joined in, and by the chorus, Micah has, too. As our voices blend into one, I lift my eyes to the cross at the far end of the stage and thank God for the way He intervened in my mama's life right here so many years ago.

And then I thank Him that He never, ever stopped.

# 33

## Micah

The last hour has been one of the most surreal of my life, and I've had several to choose from as of late. Though we'd moved our conversation outside the chapel to the picnic tables above the river trail, I'm still operating under a cloud of disbelief.

Luella named me and my brother partial owners of a campground only ten miles from where we grew up. That scale of generosity and kindness didn't seem plausible, and yet, so much about these last two weeks has defied logic.

Luella just started her tour of the grounds with Adele and Hattie, which gave Raegan and me a much-needed moment to catch up in private. As we walk hand-in-hand down a path I know almost as well as the house I grew up in, I ask her to tell me what happened on the road with her sisters. And when she does, the pride I feel for her soars above the rest of the emotions lurking in my chest.

We edge closer to the fork in the path—one trail leading to the water, the other leading to the common area. "I have a few things to fill you in on, as well."

Her expression shifts to one of concern, but as soon as I start to speak again, my phone chimes in my pocket. Five times.

"Guess we know where we can find cell service on the grounds," I say.

I pull my phone out and read the screen.

"Two texts from Adele, one from you, and . . . oh." I swipe to check the time stamp on the text. "Two from my father from just over an hour ago. He says he's in Skagway for a couple of hours and was hoping to reach me."

"Then go," Raegan says, pushing my shoulder. "Go talk to him. I'll wait here."

Whatever she reads in my face when I hesitate has her taking in a breath. "Oh, Micah, you found something, didn't you?"

"I did."

She purses her lips and nods. "Then I'll wait until you come back from your call."

I grip the back of my neck, willing myself to move as my heart gallops in my chest. "I don't know if I can do it—not like this."

"You can." Raegan moves in, touches my unshaven jaw, and looks me straight in the eyes. "You need him as much as he needs you. Go talk to him, tell him what you've found. I'll be right here when you come back." She places her hand over my heart. "I'll pray God gives you the words and the strength you need."

I pull her in and wrap her tightly in my arms, murmuring in her hair. "Thank you."

"He loves you, Micah. Remember that."

I swallow the thickening emotion in my throat, not sure whether Raegan is speaking of my dad or of God. Either way, I know she speaks the truth.

I'm standing at the edge of the spot in the river where I was baptized when I lift my phone to my ear. By the fifth ring, I'm certain I've missed the short window he had for coverage. And then he picks up. I can hear the wind blowing hard into the receiver. He's still on shore.

"Son? Are you there? Hang on, let me walk back up the dock. There's a shelter with a bench that will block the wind. I'll tell the guys to give me a few more minutes." His shout is muffled, but not more than a few seconds later I hear the distinct stomp of his rubber boots, and then the wind is silenced. "Is this any better?"

"Yes, it's good, Dad." The word resonates in my chest.

"Today must be my lucky day. I spoke to your brother a couple hours ago. He and Kacy put the kids on video, and I laughed so hard I thought my spleen would rupture. I've missed you boys. By the sound of your voicemail updates, you've had a full couple of weeks." He chuckles. "I was more than a little surprised to hear you took after your old man, driving a tour bus across the country, but I nearly spit out my coffee when I heard you say you were driving for Luella and her girls. Gosh . . . how old must Adele and Hattie be now? Late thirties, early forties? I never did meet the youngest one. She came along after we moved to Idaho."

"Raegan." Just the sound of her name brings me comfort. "She's a few years younger than I am." At the thought of her up at the camp waiting for me, I shift the conversation away from the Farrows. "I'm actually standing in front of the Saint Joe as we speak." I glance out at the river that runs upstream from my parents' house. My dad's house now.

"No kidding?" He huffs a rugged laugh. "I wish you would have told me, I would have tried to get back in time to meet Luella's family."

"I think we can make that a reality soon enough." I kick at a pile of rocks on the riverbank. "But first, there's something I need to tell you before I get back on the road, Dad." I pause. "And I'm afraid it's not going to be easy to hear."

My father goes quiet on the other end of the line, and I close my eyes right then and pray for guidance. For all the schooling I've had and all the hard conversations I've mediated, I don't know how to do this. I don't know how to break the heart of the man who raised me as his own and never once led me to believe I was anything but wanted.

"I'm listening," he says. It's the respectful response he taught me and Garrett to say when we were boys, and the response we still offer each other as adults.

"Before I left on this road trip with the Farrows, I learned some surprising information regarding my blood type. At first, I didn't think the findings could be accurate, but after some more testing, Garrett confirmed it at the lab." I fight for the return of moisture to my mouth. "What I'm about to tell you—is not a theory, Dad. It's fact."

He's quiet on the other end, yet I know he's there. I know he's giving me room to say whatever it is I need to say. That's always been his way of parenting. His patience has been my guide in navigating both the still and raging waters of life.

On the tail end of an exhale, I let it out. "I'm not your biological son."

I wait for my father to absorb what I've just said, allowing him the same space to process as he allowed me, only when his reply comes, I'm sure I've misheard him.

"I know," he says. "I just wish you hadn't found out without me with you."

For the life of me, I can't seem to interpret what he's just admitted.

"What are you saying? That you knew I wasn't yours?"

"You *are* mine," my father says in a constricted voice. "In every way that's ever mattered to me, *you are mine*." He clears his throat. "I've long wanted to have this conversation with you, but out of respect for your mother's wishes, I've stayed quiet. My plan was to tell you when I got home—I even have a letter for you from your mother."

"You have a . . . a letter?" I blink rapidly. "You knew? All this time?"

"Please, son, I'll tell you everything I know."

I close my eyes. "I'm listening."

"I was in love with your mother for several years before she trusted me enough to share the darker parts of her history with me as a friend. I drove for their summer tours and escorted her to dinners when she asked, and sometimes, on the rare nights when she felt particularly open, she would stay up late with me to count the stars. Those were the nights she'd tell me about the monster who lived in her home when she was growing up and all the reasons she vowed never to marry or have children of her own. She didn't want to carry on her pain, and she struggled to believe she could ever be truly healed. I was honest about my feelings for her, but I respected her enough to honor her wishes and learn to love her as my friend, even though I wanted her as my wife."

I search the waters beyond, mirroring my father's words with my mother's voice in her journals.

"Your mom was at the peak of her career in the early '90s, but she wasn't happy. I remember being shocked when I saw her on that last summer tour with Luella. She'd lost so much weight due to whatever new prescription she was hooked on at the time, and her relationship with Luella was a constant guessing game—sometimes up, sometimes down, sometimes nonexistent. The stresses and pressures of fame had taken a toll on them both." He takes a breath. "The night before we rolled into Nashville, I told your mother I loved her, but she replied with all the reasons it would never work between us. Despite what I wanted, I left to go back home to Montana without her. I've never regretted a single decision more in my life."

He's quiet for so long this time, I'm not sure if he's still there.

"Dad?"

"I'm sorry, son. I'm trying." He takes a breath. "Your mother and Luella got into an argument after I left, and she met up with a man she used to trust, someone who'd known her a long time." Bile rises in my throat, and everything in me wants to tell him I've heard enough, but the sound of my father's hoarse baritone on the other end of the line keeps me quiet. "He consoled her and offered her the validation she was desperate for at the time. He took advantage of her trust in every way possible."

I try and fail to block the smug face of Troy from my mind. "And she found out she was pregnant soon after," I surmise. "How did she tell you?"

"She flew to Montana. She quite literally showed up on my doorstep and asked me if I'd meant what I'd said. I confirmed that I did. And then she asked if I'd be the father of her baby." His words are choked, strained. "She told me I was the only man she'd ever known to show her love, and she wondered if that love was big enough to include a child that could never be mine by blood."

"And you . . . you just agreed?"

He's quiet for a moment before he says, "There was no alternative, Micah. I loved her—*all* of her. Her past, her present, her future. I loved her through her pain, through her grief, through her trauma, and through all the healing that would eventually come. *I loved her.* There was no question I would love her unborn child, too."

It takes me a minute to find my breath. "Why didn't either of you ever tell me this?"

"We went round and round about it. It was the biggest conflict in our marriage for years. Ultimately, we were on two different sides of the fence. I saw it as necessary truth, and she saw it as a necessary protection in light of who and what that guy was. She did agree to a compromise when you were a boy, though: if there was ever a medical or safety reason to divulge the details for your sake, she would. Yet as active as you were, you never so much as broke a bone."

I wipe my nose with the hem of my shirt. "I'm thirty years old now, Dad. Was she *ever* planning on telling me?"

"She always said she would tell you before you started a family of your own. But once we received your mother's prognosis, she asked me if I would talk to you after she was gone. Neither of us wanted your last memories of her to be tainted by this, and I . . . I can't say if that was the right choice or not. It's certainly not the first time in parenting I've felt out of my depth. I've been praying about the timing of this conversation since I got to Alaska. I'd planned to take you out on the boat once we were both settled at home—figured we'd discuss it while fishing." His honesty nearly makes me laugh. My dad was forever saving significant conversations for fishing. Only, this time, I got to him first.

"Micah, when I held you in my arms that first time, I prayed God would allow me to be the father you needed, and wherever I fell short, that He would fill in the gaps. I knew, even then, that keeping your mother's secret for her would come at a cost. I just prayed that the cost would be less than what it cost her to keep it."

"I found him, Dad," I say. "I sat with Troy Rigger at a bar last night at the Gorge Amphitheater."

There's a brief pause. "Oh, son."

"He doesn't know who I am, but I needed to know who he was. And now that I do, I want nothing more to do with him."

"I'm sorry. I wish there was a better ending I could offer you than this."

"There is," I cut in. "I'm living it. I don't even want to imagine the man I would have become under his influence. Or the kind of pain he would have caused Mom if she'd stayed with a guy like that."

"I've laid awake many nights thinking the same thing. To me, you were always meant to be Micah Franklin Davenport. I love you, son. I hope you can forgive me for keeping this from you for so long."

It's several beats before I can speak again as I watch a hawk fly the distance across the river. "I do, Dad. And I love you, too."

We're quiet on the line for some time, each of us lost in our thoughts. It's a familiar and comfortable silence, one we've practiced at campfires, hunting excursions, and hours upon hours of fishing trips. But today we're not side-by-side, we're an ocean apart, which means I can't read him the way I normally can.

I wipe my cheeks with the back of my hand and clear my throat. "I have other news to share if you have another minute. It's of the good variety."

"I think we're both due some good news right about now."

"Camp Selkirk has a new owner."

"Really?" he asks. "Do you know who it is yet?"

"Well, technically, as of today, I'm one-fifth owner. Luella purchased it and gave it to her three daughters and to me and Garrett as a living inheritance. The deed is in all five of our names." I hesitate. "I'm not sure where you stand with her, Dad, but . . ." How do I even try to summarize what I feel for Luella after these weeks on the road with her? "But she's not at all like I thought she would be."

"I've always cared for her, but even more so after she made your mother's last few days on earth so peaceful. That's a debt I'll never be able to repay. But I'm afraid I'm still struggling to wrap my mind around your name on a deed to a camp."

I laugh. "That makes two of us, then. She's asked me to do a bit of vision casting with her on our trip home to process through how we can use these grounds to give back to the community while keeping its core values intact."

"Sounds like a dream come true for you."

"One of them."

I turn then and spy Raegan standing at the top of the river trail, her gaze fixed on me. I lift my hand and smile to let her know I'm okay, and then I tell my dad everything I can about the woman I fell in love with on a tour bus this summer . . . the same way he fell in love with my mother on the same bus more than thirty years ago.

# 34

## Raegan

I don't realize how long I've been holding my breath until Micah seeks my gaze from down below. *He's okay.* It's as if a valve to my lungs has opened and I'm discovering oxygen for the first time. A mix of relief, elation, and gratitude swells inside me on his behalf, and it's a sensation unlike any I can name. Only, perhaps that's not true. Perhaps I can name it.

Once he slips his phone into his back pocket, he strides up the rocky riverbank and the dirt-covered path to where I wait at the trailhead. I'm not sure what expression I expected to see etched into his striking features after such a critical conversation, but the weightlessness of his countenance is so contagious, it captures me in its undertow and refuses to let go.

A dust cloud plumes behind him, the particles shimmering in the sunlight, as he reaches for me in a wordless invitation I readily accept. He scoops me into his arms and nuzzles his face into the crook of my neck. And everything about this moment—my feet lifted off the ground, Micah's embrace holding me tight, his lips pressed firmly against my collarbone—is everything I want to hold on to forever, and yet the instant he sets me back on solid ground, I feel a breathless kind of foreboding I want to ignore.

"My dad wants to take you bass fishing," he says, lacing his fingers behind my lower back. "He wants to make sure you know he's the resident expert on the best spots around here and that I'm not to take you to any of them on my own."

I blink, confused. "You . . . you talked to him about fishing?"

Micah smiles and bends to kiss one of my cheeks. "You should probably know, we often talk about fishing."

"But what about—"

"We talked about that, too, and I promise to tell you every critical detail of that conversation as soon as we're back on the road." He presses a kiss to my other cheek. "But the highlight of the call came at the end. Care to guess what it was about?"

My cheeks ignite from the imprint his kisses leave behind, and the urge to hold on to him strikes me again.

"You," he answers. "We talked about you, Raegan Lynn." Tenderly, he brushes his lips against mine. Soft, sweet, perfect. "I told him that I don't know how I lived in a world without you before now." Another tender kiss. "And most importantly, that I hope I never have to again."

"I feel the same way, Micah." I touch his face as if to memorize every strong curve as my breath shallows with a desperation I'm fearful to expose.

His kiss only amplifies the longing inside me.

But when he pulls back, he must see it. The coming good-bye I don't want and yet can't pretend away. Not even with the vivid imagination God's given me.

I can't swallow the ache away, but I manage a shaky smile. "Ever since we arrived today, I've had the strangest feeling—almost like I've been here before, despite having never visited Idaho." I touch the collar of his T-shirt. "I couldn't figure it out until just a few minutes ago when I watched you hike back up the trail from the river." My chin quivers. "This is how I pictured Birch Grove, Micah. It looks so much like the beautiful mountain town I dreamed of when I wrote my novel—"

"So stay," he whispers. "Stay here with me."

For what has to be the tenth time this afternoon, tears well in my eyes and spill over my cheeks. "I want that. You have no idea how much I want that, but . . ." I drop my chin and study the dirt under my sandals, willing myself to be stronger, to be braver, to be more like the man whose arms are wrapped securely around my waist as if nothing could ever break his hold.

I lift my head and search the ground around us. It's impossible not to imagine how much of a blessing Micah will be to this community he has loved for decades, or to see how providential the timing is . . . even if that timing includes a sacrifice for us both.

"This is right for you," I say in earnest. "The answer you've been praying for is here."

"You're an answer I've been praying for, too."

The conviction in his voice ripples through me, and I can't utter a word in reply.

"You could write here, Raegan. First your mom's memoir and then the sequel to Birch Grove and then whatever comes after that. Can't you see it?"

"Micah—"

"I know it's fast," he breaks in, "and if there was a way for me to pick this campground up and move it south to Tennessee, I would. Without question." He dips his chin to catch my gaze. "You could write every day while I oversaw the project-development phase of the camp, and then in the evenings, we would be together." His face and tone fall serious. "My sister-in-law has a loft apartment over her Pilates studio not fifteen minutes from here. You could live there until we're ready to . . ."

More tears track my cheeks as I yearn for him to finish that statement. "Until we're ready to what?"

He steadies my shoulders with his strong hands. "I've known what I desire in a life partner for a long time. I just never imagined I'd find her on a road trip. If it wasn't completely selfish on my part, I'd ask you to marry me right now."

Some irrational, ultraromantic part of me wants to fling my arms around his neck and tell him my answer would be yes, that if he can march me back up to that chapel and call in a preacher, I'd happily become Raegan Lynn Davenport while wearing flip-flops, shorts, and a messy bun just so we'd never have to be apart again. And maybe if this conversation had occurred yesterday, that's exactly what I would have done. But something holds me back. Chances are high it's the same something that's holding Micah back from officially asking.

I've spent a large part of the last few years resenting the ties that bound me to my family. I'd daydreamed about an escape, whether through a marriage that was never meant to be mine, or through creating a whole secret identity that would cut them out of a huge portion of my life entirely. But now that I have the choice to run away with the most incredible human being I've ever known—the pinch in my chest at the thought of leaving gives me pause.

And I can't ignore it. Not even for Micah.

The healing that started with my family on the side of the road today, the healing I wrote about in my fiction and prayed about in my real life after Daddy died, is still in process. And if I leave them now, I'm not sure it will continue the way it needs to.

Long distance doesn't seem like a viable option for the healing that still needs to be done.

And yet, the idea of saying good-bye to Micah is . . .

"You can't leave your family yet." His gentle statement is paired with a knowing look that both breaks and restores my heart at the same time.

I shake my head and whisper what might be the most difficult words I've ever spoken. "Not yet."

"I know," he says, pulling me close and kissing my hair. "I know."

"What happened today was . . ." My words catch in my throat as I remember Hattie's confession and Adele's breakdown and our collective honesty and commitment to move forward together rather than apart. "It's the start of something new, something healthy and right. And after so many years of living emotionally disconnected from one another, I can't walk away now. Especially when there is so much left to be resolved." I pull back and reach for his hands. "If I'm going to write this book like Mama's asked, then I need them all to be a part of it, too. I want to include their perspectives and memories during the years I was too young to remember. We're all a part of Mama's legacy."

My heart constricts as he searches my face.

"I can see myself here, Micah," I say with the same conviction he spoke with earlier. "The same way I can see myself with you. I just need a little more time."

His pointer finger grazes my jaw and stops at my chin. "I can give you that." His gaze lowers to my lips. "When is your deadline to Fog Harbor Books?"

I can barely think from want of kissing him. "If the contract remains as is, then I think my final draft will be due in November."

"Four months." He breathes out. "We can do that."

"We can." I nod in agreement. "How about we plan to host your entire family for Thanksgiving dinner at Mama's this fall? I'm sure we'll all have plenty to discuss regarding Camp Selkirk by then."

"It's a date." His smile is just short of reaching his eyes. "In the meantime, you can read me your new chapters over video chat."

"Of course," I say over the rising emotion in my throat. "And you can take me along with you on your trail hikes and fishing adventures."

"Yes and yes." He tilts my face to his. "To paraphrase my mother, 'Life's too short to be questioning what to do with the time we've been given.' And, I think it's safe to add, *who* we spend that time with." He brushes his lips against mine. "And I want to spend my time with the woman I love."

Tears slip over my curved lips. "I love you, too."

When he presses his mouth to mine, he kisses me like it's the start of a much-anticipated homecoming rather than the start of a long and difficult good-bye. Deep down, I have faith it's not the latter. Our original route might have been full of bumps and detours, breakdowns and secrets, but even still, we found our way here together once.

I have no doubt we will find our way back to each other again.

# Epilogue

## Raegan

The beautiful end-of-summer décor and fresh flowers Hattie used to transform today's intimate back-patio brunch at the Davenport house into a feast suited for royalty were nearly as jaw-dropping as the stunning vision she brought to life inside Camp Selkirk's chapel yesterday afternoon. Equally as spectacular was the menu Adele curated for our special guests this morning: sweet and savory crepes, made-to-order omelets, a customized juice bar, and yogurt parfaits worthy of their own Instagram feed. The entire weekend has been as fairy-tale-like as my sisters promised it would be. With one exception: I've barely had a minute alone with either of them since they arrived in Idaho seventy-two hours ago.

And no matter how many times Micah has hinted at his own desire for some alone time with me, I know I can't leave here without saying a proper good-bye to Adele and Hattie. Not after everything they've done for me this weekend, and certainly not after everything

384

the three of us experienced together this year. As much as I long to start a new chapter with the man I love, I want to close out the last one with the same grace and love they've shown me in the last thirteen months, which is why the second Micah's brother, Garrett, challenges him to a celebratory basketball game, I use the distraction to locate my sisters.

Where on earth are they? I glance down at the text from Mama again, asking me to meet her in the garden. Perhaps my sisters are with her?

I pass through Frank's open, farm-style kitchen and thank the incredible camp staff employees for all their help this weekend—as well as for their graciousness in navigating the media circus upon Mama's arrival. It didn't take long for this sweet Idaho town to fall hard for Luella Farrow. Anybody who had reservations about the big country music star from Nashville purchasing their favorite summer campground came around after the grand opening this past June, when Micah's vision caught like wildfire. Local and national sponsors have donated and committed to advertising for teens and hurting families of all kinds to find the support they need at Camp Selkirk.

As I weave across the manicured portion of the Davenport acreage, I hear Garrett egging his big brother on while my two nieces, Cheyenne and Annabelle, act as their cheerleaders. By the sound of their engaging and humorous chants, it seems my nephew, Aiden, along with my editor, Chip—who arrived at the weekend festivities shortly after Cheyenne's best friend, Allie Spencer—have been added to the spontaneous pick-up game. If not for the case of my missing sisters, I'd be out there rooting for my favorite player.

The early September breeze lifts my hair from my shoulders and flows through my white eyelet sundress as I walk toward Chickee's old prayer garden, the same one I read about in Lynn's journals. It's hard to believe an entire year has passed since I opened those early entries that started a stone's throw away from here. I hope Lynn can see all the improvements her son has implemented at the campground she loved. Though she's not here to tell either of her boys how proud she is of their accomplishments on earth, I often think their character speaks of her love, support, and even her pride as a mother. As does the last letter she wrote for Micah to read after she passed, explaining her decision and asking for his understanding and forgiveness.

As I approach the entrance to the garden, I spot my mother waiting inside the fenced perimeter. She's alone, seated on a bench.

Though I never had the opportunity to meet Lynn Hershel Davenport in the flesh, this is the place I imagine her whenever she comes to mind now. Maybe that's because of the interviews I conducted with each of the Davenport men while drafting Mama's memoir and the memories they shared of her here. Or perhaps it's because of the framed photograph hanging outside Franklin's room of her sitting on this very bench at sunrise, her Bible open on her lap and her eyelids closed. Whatever the case, every time I venture inside, I feel a similar sacred influence as when I put pen to page. Her journey was different from my own, and yet my story will forever be intertwined with hers.

Mama's bright and contagious grin fills her face as she takes my hand and pulls me inside the special space. "You looked so happy at brunch this morning, sweetheart."

"I am happy," I say easily.

She angles her neck and studies my face. "And yet something's bothering you." She purses her lips. "Does it have to do with your trip? Or perhaps with all the see-you-laters you'll be hearing when you go?"

An unexpected lump rises in my throat as I imagine pulling out of Frank's driveway with Micah in the blue Bronco I drove here from Nashville three months ago for the camp's grand opening. It's strange how long a person can anticipate a special milestone in their life and still feel the bittersweet tug of change clinging to their coattails. Good-byes are hard, even when they're framed in a *see-you-later*. "I'll miss you and the girls so much."

"I know, sweetheart. And we'll miss you, too. But we're only a

flight away—or a week-long road trip, depending on the traveler."
Mama winks, then peers steadily into my eyes. "I was just praying
for your safe and happy travels on the road. I know it will be special."

"You were?" Again, the temptation to cry surprises me. After all
the emotions of the weekend, I would have sworn I had no tears
left in me.

"Of course I was." Mama pulls me into a hug and rubs my back
with comforting circles. "It's been one of my greatest joys watching
you grow into such a capable, strong, creative, passionate woman,
Raegan. Between your dedication to writing my memoir and your
support at the camp alongside Micah and your sisters, it's no wonder
why that man of yours is so smitten with you. You've both worked
hard at the pursuits and relationships God has given you, and now
it's time to put that same kind of focused energy and love into each
other."

I think of Micah then, recalling the way he smiled while tears
trailed his cheeks at the sight of me in that chapel yesterday. And
soon, my bottom lip begins to quiver. "I love him so, so much,
Mama."

"No one would ever doubt it." She chuckles sweetly at that. "Your
sisters adore him—and that's high praise for Adele and Hattie."

The truth of her statement hits me afresh as I think back on
Micah's proposal at Thanksgiving and the way they'd both played a
part in his plan, all while knowing what a future with Micah would
mean. Yet, a cross-country move is hardly the only challenge we
Farrow sisters have faced since we parked Old Goldie in Nashville
last summer. Not only did Hattie's ex-husband get dumped by the
Grecian goddess he claimed was his soulmate, but he's currently
facing allegations of fraud based on new evidence brought to light
by the same Grecian goddess. Despite Peter's legal battle for damage
control, Hattie's lawyer is convinced her hopes for full custody of
Annabelle and Aiden will soon be realized.

The only moment in Hattie's recent history that rivaled such good
news was the evening Adele waltzed into Mama's dining room for

family dinner to announce that Hattie's contractual obligations to Willow House Publishing had been terminated. When we pressed her for details on how exactly that had happened, she simply smiled and said, "Let's just say my new motto of working smarter, not harder is paying off." Turns out, when Adele decided to anonymously alert Peter's legal team about a tell-all being written that would surely paint their client and his dealings with the Farrow family in a poor light, they weren't thrilled about it.

As soon as they threatened to file a lawsuit against Willow House Publishing, Adele was right there, pushing for Willow House to release Hattie from her contract while allowing all of the negative press to be reflected on Peter San Marco. For a woman who barely had enough time to drink a protein shake between CEO meetings at Farrow Music, she now has enough time on her hands to bake on the weekends, go on empty-nester dates with Michael, and keep tabs on the retribution of her ex-brother-in-law. All thanks to the partnership with Sweet Home Records, the investor she and Mama signed with last September.

"Have you seen Adele and Hattie?" I ask Mama.

"I haven't, but I'll give them a call."

She takes out her phone as I walk along the assortment of flower beds, studying the prayer stones in the garden Lynn inherited from her grandmother. Printed on each stone is a name, followed by a request—most often written as a single word or phrase, and accompanied by a date. It seems that depending on the answer, the date was either left open or closed by the addition of a second date. On my very first visit out to the garden last fall, I spotted the stone with my mama's name on it. The date had been printed over a decade ago, but it had been closed by Frank just a few days before Lynn went to meet her Savior.

There has to be at least three or four hundred stones along these flower beds. The sight actually gave me the idea for the second book in my Birch Grove series. After the initial sales number came in for the launch of Mama's memoir in May, Chip got the approval to contract a three-book series set in Birch Grove with Fog Harbor Books. Our negotiations went splendidly, and as of right now, I'm on schedule to release one book a year for the next three years. *The Sisters of Birch Grove* will release this coming January.

"Neither of your sisters are answering," Mama says with a shrug, as if it's normal to lose two grown women on a five-acre property. "And their location on the family app is turned off."

"But Adele never turns her location off—"

Two familiar arms encircle me from behind, and I'm suddenly overcome by a scent even more intoxicating than the flowers in this garden. Micah kisses me on the neck and holds me in an embrace that causes my knees to weaken. And then I catch the sparkle of sunlight glinting off his wedding-ring finger and can't help but swoon all the more. *He's mine. Forever and ever.*

"Hello, wife." He turns me to face him, and what I find there makes me want to move in even closer. I wrap my arms around his waist, and he sets his hands on my shoulders. "I was starting to worry I'd have to go on our honeymoon without you."

I feign offense. "Micah Franklin Davenport, you know as well as I do that you'd be bored out of your mind without me in the jump seat."

He laughs and then lowers his voice to an alluring tenor. "That's not the only place I'd be bored without you."

A montage of sacred memories flashes through my mind as I recall our short drive from the chapel to the Craftsman-style home we recently purchased just a few miles south of the campground on the other side of the river. Neither of us had stayed there until last night. And all of it—the long-distance relationship we prioritized, the late-night video chats, the weekend flights, the pressing editing deadlines, the challenging projects and meetings at the camp for Micah, the family work days on the grounds, the Luella Farrow memoir book signing in May, the camp's grand opening in June, the wedding date set for September 2nd after the rush of the summer had finally died down—had been worth it. We'd said as much to each other this morning as we tangled together, watching the sun rise over the river.

And there is so much more to come.

"How 'bout I leave you two lovebirds alone and I'll see if I can locate your missing sisters?" Mama winks at both of us as she opens the gate to leave.

Micah hitches an eyebrow. "Given Hattie's paranoia of wildlife, I don't think you should be too worried."

"She's getting braver."

"Only because she's watched every YouTube possible on whatever fill-in-the-blank animal or reptile she might encounter in the outdoors." He laughs. "But I'm glad Aiden and Annabelle love it here."

I shift my stance to block the sun from my eyes. "If Hattie gets full custody, she mentioned coming to help for the whole summer next year."

Micah grins. "I thought you weren't a fan of family employees?"

I swat his chest and roll my eyes good-naturedly. "I'm not. They'd all be volunteers, not employees." I smile up at him. "I have boundaries now, sweet husband, remember?"

"You better stop with all that sexy boundary talk. We have a long drive ahead of us until our stop tonight."

This time when I laugh, I start toward the garden gate. Only, Micah stops me with a gentle tug at my wrist.

"Wait, Rae," he says with an arresting tone that brings me up short. "I came down here because I wanted to show you something first. I found it right before I went to the chapel to marry my stunning bride yesterday."

"Found what?" I follow him through the garden and trail over stones with names of his family members and life events that have come and gone. And then I stop. Micah crouches down and lifts a small stone I've never seen under the sunflowers. It reads: *Micah's future wife.* Underneath it, in a much bolder black, is our wedding date.

Tears spring to my eyes. "Your mom prayed for your wife?"

"My mom prayed for you, Raegan Lynn." He twists to smile up at me. "I ran back up to the house in my suit to find a Sharpie just so I could add our wedding date. It felt important to show my mom another one of her prayers had been answered." He stands and takes my hand. "And I'm so thankful the answer was you."

I kiss him then, bold and unashamed, and I silently thank God right here in the garden for the gift I have in Micah. Breathless, I pull back just long enough for him to ask, "Does that kiss mean you're ready to leave? Because as much as I love family time, I'd really like to start our honeymoon sooner than later."

I laugh and tug him toward the gate. "I promise we can leave as soon as I say good-bye to my sisters."

Before he can respond, the sound of a funny horn tooting merrily in the distance causes us to pause.

"Is that coming from the camp?" I ask, looking down the road.

"I've never heard that sound in my life."

But then we hear other sounds. Cheering and clapping and then the chanting of our names: *Micah and Raegan! Micah and Raegan! Micah and Raegan!*

Hand in hand, we sprint up the grassy knoll toward the driveway, where our extended family and closest friends from this morning's after-wedding brunch are lined up shoulder to shoulder. It's an effort to see over the excited crowd, but it's not until Allie and Chip allow us to break through the chain of people that we see the vintage lime and white VW bus idling in the driveway.

My sisters wave at us through the windows.

"Say hello to Lima Bean, Junior," Mama says in my ear. "I pray she'll be the best road-trip vehicle you ever have."

Micah and I turn toward her in shock and ask in tandem, "This is ours?"

"It's a wedding gift. Your sisters have searched high and low to find it."

I know we both want to protest this, as all the traveling here and back by our loved ones is gift enough, but Mama is not going to argue this point with us again.

Adele and Hattie wave us around to the open side door opposite to where we stand, and soon everyone is crowding behind us. Both my sisters are talking at once, trying to show us all the beautiful features of this gorgeously restored vintage bus, but I'm too overcome with gratitude to hear them. We were prepared to take my Bronco as our road-trip vehicle across the country, but this is exceedingly better. On the far wall hangs a wooden map, and each carved state is open and filled with a soft corkboard material so we can easily pin where our travels take us. The words *Micah and Raegan's Epic Adventure* are burned into the wood grain at the top of the map.

"This is incredible," I say to my sisters as they climb out of the Volkswagen to give my husband and me a chance to look around for ourselves. There are white curtains and a retro mini table and chair set inside, even a little countertop and sink and makeshift bed covered in coordinating sheets and blankets. It's all utterly adorable.

"We think you're pretty incredible, too," Hattie says, hugging me tightly. "We wanted to send you off in a road-worthy vehicle so you'd be inspired to visit us more often."

"We already transferred your luggage onto the racks above so you'll have plenty of space in here," Adele adds. "And you'll find both your favorite road-trip snacks and drinks in the mini cooler between the seats." She smiles. "Cheyenne made you a playlist, and Michael added a few of his favorite songs on there, too. Sorry in advance." My oldest sister rolls her eyes playfully at my brother-in-law, Michael, who promptly informs us that early '90s grunge has its place on road trips, too. We all laugh, especially Garrett, who seems to have found a new BFF in Adele's husband.

"Thank you all," Micah says. "I know I gave a lengthy speech at the rehearsal dinner, so I won't repeat it all here again—"

"We appreciate that," Garrett calls out with a laugh. "Some of us have toddlers to put down for a nap!"

"Thanks, Gar." Micah chuckles. "But really, Raegan and I feel so blessed to have two loving families supporting our marriage."

"I'm just hoping there's talk of grandbabies soon!" Frank calls out.

I giggle and blush at this as my new father-in-law moves toward me and kisses my cheeks. "Now, you call me if this one here gets out of line."

I hug him and assure him he'll be my first call.

Micah and I are both making our rounds through friends and family until there's nothing left for us to do but climb into the driver and passenger seats of Lima Bean, Junior. Nothing, that is, except for pulling my two sisters aside and locking them into a tight embrace. A year ago, hugging was a semi-strange phenomenon between us. But not anymore. Not after hours of long, important conversations, dozens of meals at Mama's, weekend flights to Idaho, and plenty of memory-making at the campground. And especially not after the two of them read *The Sisters of Birch Grove* and then hosted a surprise book party for the author.

"I love you both so much," I say through a tangled web of emotions.

"We love you, too, Sunny Bear," Hattie whispers through tears of her own. "This is just *see you later*."

"Michael and I already have our next trip to Idaho scheduled on the family calendar," Adele says huskily. And for what is likely the first time, I'm grateful for that stupid calendar.

"Okay." I sniff.

"This is where you're meant to be, Raegan," Hattie encourages. "You'll make a beautiful home here—and we'll be here often. Promise."

Adele nods and wipes her eyes. "Keep your location on when you travel these next two weeks."

Hattie and I laugh.

"I mean it," she insists, which makes Hattie and I laugh even harder. Some things never change.

After my mama gives me a final hug good-bye, I plant myself into the passenger seat of Lima Bean, Junior, and smile at my husband. He starts the engine, and the sound is so sweet it's almost musical. This moment is as serendipitous as they come as Micah takes my hand and pulls out of the same driveway our mothers pulled out of fifty years ago.

Here's to another epic adventure.

## The End

# Acknowledgments

To my savior, Jesus Christ: thank you for the many adventures you've allowed me to travel thus far . . . and for all the ones still yet to come.

To my husband, Tim: Thank you, as always, for your unwavering support of me and my dreams. Without your persistent encouragement to "get your stories in to the hands of readers everywhere" back in 2012, I never would have been brave enough to do it on my own. Thankfully, I've never had to. You are both my very first and my very favorite reader (and you always will be).

To my writing sisters—Connilyn Cossette and Tammy Gray: I am so incredibly blessed to call you my people. Thank you for the MANY hours you poured into brainstorming this book with me and for never letting a single one of my texts go unanswered, especially the ones that started with "What if . . ."

To my Coast to Coast Plotting Society sisters—Christy Barritt, Connilyn Cossette, Tammy Gray, Amy Matayo: This is our NINTH year together, and I am even more giddy about meeting with you now than I was when we first started our little plotting retreat. You are all incredible writers, mentors, creatives, and sisters. I love you.

To my early readers/reviewers—Renee Deese, Amanda Dykes, Kacy Gourley, Rel Mollet, Dana Paduraru, Joanie Schultz: Thank you for making time to read my early draft and for supporting my efforts to bring this story to final publication. What a treasure I've found in each one of you!

To my family at Bethany House Publishers and specially to my editors—Jessica Sharpe, Sarah Long, and Bethany Lenderink: Thank you for your expert feedback, brainstorming sessions, patience and flexibility with my schedule, as well as your sharp attention to detail. Thank you also for taking such good care of me as a writer as I work to balance my fiction life with my actual life.

To my church family at Real Life Ministries in Post Falls, Idaho (and specifically to my Life Group): Thank you for leading by example and for loving on me and my family this past year. It has been a joy to meet each week and to laugh, cry, pray, connect, study, challenge, encourage, and serve with each one of you. This group proves why a life lived in community is FAR better than a life lived alone.

To my cherished readers: Thank you for taking a chance on my stories and for spending your precious time with these characters who have become near and dear to my heart. Your loyalty makes a huge difference in the life of an author . . . so thank you for continuing to keep my writing dreams alive. I love you all.

Special thanks to: Connilyn Cossette for the incredible hand-drawn map she created of Lynn and Luella's original road trip in 1975. You, Conni, are the epitome of a go-the-extra-mile kind of friend, and I'm so, so blessed to have you in my corner.

**Nicole Deese** is a Christy and Carol Award–winning, bestselling author of hope-filled, humorous, and heartfelt contemporary romance novels. When she's not sorting out character arcs and story plots of her own, she can usually be found listening to an audiobook and multitasking at least four different chores at once. She's a hoarder of sparkling water, a lover of long walks and even longer talks with friends, and a seeker of fun and adventure at all times. She lives in small-town Idaho with her happily-ever-after hubby, two freakishly tall teenage sons, and one princess daughter with the heart of a warrior. For more, visit NicoleDeese.com.

# Sign Up for Nicole's Newsletter

Keep up to date with Nicole's latest news
on book releases and events by signing up
for her email list at the link below.

## NicoleDeese.com

**FOLLOW NICOLE ON SOCIAL MEDIA**

Nicole Deese, Author   @NicoleDeeseAuthor   @NicoleDeese

# More from Nicole Deese

After Ingrid Erikson jeopardizes her career, she fears her future will remain irrevocably broken. But when the man who shattered her belief in happily-ever-afters offers her a sealed envelope from her late best friend, Ingrid is sent on a hunt for a hidden manuscript and must confront her past before she can find the healing she's been searching for.

*The Words We Lost*
A Fog Harbor Romance

After moving cross-country with her son and accepting a filmmaker's mentorship, Val Locklier is caught between her insecurities and new possibilities. Miles McKenzie returns home to find a new tenant is living upstairs and he's been banished to a ministry on life support. As sparks fly, they discover that authentic love and sacrifice must go hand in hand.

*All That It Takes*

Molly McKenzie has made social media influencing a lucrative career, but nailing a TV show means proving she's as good in real life as she is online. So, she volunteers with a youth program. Challenged at every turn by the program director, Silas, and the kids' struggles, she's surprised by her growing attachment. Has her perfect life been imperfectly built?

*All That Really Matters*

## ◊ BETHANY HOUSE